STILL BURNING

The Still County Thrillers
Book 3

LAUREN STREET

STERLING & STONE

STILL BURNING

Chapter One

RITA CUT the engine and listened to the truck's engine fall silent. A last gasp of exhaust drifted past the windshield and dissolved into the starry bowl above. She glimpsed a shooting star. No clouds. It'd be another day hot as hell in Still County, Wyoming.

Although it was late enough that the air outside must have a cooled a little. She'd take her blessings where she found them. She popped the door and climbed out of the truck.

And broke out in a sweat as heat rose from the pavement. She sighed. So much for cooling off in the middle of the night. She locked the truck with a punch of the fob-button.

And stopped short at the sight of her hands. Dried blood — *Arnold's* blood — stained both her palms and coated each finger as if she'd dipped them like candles.

Shit.

On leaden legs, Rita marched across the parking lot. Throbbing tungsten street lights did little to hide the fact there weren't many visitors at the hospital tonight. Of the half-dozen vehicles in the lot, one truck she recognized: a shiny black Dodge Ram with a logo on the side panel.

Quick Cash Auto Repair.

For a moment, her heart rate stopped hammering. Except she wasn't here to see *him*.

Rita entered Casper Hospital and walked past the Patient Registry, following signs to a restroom. Thankfully, like in the parking lot, Rita was the only sign of life in the bathroom. And that was a good thing, considering she looked like death warmed over.

She scrubbed her hands clean, then wiped the pink soap-foam from the sink with a paper towel. Then she surveyed her reflection. There'd be no way to hide the fact she'd been crying on the drive to Casper.

She splashed cold water on her cheeks, then swept up some stray strands of hair into her bun. The bun was lopsided, like it'd fallen in the oven, or the yeast had never activated in the first place. She yanked it out and started over. That was better.

But there wasn't anything she could do about the bloodstains on her uniform. Blood that wasn't only on her uniform, but also Walter's. And the silver pick-up. And splattered all over the dusty, dirt road. Blood pouring out of Arnold.

She buckled over the sink and gagged. She squeezed her eyes shut, trying to shut out the image of Arnold, shot and bleeding at the reservoir. Same fucking reservoir where Clyde and Ken had baited and pummeled her. She gagged again, sagging against the sink.

Pull it together, Rita.

She faced her reflection in the mirror. "I can do this."

"Sure as shit can," she answered herself. "It's your job."

She stuck out her tongue at the mirror. "Nice pep talk."

2

"Okay, wise cracker. Try this one: You're Otto's kid. You're born to do this."

She cracked a smile. "Why the hell not? Wasn't the speech I had in mind, but it'll do. And you're right. I am Otto's kid." She winked. "I can do this."

Taking a steadying breath, she exited the bathroom and headed for the elevator.

She passed a row of vending machines, silently standing at attention as though they were officers at a commemorative memorial, silently saluting one of their own.

She stopped at the last machine, which promised coffees and extra dry-looking biscotti (the kind of 'past due-date' dry), and jammed in a credit card.

The machine spit out an espresso in a styrofoam cup.

As she took a first sip, her phone pinged in her pocket. She checked her texts: Jason.

Good news

She smiled and shot back a message. *Could use some about now*

Got a sec to talk?

She hit Jason's number, and a moment later, the line connected.

"Hey, Jason," she said.

A nurse walking past cut Rita a look, pointing at a sign on the wall above the vending machines: USE OF CELL PHONES PROHIBITED

Rita pointed to her phone and mouthed the word *emergency*.

"We found him." Rita could hear the smile in Jason's voice. "We found Adrian."

"Alive?" she asked, even though Jason had said the news was good.

"Yup. But it was a close call. Shot, too. He's stabilizing at the Apex Care-Unit."

"Thank God," Rita said. "How's Walter?"

"He's with him there now. Won't leave his side, of course. Tomorrow, Adrian will be transferred to Casper Medical Center for surgery."

"Jesus," Rita said, reaching forward. "What a night." She took another sip of coffee, but it was already cold. "How are you holding up, Deputy?"

She could hear him smile again. "Don't worry 'bout me, Sheriff. How are *you* doing?"

"I'm at the hospital now," she said, as if that answered his question.

"Good luck."

"Thanks, Jason." Rita disconnected and headed for the elevator.

For what seemed like eternity, she rode to the third floor. The elevator bell chimed and the doors slid open.

She exited the elevator and stepped through the sliding glass doors of the ICU.

A nurse in Winnie the Pooh scrubs noticed her and came over. "Excuse me, Sheriff, no hot drinks in the ward, please."

Rita blinked at her. Then she looked down at the brown sludge in her cup. "It's cold."

The nurse pointed to a nearby waste-bin. "If you would—?"

Rita blinked again. "Oh, yes," she said, shaking her head clear. She was slipping into a stupor of exhaustion. Or starvation. Probably both.

She walked over to the trash and dumped the coffee cup. "Sorry about that."

The nurse smiled, her gaze flickering over Rita's bloodied uniform. "That's all right, Sheriff. I'm sure you need more than one midnight coffee to get you through your shifts."

Rita relaxed. "I'd say." She checked out her surroundings, scanning the room numbers. As if they would tell her behind which door she'd find Otto.

"The patient manifest is at the front desk," said the nurse, anticipating her question. "But I don't think we've got anyone here facing charges tonight."

Rita swallowed, her mouth feeling even drier since the coffee. "I'm here for personal reasons. To see someone … personal to me."

The nurse gave her a warm smile. "Sheriff Jonas."

"Yes, that's him," Rita said.

The nurse smiled wider, her eyes crinkling. "I mean, you're Sheriff Jonas."

Rita took a breath and nodded. "I haven't been here to see yet. To see him."

"I know," said the nurse.

Rita stiffened. She'd gotten here as soon as she could. Otto would understand. About the demands of her role, that is.

But the nurse's brown eyes were soft. "Why don't I take you down to 303?" Her voice matched the gentleness of her gaze. "It'll be a bit of a shock, seeing him like this."

Rita swallowed and nodded again. She didn't know if she liked the nurse's matter-of-fact manner. Even though it was the same approach she herself used on the job. But somehow, she wanted this nurse to reassure her that he'd be all fixed up. Her heart cramped. She should have googled his condition before coming upstairs.

The nurse paused in the corridor. "Here we are, 303. Thanks to his long service to the county, his pension puts him up in a private room."

She opened the door, and Rita followed her inside.

Otto lay on the hospital bed, shrouded in a lightweight, pale blue blanket. He could have been merely sleeping — if it were not for the tubes twined around his face. The hiss of his breath, and what sounding like the beep of an electronic metronome, filled the room.

Rita walked forward and touched his arm. It seemed thinner. Everything about him seemed thinner — or grayer — than the last time she'd seen him. And that had only been twelve hours ago, when he'd closed the door in her face.

She took a steadying breath, then squeezed his hand and released it. She stepped back and looked at the nurse.

"What happened?"

The nurse met her gaze briefly, then settled it on Otto. "Probably a stroke. We're running more tests."

Rita chewed on her lip again. "Is there a chance he might … pull out of the coma?"

The nurse flattened her mouth. "I'll call the doctor to answer your questions."

"That won't be necessary," Rita said quickly.

The nurse paused.

Rita scratched at her bun. "I don't want to hear the medical explanation right now. I'd just like to know what you think. You seem experienced."

The nurse smiled. "It can be hard not to have answers."

Rita nodded. "I hate guessing."

"I hear you, honey," said the nurse. "Some things about our jobs are similar, like delivering bad news."

Rita glanced at the nurse's nametag. *Larissa.* "Thanks, Larissa." Then she looked down at the blood on her uniform. "Trust me when I say I can handle it." She gave Larissa a glance. "Especially tonight."

Larissa nodded, the cartoon characters on her bosom

dancing up and down. "Given your dad's cancer, it's not likely he'll revive."

Rita took a sharp inhalation, her gaze locked to her father's fragile form.

"I'll leave you with him for a chat now," Larissa said. She padded through the room and slipped out of the door, taking Pooh and his entourage with him.

Rita blew out a breath. "Dad."

The machines beeped back at her.

"This is some hider-hole you got here."

But Otto said nothing.

And then Rita said nothing.

She had nothing to say.

His voice echoed in her mind:

Come on, Honeybee. You'll think of something. You always think of something.

She pulled up a chair upholstered in salmon-pink vinyl and sat down beside Otto. She touched his hand again. There were no tubes in his right arm, although they seemed to be going everywhere else.

His chest rose and fell with mechanical evenness that made him sound nothing like himself. She hadn't realized it until now, but Otto's breath had been ragged her whole life. It was the years of cigarettes that did it.

She remembered sitting on his lap and the sound of his breath when he talked. Not that he'd ever read her books of any kind. Instead, he told her stories about his day "at the office," which usually referred to the Still County free-ways, or else the home of someone in town they knew.

Sometimes his stories were sad, like a bighorn sheep that got hit and Otto had to shoot it to put it out of its misery. And then Walter would take the carcass and dress it and turn it into sausage.

Other times his stories were fun, like a high-speed car

chase to Casper, during which they sideswiped the weathered wooden welcome sign, after which — until the bucked-off board was replaced — announced Still's population to be 100 instead of the 1000 it so proudly boasted back in Otto's day.

But no matter the story, each one he told her was breathless with laughter, and sometimes with sobbing, and always with coughing.

It was Rita's turn to tell a story. And Otto wasn't going to care if she laughed or cried or coughed her way through it.

But she couldn't think of anything to say.

Come on, Rita. You always know what to say.

But she didn't.

Maybe it was because she hadn't slept in twenty-four hours. Or maybe it was because she had a teenager's blood all over her uniform. A teenager who was the half-brother of Rita's newly discovered and recently departed half-sister.

If that wasn't fucked up enough, her co-worker's kid had been shot. And while she didn't particularly like Walter, he was someone Otto cared about. And no one should experience the kind of suffering a parent endures while awaiting word of a child's wellbeing.

She didn't need to be a parent to know this. She had witnessed that kind of suffering on the job. And it'd made her question if she'd have the strength to be a parent. To care for something so vulnerable, knowing what she did about the world. And the people in it.

Rita pushed up from the chair. She bent over Otto's tubed head. She kissed his brow, the only exposed part of his face.

"Good night, Dad."

She headed for the door, then paused. Maybe he

wouldn't recognize her, using those words. "Good night, Otto," she added.

Then she walked out of the room and returned to the elevator. Rita rode downstairs to the cafeteria, where she spotted Cash asleep in a chair.

Beside him sat Helen, wearing his jacket. Her bottle-blonde head bowed over her phone. By the speed of her thumbs, she looked to be playing a game.

Rita walked over, her stomach twisting in knots. "Helen."

Helen looked up. The fluorescent hospital lights turned her ponytail an impossible shade of yellow. Like the discontinued neon paint her son had graffitied around town.

"Only reason I went over to his house is because I wanted to talk to him again," Helen said. "Wanted to explain my side of things. But instead I — I found him lying on the floor." Her eyes narrowed on Rita. "Can you imagine if I hadn't gone over?"

"No." But Rita wasn't sure if she spoke the word aloud or not.

Anger burned in Helen's eyes. "If you hadn't upset him so, he'd still be doing fine."

Cash stirred.

"That's insensitive, Helen," Rita said.

"Who's calling who *insensitive?* After the claims you've been making about me to your father?"

"Stop talking and listen, Helen," Rita said. "This is not the time to talk about that."

Cash blinked his eyes open. He glanced between Rita and Helen, sensing the tension.

"Rita," he said. "Your dad—"

"I'm not here to talk about Otto," Rita said, cutting

him off. "At least not right now. I need to talk to Helen about something."

Helen flinched, her ponytail bobbing. "My God, it's George, isn't it? Something's happened to him in prison. First Otto, now George. I knew it!"

Rita shook her head.

Cash pulled up a chair for her, placing it so Rita could sit facing Helen.

But she declined it with a wave of her hand.

"Prefer to stand," she said, her mouth having gone dry again.

Cash gave her one of his sexy half-smiles. "No sittin' down on the job for you, huh?"

"It's not George," she said to Helen, ignoring Cash as he replaced the chair.

Helen blinked at Rita, seeming to stare through her.

Rita inhaled a deep breath. "It's Arnold."

Helen's eyes widened. Her lower jaw worked as if hewing words out of stone. But aside from her teeth grinding, she made no sound.

"He was shot earlier this evening," Rita said. "And died fleeing his killer."

Helen screamed.

Chapter Two

RITA HELPED Helen into the passenger seat of the brown and white SCSO truck, then slammed the door. She turned around and bumped into Cash. He still was without his jacket (having lent it to Helen), and she could smell his skin through his cotton checked shirt. He smelled amazing.

"You sure you're up for the drive?" he asked. The concern in his voice was sincere. "I can take you both back to Still. And grab your wheels for you tomorrow."

"I'm fine," Rita said, without missing a beat. But was she? "I'll get Helen home safe."

Cash pulled her into a hug, but she wriggled out of his grasp.

He frowned. "What's wrong?"

"I don't know." Rita ran her hands through her hair, undoing the work she'd put into her bun. "I feel like I'm gonna shatter. Like I'm so brittle that if you touch me, I'll disintegrate." She walked around to the driver's side door. "Like dust."

Cash followed. "I just want to help, Rita."

She opened the door, giving him a look. "I'm fine, Cash. I'm doing my job."

His jaw tensed. "Right. I forgot."

She softened. "I'm sorry for being short. Thank you for staying with Otto tonight. That's a huge help."

He smiled. But he didn't look happy. "Any time."

Rita got in the driver's seat. "Goodnight, Cash."

He stepped back from the truck, shoving his hands in his jeans' pockets. "Text me when you're safe and sound."

She saluted him, then shut the door.

In the passenger seat, Helen sat staring ahead through the windshield.

She said nothing as Rita wove the truck through the hospital parking lot and onto the freeway back to Still. In the pitch blackness, few headlights passed, mostly transports. Even the rowdiest crowd in town was fast asleep at this hour.

Rita preserved the silence as though it were something sacred. And the only thing she could think to give Helen while driving.

Or maybe the silence was for Rita's own benefit, as her mind crawled back to the sight of Otto in the hospital bed. Of course, the natural ebbing of her father's life as he succumbed to disease was nothing compared to the devastating tsunami of Arnold's death. Only a young man, taken too soon. And in an abrupt moment of terror.

Rita blinked, squeezing back tears, trying to focus on the road.

From time to time, Helen emitted a small sob. But mostly she stared through the window as though there was something to see in the darkness.

They passed Still's old wooden welcome sign, last updated in 2016, now citing a population somewhere between 120 and 1200, since the last digit had been partially scratched off. Half the town said snow did it. The other half said Stu and Vic did it. And Otto said he could settle the manner once and for all by nicking off a corner, like he had back in the '70s.

Rita wondered why anyone even cared about the damaged zero, given that the truly egregious error was that the town's population was now closer to 3,000 — thanks to Apex setting up shop. Maybe town council didn't want to include Apex employees in the census. And considering how much murder and mayhem the corporate giant had caused, Rita couldn't fault them.

She pulled the truck into the Apex Medical Center's parking lot, taking the stall beside a charcoal, modified SUV parked in the space marked *Medical Examiner*.

"Here we are," she said, rubbing her sweaty hands on her thighs. She'd followed this routine dozens of times in New York. But here, tonight, in Still, with Helen, circumstances were painfully personal.

She glanced sidelong at her passenger. "Ready?"

But Helen didn't answer, instead blowing her nose. Then she fumbled for the door latch.

"I'll get it," Rita said, getting out of the driver's seat. She walked around to the passenger's side and popped open the door.

"It's a mistake," Helen said. Her wide eyes seemed to stare through Rita.

Rita extended a hand to touch Helen's. "I'm sorry you have to do this, Helen." And then, dropping her cop persona, she talked to Helen as Otto's girlfriend. "And I wish I had more encouraging words for you."

Helen shook her head. "We shouldn't be here. It's a mistake."

Rita touched her arm. "We could wait until morning. But I don't think either of us would sleep. It's for the best if we do this now. Together." She cocked her head toward the entrance. "They're waiting for us."

Helen shook her head. "No." She pointed a shaky finger at the pavement. "Being here's a mistake."

Rita forced a smile. "Not to worry, Helen, I know my way around Still. Even if it has been a decade and a half."

Helen's eyes looked wild. "I know where the goddamn morgue is, Sheriff. You don't seem to understand it's a good goddamn mistake that we're here for my son."

Rita touched her arm. "We can do this, Helen, okay? Together we can do this."

"Let go of my hand," said Helen, pulling away.

Rita dropped her hand. "All right."

Helen slid out of the truck. The tungsten lights painted her hair orange. "You walk ahead. I don't want nobody thinking you're bringin' me back here for bad news. 'Specially since it's all a mistake."

"I understand," Rita said.

She led Helen down a long corridor leading to an elevator at the back of the building. The green painted walls reminded her of a nail-polish with a name something along the lines of *Morning Gangrene*. But unlike Kimmee at Cactus Creek Cosmetics, Rita didn't think the hospital chose the color to be trendy. Or, maybe Kimmee, like the hospital, had gotten a deal on the paint.

She glanced back at Helen. Now, the green walls cast a murky hue on her hair, as if she floated submerged in a marsh. Tears streaked her black eye makeup and cut slashes through her rouge. And her entire body seemed to shake with each step.

Rita wished Helen would have accepted the support of her arm. At least she accepted Rita's gesture to enter the elevator first. Rita followed her in and punched the numbers to take them downstairs.

When the doors opened, Rita took Helen's arm without question and guided her into the darkened foyer. Awaiting them, Jason popped out of a chair when he saw them.

"Hi, Rita," he said, looking as exhausted as she felt. He glanced at Helen. "I mean, Sheriff. Evening, Mrs. — Miss — Ms. Myers."

Helen said nothing, staring through him as she swayed on the spot.

Rita led her to the chair Jason had vacated. "Have a seat, Helen."

Helen sat and Jason crossed to a buzzer on the wall. He pressed the button. "I'll call for the medical examiner."

The buzzer made a faint sound, then a door opened onto the foyer. A morgue attendant wearing blue scrubs and a hairnet stepped through the doorway.

"Good evening, Sheriff Jonas. Deputy Perry. Mrs. Myers?"

Helen didn't respond.

The attendant's mouth was hidden behind a mask, but a sympathetic smile was evident in his eyes. "This way, please."

The attendant led them down a hallway to a viewing room with gray carpeting and shady blue walls. Dim pot-lights lit the perimeter of the room, and a blind covered a window on one wall. Two upholstered chairs faced the window, and a bench sat against the back wall.

"This is where we'll view the body, Mrs. Myers," the attendant said, gesturing for her to take a seat. "I'm Chris. I'm going to be here to assist you every step of the process. If you need to pause the process at any point, please inform any one of us."

Wordless, Helen nodded.

"After I leave," Chris said, "it'll only take me a moment

to prepare the body. When it's ready, that light will illumi-nate." He pointed to a fixture on the wall. "When you see the light turn on, you can raise the blind." He pointed to a button on the wall. "It's automated. After you've had enough time with the body, you can press the same button to lower the blind. Then I'll be back with some paperwork for you to sign."

Again, Helen nodded.

Chris gave Helen an encouraging smile, then left the room. Helen's grip tightened on Rita's arm. Rita gave her another smile, hoping hers looked as reassuring as the morgue attendant's had.

Then she exchanged a look with Jason. He swallowed, still looking ghostly. She didn't blame him. He was still seeing a therapist about being shot himself a few short weeks ago.

Rita swallowed too, feeling like the room was closing in. Like Moses' mineshaft at the Lower Peak. Rita inhaled.

1, 2, 3, 4.

Hold. 1, 2, 3, 4, 5, 6, 7.

Exhale. 1, 2, 3, 4, 5, 6, 7, 8.

The light fixture illuminated.

Rita squeezed her hand. "Breathe with me, Helen."

"I'm not supposed to be here," Helen said.

Rita hugged Helen's hand to her chest. "No matter what truth you face here tonight, Helen, I will find the people responsible."

The door opened and the attendant, Chris, re-entered. He moved to the back of the room and stood by the dimly lit wall, holding a paper folder.

Helen's lips were moving, but she said nothing.

"We're good to go when you are, okay?" Rita said. She faced the window, gripping Helen's arm. "Are you ready?"

Helen's teeth ground together. "It's a mistake."

"Are you able to press the button, Helen?" Rita asked, leading her to the wall.

Helen blinked at the button.

"The blind, Helen," Rita said, indicating the window. "Are you willing to open the blind?"

"Oh," Helen said, shuffling forward. "Yes."

She pressed the button. Slowly, the blind rose.

Together, Rita and Helen looked through the glass pane into a brightly lit antechamber of the morgue. A gurney sat in front of the window. A body lay on it, shrouded in a sheet, folded back to reveal the cadaver's head.

A shock of hair.

High cheekbones.

A large nose that promised the boy would one day be a tall man. Would *have* one day been a tall man.

It was unmistakably Arnold.

Helen shrieked and collapsed, dragging Rita by the arm. Rita stumbled and caught herself, as Jason stepped forward. Together, they lowered Helen to the floor.

"Mind her head," Rita said. "She's fainted."

They propped Helen upright in one of the plush chairs. Chris approached, offering a chilled bottle of water.

"Thank you," Rita said, taking it and cracking the lid. "Water, Helen."

Helen's eyelids fluttered open, and Rita put the bottle to her lips. Helen drank. Then she pushed away the bottle, sloshing Rita with water.

"No!"

Rita didn't know whether Helen was declining the water or the truth of her son's death, but she figured it didn't matter. She opened her mouth to say something she hoped was sympathetic, when Helen pitched a cushion at Rita.

"*No!*" Helen said.

Rita took the cushion on her chest.

"I'll get a nurse," Chris said, crossing to the door. He punched the button on the wall, lowering the blind, and met Rita's eye. "You okay with her for a moment?"

Helen threw another cushion, this time hitting Jason.

"For now," Rita said. "But eventually she's gonna run out of pillows."

"I'll be right back," Chris said, stepping out of the room.

Helen lobbed another missile — this time the seat-cushion. Rita ducked. Helen's eyes rolled back. Then she slumped to the floor again.

"Shit," Rita said, darting forward. "Should've been ready for that."

Jason scooped her up under the arms, then he and Rita popped her back into the chair.

"Water, Helen?" Rita asked, crouching beside her.

Again, Helen's eyelids fluttered open. With a shaking hand, she accepted the bottle and put it to her lips.

Chris returned with a nurse wearing coral-pink scrubs pushing a mobility chair. He and the nurse transferred Helen into it. Then the nurse wrapped one of the pale blue hospital blankets around Helen's shoulders and rubbed her arms vigorously.

"Good evening," the nurse said, looking Helen in the eyes and smiling, "I'm Brené."

Helen stared back at her, listless.

"This is Helen Myers," Rita said.

"Seems you fainted here tonight, Helen," Brené said. "Can I call you Helen?"

Helen blinked at her, then nodded.

"Do you know where you are, Helen?" Brené asked.

Helen blinked and glanced around the room. "They said I was going to the hospital."

"That's right," Brené said, squatting to be able to keep looking Helen in the eye. "You're at the hospital. Do you remember why you're here?"

For a moment, Helen's lips moved silently. Then she said, "Arnold."

Rita touched her shoulder. "Yes. We came here to see Arnold."

Helen let out a strangled sound. "My boy. Arnold — he's — they—"

"Did you see Arnold here tonight, Mrs. Myers?" Jason asked.

Helen whirled on him, hissing.

"You don't need to talk about your son right now, Mrs. Myers," Chris said. "We only need you to identify if the deceased is your son, Arnold—" He paused to consult his paperwork. "Arnold George Myers."

Helen looked up at him and blinked. "Arnold?"

Chris extended the paper folder he'd been holding. "This is the paperwork, Sheriff Jonas." He glanced at Brené. "If Mrs. Myers is fit to sign."

"She can't sign if she's assessed and committed for psychiatric care," Rita said. She touched Helen gently again. "Are you able to sign some papers, Helen? About who you saw through the window tonight?"

Helen glanced over her shoulder at the window, the blind lowered once more. "He's in there," she said.

Rita nodded, opening the folder. She took out some documents with Post-It tabs directing Helen where to sign. Rita offered her the pen.

"I'm not doing this," Helen said, refusing the pen.

"You've gotten through the hardest part, Helen," Rita said. "If you can fill out these boxes and sign your name at the end, we can move onto other important matters. The important matter of making things right."

Helen's gaze hardened. "Make right? Make *right?* How can anything be made right?"

Rita swallowed, searching for words. "I know this is difficult—"

"You don't know," Helen said, spraying spittle. "You don't know what it's like to lose a child. And you'll never know! You're not a parent. You don't know a mother's pain."

And she snatched the pen from Rita.

Rita blinked back tears of her own, forcing a professional smile. "You're right, Helen," she said, "I don't know. And I am so sorry for your loss. We all are—"

"Otto said you weren't the type, you know," Helen said, scribbling her signature on the documents. "The type to be a mother. Said you'd never played with dolls. Instead spent all your time telling off the neighborhood bullies." She dropped the pen on the signed papers. "And chasing down kids who stole shit."

"Thank you, Mrs. Myers," Chris said, gathering the papers and putting them back in the folder.

"Now that that's done, let's get you somewhere more comfortable, shall we?" Brené said, releasing the brakes of the mobility chair. She looked at Rita. "We'll keep her overnight. It's a slow one, so I'm sure we can find her a quiet corner."

"Thanks," Rita said.

Brené turned back to Helen. "I'm going to take you to the psychiatry ward for observation, Helen. Do you know what that means?"

Helen scowled at her. "Psychiatry? It's for people who are broke in the head."

Brené hid a smile. "Not necessarily. More like broke in

the heart. And that can affect our thoughts. Psychiatry is medicine for our thoughts and our feelings — in those times when our heart may have been broken."

"Okay," Helen said, as though all the fight had gone out of her.

"But I was actually asking if you knew what it meant to be here under observation?" Brené asked.

Helen looked at her dully. "Sounds like you're going to keep tabs on me."

"In a manner of speaking," Brené said. "We'll find you a cozy spot where you can get help with anything you need tonight, okay? And after what you've been through, Helen, it'll be good to have the help, right?"

Helen blinked. "Okay."

"Good, we're all on the same page," Brené said, patting Helen's blanket-draped shoulder. "Now don't let me catch you trying to get things for yourself upstairs, all right? You're to put up your feet and drink as much juice as I can offer you."

For a minute, Helen ground her teeth. Her four attendants stood by, silent. At last she said, "Okay."

"I'll get the doors," Chris said, stepping forward.

Brené rotated the mobility chair, then wheeled Helen through the door, listing her beverage options.

"Pineapple, orange, apple, and passion fruit, which some folk say tastes just like cantaloupe. But other folks say it turns up the passion, if you know what I'm saying. And we could all do with a little more passion, don't you think?"

Chris closed the door behind them. Rita blew out a breath.

"You know, Jason," she said, "I never thought to ask Helen if she viewed Lisa's remains. Not that there'd been much left to identify of her body. Although maybe George did. Because Apex had handled Lisa's death, I wasn't in the loop. And so I never thought to ask. But I should have thought to ask — I've taken the fucking Trauma-Informed Policing course more than once. What was I thinking? Oh, right, I wasn't thinking. Otherwise I wouldn't have fucking informed a mother that her kid was dead while wearing a uniform soaked in his own goddamned blood. So obviously I'm kicking myself now. Except I can't get my fucking boot any farther up my own ass, which is exactly what I deserve because what a way to fucking re-traumatize a poor woman—"

"Stop," Jason said, putting his hands on her shoulders and giving her a shake. "You're spiraling."

Rita rubbed her hands over her face. "You're right. I'm spiraling. Because I'm exhausted. And hungry. I need sleep. And food. Probably both."

"Yup," Jason said. "And then there's the matter of your family."

Rita bit down on her lip. "That's my half-sister's half-brother lying on that gurney. I don't know what that means, but I think it's gotta mean something."

"Yup," Jason said, "it does. I got six sisters, Sheriff. Some of 'em don't even wanna be sisters anymore. All's I know is I love 'em all. Always have, always will. Easiest love on the planet, siblings."

"I wouldn't know," Rita said, feeling hollow. "Never had any." An image of Carol, enraged, flashed across her mind. In the memory, Carol was angry because Rita had hidden the keys to the station wagon, to prevent her from driving.

"—and your dad's unwell, too," Jason's voice said, breaking into her thoughts.

Rita nodded. "Really unwell."

Jason squeezed her shoulder. "Mary Lou said it was bad."

Rita looked up at him. "Mary Lou? How does she—?"

"It's Mary Lou," Jason said. "She always knows."

"That's true," Rita said. "And we all love her for it." She took another deep breath. "How are you doing? A gunshot fatality is bound to trigger a response in you."

Absentminded, Jason rubbed his right thigh, where he'd been shot during an invasion at the SCSO. Rita wished like hell she could have tested the bullet casing against the Apex ballistics records.

"Of course I can't help but think about it," he said. "But it's not so bad, to be reminded."

Rita's eyebrows popped up. "You aren't haunted by it?"

"Used to be," he said. "But ever since it happened, I've been going to prayer circle with Loraleigh, and I've come to realize that getting shot gave me new life." At that, his cheeks flushed. "Can't help but think God saved me for a purpose. That I'm truly meant to be here, no matter what my ma says. And now that I know what it feels like to think I might not be here, I don't want to not be here."

Rita blinked at him. "You mean, reliving the experience makes you appreciate being alive?"

Jason tilted his head, thinking. "Well, when you say it like that … yeah."

"Jesus," Rita said, "the NYPD could use more officers like you, Jason."

His cheeks flushed a deeper pink. "Oh, yeah?"

"Yeah," Rita said. "Except those flatlanders don't deserve you. So don't you go anywhere, y'hear? Otherwise, I'll fire you."

Jason laughed. "Thanks, Sheriff. I mean, Rita."

"We should get out of here," Rita said. Then stared down at her pants. "I can't believe I'm still wearing this."

Jason nudged her shoulder. "I've got some power bars out in the Casper PD cruiser, if that helps."

"You're a fucking godsend," Rita said, her stomach growling in agreement.

"See?" Jason said, grinning. "I told you God kept me here for a purpose."

Rita laughed aloud, for fear that she otherwise might cry.

Jason led the way out of the viewing room, and she followed him out of the morgue and back to the foyer. The elevator door closed behind them and Jason punched the buttons. In silence, they rode upstairs.

Chapter Three

"I'LL LET Officer Hutch know you're here," the receptionist at the Apex Medical Center said.

"Thanks," Rita said, taking a seat in the corner of the reception area.

"I'll get us some coffees," Jason said.

"At two in the morning?" Rita said. But Jason had already walked away. Five minutes later, he returned from the cafeteria, carrying two paper cups of coffee. He handed one to Rita.

She popped off the plastic lid and sniffed the steaming liquid. Then she took a tentative sip.

"Dammit," Rita said, crinkling her nose, "this is even worse than the sludge back in Casper."

The coffee hit Jason's tongue and he grimaced. "Nothing compares to Skyler's. Sure bet it's nice living above the Bighorn Bean."

Rita shrugged. "Apartments are overrated. Plus, I've only lived there a couple months, and I've already got an infestation of dust-bunnies."

"I meant it must be nice living above a coffee shop."

Rita frowned. "It's a drawback, actually."

Jason peeled back his lips and hazarded another sip. "How can that be?"

"Because it makes all other coffees intolerable to Skyler's," Rita said. "She's ruined me." She dropped the coffee cup in a trash-can beside her chair and sighed. "So what's going on with the crime scene?"

Jason peeled back his lips again, braving another mouthful. "Apex is holding the scene for us, and Casper forensics are already on site. Casper also put up a road-block. As did Beaumont. But there's no sign of the copycat Apex vehicle."

"Ain't gonna find it," Rita said. "Van's gonna be dumped and torched."

Jason nodded and sipped some more coffee. "How's Otto?"

Rita chewed on her lip for a moment. "I don't really have an answer."

Jason nodded again. "I understand."

"You should go home and sleep," Rita said. "I'll talk to Walter."

Jason looked at her. "You sure?"

"I'm sure that we've both been running on fumes, seven days with no break. In fact, the days are completely muddled together. And quite possibly I'm gonna bankrupt the overtime budget. If I haven't already."

"Hmm," Jason said. "Mary Lou would know."

"Yeah?" Rita sighed. "Well, don't ask her."

"Good night, Sheriff," Jason said, giving a wave as he turned to leave.

"Good night, Deputy," Rita said.

Jason walked out the sliding glass doors, each one emblazoned with the Apex logo. Rita headed down the hall to urgent care.

In the hallway outside the waiting room, Walter sat waiting in a white frame chair that looked too small for him. He looked up when she approached.

"Adrian's still with his doctors," he said. "They're getting ready to transfer him."

Rita laid a hand on his shoulder. "How are *you* holding up, Walter? I can't imagine what you're going through."

"All these years on the job," he said, "didn't see too many GSWs. But there were some, you know, even out in this neck o' the woods."

She nodded. The number of times Walter and Otto had seen GSWs in their careers probably equaled what Rita has seen during a single shift-cycle at the NYPD.

"Your dad ever tell you 'bout some of them shootouts?" Walter asked.

"Yeah," Rita said. "Mostly the tale of the moonshine shack shootout."

Walter chuckled. "Jesus Murphy, good on him. Anyway, it was always damn bone-chilling, you know, seeing a bullet in a body." A shudder coursed through his broad shoulders. "But it's a fuck of a thing when the bullet's in your kid, Jonas."

Walter had never called her Jonas before. That was how he addressed her father.

"I'm so sorry, Walter," Rita said. "I can't imagine."

He rubbed his face with his big hands. "It's moments like this, Rita, you can be thankful you're not a parent."

Rita stiffened. And refrained from asking what the hell Walter meant by a comment like that.

Then she relaxed her shoulders. The guy was on edge. And he wasn't the only one — she was right there on the cliffside alongside him. And Helen was dangling over its metaphorical edge. Everyone had had a long night — too long — and Rita had better get on with her business so she could go get some sleep. Tomorrow was already here, and there was already a Casper Mountain-sized pile of work to be done.

"Did Adrian tell you what happened?" she asked.

Walter shook his head, then nodded it, bobbing it around without committing in any one direction. "Only said that he and Arnold were chased and shot at. He said the shooters wore masks and drove one of them Apex trucks — presumably a fake one, one of them portable drug-buses."

"Shit, Walter, Adrian must have been terrified."

"They were forced off the road near the reservoir. Adrian jumped out and ran, but he's not sure what happened to Arnold."

"So Adrian doesn't know Arnold's dead?"

Walter shook his head.

"Let's keep it that way for the time being," she said. "There isn't anything that can't wait till after his surgery."

Tears welled up in Walter's eyes and he nodded. Then he cleared his throat.

"Better get myself ready," he said. He stood, the chair creaking as he shifted. "Winona's gonna meet me at Casper Hospital."

"I'll be thinking of you, Walter," Rita said.

The door opened and an ER nurse popped out his head. "Mr. Hutch? We're moving Adrian now. You can ride in the ambulance with him."

"Coming," Walter said, heading in the nurse's direction. Then he looked over his shoulder. "See you, Jonas."

Rita went out to the parking lot. Before climbing in the SCSO truck, she watched the ambulance drive away. The medical examiner's gray SUV was also gone, leaving the space beside her empty. That meant Arnold's body, as well, was on its way to Casper.

Rita drove the truck away from the hospital in silence, zero interest in listening to music. She drove out to the reservoir where they'd picked up Arnold.

A figure stood by the entrance-gate. She knew the man immediately. Funny that only four months ago, when he'd lured her out here on nefarious terms, she hadn't been able to identify him beyond his balaclava. Now, Ken Saunders' thick, boxy silhouette was as recognizable to her from a distance as if he were Sponge-Bob himself.

Rita parked the truck and hopped out.

Ken sauntered toward her. For once, he wasn't wearing shades. Somehow, she supposed he'd wear sunglasses even in the pitchiest of darkness.

He tipped his crewcut head. "Sheriff. You're up early."

"Nope," she said forcing a smile. "Out late."

He squared his already squarish shoulders. "You don't seem pleased to see me."

She frowned at him. "Guess I'm still getting used to you and your new position. That night when you pummeled the living daylights out of me, this wasn't the career path I envisioned for you. I'd been thinking along the lines of demotion, not promotion." She wiggled a finger at his shoulder, as though he were wearing epaulettes. "Did beating me up earn you your stripes?"

"Hell, Sheriff Jonas, I know we didn't get off to a good start." Ken spread his beefy hands. "But here we are now."

"Bad start, wrong foot, what does it matter?" Rita said.

A muscle tightened in Ken's jaw. "I can't blame you for being angry at me. But can't we forget about what happened?"

"Did you honestly expect me to *forget* about having the living daylights beat out of me, Ken?"

"Well, shit, maybe not forget about it *altogether*, Sheriff. But I'd sure prefer if you didn't mention it so much."

"You'd prefer it, huh?"

"I've made an effort to work in a spirit of cooperation."

Rita frowned at him. "How the hell d'you think you did that?"

"By transferring Peggy."

"That was supposed to appease me?"

"Isn't that what you wanted?"

"See? This is my problem: You nearly kill me. Then you fail to uphold the law because you think that'll appease me. This is very confusing for me, Ken. I hope you can see that."

"Peggy's transfer to Brazil was Angela's order." Ken tipped his chin. "But I could have refused."

Rita snorted. "Refuse orders from Angela Ruiz?"

"All right, Sheriff Jonas, I can see you're not easily won over. I'm just tryin' to make peace." He pulled on his chin, looking mildly distressed. "If you need any support, I'm here."

Rita refrained from telling him she was pretty sure her bra could provide better support than him. And that was despite having yanked out one of its underwires.

"See you around, Ken," she said. "Thanks for managing the scene here."

He held out a business card. "Call me anytime, Sheriff Jonas."

She hesitated. "Yeah, I got the number."

Then she caught herself. Ken was operating under Angela's "spirit of cooperation." And if Ken could … well, then she could.

She snagged the card from his fingers. "Thanks." She flashed a smile. "See you around. Ken."

Chapter Four

FLOODLIGHTS LIT up the crime scene, casting an artificial daylight. Rita followed the corridor of yellow tape down to the reservoir, slicing the borders of a polygonal shape through the dry brush. Apex security moved along its perimeter like worker ants.

Rita drew in a deep breath. It was impossible not to think about her half-sister, Lisa, losing her life less than half a mile from here. For all the messes that George and Helen — and Otto — had created in their kids' lives, hopefully Lisa and Arnold had found peace on the other side.

If there was another side.

Rita took another breath. She had to believe there was another side to Apex. To Still County. To herself. She had to believe there was more to this life than cleaning up after beheaded accountants and hunting down shooters who killed kids.

But what had Helen said — that Rita wasn't mother material?

No, it was Otto who'd said that. Rita was cut out for the beat, and that's where'd she stay.

A figure clad in a white Tyvek suit straightened and waved at her. Even though it was hard to tell in the bright lights, she was certain it was Tilda, head of Casper Forensics.

The pale figure headed toward her and Rita closed the gap, meeting her at the yellow taped line.

"Goddamn," said Tilda. The form-fitted hood of the suit did nothing to hide the fact that she'd shed some tears. "Doesn't seem right."

Rita blew out a breath. "Ain't wrong about that."

Tilda cracked a smile. "You don't sound like a flat-lander no more."

"Please," Rita said, matching Tilda's hollow smile, "I can't take any more bad news tonight." Then she gestured over Tilda's shoulder. "How are things going here?"

"We got tire impressions and a boot print," said Tilda. "We also got a whole lot of blood and bullet casings."

"You'll be getting another bullet from Casper soon. Victim is having surgery at some point tomorrow — actually, that'd be today now." Rita rubbed her temples. "It's hard to think straight when I haven't slept in twenty-four hours."

"Yeah, you look like hell," Tilda said. "And I say that with love because I know you'd tell me if I looked like hell. So go home and rest. We'll be finishing up here shortly. I'll need a day to process, and then we'll review everything."

"Thanks, Tilda," Rita said. "Talk to you soon."

She headed back up the hill toward the parking lot. Finally, the land had cooled off and Rita could walk without breaking out in spontaneous sweat. As she moved away from the floodlights, the Wyoming darkness swallowed her again.

She pulled out her phone and used it as a flashlight. Upon arriving at the truck, she climbed into the driver's seat and texted Mary Lou.

You still at HQ?

When she didn't get a reply, Rita hoped Mary Lou had gone home to bed. Which is where Rita needed to be. The nocturnal coolness would soon melt into midmorning heat, and Rita intended to sleep before the day heated up.

She scanned the parking lot for Ken. But even he had wisely gone home for some shut eye. Rita yawned.

Then she pulled out of the gravel lot and drove home. She parked in her usual spot behind the Bighorn Bean. Already, the lights burned bright inside, and Rita detected the aroma of freshly baked goods. But she didn't think she could tolerate the smell of any more coffee right now. Not even Skyler's.

She restarted the ignition and drove out of the lot, straining to see through the headache behind her eyes.

Arriving at Otto's, a sense of relief settled over her when she spotted Jason's Kia, parked next to the camper. She wouldn't be alone at Otto's property — even if he, like Mary Lou, was sleeping like a stone. As to whether or not Ken was catching up on his beauty rest, Rita couldn't care less.

As was expected, Otto's door wasn't locked. Rita entered the house, closed the door, and latched it behind her. She removed her shoes and hung up her coat, as though she were one of the guests arriving to his birthday party.

She padded through the foyer into the living room, feeling the need to be silent even though no one was there.

A stack of Otto's birthday gifts sat on the coffee table, still wrapped in shiny gold and silver paper. One item was wrapped in a newspaper article about septuagenarians, and how seventy is "the new forty." At thirty-five, Rita wasn't so sure about that.

On the sideboard sat the remains of Otto's birthday cake. Once a decadent masterpiece decorated in pearly scrolls of icing, it now resembled the inter-state freeway following a snowfall, as the dregs of vanilla frosting formed miniature snowbanks, scraped away from the silver-gray cake pan by a horde of forks doing the work of a snowplow.

She picked up the pan and walked into Otto's kitchen. She supposed she should put the leftover cake in the trash. But then the bag would have to go outside to the can, so as not to stink up the house. And Rita was too tired to do all that. She opened the fridge and shoved the cake on the top shelf, on top of a half-eaten charcuterie board. The cocktail wieners, as well, were definitely destined for the trash, and she made a mental note to do so in the morning.

Otto's refrigerator otherwise held similar treasures to those in Rita's: half a carton of milk; half a tub of yogurt; half a tray of eggs; a block of margarine too old to consider edible; ditto for the sliced cheese. There was also a single-serving lemon custard pie in a clear plastic cup. She didn't know Otto liked lemon custard. Maybe the pie was a relic of Helen's tenancy.

She closed the fridge door and turned, her toe kicking a piece of crockery on the floor. A broken coffee cup rolled toward the sink. Then her eye tracked a dried coffee stain spread across the floor.

She fetched Otto's broom from the closet and swept up the broken shards, then dumped them in the trash. Then she dampened a sponge and scrubbed the floor clean.

While down on hands and knees, Rita noticed Otto's cell phone lying beneath the kitchen table. She picked it up and pressed the power button.

But there was no life in the battery. She pushed onto her feet and placed the phone on the counter. She hooked it up to its power charger, which Otto kept plugged into the wall socket next to his landline.

She wondered how long Otto had been lying on the linoleum, alone and inert, like his phone. Thank God Helen had found him. Otherwise, who knows when he might have been found? It wasn't like Rita was checking on him daily, like when she was living in the camper. Since she'd moved to the apartment, she saw him only once or twice a week. And it wasn't Jason's duty to look in on him. Now she wished she had said something to Otto at his bedside.

But in that moment, she had felt so distant from him. Even though she'd been holding his hand. And now she felt an even greater distance between them. If only she could have known then how she'd feel standing in his kitchen now, watching his phone slowly come back to life.

She walked away from the phone on the counter and entered the living room. The drapes were still closed. Yesterday, like every day, Otto would have pulled them against the late-afternoon sun that otherwise blasted his eyeballs while he sat in his west-facing dining room.

Rita left the drapes as they were and sat on the sofa, which wore a handsome, handmade slipcover. Clearly one of Helen's touches. And a good one. More than changing the sofa's appearance, the nubby fabric provided a barrier between the smoke-steeped cushions and whoever chose to sit down on them.

She pulled a blanket off the back of the sofa, unfolding it to reveal an enormous image of a wolf's head. She pulled the plush fabric up to her nose. Despite having been laundered with a highly floral detergent (Helen again?), the blanket still exuded the faint stench of smoke, reminding

Rita of her father's shirt, when he used to tell her his stories.

Rita rolled onto her side and curled into a ball, tucking the blanket around her shoulders even though the day would be warm.

Eventually, she fell asleep.

Chapter Five

RITA AWOKE to the alarms in Otto's hospital room. Lights flashed on the ventilator next to his bed. His eyelids fluttered open and she reached for his hand.

But it was no longer Otto's hand. Adrian stared back at her, a bullet wound in his forehead. His mouth moved but emitted only the beeping alarm.

She wanted to tell him he hadn't been shot in the head, that it was all a mistake. But Adrian had disappeared, and now Arnold lay in his place in the bed. The deceased teenager twitched, then turned his head toward Rita—

She sat up, throwing off the blanket.

She wasn't at the hospital in Casper. She was lying on Otto's sofa, and the alarm was only her phone, vibrating on the coffee table. She groaned and reached for the device.

"Hi, Mary Lou."

"Hate to break it to you, Sheriff, but we got a domestic."

Rita groaned in silence. She'd never been a fan of domestics in New York, where life mates hurled one another's belongings off apartment building fire escapes, but she disliked them even more in small towns where there was a decent probability of recognizing the couple.

Rita wiped the sleep from her eyes. "Where am I going?"

"The Myers' old house. Heather Bannister called it in. Her husband Max is there, and he's raisin' hell."

Rita thanked Mary Lou and signed off. Then she let out a sigh. So much for sleep.

She climbed to her feet and straightened the sofa, refolding the wolf blanket and returning it to the backrest.

Then she washed her face in the downstairs bathroom. Two hours of sleep wasn't going to last her for long. She threw back a cup of water, then fetched her coat.

She stepped outside and locked the door behind her. Turning around, she saw Jason awaiting her in his Kia. She crossed to the vehicle and climbed into the passenger seat.

"Deputy," she said.

"Sheriff." Jason looked her over. "You haven't changed your uniform yet."

"Nope," Rita said, fastening her seatbelt.

Jason pulled out of the driveway and headed for town.

"Well, isn't this familiar," Rita said, leaning back against the headrest. "Headed to the Myers' house in the dead of night."

"Isn't the dead of night," Jason said, pulling onto the freeway. "It's practically dawn."

"Really?" Rita said. "Damn. I was gonna sleep."

Jason glanced over at her. "Long night?"

Rita scoffed. "Hasn't even started. Could use a dinner and a bath and a cozy set of PJs." She stared out at the darkness sliding by. "New York never really sleeps. But out here in the mountains … it's as dark as the boogie man's shadow."

Jason smiled. "Ain't no such things as the boogie man."

"Double damn," Rita said. "Think how much easier our jobs would be if we could stick everything on that guy."

Jason laughed.

"You should probably speed up," Rita said, indicating the dashboard.

Jason punched the gas, and the Kia shot forward.

"Thanks for driving," Rita said. The scenery whipped past. "You don't want to take the SCSO's truck?"

Jason shrugged. "Figured we wouldn't be out long." He glanced at her again. "This way, I can drive you back to Otto's for a bath."

"You make me sound like a dog," Rita said.

"Well, you do smell."

"Shut up."

Jason turned onto a side street and pulled up to the Myers' former family home. It was easily spotted, because every light in the house was switched on.

Rita sighed. "Dare I say this place has a curse?"

Jason scrunched up his face. "Some people's circumstances are just unlucky."

"Or maybe it's just damn unlucky that Apex set up shop in our county."

"Apex isn't the only bad news in town," Jason said. He pointed to a black BMW in the driveway. "Check out those fancy wheels."

"Definitely not Heather's," Rita said.

But she wasn't looking at the Beemer. Next door, Lydia stood watching through the living room window. As Rita's gaze meets hers, Lydia withdrew, letting the curtain fall.

Rita got out of the Kia and walked with Jason toward

the house. Shouting issued from within, then something shattered. Swapping a look, she and Jason picked up the pace.

Rita jogged up to the door and knocked. The shouting subsided. But nobody answered. She knocked again, this time louder.

"They can't hear," Jason said.

Rita put her lips to the paneled window beside the door and shouted, "This is Sheriff Jonas and Deputy Perry of the SCSO. And we aren't leaving until we talk to Heather."

The door opened. A man stood in the foyer, wearing an expensive suit. Not New York-expensive, but expensive for Still County. His tie hung loose and sweat beaded his face. His hair, which clearly had been cut, combed, and gelled with precision, now fell lank over his forehead

He breathed heavily, his chest rising and falling. "My apologies, Officer—"

"Sheriff."

"My wife and I were having a disagreement. We didn't realize we'd raised our voices so loud." He flashed a smile and gestured to Lydia's house. "Apologies for disturbing the neighbors."

"Please step outside, Mr. Bannister," Rita said.

Max Bannister blinked at her. "Is something wrong, Officer?"

"Yes. And there'll be two things wrong, Councilor, if you keep calling me officer. So I'd like you to step outside so we can chat."

"No need for a chat, Sheriff. It's late, and I'm sure we all want some sleep." He winked and wagged a thumb toward next door. "Especially Lydia. I can assure you it won't happen again."

Rita raised an eyebrow. "Let me rephrase it this way,

Mr. Bannister. I need you to come outside now, so that we can have that discussion."

For a moment, Bannister hesitated. Then he took a step back and started to close the door. "Another time, Sheriff."

Rita set her forearm against the door and pushed against it, stepping inside. Jason followed, spinning Bannister while Rita sidestepped behind him, snapping cuffs on his wrists.

"Take him outside, Jason."

"Fuck you," Bannister said.

"May as well put him in the Kia," Rita said. "We'll talk down at the station, Mr. Bannister."

Jason steered him outside and Rita shut the door behind them. The house quieted at once and a shiver passed over her. The last time she'd been here, she'd been checking in on Arnold Myers. Making sure he was okay, in the wake of his sister's death. Of Rita's half-sister's death.

And now Arnold was dead.

Upstairs, someone sobbed.

Rita followed the sound, walking across the living room carpet in her shoes. Unpacked cardboard boxes crowded the room.

Heather sat on a box, her face swollen from crying. Or worse.

"Did he hit you?" Rita asked.

Heather shook her dark head. "Just raging."

Rita stepped closer and gestured to her arm. "Those red marks on your arm look painful."

Heather looked at the marks, then touched them gingerly as if noticing them for the first time. She glanced at Rita. "I ain't testifying against him, Rita. He's the father of my kids."

"You need to consider their safety, Heather."

"He doesn't hit the kids."

"Just you?"

Her gaze flickered away. "Didn't say that. I just want him gone."

"What was the argument about?"

Heather lifted her chin. "I left Max. And now he ain't happy about it." She rubbed at the marks on her arm. "Can you get him gone?"

"If you want him to not come back, you'll need to go to court and file the paperwork. Then the judge will issue a restraining order."

"Shit," Heather said, biting her lip. "Never thought things would go like this, back when we got engaged. Thought I'd do better at marriage the third time round. But I only fucked things up worse."

"*You* didn't fuck up anything," Rita said.

For a moment, Heather studied her arm, silent. "Fine," she said at last. "I'll do it."

"In the meantime," Rita said, "I'll put Max in the cells. I'll release him sometimes tomorrow morning on the condition that he not visit this address."

Heather nodded.

"Or contact you in any way."

Heather nodded again.

"Anything else you need?" Rita asked.

Heather rubbed at her arm. "Just for you to go now. I need to be with the kids. They haven't slept much."

"Of course," Rita said. "Do the kids need anything — aside from sleep?"

Heather shook her head. "We're sorted. Cash has been great, bringing by groceries and anything else that we need."

Rita gave her a forced smile. "That's good to hear."

Heather managed a weak smile of her own. "Yeah.

He's a hell of a godsend. Wish I worked harder at being his wife." She ran her hands through her hair. "What we don't appreciate when we're young, huh?"

Rita nodded, her throat closing up as she remembered leaving Cash at the altar. "Uh-huh," was all she managed to say.

Heather slid off the cardboard box. "Thanks, Rita," she said. "I'm gonna go make the kids some hot cocoa."

"Good idea," Rita said. "I'll let myself out." She handed Heather a business card. "This is my direct number. Don't hesitate to call it if anything comes up. Anytime. Got it?"

Heather took the card. "Thanks."

Rita walked to the front door. "Get some better security around here, huh?"

Heather blinked at her.

Rita cocked her head toward the door. "Stronger locks. Get a chain across the door."

Heather glanced at the door, chewing on her lip. "I'll keep it in mind."

Rita bade her goodnight and went out to the Kia. Jason had put Max Bannister in the backseat of the Kia and was leaning against the driver's side door.

He looked up as she approached. "Good to go?"

"Yup," Rita said, moving toward the passenger side.

"Good," Jason said. "'Cause this guy's jumpy as hell."

Rita climbed into her seat as Jason slid behind the wheel. They fastened their belts and Jason pulled out of the drive.

An alarm on the dash chimed.

Rita glanced in the back seat. "Did you unbuckle your seat belt, Mr. Bannister?"

"Fuck you!" Bannister said.

"Please put on your seatbelt, Mr. Bannister," Rita said.

"I can't, can I?" he said. "I'm handcuffed."

Rita frowned back at him. "Well, you go it off while handcuffed."

"Fuck you, Sheriff," Bannister said for a second time. "I ain't a criminal, and you can't arrest me for riding without a seatbelt!"

Rita looked at Jason. "He's right. We can't arrest him. But we can fine him."

Jason ground his teeth as the beeping droned on. "Can we fine him for childish behavior, too?"

"I wish," Rita said, over the alarm. "I think he's the most juvenile perp we've met. And that's saying a lot, considering Stu and Vic."

"Ma used to belt us if we didn't buckle in," said Jason. "She also expected us to cram more than one kid into the same belt. That's what you gotta do when you got seven."

"What would anyone do with seven kids?" Rita asked, mystified. She looked over her shoulder at Max Bannister.

"Doesn't the beeping bother you, Councilor?"

"What do you think?" Bannister said.

"I think you're acting like a child," Rita said.

"Not a problem for me," he said.

"I can see that," Rita said. Then she sighed and faced forward again. She glanced sidelong at Jason. "Any way to disable the alarm, Deputy?"

Jason shrugged. "I dunno. You could look it up in the manual."

Rita curled back her lips. "The *manual?*"

Jason reached past her. "Sure, it's right here in the glove—"

"No thanks," Rita said, brushing his hand away. "Thanks, but manuals aren't really in my wheelhouse."

Max Bannister laughed. "Maybe next time you two

zipperheads should bring a patrol car. What kind of outfit—"

"This kind of outfit wasn't expecting to arrest your sorry ass," Rita said, teeth clenched. "I'd hoped we could all have a civil chat, Councilor. But you proved me wrong."

Bannister's eyes burned with fury. "You know, I could sucker punch either one of you right now, and neither of you'd ever see it coming."

"I don't think so," Rita said. "You're handcuffed, remember? Besides, any attempt to throw around your weight, and you'd probably cause Jason to roll the Kia. And since you're not buckled in, I doubt things would work out in your favor."

"Fuck—"

"Shut up," Rita said. "Or I'll tell Jason to drive you to Natrona County and process you there. And that ain't gonna look good at work, is it, Councilor Bannister?"

Bannister grumbled under his breath.

"I didn't think so," Rita said, facing forwards again. She looked at Jason. "Look what I can accomplish on a sleep debt? And would you believe Otto thinks I'm not the parenting type?"

Chapter Six

Jason poked his head in Rita's office. "I processed Max Bannister, Sheriff."

"You make him sound like a ham," Rita said.

Behind Jason, Max sat handcuffed to a chair, scowling.

"He'll be more cheerful in the morning when he's released from the cells."

"I still haven't told him he's spending the night here." Jason glanced back at Max. "He's not gonna like that."

"Boo hoo," Rita said. "At least he'll be relieved to pick up his vehicle in the morning, considering once he has done so, he will never again be permitted on Heather's property."

Jason grimaced. "Very relieved."

"But let him make his call first."

Jason nodded. "I'll take him down to the holding room."

"Thanks, Jason. I appreciate you watching him overnight. But it anything comes up, like you're gonna fall asleep, give me a call."

"No need, Sheriff." Jason held up an enormous mug. "I'll stay awake."

Rita blinked. "Is that a beer stein?"

"Coffee," Jason said, grinning. He rotated his wrist so Rita could read the slogan on the side: *Good men are like coffee … rich and hot!* "I got enough medium roast in here to keep me up till Wednesday."

"Enjoy the heart palpitations," Rita said, yawning. "I'll see you after what I hope will be a deliciously sound sleep."

She headed to the parking lot and drove the truck to Otto's. Trudging through the front door, she kicked off her shoes stumbled to the slip-covered sofa, where she collapsed.

For a moment, she debated the merits of taking a bath or a shower.

Her eyelids fluttered open. Daylight streamed through the crack in the drapes.

She sat up, rubbing her head. The headache was still there. But the aroma of fresh coffee snapped her awake.

She shuffled into the kitchen. Jason stood at the stovetop, fiddling with an old-looking percolator. He looked up at her, grinning. "How happy was I to find this in Otto's cupboard? And not a speck of rust. How about some espresso, just made the way my granny makes it?"

By the speed of his words per minute, Rita gauged Jason was still running on the contents of this morning's beer stein.

"Smells fucking amazing," she said, her mouth dry as a desert.

"I hope it's okay that I let myself in," said Jason. "By the volume of your snoring, I figured you'd be needing some caffeine." He glanced at the clock above the stove. "Even if it is almost lunchtime."

"You're a lifesaver," Rita said, accepting a mug. She

took a seat on the banquette. "But shouldn't you be putting yourself to bed, now that you've sorted out Max Bannister?"

Jason smiled. "I'll go have a nap when I've finished up here. And yes, I dropped off Councilor Bannister at Heather's place to pick up his Beemer. Then I followed him out of town."

"Please tell me he wore his seatbelt," Rita said.

Jason laughed. "Begrudgingly."

Rita tried for a smile, but even her face hurt. "Good work, Deputy. What else is happening?"

"Walter called earlier." He consulted the clock again. "About an hour ago. Adrian's out of surgery. Walter's going to stay with him for the next little while."

"Good idea," Rita said. "At least until we find out who targeted the boys." She drummed her fingers on the table. Then she picked up her phone and sent a text message to Ken.

Pls arrange for me to speak with whoever found Adrian at Apex

She wondered if she were too informal. Not that they weren't on punching terms. She typed again.

Thanks in advance

Then she hit send. Now it was up to him and his "spirit of cooperation."

As she set down her phone, she noticed a text notification. Cash. She'd forgotten he'd messaged. She resisted the urge to swipe it open.

"We need to talk to Castor and Beaumont Drug Units," Rita said. "See if they have any ideas who's running meth through the county. I'll meet you at the office after I go change my uniform."

Rita lifted a spare set of Otto's keys from a hook on the wall by the phone and gave them to Jason. "These are spare keys for the house," she said. "Maybe you'll need to get in here again. I think that little one is for the crawl space."

"Thanks," Jason said, taking the ring. Then together, they walked outside to their vehicles.

Rita drove to her apartment, her head pounding as the sun beat through the truck's windshield. Maybe going without any sleep would have been better than cramming in just a few hours. She parked behind the Bighorn Bean and dragged herself upstairs.

The hot shower felt like heaven. Reluctantly, she got out and toweled off. She dressed in a clean uniform and tied her hair in a bun. She took a moment to meet her gaze in the mirror. The last conversation she'd had with herself had been in the hospital.

"It's okay, Rita," she told herself. "You're gonna get through this."

And then, with a sudden wish that Cash was there to echo her words, she remembered his unread text.

She grabbed her phone and opened her messages.

Ottos resting nicely I'm headed home

Rita felt a mix of relief and worry. Relief that Otto rested, worry that he was alone.

Another message crossed her mind, and she walked to the safe. She dialed the combination and opened the door. Inside sat the shoebox storing letters from Lisa.

Her heart pounded. Rita opened the box and took out the first envelope.

But her stomach felt raw. She couldn't. Not yet. She put back the envelope and shut the safe. Standing up, a wave of dizziness washed over her. Her stomach felt raw, most likely having drank coffee on an empty stomach.

She needed food.

She pulled open her fridge and stared at the salad supplies Cash had brought. When it became apparent that the salad wasn't going to make itself, she slammed the door shut and went downstairs to the coffee shop.

Skyler greeted her with her unusual enthusiasm. The teenager's pink and purple hair had been shorn off one side of her head.

"What happened to your hair?" Rita asked.

Skyler smiled wider. "I shaved half of it off last night."

"I can see that," Rita said.

Skyler shrugged. "Didn't like the purple and pink streaks."

Rita pointed to the side of her head. "I can see your piercings better."

"I'm thinking about getting some more," Skyler said, fingering the dozen or so rings in her ear. "So what'll you have? The usual?"

Rita shook her head. "Not today. I think I rotted my gut with bad coffee. And then I made it worse by not eating enough food. Someone left salad in my fridge, but I just couldn't do it."

"Oh, no," Skyler said, looking concerned.

"I don't think it'll be permanent," Rita said. "I think it's a symptom of starvation. Or sleep deprivation. I'm too tired to figure it out." She pointed to a menu board. "I'll take one of those."

Skyler glanced at the board, following Rita's gaze. Her frown deepened. "Tea? Herbal?"

Rita nodded. "Something for the gut. Peppermint's good for that, yeah?"

Skyler pursed her lips. "Dandelion's best."

Rita crinkled her nose. "I'll have the peppermint, thanks. To go."

Skyler selected a tea bag. "Right away, Rita. Keep in mind, it might make you a little sleepy."

Rita arched an eyebrow. "No shit?"

Skyler filled a giant paper cup with steaming water. "Peppermint puts me out every time. And you look a little tired today."

Rita tried for a laugh. "Don't I always?"

Skyler passed her the paper cup. "I mean, you look *exhausted*."

Rita took the cup, the size of a thermos. Or a beer stein without its handle. "Been working too many shifts in a row. I need a day off. And a box of muffins."

Skyler smiled. "That I can get you." She grabbed a paper muffin box and indicated a wheeled cooling rack behind the counter. "Fresh batches came out a few minutes ago. What'll you have?"

"Cover all the food groups, please," Rita said. "Spiced carrot pecan, lemon ginger, bacon and cheese."

"And chocolate chip," Skyler said, working the tongs. "Chocolate's definitely a food group."

Chapter Seven

RITA LEFT the Bighorn Bean and drove the truck around the block to SCSO Headquarters. When she entered, Mary Lou was already there, along with a lingering odor of burnt coffee.

Rita's stomach flip-flopped. She burped.

Mary Lou looked up, then marched across the bullpen. "Good god, Rita, I don't know whether to ask after Otto or Adrian or Arnold. And Lord, that's a tongue-twister."

Rita pulled up Walter's chair, which once had been Otto's, and gave Mary Lou the box of muffins. "Help yourself."

Mary Lou selected a muffin and sat at her desk. "Thank you kindly, Sheriff."

"Adrian is now at Casper hospital, his GSW now stabilized," Rita said. "Walter is staying with him, of course. Arnold, unfortunately, is dead. And Otto seems to have had a stroke." Then she sat her elbow on the desk and dropped her head in her hands. "Oh, and Helen is hospitalized."

Mary Lou shook her head. "Hell, you need a day off, that's what."

"That's what I told Skyler at the Bighorn Bean," Rita said. "But I know I'm not going to get it, so what I really need right now is to talk to Hunter Green. There's too much for us to do around here with Walter on leave."

Mary nodded. "And with Otto in the hospital — well, hell, you'll want to be with him, won't ya, honey?" She pushed the muffin box toward Rita. "Eat something. Especially if you're wanting to get something from Hunter Green. You'll need all the gas in your cylinders you can get."

"Thanks," Rita said, "I think." She dug in the box for the spiced carrot-pecan muffin.

Suddenly, someone jabbed a pocketknife into Rita's shin.

"Jesus Christ!"

"Shoo, Ted, I told you to use the scratching post."

Mary Lou reached over to pluck the Siamese cat from Rita's leg.

Rita rubbed at the puncture wound through the pantleg of her uniform. "What's Theodore doing back here?"

"Keepin' out of harm's way," Mary Lou said. "Bathroom's gettin' a lick o' paint."

"Paint fumes can't be good for him," Rita said.

"Nope," Mary Lou said. "Neither is gettin' stepped on by Lucky."

"The electrician?"

Mary Lou nodded, her silver stack of hair wobbling. "Yep. Turns out he can paint, too."

"Why?"

"I suppose because the menfolk in his family exposed him to all sorts of handy trades," Mary Lou said, nibbling

53

her muffin. "He can lay tile, too. They say he's a triple threat."

"I meant, why is he painting your bathroom?"

Mary Lou shrugged. "He needs something to do all day. While I'm here at work."

Rita blinked at her. "Isn't he busy being an electrician?"

Mary Lou laughed. "Silly! He's busy dating me."

An unresolved mystery suddenly came to Rita's mind. "That reminds me, Mary Lou, you never did tell me what they say about dating electricians."

Mary Lou blinked at her. "Isn't it obvious?"

Rita pursed her lips. "Nope, sorry. Thought about it all the way on the drive to see Otto. But I got nothin'."

Mary Lou's eyes twinkled. "They really *turn you on*."

Rita groaned.

Mary Lou shrugged. "To each her own." Then she grinned. "You always preferred grease monkeys."

Rita stuck out her tongue at her. "What do they say about painters and tilers?"

Mary Lou crinkled her nose. "Damn, girl, I couldn't tell you. But I'm gonna find out."

"I'm sure you will, with your powers of investigation," Rita said. She pushed up from Otto's old chair and headed for her office. "Gonna go talk to Hunter."

Rita shut the door behind her and sat at the desk, Ted following at her feet. She settled into the chair and peeled the parchment paper from the muffin.

As she took the first bite, Ted jumped on her lap, stabbing her thighs with his claws.

"Ouch," she said, spraying muffin crumbs.

Ted lay, stacking his limbs on her lap. A moment later, he started to purr. Rita resisted petting him, given her fingers were sticky with cream cheese icing drizzled with a brown sugar glaze.

She studied the muffin. It was the perfect mix of ingredients: cream cheese, spices, carrots, pecans, raisins, wheat, and eggs holding it all together. A complete meal. Full nutrition. Who needed more than a muffin?

Rita finished the muffin and licked the icing off her fingers. Mary Lou was right — she felt better, calmer.

She picked up the landline and called the hospital in Casper.

The automated menu put her through to the ICU, and she asked after Otto. The desk nurse informed her that his condition was unchanged since the previous night. Rita thanked her and asked the nurse to verify the visitors' hours.

While the nurse recited the schedule, an Apex vehicle pulled up in front of the office. For a moment, she stared at it, searching for anything unusual.

When the nurse finished speaking, Rita thanked her again and said she'd try to stop by in the afternoon. Then she hung up and called the DA.

Hunter Green had already heard the news that Walter's son had been injured in a shooting, and that Otto had had a stroke.

"I'm turning the investigation over to Apex," he said.

Rita scoffed. "No way. It's SCSO jurisdiction."

"Without Hutch, you're down a number. And with your dad ill, how present are you?"

"We've got it handled," Rita said. "Only I need some interagency support. An additional officer, only while Walter is out."

"So then you don't have it handled," Hunter said.

Rita seethed. "Of course we have it handled," she repeated. "We just need more hands."

Hunter's voice was flat. "Use Apex."

Rita scoffed.

"They're offering their manpower free of charge," said Hunter.

"In a spirit of cooperation," Rita said.

"You sound sardonic," Hunter said.

"You guessed right," Rita said. "This move has Angela Ruiz all over it."

"So?" Hunter said. "It's assistance."

Rita rolled her eyes. "They're only trying to clean up their reputation."

Hunter let out an impatient sigh. "Their policing reputation is fine, Rita."

Rita snorted. "According to who? Have you met Ken and Clyde? Besides, I'm talking about their corporate reputation. All they can see is someone is tarnishing their name by using fake Apex vehicles to traffic drugs. You can bet that makes their skin crawl, and they'll do just about anything to manage the damage. Including shoot my deputy."

"You can't prove they shot your deputy," Hunter said.

Rita scowled at the receiver. "Sing me another song, Hunter, 'cause I ain't interested in that one."

"Have *you* tried a spirit of cooperation?" Hunter asked, a scowl of his own evident in his voice.

"I'd love to cooperate with an officer on loan from Beaumont or Casper," Rita said sweetly.

She could almost hear Hunter shaking his head through the telephone line. "You can either accept the help from Apex, Rita, or go it alone."

Rita swore under her breath and threw up her hands, startling the cat. Ted shifted, digging his claws into her thigh. She bit back another curse.

"May I remind you, Hunter," Rita said, drawing out

each word, "that Ken beat me up? I'm not exactly keen to play Sherlock to his Watson."

"Who's asking you to play, Rita? It's time to get to work. And the condition of Ken's release states that the two of you can be in contact for professional reasons."

"Professional?" Rita asked. "We're talking about a primate here." Then she hung up, pissed. Ted, on the other hand, continued to purr.

Knuckles knocked on Rita's office door, and Ted bolted from her lap.

"Ouch," Rita said, rubbing a new set of claw tracks. Then she said, "Come in."

The door opened, and Mary Lou's silver head poked through.

Her gaze skated around the room, first passing Ted, who perched on the desk smoothing a ruffled patch of hair, then settling on Rita, rocking in her office chair. "Looks like that didn't go very well."

"What?" Rita asked. "The conversation with Hunter, or lap time with the carnivore?"

Mary Lou walked over to the desk and rubbed Ted's cheek. "Theodore's not a carnivore. He eats kibble."

"I suggest you read the ingredients," Rita said, brushing the hairs from her uniform. Except her efforts seemed to make things worse, the hair forming a thick mat on each thigh.

"I'm not here to talk about Ted," Mary Lou said. "Ken Saunders would like to talk to you."

"I'm not taking any calls until I get this damn cat hair *off*," Rita said, with a huff. "I just put on this uniform. I need it to last at least a week like the last one."

"Ken's not on the line," Mary Lou said, looking glum. "He's here at HQ."

"Here-here?" Rita asked, pointing at the floor. Then

she went back to brushing her pants. "Unless you want to tell him I just got back from wrestling a mountain lion, I'm not taking appointments until this stuff comes off." She stopped rubbing at her pants and began picking off the hairs one by one. "And this is liable to take a while."

"Wait here a moment," Mary Lou said, leaving the office. Ted jumped off the desk and followed her out of the room.

"What am I, chopped liver?" Rita asked.

A minute later, Mary Lou (but not Theodore) returned with an adhesive roller. She passed it over Rita's thigh, removing Ted's hairs.

"Well, that's a fucking miracle," Rita said.

Mary Lou grinned and rolled Rita's other thigh. "This baby was indispensable the other night when Ted's hairs were all over my lingerie. Lucky's allergic to cats, you know. Couldn't have his eyes swelling up."

"Heaven forbid," Rita said. "Don't want anything swelling up that shouldn't be."

Mary Lou stepped back to admire her handiwork. "Much better," she said. "Oh, while you were talking to Hunter, I asked my friend what they say about painters."

Rita's brow lifted. "Oh, yeah?"

"Yeah. Unfortunately she didn't know. But she *did* tell me what they say about gearheads."

Rita's brow puckered. "Oh, yeah?"

Mary Lou twerked. "They're sure good at grindin'."

Chapter Eight

Ken Saunders walked into Rita's office. He wore a light gray suit jacket over a black button-down, reflective sunglasses hooked in the breast pocket.

"Afternoon, Sheriff," he said, closing the door. He walked over and sat in one of the chairs facing her desk.

It wobbled and creaked under his weight.

"That one has a broken backrest," Rita said.

Ken pried himself out of the chair and moved toward the other one. "Then why is it in here?"

Rita pointed to the chair he was about to sit in. "Because that one has a broken leg."

Ken paused. Grumbling under his breath, he returned to the first chair, arranging his weight so it didn't creak. Then he folded his meaty hands on his lap.

"I spoke to Angela Ruiz this morning," he said.

"How's the weather in Brazil?" Rita asked.

Ken didn't answer. "Ms. Ruiz advised me that we'll be helping the SCSO on this case."

Rita raised an eyebrow. "The DA and I were just

discussing Apex's intentions. And I have to say, they're usually duplicitous."

Ken spread his hands and smiled. "I'm not sure what you mean by ducipibliss — duplissibiss — ducidious. But whatever you need in respects to this case, just let me know."

"Hm," Rita said. Now more than ever, she was convinced Angela was using cooperation to woo her over to Apex.

"All right," she said. "We'll cooperate on this one. Tell me what you got."

Ken drew himself up, jiggling the chair. "I'm the one that found Adrian."

Rita pulled out her phone, opening the voice app. "I'm going to record this."

Ken nodded. "When the front-gate alarms went off," he said, "I figured there was more vandalism. I found Adrian hiding along the perimeter fence."

"Poor kid," Rita said. "Terrified and shot."

Ken rubbed his palms along his thighs. "He was downright hysterical. I got him up to Apex's medical center right away."

An image of Boyd with hands on Lisa Myers flashed through Rita's mind. "You get any of this on tape?"

Ken shook his head. "No footage. Security cameras are still broken."

Rita scoffed. "You're kidding."

Ken flushed. "Apex has had quite a bit to deal with lately, Sheriff."

"No shit," Rita said. "So you didn't see a copycat Apex truck?"

Ken frowned. "Wasn't looking for one. And the kid didn't say nothing. I had no idea about the shootout at the reservoir until your call came through."

Rita studied him for a moment. "Did you know about George selling drugs at Apex?"

"No," Ken said. He frowned. "And this feels like an interrogation."

"Wasn't it mentioned in Boyd's files?"

"What, George's side gig? No. Before Boyd left, he destroyed all his personal files, paper and digital. Or maybe Victor Price did." Ken rubbed a hand over his bristle-brush hair. "D'you think George has got anything to do with the copycat trucks?"

Rita shook her head. "George was low key. Plus he wasn't that organized. You got any other leads?"

"Nope. But we'll find it," Ken said. "Took your earlier suggestion and put a notice in the paper, with a digital rendering of the truck."

"Nicely done," Rita said. "What else is Apex doing?"

Ken shrugged his enormous shoulders. "Generally beefing up security."

Rita looked him over. "And by that, I'll assume you mean replacing the broken security cameras, not increasing your workouts and protein shakes."

"Yeah, cameras," Ken said. "But Apex police are out searching for the van now. It's only a matter of time."

"What's their plan if they find the shooters?"

Ken gave her a look. "Arrest them, of course."

"They shot and killed a sixteen-year-old boy and nearly killed another kid. I know throwing a few punches is all fun and games for types like you and your pal Clyde, but this pair is armed and dangerous. Your crew's gotta be careful."

Ken gave her a grim nod. "I understand."

"Good," Rita said. "I need to be able to get a good night's rest, without worrying about any more officers getting injured."

"You do look like you could use some rest," Ken said.

"Thanks," Rita said, her tone dry, "I didn't know." She stood up, indicating the end of the meeting. "Goodbye, Ken."

But Ken stayed seated. "What can I help *you* with, Sheriff?"

Rita moved toward the door. "Looking for the van is helpful, thanks."

"All right," Ken said, pushing up from the creaky chair. He hovered by Rita's desk. "Well, let me know if I can, you know … cooperate."

Rita smiled, reaching for the doorknob. "I think we already are."

Ken nodded, his thick fingers fidgeted with a button his suit jacket. "Er — did Ms. Ruiz offer you Boyd's position at Apex?"

Rita's hand paused on the doorknob. "Why would she do that?"

Ken shrugged. "Before she left, she told me she wasn't ready to make a decision about filling the position. She said she was waiting for a response from one more candidate."

Rita kept her face impassive. "And you think that candidate was me?"

Ken scratched his head. "It might have been."

Rita found a stray cat hair on her cuff and plucked it off. "Do *you* think she was considering me?"

Ken thought for a moment. "You're right," he said. "Probably not." Then he walked toward her and held out his hand for a shake.

Rita ignored it, instead opening the door for him. "Goodbye, Ken."

He tipped his head at her, then walked through the door. Rita watched as he left the office, then blew out a sigh.

She strode out to the bullpen and chose another muffin: this time, lemon ginger. She passed the box to Jason, who was now seated at his desk. "Have some muffins, Jason."

Jason selected a bacon and cheese. "Thanks."

Rita gestured to Edith Mae's desk empty. "Take one for your sister."

"She's with her friend Gail's family," Jason said, peeling the wrapper. "They've gone to California for the week.

"Well, that was a sensible thing to do," Rita said, biting into her muffin. "Wish I'd thought of it. Though I'm surprised Esther let her go."

"Ma didn't," Jason said, biting into his muffin. "But I said she could."

Rita slapped his shoulder, then brushed a lemon crumb from his uniform. "You're a good brother, Jason."

Jason coughed on a muffin crumb. "I know."

Chapter Nine

"THAT WAS DYLAN BRUCE," Mary Lou said, hanging up the telephone. "He's scheduled Arnold's autopsy for nine a.m. tomorrow."

Rita licked the last of the lemon-ginger frosting from her fingers. "I'll head to Casper this afternoon. I'm hoping Adrian is well enough for an interview. Could you book me a room at the Best Western Lodge for tonight?"

"Ten-four," Mary Lou said. "But are you sure, Sheriff? You look darn tootin' tired."

"I know, I've heard it already."

Mary Lou tapped her pink lip. "Why don't you send Jason to the autopsy?"

Jason turned white.

Rita rubbed her face. "Because Arnold was Lisa's half-brother, and Lisa was my half-sister."

"And that means something," Jason said.

"You mean a conflict of interest?" Mary Lou said.

"Look who's talking," Rita said. "Your personal escapades around town make talking to anyone about anything a conflict of interest."

Mary Lou stood and put her hands on her hips. "That's not entirely accurate. Lucky's from out of town."

"I stand corrected," Rita said. "Besides, if I overnight in Casper, I can fit in a visit with Otto. Hunter says if I take leave, he's handing the whole investigation over to Apex."

Jason's eyes widened. "That's not fair."

From his perch, Theodore meowed.

Rita sighed. "Fair or unfair, that's policy. Or at least according to Hunter. And if the D.A. pulls the case from us, it could jeopardize the SCSO."

Mary Lou folded her arms. "It would be another step toward shuttin' us down altogether."

Jason rubbed the scar on his thigh. "So we play nice with Apex, huh?"

"Sorry, Jason," Rita said. "I gotta cooperate with Ken." She turned to Mary Lou. "And no throwing dirt. We keep the dirt in *our* sandbox as much as possible."

Mary Lou gave a pink pout and a curt nod, her beehive bobbing. Rita always wondered how she crammed it all inside her motorcycle helmet.

"I'll check in with Beaumont and Casper drug units to see if they have any leads," Jason said.

"And I'll call with any updates from Apex about the suspect van," Mary Lou said.

"Thank you, thank you very much," Rita said, hoping for Mary Lou's benefit that she sounded at least a little like the King.

Mary Lou smiled. "For that, I'll book you a King-sized bed at the Best Western."

"See you tomorrow, you two," Rita said.

She snagged the last muffin in the box and walked out to the parking lot. A few minutes later, she was parking in the lot behind the Bighorn Bean, and a few minutes after that she was climbing back into the truck, carrying a packed overnight bag.

Then she was on her way to Casper, picking at the apple-walnut muffin that would have otherwise been Walter's.

On the drive, images of Arnold at the morgue flashed through her mind.

Then images of Helen, distraught.

And Otto, unconscious.

Rita focused her eyes, concentrating on the road. She was gonna have some hellish nightmares if she didn't clear out the images of everything she'd seen in the past twenty-four hours.

She tried to envision Cash, shirtless. But why stop there? She imagined him without any clothing at all. And then outside, by a river. Then she imaged herself by the river, also without clothes.

But it was no use. Unwanted thoughts continued to crowd her mind.

In this instance, Heather Bannister. Formerly called Heather Gabriel. AKA Cash Gabriel's first wife.

Rita felt her brow puckering and tried to smooth it out with her fingertip.

"Damn it," she said to her reflection in the rear-view mirror. "Why does he have to be so sexy?"

"It's the hair," she said back to herself. "Always looks like he just rolled out of bed."

Rita grunted. "You're right."

"Of course I'm right," her reflection said. "I wouldn't leave you guessing."

She pulled into the hospital parking lot and turned off the ignition.

But she felt frozen, even in the sticky heat.

"Last night I didn't know what to say," she said to her reflection. "Now I don't know what to do."

"Breathe," she said back to herself. "That's what to do."

She nodded. "You're right. Breathe."

"I'm right. No guessing."

Together, she and the Rita in the rear-view mirror breathed.

Inhale deeply. 1, 2, 3, 4.

Hold. 1, 2, 3, 4, 5, 6, 7.

Exhale. 1, 2, 3, 4, 5, 6, 7, 8.

Then she unfastened her belt and headed inside and upstairs to Adrian's room. As she rounded a corner in the corridor, she came upon Walter and his ex-wife, Winona.

Although only a handful of years apart, the couple appeared to have a difference in age of twenty years plus. In reality, Walter was only a half-decade older. But he'd collected weight around the middle, while Winona had whittled away every extra pound. And where Walter's hair had receded, Winona's had grown to an impressive length (thanks to extensions).

"You were supposed to be looking after our kid," she said, her long ponytail bobbing. "Not lettin' him turn into a felon. Some cop you turned out to be! Or should I say, some father?"

Walter stiffened and Rita strode toward them.

"The only one at fault is whoever shot those boys," she said, interrupting the scene.

Winona turned, her face purple with fury. "Oh, Rita — I'm sorry to hear about your dad."

"Thanks, Winona." Rita said. She cleared her throat. "I'm sorry, too, for what's happened to your son." She glanced at Walter, whose face had also turned a shade of purple. "Walter."

He swallowed. "Rita. Been meaning to let you know, Casper P.D. picked up the bullet from the surgeon."

"Thanks," Rita said. "How's he doing?"

Walter's face relaxed. "Pretty good, actually. Doc says he ain't gonna have any lasting mobility issues with his shoulder. He's got a long road of physiotherapy ahead of him, but he likes to swim."

"That's great to hear," Rita said. "Is he up for some questions?"

Winona stiffened. "What's the meaning of this?" She glanced at Rita, then at Walter. "Does Adrian need a lawyer?"

Walter made an impatient sound. "No, Winnie, he's not being charged with nothing. He's a goddamned witness."

"He's our only witness at the moment," Rita said. "Wish it were another way, Winona."

"The nurse is changing his wrappings," Walter said. "She ought to be done in a tick."

"Have you told him about Arnold yet?" Rita asked.

Walter and Winona glanced at one another, then shook their heads.

The nurse emerged from the room. "You may go in now," she said. "He's comfortable."

Winona rushed inside the room and Walter followed. Rita waited a heartbeat, then joined them at Adrian's bedside.

He looked pale, but better than the night before. Winona and Walter gave him kisses and said encouraging words.

Then Walter gestured to Rita. "This is Sheriff Jonas. She's got some questions for you."

Adrian nodded, pushing up on his pillows. A hospital-issue nightgown covered a large, fresh bandage on his left shoulder. "I figured."

Winona and Walter shuffled back to lean against the wall, side-by-side. Rita drew up a chair and sat beside Adrian.

A familiar feeling of sitting at Otto's bedside coursed through her. Her pulse quickened and she took a deep breath.

"Adrian," she said, meeting his eye, "I appreciate you seeing me." She paused for her own benefit, collecting her thoughts. "How are you feeling?"

He shifted against the raised mattress of the electrical bed. "Could do with a fucking decent pillow." He nodded toward the one behind his back. "This thing's like a slice of fucking Wonder Bread. And my shoulder hurts like fuck if I'm not jacked on pain meds. Though the doc says I'm lucky since I'm right-handed and the bullet grazed my *left* shoulder. And she said I shouldn't expect any lasting injuries."

"I've got a whole home-based recovery plan in mind for him," Winona said. "Based on Pilates, Yoga, and yodeling."

Walter narrowed his eyes at his ex-wife. "Adrian needs to follow doctor's orders, not yours."

Adrian frowned at his father. "Mom knows what she'd doing, Dad. She made me use the netty pot last year when I had a sinus infection, and you wouldn't believe what—"

"That's wonderful, Adrian," Rita said. "I'm happy to hear you won't have lasting problems with your shoulder."

Adrian beamed. "Just a scar. And that's sexy as hell, ain't it? A bullet-wound in my shoulder … Imagine the girls that I'll score when I'm twenty."

"Imagine," Rita said. "Your luck will really be flowing then."

"He's lucky the bullet didn't hit any major blood vessels, that's what," Winona said, her voice tight.

"Right," Rita said, as Jason came to mind. "That can be a risk in a large muscle."

"Well, that's good, son," Walter said, winking at Adrian. "'Cause y'ain't got any of those."

Winona hit him on the arm. "Who are you to talk?"

"Ouch," Walter said, rubbing his biceps. "You been doing somethin', Winnie? Besides yoga?"

Winona flicked a long strand out of her face. "Kettlebells."

Walter whistled. "Jesus."

"Cool," Adrian said.

"I'm enrolled in a course for a kettlebell work-out," Rita said. "It's an online thing."

"How do you like it?" Winona asked.

"Dunno," Rita said. "I don't have a kettlebell."

"You won't regret it," Winona said.

"Good to know," Rita said. "Shall we get on with things?"

Adrian nodded. "Sure."

"Is there anything you need before Sheriff Jonas starts?" Winona asks.

"Pillows," Adrian said. "Plumper ones."

Winona blinked at him a couple of times. "Certainly, honey." She stepped away from his bedside to rummage in the wood veneer cupboard. "I'll see what they've got."

"This isn't the Ritz," Walter said. "There ain't going to be extra pillows in the wardrobe."

Winona closed the cupboard door. "No spare pillows," she said, as if Walter hadn't spoken.

"You'll have to tough it out like a Spartan," Walter said.

"Damn," Adrian said.

"Stop cussin'," Winona said.

"Ain't cussin'," Adrian said. "Just cursin'."

Winona snorted. "Cursin'? How's that different than cussin'?"

"Angels don't mind curse words. They know you got to cast out the devil, so they'll let you damn things and piss on things and shit on 'em, if you have to. But try to fuck things or suck things or—"

"We understand," Winona said.

"—those are cuss words," Adrian said, "because you're tryin' to make someone feel downright dirty 'bout something. And even I know that ain't right."

"You and Arnold spray-painted both cuss words and curse words," Rita pointed out.

Adrian flushed a shade that would complement the neon yellow spray-paint. "That's right, Sheriff Jonas," he said. He paused to look at his parents. Then his gaze returned to Rita. "I won't do it again, Sheriff Jonas."

"That's great to know, Adrian," Rita said. "But we'll talk another time about how to make amends and move on from this. In the meantime, I appreciate you answering my questions about last night." She broke eye contact to give him some space. "Some of them might be uncomfortable."

Again, Adrian glanced at his parents. Walter nodded. Winona looked wooden. Adrian turned back to Rita, "Okay."

"Please tell me what happened last night," Rita said.

Adrian licked his lips before speaking. "We were leaving the Gas N Go when we noticed an Apex van start to follow us. At least we thought it was an Apex van, when we first saw it. Just a regular ol' set of Apex wheels. Except it was kind of a junker. Had some rust spots. Painted over, but you could still tell."

"Then what happened?" Rita asked.

"They stuck to us. We figured it was some hot-headed security type that we must've cut off without noticing. But they never put no siren or lights on, so we decided to lose 'em on the freeway. We hit the gas, figuring we'd get the hell out of there. And that's when we knew they were chasing us, 'cause they damn well near drove us off the road."

Rita wrote some notes. "Who was driving, you or Arnold?"

Adrian glanced at his parents again. "Me."

"You're a good driver, son," Walter said.

"Go on," Rita said.

"They caught up with us," Adrian said, trembling. "And then they fired at us."

Winona came to his bedside and took his hand.

"Did you see the drivers?" Rita asked.

"All we saw was there was two of them. But they was both wearing ski masks."

"That must have been very frightening."

"Sure as fuck was," Adrian said. "Um, sorry 'bout the cuss words."

"And then what?" Rita asked.

Adrian gripped the blanket. "We weren't sure where to go at first. Then Arnold mentioned the reservoir. We used to hang out there lots." He glanced at his father. "You know, parties and such. Anyhow, we headed there. Figured we'd jump over the railing and swim to the other side." His fingers gripped tighter. "We *agreed* on it, man. Adrian said he could do it. So I got out and jumped in and started swimmin'. I thought Arnold was right there behind me. But we got split up—"

His voice broke off in a choke.

Rita reached for the bottled water on his bedside table

and handed it to him. "What happened when you started swimming?"

Winona rubbed Adrian's back. "Must you keep goin', Sheriff? We can all see how tired he is."

Adrian swallowed back the water, then wiped his lips dry on the back of his hand. "I figured that if those fuckers from Apex — sorry, Ma — but I figured if those fuckers *were* from Apex, they wouldn't shoot at me on home turf. So I headed for the property."

Rita refrained from mentioning his assessment of Apex was probably flawed. "And you made it to the Apex perimeter fence?"

Adrian nodded. "Think I might have set off some alarms, first trying out the gate. Big guy in sunglasses found me and helped out." He took another sip of water, his hands shaking. "Is Arnold here too?" He glanced at his father. "At the hospital, I mean? Dad hasn't said anything."

Rita sat forward, taking the water bottle from his hands. "I'm sorry to tell you, Adrian, Arnold was killed."

Adrian's mouth opened. Then he buckled over, a cry finally emitting from his throat.

Chapter Ten

WINONA THREW her arms around Adrian, but he pushed her away.

"No, Ma."

Winona released him and glared at Rita. "No more questions," she said. "It's too much for him. It's too much for all of us."

"Too much for *you*, Ma? How 'bout me? Arnold's *my* friend!"

"See how upset he is?" Winona said, staring down Rita.

"You're damn right I'm upset," Adrian said. "'Cause it was all my idea, Ma. I'm the one who stole the van!"

"Stop talking, Adrian," Winona said. "We don't need to do this now. What you probably need is a lawyer."

"I want to talk to Sheriff Jonas alone," Adrian said.

Winona gripped his shoulders again. "Adrian—"

"Fuck off, Ma." Adrian shook her lose. "It's your fault."

Winona stepped backwards, her ponytail swaying. "What's my fault? What are you saying, Adrian?"

Adrian's cheeks burned red. "If you hadn't moved us to

Beaumont, I wouldn't have had to leave my best friend alone in that shithole. And I could've been there for him when his sister died."

Winona touched his shoulder with a tentative hand. "But Adrian, it's not up to you to take care of Arnold—"

Adrian screamed. "He was my friend!"

"We'll take a break, Adrian," Rita said, stepping back. "And give you some time alone."

But Winona wrapped herself around her son. "I'm not leaving Adrian right now."

"Get away from me, Ma!" Adrian wrestled his pillow out from under his injured shoulder and swatted his mother with it. "Get out!"

Rita traded a look with Walter.

He took the cue, moving toward his wife. "Come on, Winona." He tugged her away. "And Adrian, son, take it easy—"

Adrian threw the pillow, striking Walter in the head.

"Get out!"

Rita scooped up the pillow from the floor and put it on the foot of the bed. "We're going Adrian, but anytime you—"

"No, stay," he said, swiveling his gaze on her. "You stay, Sheriff Jonas."

"Sure," Rita said, freezing. Then she sat in the chair by the bed.

Winona cut her eyes at Rita. Walter nudged her and she allowed him to lead her from the room.

"Take care, Winona," Rita said. Then she nodded at Walter. "Walter."

Walter nodded and gave her an uncertain smile.

Rita smiled back, then faced Adrian again. He was watching her closely.

She took out her phone. "I'm going to record our

conversation," she said, swiping open the voice recorder app.

"Okay," Adrian said. He sounded relieved. "What do you know? Everything?"

"I know about the vandalism," Rita said, pressing record. "And now I know that it was your idea to steal the van. Why'd you target that one?"

"We didn't think nobody would notice us drivin' it around 'cause it looked like all the other Apex vans. More or less."

"So you drove it around a bit, committing random acts of vandalism, and keeping a secret about Arnold moving back into the Myers place?"

Adrian nodded.

Rita gave him an appraising look. "Bold moves."

Arian stuck out his chin. "Apex doesn't scare us."

"But then you ditched the van and torched it?"

He nodded again, screwing his hands around the water bottle.

"Why did you do that?" Rita asked.

The bottle crinkled in his fists. "'Cause we figured out it wasn't a regular maintenance vehicle."

"How so?"

"It was a fucking chemistry lab."

Rita gave him a wry smile. "A *chemistry* lab?"

Adrian blushed. "It was drugs, okay? But I don't do nothin' with drugs and I don't want my dad thinkin' I do." His cheeks burned a little hotter. "Mom and me love Jesus, okay?"

"Got it," Rita said. Then she gave him a slight frown. "Brave choice, torching that van."

Adrian crinkled his brow. "What d'you mean?"

"Could have exploded. All those chemicals."

He scratched his head. "Didn't think of that. Just

wanted to be rid of it. Hoped Apex would clean up its burned-out shell and nothin' more would come of it."

"Except it never belonged to Apex in the first place, so that was never going to happen."

"Damn logo on the side wasn't painted," Adrian said, setting his jaw. "Just a fucking decal that started to shrink and peel in the heat. When we saw that, we tried to put out the fire. But it was too late."

"Well, I'm sure you knew why they'd disguised it," Rita said. "Did either of you have any ideas about who owned the van?"

Adrian shook his head.

"Do you think whoever you stole it from saw you do this?"

Adrian shrugged. "Like they were tailing us before that night?" He shrugged again. "It's possible."

"Where did you steal it from?" Rita asked.

"We first saw it on the freeway, traveling a ways ahead of us. When it turned onto Windset Lane, I got the idea and followed it."

"That's the rural road that runs a couple miles parallel to Miners Way?"

Adrian nodded. "Yeah. Bunch of ol' farmhouses. Except no farms no more. Dad says we used to get produce out that way. Berries and shit, when I was a kid. But not since they put Miners Way through that land."

"I see," Rita said. "So you headed down Windset Lane with intent to steal the van?"

"It's real quiet out that way. Not many folk around." Adrian flushed. "And a long way from the SCSO."

Rita nodded. "Go on."

"The van stopped."

"At an address?"

"Yeah. A crummy yellow house. Bunch of overgrown

bushes around it. If we lived there, Dad would make me prune them."

"What happened?" Rita asked.

"Two guys got out of the van and went to the front door. They looked like maintenance men."

"Did they go into the house?"

"No, they only talked to the lady for a minute."

"Did you happen to overhear their conversation?"

"No. But I could hear some kid wailin'."

"Then what did the men do?"

"They walked 'round back of the place. So I took my chance."

"Did you get a look at them?"

"No. They were walking away from us. Plus they were movin' fast and I was movin' fast, too. I found the key in the ignition, so I started it up."

"Where was Arnold?"

"He took the wheel of my Ford and followed."

"What did you do after that?" Rita asked.

Adrian took a moment before answering. "Partied."

Rita raised an eyebrow.

"Edith Mae Perry stole us some six-packs and we drank 'em at the reservoir."

"Edith Mae Perry is sixteen."

Adrian looked impressed. "No shit?" He scratched as his bandages. "Guess it's the black lipstick that makes her look so mature. I thought she'd graduated."

"I believe she dropped out," Rita said. "So you went down to the reservoir with the beers. Why?"

"To celebrate bein' real anarchists." Fresh tears welled up in Adrian's eyes. "And now Arnold's died for the cause."

Rita bit down on her lip, stopping herself from saying Arnold's death had been senseless. Instead, she asked: "I meant, why'd you go to the reservoir?"

Adrian choked back a sob. "Because we liked to throw the empty cans in the water."

"I see." Rita closed the voice recorder app. "I appreciate the information, Adrian. It'll help us find out who did this to you, and who's responsible for Arnold's death."

More tears flowed down Adrian's face. "You're welcome."

"You might want to google 'survivor's guilt,'" Rita said. "Just in case you're feeling it."

Adrian looked up at her. "What's that?"

"Something people sometimes feel when it's not their fault."

Adrian's gaze dropped again. "Okay. Thanks."

Out in the hallway, Rita approached Walter. He stood with his back against the wall, staring into space. More than an arm's length away, Winona also leaned against the wall, her head bowed over her phone.

"Walter," Rita said.

He looked up.

"I'm putting you on compassionate leave for the remainder of the week."

Walter's gaze hardened. "I ain't taking leave."

"You need to, Walter," Rita said.

"What I need is to find my son's shooter."

"And we're doing that," Rita said. "But the best way you can help is by staying close to your son. It's possible he might start to remember more once the anesthetic and adrenaline wears off. Not to mention the grief. Keep him talking."

Walter sighed. Then he nodded. "Will do, Jonas."

"Hang on," Winona said, approaching. "Adrian ain't goin' back to Still."

"He's our only witness to Arnold's murder," Rita said. "If that's where——"

"I'll keep him safe," Walter said. "If the shooters know Adrian's fit to testify, he could be in danger."

"Jesus Christ," Winona said, her eyes wide as saucers.

"Good idea," Walter said, throwing her a look. "Call on Jesus. We can always use his help, too."

Winona stiffened. "Walter can come here," she said, speaking to Rita as if Walter wasn't there.

Walter looked at his ex-wife. "What'd you say?"

Winona tossed her extensions, and Rita noticed her breasts were also artificial. "I said, you can stay here. At the house. With Adrian. And me."

Rita nodded. "Good plan, Winona." She looked at Walter. "Keep me informed."

Walter gave a nod. "Sure thing, Sheriff." Then he glowered at Winona. "You plannin' on givin' me the futon?"

Rita wished them a good night and went downstairs to Otto's room.

Although it had only been twenty-four hours, she was shocked by his appearance. He looked frailer, paler, lighter.

She sat on the edge of his bed, holding one of his hands in both of hers. How much less of it there was to hold than only yesterday.

"Hi, Dad. Otto. It's me. Rita. I'm here."

The machines helping him breathe beeped without pause. Persistent. Rhythmic. She watched their flashing green, red, and blue lights, unable to look at Otto's face where it seemed all the lights had dimmed.

For a long while, she sat.

Unable to think of anything to say.

Eventually, she tucked the blanket around him and left.

Chapter Eleven

RITA WALKED through the hospital parking lot to the truck. She dropped into the driver's seat to rest her head against the seat. For a moment, she sat, listening to the sound of her own breath.

Inhale.

Exhale.

When her head felt clear, she found Tilda's number in her contacts. The call rang through to her voicemail.

Rita left a message, asking if Tilda would be available to meet following the autopsy to review the evidence.

She rang off and checked the time. It was early. She dumped her phone in the car console and started the ignition, headed to the Natrona County Jail.

After a swift drive, Rita arrived at the courthouse, slowing to turn into the parking lot beside it. She parked in one of the stalls along the perimeter fence, reserved for law enforcement vehicles. The penitentiary, a one-story brick building, adjoined the courthouse via a covered pedestrian walkway.

She entered the purple-painted reception area and signed in, requesting to speak to George Myers.

While she waited, Rita browsed the covers on a wall-mounted magazine rack. One read: *Coffee: Six Surprising Health Perks of Your Daily Brew.*

Rita was trying to work out how to feed the magazine through the series of metal rods that constructed the rack when the receptionist called out.

"George Myers for Sheriff Rita Jonas." A light lit up on one of the booths. "Number five, please."

Rita slid the magazine back between the rods. Or tried to. It sagged over the rods, pages fluttering open.

Rita sighed and walked over to the booth. She took a seat and picked up the telephone receiver.

On the other side of the bulletproof partition, George mirrored her movements. He looked heavier than when he'd come in here. The redness of his eyes indicated he'd recently been crying.

"Hello, George," Rita said. "I'm so sorry for your loss."

George took a breath. "Warden told me about Arnold last night."

"It's an immense shock to all of us," Rita said.

"It's a fucking shock, all right," George said. "I didn't know how I would survive losing Lisa." He gave a bitter laugh. "And turns out, she wasn't even my fucking kid." He dropped his head into his hands, shoulders shaking as he sobbed. He lifted his head again, his eyes imploring. "He was my son, Rita. I gotta know who did this."

Rita touched the glass between them. "We're doing everything we can. Everyone. Beaumont. Casper."

George gave a weak nod. "Did this happen because I killed Matt Kirkland?"

"I don't believe it's related. I think this has to do with the torching of that meth van."

George leaned back and slapped his thighs. "Arnold had nothing to do with that shit. He ain't a seller and he ain't a user."

"That's not quite what I meant," Rita said. "Adrian and Arnold stole the van because they thought it belonged to the Apex fleet and would go unnoticed." She shrugged. "Taking an Apex van appealed to their anarchistic tastes. And unbeknownst to them, it was a meth lab on wheels. They made a rash decision to torch it, then discovered it had only been disguised to be a van from the company." She paused to take a sip of water. "Who's running meth in Still?"

George blinked at her. "I got no clue."

Rita scoffed. "Come on, you gotta have a lead. With you in here, someone's picking up the slack. Who's keeping your regulars happy?"

"Piss off, Sheriff. If I had anything to share that would help you find Arnold's killer, you'd know in a heartbeat."

"You're right, George. I'm sorry. We're all shook up over this tragedy, and I'd damn near do anything to solve this."

George wiped away a tear. "How's Helen?"

"She's in shock, too. Not sure how much more she can take. She spent the night at the hospital."

George nodded but stayed silent.

"George…"

He met her eyes. "Yeah?"

Rita licked her lips. "I want you to know … Arnold … he wasn't alone." She paused to swallow. "He wasn't alone when he died."

George licked his lips too, his mouth close to the receiver. "I'm glad." His voice was barely more than a whisper. "Were — were you there?"

Rita nodded, even though he was staring down at the

floor. "Yes. And my deputy, Jason Perry. And Walter Hutch. You'd know him, of course, from your tenure as Fire Chief."

"Sure," George said, rubbing his neck. "I've played a few rounds of cards with him, too." His voice cracked.

"He held him, George. Walter held him in his arms. Me too. We held him together."

George started to nod, then hung his head, resting his forehead in his hand. This time, his voice sounded strangled. "I'm glad."

Rita gave him a moment of silence. Then she said, "Walter understands your pain, George. He didn't lose his boy, but he felt the fear of it. And despite being distracted by worry for his own son, he stayed with Arnold. And went with him, in the ambulance."

This time, George said nothing.

"I'm going to find who did this, George," Rita said. Then she stood, pushing back the chair. "Take care, George. I'm gonna go back to work now."

Face still buried in his hand, George managed a slight nod.

"I'll keep you updated," she said. Then she hung up the phone.

Rita walked through reception, but instead of exiting the building, she returned to the sign-in desk.

"May I speak with Thomas Gabriel, please?"

The receptionist looked up from her keyboard, blinking at Rita through glitter-framed glasses. "He only meets with his lawyer."

Rita smiled. "Please try."

The receptionist nodded. "Will do, Sheriff Jonas."

Choosing a chair beside the window, Rita sat to wait. She crossed and uncrossed her legs, trying to get comfortable on the plastic chair. A clock on the wall kept track of the minutes.

Tick, tick, tick.

She stood and walked over to the water dispenser. She filled a paper cup, then wandered by the magazine rack, sipping her water. The article about coffee sagged another inch before her eyes. Then it slipped free of the metal rods of the magazine rack and crashed to the floor.

Rita bent to pick it up when the receptionist announced her name.

"Sheriff Jonas?"

Rita stuffed the magazine back in the rack and returned to the desk. "Yes?"

"I'm sorry, Sheriff Jonas, Mr. Gabriel declines the visit."

"Thanks for trying," Rita said.

She crumpled and tossed her paper cup in the trash and headed outside.

Back in the truck, she stared through the windshield, drumming her fingers on the steering wheel. She couldn't help but think of the Myers family. In a few short months, both children were dead, one parent was in prison, and the other parent in the hospital.

Inhale.

Exhale.

She turned the ignition and pulled out of the lot, headed for the closest McDonald's. In the drive-thru, she ordered a burger and fries. Then she headed in the direction of the Best Western.

She passed a community park and braked to swing into the parking lot. She hopped out of the truck and chose a picnic table in a shady patch beneath a tree.

But the smell of her food turned her stomach. What was going on with her these days? Maybe Ruby Joe's home-cooking had ruined her tolerance for anything else. She picked off a corner of the hamburger bun and tossed it to a chipmunk.

"Enjoy," she said, grabbing the paper bag and heading back to the parking lot. In the truck, she pulled out her phone and googled the property on Windset Lane where Adrian had stolen the van. The yellow house was one of only a few addresses on the old road.

She texted Mary Lou the house address, then followed up with another.

Please find out what you can about the place. When you've ready to review, send me a Zoom link. Jason too

Mary Lou texted back right away. *10-4*

Thanks, Rita typed. *Headed to the Best Western now*

Mary Lou thumbs-upped the message and Rita hit the road, the scent of McDonald's filling the cabin of the truck. She opened the window and gulped in the fresh, windy gusts.

At the Best Western, she checked into a basic room with a king-size bed. Insipid framed floral prints hung on the walls, offering little competition to the view through the window of Casper Mountain.

Rita poured herself some water and oriented the armchair to enjoy the vista. Then she opened her tablet and logged onto the Zoom link awaiting in her email.

Mary Lou's and Jason's faces popped up on the screen.

"Howdy, Sheriff," Mary Lou said. "Got the scoop on the Windset Lane place."

"Go ahead," Rita said.

"It used to be owned by the Willow family. They moved away over ten years ago, but they still own it."

"Rented?" Rita asked.

"Or maybe vacant," Mary Lou said. "Don't know that yet, so I'll find out."

"Great. Could you also request a warrant for search of the property, please? It's where the boys stole the Apex van." Her eyes searched the summit of Casper Mountain, as if the scraggy peak contained the answers to her questions. "We need to find out that van's history."

"I checked with Beaumont," Mary Lou said. "Turns out the VIN number for the van was removed."

"Of course it was," Rita said.

"But we know it's an older model GMC," Mary Lou added.

"That's good info," Rita said. "Jason, check with the local dealerships. Find out what vans have been sold over the past six to twelve months."

"Sure thing," he said. "Also, I've been in touch with Bowman and Casper drug units. They've been hearing rumors about a new player in the region. But so far, they don't have any leads on who it might be. Maybe someone out of Cheyenne, but they can't verify that."

"Okay, thanks," Rita said.

"Oh, and Randy called," Mary Lou said. "He's repaired your Honda."

"Fantastic," Rita said. "Mary Lou, could you please ask him to tow it to the station and leave the keys with you?"

"Ten-four."

Rita's phone buzzed with a message. Maybe about Otto.

"Mary Lou," she said, "could you please check up on Helen Myers?"

"Already done," Mary Lou said. "She had a rough night. But she's resting now, with the aid of sedatives."

"Thanks," Rita said, her chest feeling hollow. "I appreciate you checking in with her."

"Happy to do it," Mary Lou said with a smile. "I like to help folks keep on keepin' on, if you know what I mean.

Like Elvis used to say, 'When things go wrong, don't go with 'em.'"

"Wise advice," Rita said. "All right, everyone, let's sign off. Good work."

Jason saluted and Mary Lou bobbed her beehive, and Rita closed the meeting. She put the tablet to sleep, then swiped open her phone.

The message was from Tilda.

Not about Otto. Rita felt a mix of disappointment and relief not to be called back to the hospital.

Hey, Tilda's message read, *no need to be alone in the city tonight. Taking you to dinner. Pick you up in 10*

Rita messaged back. *10-4*

Chapter Twelve

RITA SLID into the passenger seat of Tilda's Toyota.

"Rita, this is Bennett," Tilda said, gesturing to the backseat, where her eight-year-old daughter sat reading. She wore a headband with flashing LED stars. "Bennett, this is Rita."

Bennett raised a hand in greeting but kept her eyes trained on her comic book.

"It's a big night in our small world," Tilda said, "so Bee and I are going out on the town."

"So what are you two celebrating?" Rita asked.

Bennett looked up from her comic book, flashing a gap-toothed smile. "We won our hockey game."

Rita matched her grin. "Nice! Congratulations."

"Did you see me score the final goal?" Bennett asked.

"Sorry, no," Rita said, "I didn't catch the game. I was working all day. That's how your mom and I know each other."

"Okay," Bennett said, returning to her comic book. "It was a good game."

"And a good game always works up an appetite," Tilda said, pulling away from the curb. "Not just Bennett's, but mine too." She shivered as though she were still in the arena. "All that cheering in the chilly air."

"Sounds divine," Rita said, blotting away some sweat on her brow.

Tilda drove to a few blocks away to a family restaurant called The Range-Rider's Diner.

Aside from a row of arcade games, the place was a cozy throwback to a bygone era, with cowhide booths, wagon wheel lamp fixtures, and burnished wood tables.

Tilda waved down a server, then pointed to a family across the diner.

"Looks like more than one victory meal here tonight," Tilda said. "Amy's a teammate of Bennett's."

"Amy's the goalie," Bennett said, waving to her friend.

The server showed them to a booth and handed out laminated menus as dense as the Bible.

"It's gonna take me all night to read this," Rita said, flipping over the placard.

"Don't bother," Tilda said. "We only come here for shepherd's pie."

The server returned, and Tilda ordered three servings.

"Extra cheese, please," Bennett said.

The server made a note. "You got it."

"She earned it tonight," Tilda said, beaming with pride. "Big win at summer hockey camp."

"Way to go," the server said, smiling. "What are we toasting with?"

Bennet tapped her chin for a moment, relishing the decision. "Iced tea, please."

The server glanced at Tilda, then Rita. "Iced teas all around?"

"Absolutely," Tilda said. "We're living large tonight."

The server laughed and gathered the menus, then left to put in the order.

"Can I go play arcade games with Amy?" Bennett asked.

Tilda nodded and opened her purse. She dug out a handful of coins and gave them to Bennett.

Bennett thanked her mom, then headed to her friend's table.

When she was gone, Tilda leaned forward. "I heard through the grapevine that your father isn't well."

"He may have had a stroke," Rita said. "But we're waiting on test results to be sure."

"Aging parents," Tilda said with a sigh. "Looking after Mom was the reason I moved back to Casper in the first place. Rick thought she should have moved in with us. But she never could have done it, not with dementia. And definitely not in Chicago." Tilda shook her head. "Coming here was the only solution I could see. I always told Rick we wouldn't stay. Especially not after Mom died. But I got used to things here. And Bennett was so little then, and things seemed much easier with her in a city this size."

"But you couldn't convince Rick to stay on?"

Tilda's mouth flattened. "Eventually we divorced. He wanted his career. And so did I. But mostly I wanted to be the best mom I could be, and that seems simplest to do in somewhere more … simpler. You must appreciate that about Still, compared to New York?"

"Thanks to Apex, it's not quite as quiet as I'd hoped," Rita said. "Sometimes I miss New York. But mostly I think it's just the people I'm missing."

"Like Dale?"

For a moment Rita didn't answer, studying the tabletop. "I'm not sure anymore," she said. "There are a lot of things I don't feel so sure about these days." She crinkled her nose. "You ever feel like that?"

Tilda laughed. "All the time." She glanced over her shoulder to check on Bennett. "I'm a parent."

"I'm getting used to not having Dale around," Rita said, feeling a sudden pang of sadness. "How long did it take for you to get used to Rick not being there?"

Tilda scoffed. "Who said I got used to him not being there?" She blew out a sigh. "After we split, I dated for a while here in Casper. I was seeing a man who was caring for his mother, actually. And wouldn't you know, it's the reason I ended up letting him go." She gave a bitter laugh. "You'd think I'd have been more understanding. At least, that's what he said to me. But I *did* understand. All too well. Caring for Mom had consumed three years of my life, and I could see that caretaking was doing the same to his."

"It can be a lot," Rita said, images of Otto on the ventilator running through her mind.

Tilda nodded. "That's for damn sure. We wouldn't be going on vacation. There were no holiday celebrations. Already my job disrupted daily routines, and I knew this journey would do the same to his schedule. Having just walked that road myself, I didn't have it in me to do it again so soon, even if I was only the co-pilot."

The server stopped by with three glasses of iced tea with striped, paper straws.

Rita took a sip. "I don't know if I'll stay in Still after, you know … Otto passes. Too soon to tell. There's a lot about Still that I like. But there are also memories around every corner." She poked at the drink with her straw. "Nostalgia's a bitch."

Tilda laughed. "Tell me about it. And that's just the bad boyfriends. Tell me, you got a long-lost beau in town?"

Rita shrugged. "Sure, I bumped into an old boyfriend from high school."

Tilda grinned. "What kind of bumpin' are we talking about?"

Rita fiddled with the straw in case her face betrayed her private life. "Let's just say, it's a bumpy ride hanging out with old friends. Seems to make the changes over the years that much more obvious." Rita took another sip. "Although I don't think I've changed all that much. At least not according to Mary Lou and Ruby Joe and some of the other opinionated citizens of Still."

Tilda gave her a lopsided smile. "Don't be so hard on yourself. Life'll do that for us well enough."

Rita laughed. "Ain't that the truth?"

Tilda tapped her glass against Rita's. "Look, whether you stay or go, Rita, make sure you're choosing for yourself. Not because of what anyone else thinks. Not even for Otto. Thank God I made the decision to stay for Bennett and myself. Otherwise, I'd be back in Chicago. With Rick. Probably miserable. And we're all getting too old to stack up any more regrets."

Rita crinkled her nose. "Suit yourself. I've got to believe I've still got more mistakes to make, and plenty of time to get over them."

Tilda sat back in the booth. "Girlfriend, regrets are one thing. They're like wrecking balls. But mistakes?" She gave a one-shouldered shrug. "They're more like ping-pong balls. Light and easy to roll with. And we got all the time we'll ever need to get over, under, or on top of any mistakes we're planning to make. Especially the tall, dark, and handsome ones."

Rita blushed. "I think we should stop talking about this, in case Bennett comes back."

"Ah, shit, she's heard it all in the locker-room anyway."

"Well, that's a relief."

The server arrived with three steaming servings of shepherd's pie, one of them clearly extra cheesy. Tilda slipped out of the booth to fetch Bennett.

While she waited for them, Rita poked at her meal. It smelled delicious, and yet she had no appetite.

Tilda and Bennett returned to the booth, sitting together on the bench opposite Rita. Bennett blew the steam from her meal, but it was still too hot to eat. She dragged her fork through the melted cheese, making webbed patterns.

She fixed an eye on Rita. "Why don't you have kids?"

Rita shrugged. "Because I never married."

Rita's answer didn't appear to satisfy her. "Well, why didn't you get married?"

"Bennett," Tilda said, a hint of warning in her voice. She glanced at Rita. "You don't have to answer these questions."

Rita smiled. "It's okay." She punctured the potato crust with her fork, releasing a cloud of steam. "I didn't get married because … I changed my mind."

"Why'd you change your mind?" Bennett asked.

Rita thought. "Because I had a change of heart."

"How did it change?"

"Bennett—"

"It's okay," Rita said again. She turned to Bennett. "I think my heart got smaller. Tighter. More scared."

"Scared? Why?"

"I think the idea of having kids scared me."

Bennett laughed. "Kids *scare* you?"

"Maybe it's not the kids," Rita conceded. "Maybe it's responsibility that scares me."

Tilda made a sound like a buzzer. "I call bullshit," she said. "Cops ain't afraid of responsibility."

Rita sampled her shepherd's pie. "You might be right. Maybe it's just relationships that scare me."

Bennett's eyes widened. "Quantum," she said, with a note of awe. "That's what mom says, too."

Tilda blushed. "Bennett."

"It's true," Bennett said.

"Definitely true," Rita said. She winked at Tilda. "I won't tell anyone you're scared if you don't tell anyone I'm scared."

Tilda laughed. "Deal. Although, for the record, dating apps *are* scary. Meeting up with a stranger based on a swipe to the right and five hundred characters? How the hell is that supposed to tell me what's going on between someone's ears?"

Rita stuck out her tongue. "Dating's all about guesswork. And I hate guessing."

"It's probably a good thing you didn't get yourself a kid," Tilda said. "Parenting's a lot of guesswork."

"I knew it." Rita bugged her eyes at Bennett. "Dodged a bullet there."

Bennet pulled a face. "It's not like kids are complicated."

"You make raising kids sound as easy as pie," Tilda said. "Or in this case, shepherd's pie."

Bennett wiped her mouth with her napkin. "They are easy," she insisted. "All you got to do is play games with them. And play make believe. And sing. Maybe dance. Definitely cuddle."

Rita tried to sound light, but her voice felt brittle. "Those things aren't so easy for me."

Bennett frowned. "Why not? Did you forget how to play?"

Rita sampled her shepherd's pie. Tilda was right. It was savory and satisfying. She swallowed and met Bennett's eye. "I'm not sure I ever learned."

Bennett frowned. "Why not?"

Rita shrugged. "Didn't have any sisters or brothers."

Bennett knit her brow. "Neither do I. What about your mom and dad?"

"If you mean, did I play with them, no, not really. My daddy was always working. Often, I stood on the side of the road waiting for backup while he redirected traffic or administered first aid."

"That's sad," Bennett said, sucking back the last of her tea. "What about your mom? What did you do with her?"

For a moment, Rita was quiet, eating another mouthful. "Cleaned up, I suppose. I cleaned up a lot of broken stuff. Or spilled stuff. Tidied a lot of messes."

Bennett's brow crinkled more. "Like kitchen work?"

Rita nodded. "And bathroom work. Sometimes bedroom work. Everywhere-in-the-house work. She was sick a lot. From drinking."

Bennett squared her shoulders. "Mom doesn't drink."

Rita half-smiled. "That's a smart move. I think about it from time to time."

The server stopped by to offer coffee and dessert. Rita and Tilda declined (despite Bennett's protests) and Tilda asked for the bill.

"My treat," she said.

"Thanks," Rita said. "It was nice not to eat alone."

"You didn't eat much," Tilda said. "I hope you're feeling all right."

Rita forced a smile. "Seen a lot of death this week, that's all."

"I understand," Tilda said. "Work used to affect my appetite, too. But not so much now."

The server returned with the bill and a box for the remainder of Rita's meal. Rita noticed that Bennett had eaten more than she did.

"Thanks again," Rita said when Tilda dropped her off at the Best Western. "Good night."

"See you tomorrow afternoon at the PD," Tilda said, pulling out. Then she put up her window, and the Toyota rolled out of the parking lot.

Rita headed up to her hotel room where she showered and pulled on her PJs. She was turning down the covers when her phone rang. Immediately she thought of Otto. Then Cash.

But it was a number she didn't recognize.

"Sheriff Jonas speaking."

"Hello, Sheriff Jonas, this is Alan Crawford. I'm Tom Gabriel's attorney."

"Hello, Alan," Rita said. "What can I do for you?"

"I'm phoning to find out what I can do for you, Sheriff. Why'd you stop by to see Tom this afternoon?"

"If I answered that question, I'd be doing something for you," Rita said.

"Well, aren't you clever."

"And aren't you presumptuous."

"So you won't tell me why you want to speak with my client?"

"A private matter," Rita said.

"Is this about the dead kid in Still?"

"Can't say," Rita said. "Like I said, it's personal."

For a moment, Alan said nothing, and Rita wondered if the call had dropped. Then: "All right, Sheriff. Tom says he'll talk to you. You can come back tomorrow afternoon."

"I'm not sure I can make it tomorrow afternoon," Rita said. "I've got a meeting."

"Tomorrow or forget it."

"I'll see what I can do," Rita said. Then she hung up.

She texted Tilda next.

Can you meet earlier tomorrow?

Tilda texted back. *We can chat over lunch. Come by after the autopsy.*

Rita grimaced. *Sounds appetizing.* Then she set the alarm on her phone and climbed into bed.

But sleep didn't come. She tossed and turned, thinking about Arnold and Lisa.

She grabbed her phone again and dialed Otto's landline, listening to his voicemail:

"You've reached Otto Jonas. I'm retired now, so don't expect much from me. Leave a short and sweet message if you like. If not, you can go fu—"

A high-pitched beep cut off Otto's voice, indicating live recording.

Rita disconnected, then called and listened again. And again, dialing and listening on repeat. Years of smoking had made Otto's voice coarse. And she missed it now. She imagined the small amber light on his answering machine flashing each time it kicked in, displaying a weak sign of occupancy in the empty house.

Then she recalled that his cell phone was sitting on the counter beside his landline, charging. She dialed that number too.

"Hi, Honeybee. You should probably text me because I don't know how to check voice mail on this dad-blasted thing. And if you're not Rita, I don't know why the hell you're calling me on this fangled contraption 'cause I ain't gonna answer it anyway."

The message made her laugh. She wasn't sure she'd

even heard it before. She disconnected and called again, listening to his voice say her name.

"Hi, Honeybee—"

"Hi, Honeybee—"

"Hi, Honeybee—"

When she'd lost count how many times she called, she texted him instead.

Hi, Dad.

But she didn't know what else to say.

So she turned off the light.

Chapter Thirteen

RITA WOKE EARLY, a full hour before her alarm was scheduled to go off.

She groaned and dropped her phone back on the nightstand. Maybe she'd woken to the drone of the ventilation system. Or the passing traffic on the boulevard. Or maybe it was the shepherd's pie.

Then she remembered listening to Otto's voicemail on repeat last night.

Sudden loneliness swept over her. She felt the urge to call Cash. Or maybe she should call Dale. Even though she'd seen him not long ago, it felt like a lifetime. And she hadn't thought of him since, until Tilda had asked after him. Hadn't his birthday passed last week?

But it was too early to call anyone. She yawned and pulled the pillow back over her head. Why the hell was she awake anyways? She could do with another few hours of sleep.

Her bladder nudged her to get up and she shuffled to the bathroom. Then she returned to bed and picked up her phone again.

U awake? she texted.

10-4

Rita switched on the bedside light and sat up in bed, cross-legged. Then she dialed.

"You're up early," Rita said.

"Went to bed early," Jason said.

"I went to bed early too," Rita said, "although I still feel exhausted."

"I was just having a coffee and reviewing my notes from yesterday," Jason said. "I finished talking to the dealerships. I talked to four lots that each sold a single GMC, similar to our barbecued one. Of course, without a VIN, I can't be certain. But today I'll follow up with the buyers to see if they still have possession."

"And we'll see if there are any unaccounted for," Rita added.

"Right," Jason said. "I've also put in a request for insurance records with the Wyoming Department of Motor Vehicles. But it's hard to be hopeful. The plates were stolen, so it's possible the vehicle was never registered after it was sold."

"Good work," Rita said.

"Oh, and Mary Lou put out a warrant for the property on Mountain Lane. We're just waiting on the judge."

"Thanks," Rita said. "I'll be back in town tonight, and we'll convene in the office tomorrow. If anything comes up, call me."

"Will do, Sheriff. How's Otto?"

"About the same," Rita said. Then she thanked him and said goodbye.

Downstairs, Rita sat alone in the hotel's dining hall, eating a breakfast of corn flakes, scrambled eggs, pork sausage, and blueberry muffins — which ought to have been named "plain with a berry on top." And coffee, of course, except she couldn't get it down.

After breakfast, Rita drove to the Casper City Hospital. At the morgue, she signed in at reception, presenting ID.

"Are you needing PPE, Sheriff Jonas?" the receptionist asked.

"Not today," Rita said. There wasn't much question about the cause of Arnold's death. "I'll view from the observation room."

Rita entered the small antechamber and sat on the bench in front of the glass partition, affording a clear view of the autopsy table. Arnold's cadaver lay on the cold surface, his flesh pallid and waxen. The few sips of coffee she'd had at breakfast turned sour in her stomach.

On the other side of the pane, a tall man in yellow PPE bent over the body. Rita recognized Dylan Bruce by his distinct, thick-framed glasses. A forensic technician worked alongside him, collecting samples.

Bruce caught sight of Rita through the glass and gestured for her to come in.

Rita sighed. She got up from the bench and punched the intercom button. "Coming," she said. Then she left the observation room, returning to reception to ask for PPE.

The receptionist handed Rita a sealed plastic packet, containing a visor, yellow gown, mask, and nitrile gloves. She tore open the bag and put on the gear. Then she entered the autopsy room.

Despite wearing a mask, the pungent odor of chemicals, cleaning agents, and biological matter hit her hard. She swallowed back her bile and gave Bruce a friendly wave.

"Thanks for stopping by, Sheriff Jonas," Dylan Bruce said.

"Anytime," Rita said, wry. "How's it going?"

"We're wrapping up now," he said. "Taking the last samples for the tox report now. We'll let you know if we find any drugs in his system."

"Thanks. What can you tell me about his death?"

Bruce trained his gaze on Arnold's body. "Victim died of two GSW to the chest. No other indications of trauma to his body. Both shots were fired at close range."

Rita gave a slow nod. "His partner in crime had the benefit of being shot at a distance and in the dark. Bullet nipped his shoulder."

"These bullets are full metal jackets," Bruce said, lifting a small tray containing two clean bullets. They clinked as they rolled against each other. "A blessing for his friend, even though it didn't help this poor kid."

"So when you say close range," Rita said, "how close we talking?"

Bruce passed her the tray. "A matter of feet. Maybe inches."

"Most likely by someone in the driver's seat," Rita said.

"That's your job, Sheriff, not mine."

The forensic technician passed Rita a small box containing some plastic baggies and labels. Rita packaged the bullets in a bag, then labeled it, entering the bullets into evidence.

When she was done, she thanked Bruce and his assistant, then left to strip off her PPE. Then she headed upstairs to Adrian's room, only to find he'd been discharged.

She found a quiet seating area by a south-facing window and pulled out her phone. She texted Walter.

I see Adrian went home

Fucking relief, Walter texted back.

Rita composed another message: *Have some questions for him. Ok to come by?*

He's asleep now, come tonight at 7.

Rita replied with a thumbs up. Then she called the Best Western to arrange staying another night. The receptionist offered Rita the same room and she booked it. Then Rita texted Mary Lou to let her know she was staying on for another night, and she'd be back in the morning.

Are you staying on for Otto? Mary Lou texted.

Need to interview Adrian again, see you in the morning

Rita left the seating area and headed down to Otto's room. He lay in the same state as yesterday.

Rita sank down into the chair beside his bed and touched his hand. Drier, lighter, thinner. Rita let out a breath.

Inhale.

Exhale.

"Excuse me," a voice said.

Rita looked over her shoulder.

A man in a white coat stood in the doorway. "Are you Otto's daughter?"

Rita stood. "Yes, I'm Rita Jonas."

The man entered the room. "Good afternoon, Rita. I'm Dr. Albright. I'm glad you're here. I need to speak with you about your father. Would you like to come to my office?"

Rita swallowed. "Here is fine."

Dr. Albright gestured to the chair Rita had just vacated. "Won't you have a seat?"

Rita sat down.

Dr. Albright then gestured to the ventilator. "You understand this machine performs your father's breathing for him?"

Rita nodded. "Yes."

Dr Albright's mouth turned down. "It saddens me to

say it's time for you to consider removing him from ventilation."

Rita watched her father's chest rise and fall. Rhythmic. Methodic. Mechanical in its precision. She'd never known her father to inhale and exhale like that. It wasn't like him not to be wheezing and coughing. Laughing especially made him breathless.

She licked her lips, searching for her voice. "If we take him off … won't he die?"

"In all likelihood," Dr. Albright said. "But he's non-responsive, Rita. He has no brain activity."

She squeezed Otto's hand. "No brain activity." Then she looked up at Dr. Albright. "I'll have to think about it."

Dr Albright gave her a warm smile. "I understand. I'll leave you to be with him now."

She thanked him and said goodbye, and he left the room, closing the door behind him.

Rita slumped in the chair, watching her father's chest rise and fall. Then her gaze drifted to the monitor on the ventilator. One red and one yellow line zig-zagged across the screen.

She dragged her gaze from the monitor back to her father. To his face, which hung from his skull in gray folds. His complexion bore barely any more vitality than Arnold's.

"I — I don't know what to say, Dad," Rita said.

But Otto didn't answer.

"What's worse is, I don't know what to do … what to do for you."

Again, Otto remained silent.

"What do you think, Dad?" For a moment, she listened to the sound air passing in and out of the tubes. "How's this working out for you?"

The machines beeped and huffed.

"That's what I was thinking, too," she said.

Then she stood and bent to kiss his forehead. "Goodnight, Dad."

Out in the parking lot, Rita climbed into the truck as though it were a cradle. She curled up in the driver's seat, jamming her knees against the steering wheel and hugging herself. Then she let the tears fall.

She sobbed until she was shivering, then took a sip from the water bottle in the console. She wanted to call Cash.

But her thumb stalled on the screen. Their earlier interaction over his father, Tom Gabriel, had left a bad taste in her mouth. And so did that fact that Cash had been running drugs — even if they were medicinal for Otto to cope with chronic pain. She knew the Gabriels had nothing do with Arnold's murder. But dammit, she'd feel a lot better if she could trust that one of them — let alone the two of them — wasn't holding back on her.

Her thumb slid down her roster of contacts and landed on Dale's name.

Then Lana's.

But her New York friend seemed so far away.

Rita called Mary Lou.

"What can I do for you, Sheriff?" Mary Lou asked.

Rita wanted to tell her about Otto not being able to breathe for himself. And what Dr Albright had asked her to think about.

Instead she said, "Jason said you put out a warrant for Mountain Lane."

"Just came in," Mary Lou said. "Confirming that the Willow family still owns the property, but they lease it to a tenant. Rental agreements are handled through Claudia Perkins at Chattum Real Estate."

"Thanks," Rita said. "I'll stop by on my way back tomorrow."

Then she drove to Casper PD where she met Tilda in the lobby.

"Cafeteria has pizza today," Tilda said, as though the news were worth celebrating.

"Works for me," Rita said, following her downstairs.

In the cafeteria, they filled their plates with slices of gooey pizza, then went upstairs to Tilda's office.

Tilda snapped on a pair of nitrile gloves. "Want some?"

Rita blinked at her. "For what?"

"The pizza, of course. Keeps things tidy around here. I don't exactly have the type of job cut out for working lunches."

Rita declined the gloves but accepted a stack of industrial-grade paper towels from Tilda and sat down on the chair opposite her desk. She bit into a slice of Hawaiian pizza. The flavor of tomato sauce and pineapple exploded on her tongue. It was the first time in days that food had appealed to her.

"Good autopsy?" Tilda asked through a mouthful of pizza.

"Uncovering answers always brings up more questions, doesn't it?" Rita wiped a dribble of sauce from her lip. "Gave you a couple presents, by the way."

Tilda nodded. "Got 'em already," she said. "We're running the bullets through the system right now to see if they match anything. Ballistics is going to be our best friend in this case, since we got no DNA."

"What other information is our friend?" Rita asked.

Tilda took a sip of water. "Blood spatter at the site confirms Adrian Hutch exited the truck and ran for the reservoir. We also found blood on a bank about a hundred yards from his entry point, indicating his exit from the water."

Rita took another bite of pizza. "That confirms what he said about swimming to safety."

"How's he recovering?" Tilda asked.

"Fairly rapidly, I'd say," Rita said, glad to have a piece of good news to report. "Bruce would say it's thanks to a full metal jacket. I'm sure his father would say it's due to his breeding stock."

"And what do you say?"

"I'd say it's thanks to his gumption." Rita crunched through her last pizza crust, completing her first full meal in days. "He thinks he's a hero."

Tilda shrugged a shoulder. "Good on the kid."

Rita wiped her fingers clean on the paper towel. "Thanks for feeding me again, Tilda."

"Anytime," Tilda said, peeling off her red-stained gloves and tossing them in the trash. "Are you headed back to Still?"

"Headed to Natrona County Jail," Rita said. "Although I'd rather head for a long shower and an even longer nap."

"Rolling stones gather no moss, huh?"

Rita half-smiled. "Something like that."

Chapter Fourteen

THOMAS GABRIEL KEPT RITA waiting fifteen minutes. And there was no way she was going to attempt selecting a magazine from the rack. She was doom-scrolling social media when the receptionist called her name.

She marched to the third phone area, where Thomas Gabriel was already seated. Not much had changed about him, aside from the color of his hair, now as white as Wyoming snow. His wiry, well-muscled arms bore the same teal tattoos of pin-ups and pot leaves she remembered from twenty years ago. As a teenager, he'd scared the shit out of her. And he still did.

"How's my kid?" Tom asked.

The likeness between Cash and his dad was apparent. Although Tom's blue orbs were menacing and cold, whereas Cash's had always been warm.

"He's fine," Rita said.

"Shithead hasn't visited me in three years."

"Small wonder," Rita said, even though the fact was somewhat surprising to her. While Cash hadn't exactly followed in his father's footsteps, she'd never thought there was bad blood between them.

Thomas grunted. "You two married yet?"

Rita frowned. "Really? Is that what you think?"

He leaned forward, studying her through the partition. "What I think is you don't deserve him." He spat on the partition. "Not after high-tailin' it like you did."

Rita rolled her eyes as the spittle oozed down the glass. "I'm not a fugitive, Tom. In fact, I've moved back to Still."

Tom leaned back and crossed his arms. "I heard. I know all about you bein' the new sheriff on the patch."

Rita rolled her eyes and hung up the receiver.

"This is bullshit," she said, even though she knew he couldn't hear her. She pushed back the chair and got up.

Tom banged his receiver on the barrier. She cut him a look and he pointed at the phone. She sat back down and picked up the receiver.

"I'm not going to sit here and be insulted, Tom. I've had a shitty couple of days."

"Dammit, Rita, you was always made of tougher stuff than Cash. Thought you could roll with a couple o' hits."

"I *am* made of tough stuff, Tom. But I've got a deceased teenager on a slab at the morgue. Shot because of drug violence in sleepy ol' Still. So I'm not in the mood for your punchlines."

Tom stuck out his chin. "That why you want to see me? You think I got somethin' to do with this dead kid?"

"I thought you might have some information," Rita said, maintaining a calm tone. "Be able to help in some way."

Tom threw his head back and laughed. "I'd rather die than help a pig."

Rita sighed. "This is a waste of my time." She hung up the receiver and got up from the chair.

Tom banged on the partition again.

"Tell Cash to come visit," he yelled, though the partition muted his voice.

Rita walked out of the county jail and back to the truck. She climbed into the driver's seat and leaned back against the headrest, rubbing her temples. But her headache refused to abate. All she could think about was going to bed. She checked the time. Still early, thanks to the brevity of her interview with Tom. She texted Walter, letting him know she was on her way and would arrive before seven.

Then she started the ignition and drove across town. Winona's two-story house, painted sage green with a cranberry door, radiated a charming presence on a nondescript street. Rita parked the truck at the curb.

She was turning to open the door when a black minivan passed. Two men sat in the front, and the passenger looked out at her as they passed. His face shadowed by a ballcap, she didn't recognize him. But the way he turned his head to track her raised the hair on the back of her neck.

Were they following her?

The van continued on its way, and Rita walked up to the front porch. But instead of ringing the bell, she paused in the shadow of the porch railings, watching.

Thankfully, the black minivan didn't return. She wished she'd paid better attention during the drive from the county jail.

She stepped out of the shadows and rang the doorbell.

Winona answered. She wore a purple tracksuit and coordinating eye-makeup.

She stepped aside. "Come on in, Sheriff Jonas."

Rita entered the house and was hit with a fragrant aroma. "It smells … pleasantly pungent in here."

"Patchouli," Winona said. "I'm using aromatherapy to support Adrian's healing." Purple fingernails flashing, she gestured toward a flight of stairs off the foyer. "Adrian's room's upstairs. He's just finishing supper. Thank goodness the gunshot wound didn't appear to hurt his appetite. Maybe made it even bigger. He's never really taken to my quinoa spaghetti, but he had a second serving tonight."

"Maybe he's a changed man since the hospital food," Rita said. She pointed over Winona's shoulder to a homemade painting of two rabbits in lotus-pose. Hand-brushed letters read: *Bliss Bunnies Live Here*. Rita smiled. "Is Adrian the other bliss bunny?"

Overhearing the question, Walter walked into the foyer. "He prefers video games and hip-hop," he said. "Although right now his mother's subjecting him to a crying bowl, whether he wants it or not. Poor kid's laid-up and can't do anything about it."

"You could buy him earplugs," Rita said.

"He doesn't need earplugs," Winona said, frowning, "because it's not a crying bowl. It's a *singing* bowl."

"Well, if he's up for singing, he'll be up to answer some questions," Rita said, encouraging.

"What is it you got to ask him?" she asked.

"I have the autopsy results for Arnold," Rita said.

"And?" Walter asked.

"The bullets were fired at close range."

Winona stiffened. "What are you saying?"

"It's very likely they were fired from the driver's seat."

"Jesus Christ, Jonas," Walter said. "Are you insinuating that Adrian killed him?"

"I don't insinuate, and I don't guess, either," Rita said. "I'm here to ask questions, Walter. Not make accusations."

"Well, it sounds like an accusation," Winona said,

crossing her arms. "There's no way Adrian shot Arnold. He's heartbroken."

"Of course I don't believe Adrian killed Arnold," Rita said. "But I need to know why Arnold didn't follow Adrian when he left the truck."

Walter ran his hands over his thinning hair. "Goddammit."

Winona looked at him. "Wally? What is it?"

Walter ignored her, his gaze meeting Rita's. "Arnold never got out of the truck. Not till after he was shot."

"What are you saying? What happened in the truck?"

Walter kept his eyes on Rita. "He was trapped inside."

Winona looked at Rita. "Trapped?"

Tears shone in Walter's eyes. He swallowed before speaking. "The passenger side doorhandle was broken on the inside."

Winona gasped. "You were supposed to get that fixed, Walter. You said you were gonna fix it."

Walter cut her a look. "I've been too busy with this case. With all this Apex bullshit."

"You mean, *your* Apex bullshit." Two pink spots burned in Winona's cheeks.

"Ah, shut up, Winnie. Don't start busting me for that Apex business now. I've just been tryin' to do right by y'all."

"Well, you didn't do right by your son, giving him a hand-me-down 150 that's falling apart."

"Jesus Christ, Winnie, the Ford ain't falling apart. It's a broken door handle. And I feel bad enough as it is, okay?"

"That's right, Walter. Winona." Rita made a point of looking them both in the eye. "It should have been repaired. But it's an oversight anyone could easily make. And you can't let that eat you up. No one here is to blame for what happened."

But Winona wasn't mollified, her eyes wild and wide. "So if Arnold had been driving, it would be Adrian that was dead?"

Walter shook his head, his jaw set. "Not a chance, Win. Because Adrian would have never let anyone else drive his goddamned truck in the first place."

Winona put her hands on her hips. "You can't know that. Arnold was a bad influence—"

"Look," Rita said. "I'll go speak with Adrian and leave you to your evening."

Winona gave a pert nod, then disappeared into the kitchen.

Walter directed Rita upstairs. "Adrian's in the first bedroom on the right."

Rita climbed the stairs and found Adrian sitting up in bed, looking much better. His hands held a gaming console, his eyeballs and thumbs rotating in unison.

He didn't break his gaze when she entered. "Evening, Sheriff Jonas."

Rita pulled the chair from his desk, where an empty plate of spaghetti sat. She placed the chair beside the bed. "I went to Arnold's autopsy today."

Adrian set down the gaming console, his character frozen on screen. "Fucking hell."

Rita sat and folded her hands on her lap. "I learned some things that may not be easy to hear."

Adrian nodded, studying the quilted pattern of the bedspread.

Rita took a breath. "Adrian was shot at close range, probably by someone in the driver's seat."

Adrian continued to stare at the bedspread. "But I ... I thought I heard Arnold splashing around behind me."

"It might have been the shooter," Rita said.

"I should have looked," Adrian said. "But I was so scared—"

"It's a good thing you didn't go back. Or you might be dead too."

Adrian felt silent. Then he looked up at Rita. "Oh, my God."

"What is it?"

"I know why Arnold wasn't with me in the water." His voice sounded wooden. "The door handle was broken." He paused to swallow. "He couldn't even get out of the truck."

"I know," Rita said. She reached for a box of tissue on the desk and passed it to him.

She gave him another moment, then asked, "Is there anything else you can tell me about that night? Perhaps something you've remembered since surgery?"

Adrian's gaze returned to the bedspread. "I only remember the shots bein' so loud. And the water so cold. And the night so goddamn dark. I thought I was gonna die, so I just kept swimming."

Again, Rita allowed silence to reign. A half-minute later she said, "Thank you. I know it's hard to talk about this, Adrian. I'll leave you now to rest." She gave him a smile, but he was still staring at the quilt, picking at a thread.

Rita returned the chair to his desk and took his empty plate downstairs to the kitchen. Winona and Walter sat at the table in stony silence.

She deposited the plate in the sink. "Adrian looks good."

Both Walter and Winona gave her a weak smile.

"I'll be in touch, Walter," Rita said. "Thank you, Winona. Take care."

Walter got up from the table. "I'll see you out."

Together, they walked through the foyer and out of the house. When the door had closed behind them, Walter asked, "How's the investigation progressing?"

Rita sighed and rolled her shoulders. "About all I can tell you is that we're following up leads. I wish I could encourage you more. But as soon as I know anything, I'll update you."

"Thanks, Jonas." Walter rubbed his face. "And thanks for the leave. Though it ain't easy bein' here with Winnie again."

"I can see that," she said.

"You ever get divorced?" Walter asked.

Rita shook her head. "Never married. Though a couple have asked."

"Well, you dodged yourself a bullet there, Jonas." Then he flushed, realizing what he'd said.

Rita shrugged. "I'm sure it's my loss."

Walter smirked. "You think Cash knows that?"

"I was thinking about Dale," Rita lied. She forced a tight smile. "He's easy to be around."

Or was he, given his affable nature that caused him to make friends with everyone, including their dog? And what about his annoying need to keep everything in its place? Maybe Cash was the one who was easy to be around, with his broken-in furniture and strong, muscled hands.

"On second thought," she said, "things are never as simple as they seem." She smiled and spread her hands. "And thus I am unmarried."

Walter blew out a breath. "Is it ever simple to live with anyone else?"

But Rita sensed the question wasn't posed to her, but rather to the first stars appearing overhead.

"Focus on Adrian," she said, slapping Walter's shoulder. "It's a common goal. It'll get you and Winnie through."

Walter nodded and thanked her and wished her goodnight. She waved as she got in the truck and pulled away from the curb.

Rita drove to the Best Western and checked in again. As she entered the room, her phone rang. It was Cash.

She kicked off her shoes as she answered. "Hi—"

"Jesus, Rita, don't tell me you actually went and saw Thomas at Natrona?"

"Okay, I won't tell you."

"Jesus Christ, I can't believe you accused him of killing Arnold!"

"I'm Sheriff Jonas, not Jesus Christ. And I certainly didn't accuse him of killing Arnold. Whoever's delivering your news has got the wrong story."

Then she hung up.

Cash rang back right away, but she rejected the call. A text came in next.

Sorry, Rita. I always lose my shit about Dad.

Rita read and reread his text but refrained from responding. She had her own father to think about. She closed her text messages and called Jason.

"How did the day go?" she asked.

"Good," he said. "I got a lead on one of the GM vans. It was purchased by the Rawhide Revue over a year ago, although it no longer looks to be insured by them. Which means it's either the van in question or they sold it, in which case whoever they sold it to never bothered with insurance."

"Or it's sitting around on the property uninsured," Rita offered.

"I don't recall seeing a van in the Revue's parking lot," Jeff said.

"Me neither," Rita said. "Nor at Jeff and Carly's house. But he's a big boy and he can answer for himself. Meet me in Beaumont tomorrow at nine."

Chapter Fifteen

RITA PULLED into the parking lot of the Rawhide Revue shortly before nine a.m. A handful of vehicles sat baking in the early morning sun, all clustered together except one. On the other side of the lot sat the SCSO cruiser, the driver's window open as Jason scrolled on his phone.

Rita parked in the empty space beside him and took a moment to check her own phone. While driving, a text had come in from Cash:

Please call

She ignored it and got out of the truck. She walked around the side to the patrol car and sat in the passenger seat.

"Nice to have you back in town, Sheriff," Jason said.

"Thanks, Deputy. So tell me about this van Mr. Jeff Jeffries bought."

"It's a 2005 GMC cargo van, no windows or seats in the back — at least at the time of purchase. And it was brown when he bought it, not white."

"A paint job is easy enough to arrange," Rita said. "But

why'd the Rawhide Revue need a cargo van in the first place? Got to be a side hustle."

"Side hustle?" Jason tapped his chin. "Like Etsy?"

"I'm talking about trafficking narcotics."

"It could have been Etsy," Jason said. "Word on the street is that Carly crochets her own G-strings. Jeff might have an Etsy page."

"Fair enough, Jason. But I don't think Jeff is hip to the gig economy."

"Okay, so it's possible Jeff didn't have an Etsy page and was trafficking drugs instead. But why slap an Apex logo on the van?"

"That, my friend," Rita said, "is one of the answers I aim to get today."

"Did you get some answers at the autopsy?"

Rita crinkled her nose. "Came away with questions more than anything. Bruce confirmed the shots were fired at close range, probably from the driver's seat."

"Doesn't look good for Adrian."

"Thankfully Tilda's blood spatter evidence supports everything Adrian told us about fleeing the scene." Rita blew out a breath. "I also went to see George Myers."

"How's he doing?"

"To be expected," Rita said, sadness seeping into her voice. "He's broken-hearted, losing both his children. And one of them wasn't even his, and yet his love for her drove him to murder."

"They say the love of a parent for a child is the greatest love on earth."

Rita nodded. "That's what they say."

"Not that I've felt that," Jason said, quiet. "George is grieving the loss of two. While my own dad couldn't care less that he had seven."

"It's hard to understand," Rita said. An image of Tom

Gabriel demanding a visit with his only child crossed her mind. She pushed the memory from her mind, deciding not to tell Jason she'd talked to him, too. Instead, she gave him a smile. "Our dads choose to bring us in into the world, but we don't get to choose them."

Jason nodded. "Did you just see Otto, too?"

Rita hesitated. Then she gave a short nod. "Yep."

"And?"

"He's stable."

"That's good. Did you know Helen was discharged from the hospital? Mary Lou said she's staying at the Still Haven Inn."

Rita blew out a sigh. "Part of me thinks I should let her stay at Dad's."

Jason blinked at her. "But you're staying at Otto's right now."

Rita nodded again. "Yeah."

"Yeah," Jason said. "You'll need to be there when he comes home. Help him settle back in, you know? He'll need his space, and so will you."

Rita nodded, unable to tell Jason she feared Otto might not come home. She popped open the door of the cruiser and got out.

Together, she and Jason walked to the entrance of the Rawhide Revue, where a bouncer stood beneath the eaves, in the shadow. He wore black jeans, a black t-shirt, and a disgruntled look on his face.

"You don't seem pleased to see us, Ollie," Rita said.

"It's in my job description," Ollie said.

"Then you'll be pleased to know we're not here to see you," Rita said. "Please let Jeff know we're here to talk to him."

Ollie folded his thick hands in front of his chunky belt buckle. "He's not in today."

Rita narrowed her eyes. "That's not like Jeff."

Ollie met her stare. "Sick day."

"Well, if Jeff's at home, then I guess we are talking to you after all, Ollie," Rita said.

Ollie's face took on a purple tinge. "What d'you want to know?"

"Do you remember the Revue ever owning a van?"

Ollie set his jaw. "Sure."

"When was that?" Jason asked.

"Dunno," Ollie said. He shrugged his massive shoulders. "Jeff sold it a while back, so I don't remember. A year ago, maybe two."

"Could you describe it, please?" Jason asked.

Ollie's eyes rolled up as he scrolled through his memory. "It were a GM, one of them boxy models. Nice shade of umber."

"Umber?" Rita asked.

"Like brown," Jason said.

Ollie fixed his eye on Jason. "No, not like brown. Shit's brown, ain't it? And stinks. The van was umber. A nice shade of earthen with a hint of burgundy."

"Got it," Rita said. "So why would Jeff need an umber van?"

"It was part of a plan to pick up clients at various hotels."

"Nice side hustle."

"Like Uber," Jason said.

Ollie bunched his fists. "Not Uber, umber."

"So how'd it all go down?" Rita asked. "This plan with the van?"

"Not so well." Ollie's brow furrowed. "Strip clubs these days are losing popularity."

Rita glanced up at the building's fading facade. A cut-out sign depicted a woman doing things on a pole Rita thought only a monkey could do on a palm tree.

"Clients not wanting to climb into a windowless van on a dark night, to be driven out here, to Still County's best skin bar?" Rita waved a hand at the decrepit sign. "I can't imagine why not."

Ollie nodded. "That's what I thought. But I'll tell you what. It's those goddamn millennials and their civic rights."

Rita blinked. "Civic rights?"

"All those kids care about is consent and who's violatin' who and shit like that."

"Thank God," Rita said. "This world could do with a generation committed to the humane treatment of one another, while at the same time exercising their right to vote."

It was Ollie's turn to blink at her.

"Well, thanks, Ollie," Rita said. "We'll let you get back to the job now."

As Rita and Jason walked across the parking lot, she asked him to follow in the cruiser to Jeff's place. Rita led the way out of the parking lot and drove across Beaumont to Jeff's house.

She parked at the curb and Jason parked behind her. Then they walked up the drive to the house.

"No sign of Carly's green Volkswagen bug," she said, glancing around.

"But Mr. Jeffries is home, like he said," Jason said, pointing to a Jeep parked in the shade of a juniper.

A bumper sticker on the left side read, *Donate to Charity … she's the best stripper in the club.* The one on the right read, *Follow Destiny … she'll show you a good time.*

Rita rolled her eyes as they walked up to the front door. As soon as Jason knocked, the door flung open. Jeff stood inside the foyer, breathing hard, one of his eyes blackened. "Goddammit, Carly—"

His voice broke off when he saw Rita and Jason.

"Looking for Carly, Jeff?" Rita asked.

"I want to file a fucking Missing Person's Report, Sheriff. And theft, because that bitch stole my property."

"When did you last see Carly?"

"Two days ago."

"What happened?"

"She just took off."

"Do you know why?"

"'Cause she's got rock for brains."

"You've been fighting lately, haven't you?"

"Couples fight. What's that got to do with anything?"

"Did you punch her again?"

"For fuck's sake, Sheriff, what has Carly been telling you? It's nothin' like that."

"So you last saw her here at the house?"

"That's what I said, Sheriff. Got your ears on backwards?"

"Then it's a Beaumont case," Rita said. "You'll need to file with them."

Jeff threw up his hands. "So if you're not here about Carly, where the hell are you?"

"I'd like you to tell me about the van."

Jeff stared at her. "What van?"

"You bought a van two years ago," Jason said.

Jeff blinked at Jason, then turned back to Rita. "Am I answering a question, Sheriff? Or am I confirming a statement?"

"I'll take that as a 'yes,'" Rita said. "Which dealership did you buy it at?"

"Well, I don't really have to answer that, do I, Sheriff?"

Jeff pumped his thumb toward Jason. "'Cause this pencil-pusher probably already knows where I bought it."

Jason swiped open the notes app on his phone.

"James Dickerson Chevrolet and GM in Casper," he read.

"That's right," Jeff said. "Jimmy Big Dick's truck lot."

Jason continued to read. "You purchased it on September—"

"What're you asking me all these questions for?" Jeff scowled at Rita, then at Jason. "He already knows all the fucking answers."

"Thanks for confirming the details, Jeff," Rita said. "Do you remember the plate number?"

Jeff's mouth flattened into a line. He studied Rita for a moment, then said, "A lotta shit happens in two years, Sheriff."

"Sure does," Rita said. "So why'd you buy the van, Jeff?"

Jeff sighed. "I made it over into a party bus, for bringing clients to the club."

"Did you get them home, too?" Rita asked.

"Sure," Jeff said. "We was aimin' to have them spend their cash in the club, not on taxis and shit."

"Preventing DUIs is a noble endeavor," Rita said.

"I invested a crap ton of money, making that thing nice." Jeff said. He ran his hands over the front of his leather jacket. "Fully upholstered black leather interior."

"Not umber?" Rita asked.

Jeff cut her a look. "What the fuck is umber?"

"A nice shade of earthen with a hint of burgundy," Jason said, reading his notes.

"Dunno about no umber, but we put nice shaggy carpet on the ceiling. Built a U-shaped bench to seat six.

Installed a flatscreen to play some pre-show videos for the customers. To get 'em inspired, you know?"

"What's a pre-show video?" Jason asked.

Jeff shrugged. "Footage of the girls in their dressing room. No kink or nothin', just them puttin' on costumes and makeup for the show. Kind of a reverse striptease."

Rita's lip curled. "How inspiring."

Jeff nodded. "I thought so. We called the operation Rawhide Rides."

"Slick side hustle," Jason said.

Jeff's mouth turned down. "Real nice. But it didn't work out."

"Why's that?" Rita asked.

Jeff threw up his hands. "Fucking millennials. All them kids makin' their own skin flicks at home. And then watchin' 'em at home, too. They'd rather stay in, squintin' at some miniature girl on a miniature screen, jerkin' off their miniature dicks."

"So the van plan didn't work out. Where's it now?" Rita asked.

Jeff squared his shoulders. "Sold it."

"To whom?"

Jeff sighed and threw up his hands again. Then he turned back in the house, leaving the front door wide open. A fly buzzed past Rita's ear and disappeared into the shadowy interior.

Another minute passed.

Rita peered into the darkened foyer. Then she traded a look with Jason. "Do you think he's coming back?"

"Maybe he's gonna prank us," Jason said.

Rita frowned. "Don't know that he has a sense of humor."

A minute later, Jeff reemerged with a handful of paperwork. He thrust it at Rita. She scanned a set of vehicle transfer documents.

"The buyer's a numbered company," she said to Jason.

He leaned over to peruse the paperwork. "That's usually a sign someone wants to stay hidden."

Rita looked up at Jeff. "Got a name for the buyer?"

Jeff thought for a moment, scratching his stubbled cheek. "Deer something. That's right. Jay Deer."

Jason frowned. "You don't mean, J. Doe?"

Jeff brightened. "Yeah, that's him."

A muscle twitched in Jason's cheek. "Could you please describe Mr. Doe, Mr. Jeffries?"

Jeff shrugged. "Tall. White. Brown hair."

"That could describe you, Jeff," Rita said.

"Well, how the hell was I supposed to know I was going to be interrogated about him five years later?"

"Two years later," Jason said.

Rita took photos of the paperwork with her phone, then returned the documents to Jeff.

"Thanks, Jeff. Have a good day."

"Nice day my ass," Jeff said. "If you see that dumb bitch, send her home, would ya?"

"Despite your wildly inaccurate description," Rita said, "I presume you're referring to Carly. And no, I won't send her anywhere."

Jeff grumbled something about the SCSO going to hell before retreating back inside the house and slamming the front door.

Rita swapped a look with Jason. "Well, there's nothing sick about Jeff today. Unless Ollie's referring to Jeff's giant umber shiner."

Jason whistled as they walked back down the drive. "More than umber, it's a full-on rainbow."

Rita took out her phone. "I'm gonna AirDrop the

photos of the transfer paperwork to you. Please look up the numbered business?"

Jason took out his phone. "Ten-four."

Rita sent the photographs. "Thanks. On my way back to Still, I'm gonna stop by the Chattum real estate office. I shouldn't be long."

"Sound good," Jason said. "Oh, and Rita?"

She paused before getting in the truck. "Yeah?"

"I think Jeff may have a sense of humor, after all." He pointed up the drive, toward the bumper stickers on Jeff's jeep. "In fact, I think that's what might be sick about him."

Rita laughed. "See you back at HQ, Deputy."

Chapter Sixteen

RITA PARALLEL PARKED in front of the Chattum real estate office. In a front window, a sign advertised Still Shadows, construction on the housing development back in full swing now that the case of the missing Apex Three had been settled.

A bell chimed as she pushed the door open. The receptionist looked up, pushing back a wall of dark hair.

"Heather," Rita said. "How are you doing?"

Heather Bannister took off her reading glasses. "Hi, Rita. I'm fine."

"Did you get the restraining order?"

Heather half-shrugged, half-shook her head. "Still thinking about it."

"Has Max been back?"

Heather fiddled with her glasses, tapping the temples against the top of the desk. "You come by to talk about Max? Or you looking to sell Otto's house?"

Rita flinched at the question. "Why would I do that?"

Heather shrugged again. "Heard he died."

Rita stiffened. "You heard wrong. I'm here to speak to Claudia Perkins."

"Oh," Heather said. "Um, she's out showing a home. Can I help?"

"I'll go meet her," Rita said. "What's the address?"

Heather put on her reading glasses. "I'll look it up." Heather clicked her computer mouse, opening a digital calendar. She read the address.

"Thanks," Rita said, turning to go.

"No problem," Heather said. "Oh, and Rita?"

Rita paused. "Yes?"

"I hope your dad gets better soon. He always seemed like a real nice guy." Heather pulled her hair into a rope and twisted it in her hands. "He pulled me over once, y'know, for rolling through a stop sign. When I told him I'd done it 'cause I didn't want to shift gears on a hill, he laughed and let me off with a warning."

Something tightened in Rita's chest. "That was nice of him."

"I'll say," Heather said. "But that wasn't the nice part. He gave me a driving lesson, right then and there. Spent an hour with me at that four-way stop, teaching me how to disengage the clutch on a hill." She swept her arm, indicating north. "It was where Esplanade crosses Ponderosa. I'll never forget."

"He's a good driver," Rita said, unsure of what to say.

Heather straightened her shoulders, pushing back her waterfall of hair. "I'm so good at stick-shift now, that when Max and I honeymooned in San Fran, I took the wheel 'cause he was shittin' bricks."

"Nicely done," Rita said, definitely referring to Heather's driving skills and not her choice to marry Max. She thanked her for the address again and exited the office.

Once outside, she blew out a big breath. Did

everyone have to ask after Otto? But then, that was to be expected; he was a public figure. In New York, a cop on the street was as much a stranger to someone as the people on the subway. But that could never be the case in a small town.

Lost in her thoughts about Otto, Rita drove to the address in question. The one-level house was an ugly old thing on the highway. A sandwich-board sign leaned against a decrepit porch, declaring, *Open House Today.* Two sedans parked on the cracked concrete drive, spikes of yellow grass growing through the fissures.

Rita pulled in and parked behind the Realtor's car; Her vanity plates read S0LD1T. Rita got out of the truck and headed up to the house.

The front door stood open. Following the voices, Rita walked down a hallway into a kitchen with peeling vinyl floors. A young couple in matching camouflage from Cabela's stood chatting with a woman in her forties wearing business attire.

"Excuse me, Claudia Perkins?" Rita said.

"Sheriff Jonas," the Realtor said. "I didn't know you were looking to buy in this part of town."

"Oh, no, I prefer renting," Rita said. "Especially since I don't have to go far for muffins." She gave the young couple a smile. "Coffeeshop's right downstairs."

The couple smiled and nodded with understanding. The woman, in her twenties, looked about eight months pregnant.

"I've even bought them in my pajamas," Rita said.

Claudia Perkins blinked at her. "Imagine that." Then she turned to her clients. "Please excuse us for a moment. Feel free to continue looking around the property." Then she turned back to Rita. "Why don't we step outside for a moment, Sheriff Jonas?"

"I'd like that," said Rita. "The smell of mildew in here is making me nauseous."

The young couple exchanged a look.

Outside, Claudia Perkins led the way across the front porch and stood in the shade of the awning, next to the porch rail. "How can I help you, Sheriff?"

"I'd like to ask you about the Willow property on Windset Lane."

Claudia tapped the railing with a manicured nail. "Yes?"

"Who's renting it?"

Claudia tapped her nail again. "I believe the name is Thorpe. A young woman holds the lease. She used to have a boyfriend, but he's not on the lease anymore."

"Do you remember her first name?"

Claudia tapped the railing. "Susan? No. Sarah? Yes, it's Sarah."

"Is Sarah Thorpe a good tenant?"

"I'd say so," Claudia said. "The best, really. Always pays her rent on time. If she didn't, I'd probably have remembered her name more easily."

"How long has she rented the property?"

"Must be three or four years. I can look it up back at the office."

"Four years is a while for a renter, yes?"

"Not necessarily for a single-family home," Claudia said.

"Even though it's run-down like this one?"

Claudia stiffened. "I'm not sure that's a fair assessment, Sheriff."

"I'm not sure it's up to code."

Claudia pursed her lips. "A building inspector will determine that."

"Yeah, at the buyer's expense."

"Are you questioning how I run my business, Sheriff Jonas?"

Rita gestured inside the house. "They're expecting a baby."

Claudia gave Rita a tight smile. "Young buyers need to enter the market somehow."

Rita narrowed her eyes at the Realtor, but bit down on her lip. Her headache was making her irritable. She cleared her throat. "So Sarah Thorpe pays on time, every month, for four years. How does she pay?"

"Twice a month," Claudia said. "Every other Monday. It's how we manage all the properties. The results have been much better than when we used to bill on the first and fifteenth."

"I meant, does she pay with automated transfers, checks, or cash?"

"Cash, actually," Claudia said. "At the office."

"Does Sarah Thorpe work at Apex?"

"No," Claudia said quickly. "Though I don't recall her employment history. But if Apex had been on the rental application, I would have remembered."

Rita raised an eyebrow. "Why's that?"

Claudia lifted her chin. "Because I don't like renting to them."

"Oh, no? They're well salaried, are they not?"

Claudia's lip twisted. "Their salaries are inflated, if you ask me." She flared her nostrils. "The problem is they come and go. I don't trust a single one of them not to break a one-year lease. And sure, they pay the stupid penalty. But the fee doesn't come near covering the headache I have to deal with in finding a new tenant. Last year I had four properties turn over more than twice because of Apex transfers."

"It's a good thing you've got Heather Bannister's

administrative assistance," Rita said, opting for optimism. "And it's a good thing you have no concerns about Sarah Thorpe as a tenant." Rita met her eyes. "Is that the case? Or do you have any other concerns about the property?"

Claudia crinkled her brow. "No concerns whatsoever, Sheriff. Why do you ask? Has something happened at the house?"

"I can't answer that question," Rita said. "But thanks for the information. You've been a great help."

Rita walked back through the house — pausing to wish the couple all the best for their baby's birth — and let herself out the front door.

Bemoaning the truck's inferior air-conditioning as she drove to HQ, her heart skipped a beat when she saw her Honda in the parking lot. She parked the truck in the empty stall next to it, hopped out, and kissed the hood of her car. Then she jogged into the office.

"Thank the Lord and Mary Lou, my Honda's back," Rita said, pumping her fist in the air.

Mary Lou laughed and fished a pair of car keys from the top drawer of her desk. "Better thank Randy, too." Mary Lou handed Rita the keys. "There's someone waiting to see you in your office."

Rita pulled a face. "Please don't tell me it's Ken Saunders."

Mary Lou pressed her lips together. "Do your job, Sheriff, I ain't tellin' you nothin'."

Rita lowered her brows at her. "It's Ken, isn't it? You don't want to tell me 'cause you know I'd walk right back out that door."

"You should go see for yourself, Rita, that's what," Mary Lou said, putting her hands on her hips.

Rita gave Mary Lou a nod. Whenever Mary Lou called Rita by her first name instead, she knew to listen up. She opened the door of her office and turned to greet her visitor.

Carly sat in the chair with the broken backrest, her head bowed over her lap where Ted purred like a Lamborghini. Next to the chair sat a backpack and fringed purse.

Rita closed the door behind her, and Carly looked up from petting the cat. Her face was a swollen mass of bruises.

"Jesus," Rita said, unable to stop herself. She dropped to her knees beside Carly, examining her face. "Have you had medical attention?"

Carly scoffed. "Course not. And I ain't here to press charges neither."

Ted hissed at Rita and jumped down.

Rita ignored him as he rubbed along her thigh, then stopping to flick her with his tail before jumping to the windowsill. She met Carly's eye. "I'm glad you came."

Carly tried to brush the cat hair from her lap. "Did … did you mean what you said about helping me out?"

Rita nodded. "Yes."

"Because I sure as shit ain't goin' home like this."

"Hell, no," Rita said. She pulled out her phone. "I need to take some photos of your injuries, okay?"

Carly's eyes widened with panic. She shook her head. "No."

"It's only for your benefit," Rita said.

"Told you, I ain't here to press charges."

Rita nodded. "I know. But in case you change your mind, it'll be helpful to have these. And it'd also be helpful for us to write down the dates and times that things happened."

Carly hesitated. Then she said, "Okay. But this don't mean I'm pressing charges."

"No charges," Rita said. She swiped open her phone and snapped closeups of Carly, face-on as well as both sides. "All right, that's enough for today, huh? Let's get out of here."

Carly's eyes widened. "Where we gonna go?"

"Well, you can't stay in here," Rita said. "None of these chairs work right. And we both know you can't stay with Jeff. Did you come in your VW?"

Carly nodded, then winced in pain. "I parked the Bug behind a fence a block away." She fingered a bruise on her cheekbone. "In case anyone recognized it."

"Smart move," Rita said. "We'll store it here in the garage at HQ. What's the license plate number?"

Carly recited it and Rita texted it to Mary Lou, along with a request for Randy to tow the car to the SCSO.

Then she put away her phone and came around to the front of the desk. "Let's go out the back door."

She picked up Carly's backpack and slung it over her shoulder. It felt like it contained bricks.

"This way," Rita said, leading Carly through the detachment to the back door.

Carly hugged her purse to her chest and followed. Rita took her across the street to the apartment above the Bighorn Bean. As they climbed the stairs, the comforting smell of coffee surrounded them.

"It's an apartment," Carly said.

"And it's all mine," Rita said, unlocking the latch. "No one else here to bother you." She pushed open the door and stepped aside for Carly to enter.

But she hesitated. "I can't stay here."

"Sure you can," Rita said, setting down Carly's backpack. Then she rubbed and shook out her shoulder. "For as long as you need."

"But it's your home. I can't kick you out of your home."

"You're not kicking me out. It's like a house-swap. Only we're paying it forward. My deputy got the crummy end of the deal, though."

Carly blinked at her. "Huh?"

Rita waved a hand. "Never mind. Just feel free to stay at my place for a while."

Carly looked around, chewing her lower lip. "But it's so small."

Rita nodded. "Quaint is the word I like to use. Although tiny might be more appropriate. But it's a lot roomier than the last place."

Carly looked unsure. "But you haven't got a guest room."

"I'm gonna stay at my dad's for a while." Rita said. "He isn't well."

"Oh, right." Carly pried off her canvas shoes and hung her purse on the handle of the coat-closet, its fringe dragging on the floor. "I heard about that."

Rita sighed. "I'm still getting used to the way word travels around here."

"The girls know everything," Carly said, referring to her network of dancers. "I bet a girl can hide a lot easier in NYC."

"The city does provide a certain level of anonymity," Rita said. "Even if you never feel like you can get a moment alone."

"Hm," Carly said, thoughtful. "I guess you never really know what a place is like till you go there."

Rita laughed. "And somehow a lot of folks around here think they know what I'm like, just because I blew in from the city."

Carly snorted. "And everyone thinks they know what I'm like, just 'cause they seen me naked."

"Guess we both know what it's like to work in uniform." Rita gave Carly a grim smile. "Prejudged before we even open our mouths."

Carly laughed, and Rita was glad to be lightening her mood. "You ain't wrong, Sheriff Jonas. But are you sure about me staying here?"

"Absolutely," Rita said. "Lie low at and get everything you need delivered, okay? And don't hesitate to reach out to me for any personal errands."

Carly nodded. "Thanks, I will, Sheriff Jonas."

"Please call me Rita. Why don't you settle in while I pack some clothes?"

She left Carly in the living room and went to the bedroom closet, where she filled her own backpack with a pair of pajamas, underclothes, toiletries, and other essentials. Then she lifted two hangers with uniforms from the rod. Lastly, she opened the safe and took out Lisa's letters.

For a moment, she sat with them in her hands, running her thumbs over the return address and the postmark.

Inhale.

Exhale.

Rita opened her eyes again and packed the shoebox of letters in her backpack. Then she put the pack on her back and left the safe open for Carly to use as she wished. Uniforms hanging over her arm, she returned to the living room.

Carly sat on the sofa, knees pressed together. Her fingers picked at the tassel on a throw cushion.

"I need to make sure Jeff ain't gonna find me," she said.

"He ain't," Rita said. "'Cause we ain't gonna tell no one you're here, aside from my landlady and the barista downstairs, who're as solid as they come. I know I won't be telling anyone else because I don't have many friends in town."

"I'm sure that's not true, Sh — Rita. You're very kind."

Rita smiled. "Wasn't popular twenty years ago, and becoming a cop hasn't helped with that fact."

Carly laughed, then winced and touched her bruises.

"You don't even need to go anywhere for a while," Rita said. "Not if you don't want to. The fridge is stocked. Sort of, if you like salad. You can order soup and sandwiches downstairs, and Skyler will send it up. Ice cream's in the freezer. The wi-fi code's on the fridge door. Unfortunately you'll have to wash the bedsheets, but there's a washer/dryer. Mind the dryer 'cause it's hot as hell, and it'll cook 'em if you're not paying attention. And it eats bras, so I wash mine in the bathtub. If you do need something that's not here, message me and I'll pop by. If it's urgent, talk to Skyler downstairs. She's the only person I've met in this town who knows everyone and isn't a gossip."

Carly hugged the throw cushion. "Thank you. I'm really grateful. I didn't actually expect you to help me. I thought it was just one of those nice things that people say from time to time. But I kept thinking of what you said and thought there was no harm in tryin'."

"I'm glad you tried," Rita said. "Oh, and you'll want to put a warm compress on your bruises. It'll help reduce the swelling and discoloration. Facecloths are in the cupboard beneath the bathroom sink. Don't worry about staining them. Half of them already have bloodstains."

Carly nodded. "Thanks."

"Do you have any cash?" Rita asked.

Carly dug in her bulging backpack. "Stole the tip jar from the Revue." She pulled out a one-gallon pickle jar filled with coins. What appeared to be several pairs of silky underpants were stuffed into the top of the jar to prevent the coins from clinking. She grimaced, shoving the jar back in her bag. "Rod's gonna be pissed when he notices it missing." She zipped up the backpack again. "He's head bartender."

Rita handed Carly the three twenties she had in her money clip. "We don't need Rod coming after you, too. If you change your mind about the tip jar, I'll have my deputy drop it back off at the Revue."

Carly tucked the sixty dollars in her bra. "Okay. Thank you."

"You're welcome. Take it easy, okay? And keep in touch. Any sign of Jeff, you've got to let me know."

Carly nodded and they bid each other goodnight. Rita left the apartment, waiting on the landing till she heard Carly bolt the door behind her. Then she headed downstairs with her backpack to the coffee shop.

"Peppermint tea?" Skyler asked.

"Don't you dare turn that into my 'usual,'" Rita said.

"So the 'usual' then?" Skyler asked.

Rita nodded. "And a pumpkin spice muffin, please."

"Glad your taste for coffee's back," Skyler said.

"Me too."

"By the way," Skyler said, "Me and my buddies are going to a party in Beaumont tomorrow night. You should come with us."

Rita blinked at her, uncertain if she'd heard right. "Come with you?"

"Yeah," Skyler said, grinning. "Great lineup of DJs. Been waiting all year to see DJ Mix Maven."

"Why?"

"Oh, 'cause she can drop the bass like—"

"No, I meant, why should I come? I mean, aside from the bass?"

Skyler tilted her head, regarding Rita. "You said the other day you could use a break."

"I fully agree I could do with a break," Rita said. "And I appreciate the invitation. But I'm twice your age and a law enforcement official. I'd only cramp your style. And probably everyone else's. Definitely the DJ's."

Skyler shrugged, a sparkle in her eye. "You're not a law enforcement officer twenty-four seven, are you?"

For a moment, Rita was mute. For some reason, the question made her uncomfortable. She rolled her shoulders. "Thanks, Skyler, but these days I've been going to bed before eight o'clock."

Skyler passed Rita a paper bag with the muffin. "If you change your mind, let me know. One of my friends is a security guard at the Beaumont Credit Union." She shrugged. "You might get along with him more than you expect."

Rita raised an eyebrow. "*'Him'?* Don't be trying to set me up, Skyler. We already talked about this."

Skyler laughed. "Not a chance. Omar's gay. But I thought you guys might have stuff to talk about." She shrugged one shoulder. "Guns?"

"He's probably twenty-five, in which case, I can't talk zillennial."

Skyler laughed. "You understand me all right, don't you? And he's twenty-three."

Rita smiled. "Have a good time, Skyler. I'll be catching up on sleep, over at Otto's. I have a guest staying upstairs in my apartment for a while. She's going through a hard time and prefers to keep to herself. If you see her around, please leave a muffin or two at the door? You can put it on my tab. But otherwise, I'm sure she'll be keeping to herself."

"Ten-four," Skyler said.

Rita winked. "Maybe you're working in the wrong shop. Enjoy the Mix Master."

"Mix Maven," Skyler said.

"Right." Rita retrieved her coffee from the counter. "I must have muffins on the mind."

She headed outside to her Honda, but before starting the ignition, she sent a text to her landlady.

Hi Abigail. I have a guest staying in the apartment for a while. Carly. She left an abusive relationship. Please keep it on the down low.

Abigail sent a thumbs up, then Rita made her way to the office.

Chapter Seventeen

RITA SAT at Walter's desk, in the chair that used to be Otto's. Maybe she should have kept it in her office after all.

"I found the address for the numbered business," Jason said, announcing the fact as if he'd won a blue ribbon at the Still County Fair. "Guess."

Rita blew the steam from her coffee. "I hate guessing."

"Well, you won't believe it."

She took a sip. "Try me."

"808 Mountain Road."

"That the abandoned place we tracked the fake Apex van to?" Rita asked. "And where my Honda got smashed?"

Jason nodded. "Yep."

She took a bite of muffin. "Owned by Elk Mountain Equity, isn't it?"

Jason nodded again. "Yep."

"So obviously the business owner knew that and is using the address as a placeholder."

Jason pulled on his chin, thinking. "So it's a dead end?"

"Not necessarily. Who owned it before the bank?"

"Graham Blake." Jason consulted his notes. "Elk Mountain picked it up four years ago when he could no longer pay taxes. Shortly after he died."

"Way before anyone started running drugs in Apex lookalikes."

Jason nodded. "Looks like."

"Hm," Rita said. "Might be a dead end." She spun in Otto's old swivel chair. "Mary Lou, we need that warrant for Windset Lane, please."

Mary Lou stopped typing to sift through her rainbow of file folders. "Comin' right up, Sheriff." She found the pink paperwork and passed it to Rita.

"Thanks, Mary Lou," Rita said. "Ready, Deputy?"

Jason gathered his gear and joined Rita at the door, and they headed out to the cruiser.

"I nominate you to drive," Rita said, walking around to the passenger's side of the patrol cruiser. "Nursing this coffee's the only thing helping my headache."

"That headache of yours is like the hiccups," Jason said, getting behind the wheel.

Rita sank into her own seat. "Oh, yeah? How's that?"

"Keeps repeatin' on you."

"Don't say that, you'll curse me." Rita lowered the window. She inhaled the fresh air, and the breeze stirred up strands of hair around her face. "I'm feeling better already." The scenery slipped past, the evergreens like jewels in the morning sun. "Nice drive out this way."

When they arrived at the yellow house, Jason parked in the drive. A Westfalia van painted in two tones of baby blue sat rusting on the southern side of the house. A layer of fallen leaves cluttered the roof and windshield.

Rita pointed. "If those are Sarah Thorpe's wheels, it doesn't look like she's driven anywhere recently."

Jason made a sound of agreement, scanning the property. "Not many signs of life around."

They walked up to the veranda, pushing past overgrown shrubs. A weatherbeaten door-mat unravelling at one end now read, 'WELCOM'.

Jason pressed the buzzer. It was broken, so he knocked.

The sound of a screaming baby drew louder until the door slowly opened. Then the sound hit them like a siren.

And stopped short as a red-faced six-month-old baby stared up at them. The infant bounced in a young woman's arms, her greasy hair knotted on top of her head. The woman appeared equally surprised to see their uniforms.

"Can I help you?"

"Sorry to disturb you," Rita said. She introduced herself, then Jason. "We have some questions about this property."

The baby continued to stare her down, now chewing on his knuckle. The woman shifted him to her other hip. "Yes?"

"May I have your name, please?" Jason asked, taking out his phone to record notes.

The woman's gaze flickered between them. "Sarah Thorpe."

"And you've lived here how long?"

"Five years."

"Your rental agreement is managed through Chattum Realty, yes?" Rita asked.

Sarah nodded. "That's right."

"Do you remember an Apex vehicle on the property recently?" Rita asked.

Sarah nodded again, bouncing the baby. "One showed up last week sometime."

"Do you remember which day?"

Sarah thought for a moment. "No, sorry. The days blend together."

"Do you know why the van was here?" Jason asked.

"They said they were here to survey the property."

"Who's 'they'?" Rita asked.

"Couple of men."

"Can you describe these men?" Jason asked.

Sarah thought again for a moment. "White guys. Tall. One was burly. One wore a skull cap, which was odd because it was hot that day."

"Would you recognize them again?" Rita asked.

Sarah shrugged. "Maybe."

"So they told you they were here to survey the property," Rita said. "What did they mean by that?"

Sarah shook her head. "I don't know."

"What did they do while they were here?" Jason asked.

"Survey the property, I guess. I didn't really see them much."

"It's very bushy," Rita said, indicating the shrubs. "Some of the windows are obscured."

Sarah sighed. "Yeah, it's hard to see out. And kind of dark in the house. I used to have help around here, with pruning and stuff. But now I don't know how I'd find the time to do it, with a baby."

"So you didn't see the men working?" Jason said.

She shook her head again. "They said they wanted to go out back, in the bush, and I left them to it."

"Did they ask to come into the house at all?" Rita asked.

Sarah shook her head. "Oh, no. They stayed outside, and we stayed inside." She rubbed her cheek on the baby's head. "Should I be worried?"

"Chances are they don't work for Apex." Rita gave

Sarah Thorpe her card. "If they come back, please get in touch with me."

Sarah accepted the card, nodding. "I will."

"And don't let them in the house."

"I won't." She nuzzled the baby's head. "It's only me and Finn here."

"We'd be happy to drive by a few times," Rita said. "If that would help you feel better."

Sarah's face brightened. "Yes, please."

"And you might want to consider pruning around the door for better visibility. For your security."

"You can call my sister, Florence," Jason said, handing her another card. "She's got a Sawzall that saws, well, through pretty much everything. Only charges twenty bucks an hour to saw stuff. Removal's up to you though."

She took the card and looked at it. "Thanks."

"We'd like to look around inside the house before we go, if that's all right?" Rita asked.

Sarah hesitated, then nodded. "Okay."

She stepped out of the doorway, and Rita and Jason entered the dim house. Earthy aromas of evergreen and lavender — and what might have been patchouli — tickled her nose. She noticed Jason rubbing at his.

The hallway led into a living room, sparsely furnished with a futon folded into loveseat position, a rocking chair, brightly patterned floor-cushions, a beat-up coffee table, and a laundry basket filled with baby toys. The stuffed Paw Patrol puppies looked practically alien amidst the hand-woven rugs and tie-dyed sarongs covering the patched plaster walls.

Strings threaded with small brown chips, like pieces of bark, hung from the curtain rod and light fixtures.

Rita fingered one of the strands. "What are these?"

"Not psilocybin," Sarah said, quickly. She blushed. "Those are boletes."

Jason examined another strand, this one threaded with ochre frills. "These look like chanterelles."

"That's right," Sarah said, lowering Finn to the floor. She rummaged in the laundry basket for a dog in a cop's uniform. She handed it to him, then glanced at Rita and blushed again. "This one's his favorite."

Rita smiled. "How do you support yourself and Finn, Sarah?"

"Mushroom picking."

Jason studied another strand, with dark brown specimens. "These are morels, right?"

Sarah smiled and nodded.

Rita fingered a piece of drying bolete. It smelled nutty. "These pay your bills?"

Jason looked at Rita. "Wild mushroom picking can be lucrative."

"Even at this time of year?" Rita asked.

Sarah nodded. "Sure, if you hike to a high enough altitude. I sell all year round, though business is more lucrative in the fall."

"Where do you sell?" Rita asked.

"I've got a buyer in Casper who sells them to restaurants."

"And what do you do with Finn when you're picking?"

"He comes with me. I have a carrier for him. And when I find a patch, he likes to crawl around in the moss."

"Do you go with anyone else?"

"My asshole boyfriend used to pick with me. But he took off for Kentucky. Decided he didn't want to have a kid." Sarah's mouth twisted into a bitter half-smile. "Little late for that."

"I'm sorry," Jason said, his jaw tensing.

"I'm not too lonely," Sarah said. "My sister's job with Casper City gives her family-related leave. Something like five days a year. She's been turning those into long weekends, coming to stay with us once a month since the dickhead left."

"That's nice," Rita said.

"Sure is," Sarah said, hugging herself. "And she always brings enough chili to last out the week."

"Maybe you can teach her about mushrooms," Rita said. "Train a new partner to go pick with you."

Sarah's brow crinkled. "I'd never thought to ask her. She's different than me." She shrugged. "Kind of corporate. She's got a condo and car payments and stuff like that."

"Walking in the woods is good for everyone," Rita said.

"Maybe especially good for people with car payments," Jason said.

Sarah laughed, and Rita took her moment.

"Jason, let's take a quick peek upstairs." She gave Sarah another smile. "We won't be long."

Sarah nodded and sat on the loveseat, while Finn rolled on the floor with his stuffy.

Upstairs, they found two bedrooms on either side of the landing. One overlooked the front yard, while the other bedroom looked out on the woods, and beyond to the Still Haven Inn. More Bohemian textiles indicated this room belonged to Sarah and Finn. The room at the front was sparse by comparison, containing little aside from a double bed and side table.

Both bedrooms accessed a main bathroom with olive-green fixtures. More puppies in uniforms cluttered the bathtub. But they found no additional signs of other tenants on the premises, least of all a man.

"Nothing suspicious here," Rita said to Jason. "Let's check outside."

They returned downstairs and Rita gestured to the front door. "Will you see us out, Sarah? And show us where the Apex van parked?"

Nodding, Sarah scooped up Finn and followed Rita and Jason out onto the porch. She gestured to a clump of trees growing along a fallen-down fence. "That's where the men parked the van. On the other side of those bushes."

"You wouldn't have been able to see much of it through the foliage," Jason said.

"I could see the Apex logo well enough." Sarah scrunched her nose. "I'd rather the darn thing wasn't so recognizable, but you can't get away from it around here."

"After you talked to the men, which way did they head?" Rita asked.

Sarah turned and pointed toward the back of the property. Above the tree line, the roofline of the Still Haven Inn was visible. "They headed back there, into the bush."

"Thanks again," Rita said. "We'll take a look before we leave."

As Sarah and Finn headed back inside, she and Jason waded through the grass to the back of the property.

Jason pushed a branch out of his face. "This place hasn't seen a tree trimmer or weedwhacker in several seasons."

Rita pointed to chunks of scuffed moss and some broken grass stalks. "We've got evidence of foot traffic. But otherwise I'm not finding anything out here but animal droppings."

"I found a chipmunk carcass," Jason said. "At least, I think it was a chipmunk."

"There's an outbuilding at the north side of the house," Rita said, leading the way. "Let's check it out."

Jason followed her into the shed, sneezing immediately. "Rat droppings."

Rita coughed. "And dust."

Jason sniffled. "Only footprints in here are ours. I don't think anyone's used these tools since the Willow family."

Rita coughed again. "Not even the dickhead boyfriend before he left." She shuffled out of the shed, gulping fresh air. "Let's go solve some more crime."

Jason fell into step with her. "Ten-four, Sheriff."

Chapter Eighteen

JASON PULLED the cruiser out of the drive on Windset Lane, headed for Mountain Road. The heat of the day was already softening the asphalt, and the sky had turned an electric shade of blue.

"I noticed something, Sheriff," Jason said, turning onto Mountain Road.

"Oh yeah?" Rita said. "What's that?"

"Our names are an anagram."

Rita thought for a moment. "Oh, you mean Jason and Jonas?"

"Yep." Jason flicked on the turn indicator and pulled into a property marked 808. "Same letters, different order."

Rita nodded. "Nicely done." Then she unbuckled, scanning the house. The building looked as empty as last time. Rita got out and they walked up to the door. A lockbox hung on the handle, and a notice stated that the bank possessed the house.

Rita looked through the narrow windows flanking the

front door. "Looks empty." She straightened. "Let's look around."

Together, they walked around the house.

"Nothing looks unusual here," Jason said.

"Let's talk to a few neighbors." Rita pointed up the road to where a man stood, leaning his forearms against a railed fence. He wore a brimmed hat and suspenders. "Looks like he spends a lot of time at that fence."

They approached the man, and Jason asked him if they could have a few words.

The man nodded. "Surely, son."

"Are you familiar with the address, 808 Mountain Road?" Jason asked.

The man pointed back the way they'd come. "The old Blake place? Sure am."

"Have you seen any recent activity at the property?" Rita asked.

The man adjusted his hat. "Nope."

"Then you didn't witness the incident a few nights ago?"

"Incident?" he asked. "You mean all them car tires squealing? Sure, I heard that."

"Did you see the vehicles?"

"Saw one of them Apex vans," he said. "Not that that's unusual."

"Are Apex vans at the property often?" Rita asked.

"No more than around the rest of town."

Rita swapped a look with Jason. It was a statement any witness in town could make.

"Aside from that night, have you seen anything unusual?" Rita asked.

"Can't say that I have," the man said. "It's sat empty for years."

"No squatters?"

"I heard Arbuckle stays overnight there sometimes in the winter," Jason said.

"Sure does," the man said. "But he ain't a squatter. He's welcome, you know? Folks drop off bottles there for him."

"People drop off bottles for Arbuckle at 808 Mountain Road?" Rita asked.

"Sure do, ma'am." He cleared his throat. "I mean, Sheriff."

"But aside from the car chase the other night, and folks dropping off bottles for Arbuckle, nothing unusual goes on here?"

"That's right, ma'am."

"Thank you for your help," Rita said, feeling like she ought to be wearing a hat of her own to tip. "Have a good day."

Then she gestured in the opposite direction. "Let's walk the other way, see if anyone on the other side of the house has seen anything."

They passed two senior women painting their porch. Rita and Jason entered the property and asked to speak with them. The women set down their paintbrushes, seemingly glad to take a break to sit in the shade.

Both women confirmed what the man had said: No squatters at 808 Mountain Road, or unusual activity of any kind — besides Arbuckle and his bottles.

Rita thanked the women, then she and Jason walked back to the cruiser.

"Let's stop by the Still Haven Inn to see how Helen's doing," Rita said on their way to the SCSO.

Jason changed route, taking Miners Way. At the far end of the road stood the Still Haven Inn, a handsome stone and lumber lodge set back behind a well-watered lawn. The evergreen shrubberies, planted only three years ago, had grown into six-foot tall sentries lining the circular drive.

Jason pulled into the lot and parked the cruiser near the front door. Rita noticed the valet kid wasn't at his post.

"You gonna wait here?" Rita asked.

Jason nodded. Rita got out and went inside.

The lobby was empty. She walked to the front desk and rang the bell. Several times. Eventually, a door behind the desk opened and the manager, Milly, appeared. Her hair looked inkier than last time, dyed to match her penciled eyebrows.

"You here about more vandalism?" Milly asked.

"Nothing official," Rita said. "I'm here to see Helen Myers."

Milly pressed her lips together. "She ain't here no more."

"Really? When she'd leave?"

"Last night."

Rita sensed there was more to the story. "Why'd she leave?"

Milly squared her shoulders. "Because I asked her to."

Rita blinked. "Why?"

Milly folded her arms. "Because she was behaving like a toddler, that's why. Acting all unruly in the lobby." She flung a finger over her shoulder. "She picked up one of them fake potted plants and chucked it clear across the room, hitting Dwayne square between the shoulder blades."

"Do you know if Helen meant for it to hit him?" Rita said.

"Of course, I'm sure she didn't mean to hit him. He was only here to clean out the furnace duct, the poor fellow."

Rita's gaze followed a layer of dust on a shelf above the reception desk. She wondered why Dave bothered.

"She's grieving her dead children," Rita said. "And that accounts for her behavior."

Milly fluttered her mascara-laden eyelashes. "Well, I didn't know that."

"Where'd Helen go after you evicted her?"

Milly's eyebrow shot up. "How should I know? It wasn't my place to ask."

Rita glanced around the vacant lobby. "Well, can I ask where the valet went?"

Milly's face was unreadable. "He quit."

Rita thanked her, although what for she wasn't sure, and walked back out to the parking lot.

Before getting in the cruiser with Jason, she called Helen. Her number rang through to voicemail. Helen had probably blocked her.

Rita sighed and ended the call. Then she sent a text message asking Helen to call her.

Then she sent a follow-up:

Want to make sure you're okay

Rita popped open the door of the cruiser and dropped into the passenger seat.

"Helen's left," she said. "Or more accurately, she was evicted."

Jason blinked. "Evicted for what?"

"Excessive mourning. And throwing a fake plant."

"So where is she now?"

Rita scowled. "Milly doesn't know."

"Maybe she went to stay with family," Jason said.

"Although impossible for you to imagine," Rita said, "she hasn't got any in the area. And it doesn't seem likely she'd go stay with George's parents."

Rita fell silent as Jason drove the cruiser back to the SCSO. Inside, Mary Lou greeted them with a wave.

"Could you run a background check on Sarah Thorpe?" Rita asked.

Mary Lou nodded. "On it."

"Don't worry about it now," Rita said. "I'm bushed. I'm going home to catch up on sleep. And maybe you two should, too."

"I'll happily call it a day," Jason said. "I'm bushed *and* famished."

"Must have been all that talk of mushrooms," Rita said. "See you tomorrow, Deputy."

"Sleep sound, Sheriff," Mary Lou said. "Without Walter here, we're all picking up the slack."

"Right," Rita said. "And we can't run full-out forever."

She headed out to the SCSO parking lot and slid into her Honda. Its familiar smell and blind spots induced a comfortableness she hadn't realized she'd missed.

She patted the steering wheel. "Good to have you back, girl."

On the way to Otto's, Rita stopped by her apartment. She trudged up the stairs and rapped on the door. When Carly didn't answer, Rita rapped louder.

"Hello, it's me," she said through the door.

A couple minutes later, the door cracked open. Carly blinked at her, her eyelids half-closed. Her bruises looked less angry.

"Sorry, Rita, I didn't hear you at first. I've been sleeping."

"You're looking better," Rita said, although Carly's pupils were as small as pinpricks. "Glad you were able to get some shuteye."

Carly patted down her tousled hair. "Seems like forever

since I had a deep sleep." Then she shrugged with one shoulder. "'Course, I took something to help."

Rita raised an eyebrow.

Carly gave a little laugh. "Don't worry, Sheriff. It's legal."

"Well, you don't need to stand around talking on my account," Rita said. "Enjoy some more of that shuteye."

"Thanks Rita. You have a good night too."

Rita gave her a wave and headed downstairs. "Call or text if you need anything, all right?" Then she got in the Honda and drove out to Otto's place.

Chapter Nineteen

RITA PULLED into Otto's driveway and parked the Honda. Then she got out and walked around to the trunk to take out her backpack and uniforms.

The smell of sweet and tangy aroma of ginger and tamari clung to the evening air. As she crunched across the gravel toward the house, Jason poked his head out the door of Otto's trailer.

"Evening, Rita. Want to come in for some supper?"

"I'll take a rain check," Rita said, in spite of her watering taste buds. "It's been a long day, and I want to unpack and settle in."

Jason wished her a good night and she stepped inside Otto's house. Despite the warmth of the day, it was cool in the house. She took off her shoes and carried her backpack and uniforms upstairs.

She hadn't been on the second floor in years. The first bedroom on the right had been hers in childhood. She set down her bag in the hallway and entered.

It smelled the same as it ever did, and looked the same too: pale pink walls (not her color choice); a framed watercolor of ducks on a pond (reportedly painted by a relation of Carol's); a nubby rag rug beside the bed that she used to rub the soles of her feet against. She even recognized the spilt juice and silly putty stains on it. Thank goodness Helen hadn't applied her decorating proclivities here, like in the living room.

Looking at her bedroom now, Rita supposed it was austere. Only a bed, a desk, and a bookshelf filled with the complete collections of *Nancy Drew*, *The Hardy Boys*, and *Trixie Belden*. Not one blue ribbon tacked to a bulletin board or poster pinned to the wall — she never would have been allowed to push a tack into the drywall. Let alone do anything else to the space to make it uniquely hers. To make it something she would like to live in.

She sighed. Maybe that's why she'd lived in such a sparse apartment in New York. Lana used to say her place looked like an IKEA catalog. And in her defense, Rita would shrug and say she could tidy it top to bottom while watching an episode of *Survivor*.

Rita went back into the hall, but instead of picking up her backpack, she entered the bedroom across the hall.

Otto's bedroom looked the same as it ever did, with framed photos from his training days and a crocheted granny-square bedspread Gramma Jonas had made for his and Carol's wedding.

She opened the closet. Otto's clothes filled half of the rod, while the other half supported empty hangers. He really had kicked Helen out for good. Rita closed the door and left the room, suddenly feeling like she'd pried too much.

She picked up her bag and uniforms and continued to the guest room. Rita set the bag by the double bed and lay the uniforms on the mattress.

In the corner of the room, a sewing machine sat on a

desk. Tucked beneath the desk was a laundry basket filled with folded pieces of fabric. Carol's fabric. She was surprised Helen hadn't tidied it away or gotten rid of it. Or even Otto himself, sometime in the last decade.

Rita thumbed through the stack of fabric in the basket. Some of it had already been cut into pattern pieces. She picked up a flowered panel for a child's dress. Carol had obviously cut this for Rita years ago and never finished. There were so many things that Carol had started and never finished. She found several more pieces, cut but never sewn. A dozen projects, born of enthusiasm until the endeavor was drowned in a bottle.

Something twisted in Rita's gut — a memory. An unpleasant one. She recognizes the scrap of fabric she was holding. She ran her thumbs over the flowered pattern. Carol had sewn it into an apron. And she'd been wearing the apron the day she'd bent over to haul Rita out from under the bed by her ankle. Rita remembered the apron wafting over the floorboards. She remembered the smell of the dust beneath the bed. She remembered the sour sweetness of Carol's breath, laced with alcohol and anger.

Rita didn't remember why she was hiding under the bed, other than to escape Carol's wrath. Even in the moment thirty years ago, Rita probably didn't know why Carol was angry.

Rita returned the flowered pattern piece to the laundry basket and selected a yardage of checked flannel. She shook it out and draped it over the machine.

Then she opened the closet door and hung up her uniforms. Carol's old clothes filled the rest of the rod.

Rita pulled them out and carried them down the hall to her room, where she piled them on the bed. On the top of the pile lay a white turtleneck with a small brown stain on the chest. Rita ran her hands over it. The sweater had been her mother's favorite. But it had always made Rita feel embarrassed when Carol wore it, because the drop of bourbon looked like a nipple when she wore it.

Rita recalled being thirteen and asking Carol not to wear the sweater around town. To which Carol had replied, "Why the hell not? If sandals were good enough for Jesus, goddammit, this sweater's good enough for me."

Rita had never really understood that statement. But she supposed Carol was right. It wasn't Rita's place to ever criticize what Carol was wearing; it was a goddamn miracle any day that Carol even got dressed.

Rita flipped over the sweater so she couldn't see the stain, then turned to leave.

And paused.

She opened her bedroom closet. Here hung Otto's off-season clothes, a hunting jacket he never used, and his dress uniform which he wore for special ceremonies.

She stood on her tiptoes and reached to the back of the shelf, her hands feeling for a familiar shape. Her fingers brushed a box, and she lifted it down.

For a moment, she sat on the bed, holding the boot box. Age had softened the cardboard. Taking a breath, she flipped off the lid.

Inside she found her high school yearbooks, greeting cards, and other mementos. A foiled heart caught her eye, and she pulled it out from the stack of envelopes.

It was a Valentine's card from Cash: *Dear Rita, You make my engine rev.*

Her stomach flipped. What was she doing, sleeping with her teenage heartthrob? When all she had to do was say yes to Dale, downsize her furnishings, and move in with him? Which would barely cause a ripple in her life, given she and Dale had all the same stuff from IKEA.

Instead, most of her stuff sat in a storage unit. Her

heart felt shut up, too, as though hidden behind a metal roll-up door.

Rita turned over the boot box, dumping its contents on the bed. She selected her grade twelve yearbook, then she returned to the guest room. She put it on the bedside table, then walked across the hall to put her toiletries in the bathroom.

She gazed at her reflection in the mirror. "What are we going to do about Otto?"

But she didn't have an answer for herself.

The doorbell rang, and Rita froze. Who the hell could that be? Everybody in the county knew Otto was unwell in Casper Hospital.

She walked down the hallway to Otto's room. She peeked out of the window at the front of the house, but she didn't see a vehicle in the driveway.

Rita went downstairs and opened the front door. A bowl of stir-fried veggies and rice sat steaming on the stoop.

She smiled. "Thanks, Jason."

Inside, Rita got a fork and a beer from the kitchen. Then she sat on the sofa and turned on the TV. As she ate dinner, she watched an episode of *Deal or No Deal*, finding herself deeply invested in a contestant named Miguel winning a million dollars.

Her phone buzzed. It was Cash again. She muted the TV, preparing to pick up.

But her thumbed stalled, unable to answer it. He'd been to visit Otto, and he'd want to talk about his condition. And she didn't want to talk to anyone about Otto in case she couldn't help but mention her conversation with Dr. Albright.

Although maybe that's what she needed — to debrief. But the phone had stopped ringing by the time she was ready to answer.

Cash left a message: "Saw Otto today, Rita. We must have missed each other. You must be concerned about everything. Please call."

She set down the phone. Miguel had taken a deal for $175,000. She turned off the TV and went upstairs to bed.

Chapter Twenty

RITA AWOKE to the familiar sound of the quaking aspen leaves on the rooftop. For as long as she'd slept here, she'd listened to that tree. Only now it was much taller and fuller, and the scratching branches sounded like an entire herd of bighorn sheep on the shingles.

She rolled over, and for a while, she counted sheep. When that didn't work, she flipped onto her back and stared at the ceiling, looking for patterns in the spackle as if they were clouds.

But all she could see was Otto's face, pallid against the pillow in the hospital bed.

Sighing, she called it a night and dragged herself out of bed. She showered and dressed in her uniform, then went downstairs for breakfast.

Happily, Otto's fridge held a wide assortment of food. But despite facing cancer, it didn't appear Otto's diet had altered in any way.

Rita pawed through packages of bacon and pork sausage, looking for the healthiest breakfast option. She settled on a bagel with cream cheese.

Afterwards, she washed her dish and knife, plus Jason's bowl from last night. Then she stepped out of the house, locking it behind her, and walked over to Otto's camper on blocks.

Before she could rap on the aluminum door, Jason's head popped out.

"Hey there, Rita, wanna carpool? Seeing as we're living here together now."

Rita held up a hand. "Let's stop right there, before everyone starts calling you Jason Jonas." She passed him the bowl. "Although that stir fry last night might tempt me to shack up with you. Thanks for dinner. It was one of the best I've had in while."

Jason beamed. "Oyster sauce with oyster mushrooms. I got the idea talking with Sarah Thorpe."

"Oyster mushrooms," Rita said, tapping her lip. "That's what those things were."

"What'd you think they were?" Jason asked as they crunched across the gravel. He looked hopeful. "Oysters?"

"I thought they might have been chicken wings," Rita said, getting in the passenger seat of the cruiser. "The boneless kind."

Jason grimaced. "Those are only at Chicken Bun on the Run." He shuddered. "Thank Jesus."

WHILE JASON DROVE, Rita typed a text to Mary Lou:

Please get in touch with Lydia. See if she can find Helen

Rita sent the message, then drummed her fingers on the passenger door armrest. Twenty seconds later, a text came in from Mary Lou.

10-4

Smiling, Rita put her phone away. She could trust

Mary Lou to get the dirt on anything, both on the job and off.

Jason slowed down in front of the Bighorn Mining building, where construction proceeded as usual. Despite them wearing hard hats, Rita spotted the redhead and the other guy crossing the site with a loaded cart of debris.

She pointed through her window at the redhead. "You noticed that guy around town?"

"Sure," Jason said, staring straight ahead through the windshield. "I see both of 'em somewhere different almost every day."

"Stu and Vic?" Rita's gaze followed Jason's.

Stu and Vic headed their way, running full out.

"What the hell are those two up to?" she asked.

Jason sighed. "Knowing them, probably another public disturbance."

Stu and Vic drew closer, waving their arms.

Rita glanced behind through the rear window of the cruiser. "Do you think they're waving at us?"

"Listen." Jason leaned his head out of the window. "They're shouting something."

Rita squinted at them, barreling down the sidewalk. "I think they want to talk to us." Resting her elbow on the door, she leaned her head out the window. "Everything all right, guys?"

"Nope," Stu said, collapsing on the hood of the patrol car, out of breath. He slid off the hood of the car and leaned over, bracing his hands on his knees and sucking in air. "Somethin' sure ain't right."

Vic, on the other hand, popped off the hood ramrod-straight and teetered on his sneakers. Running his hands through his hair, he blew out a hard breath. "Hell, yeah. Something's definitely wrong."

"Yeah." Stu pointed with a rubbery arm over his shoulder. "Something's wrong at a house on Lodgepole Street."

"That's five blocks away," Jason said. "You ran all this way?"

Vic bobbed like a pogo stick. "We was gonna call 911 when we spotted the cruiser."

"Get in," Rita said, jerking her head toward the back seat.

Stu and Vic each ran around to a side door and clambered in.

Rita popped the glove box and fished out two small bottles of water. "It's not cold, but if you'd like—"

The two teenagers snatched the bottles from her hands and cracked the lids.

"Let's go," Rita said, signaling Jason to pull out.

Victor pointed over Jason's shoulder. "Take that left."

Jason put on the indicator. "What's the address?"

"Dunno," Stu said, draining his water bottle. "All I know is it's Mr. Clark's place."

"It's coming up here on the left," Vic said. "The blue one."

"It ain't blue, it's purple," Stu said.

"Maybe it's blurple," Jason said.

Rita looked at Jason. "Blurple is not a color."

He threw a look back at her. "Have you ever gone shopping for a men's suit?"

Rita narrowed her eyes at him. "I wasn't Dale's *mother*."

Jason fixed his eyes on the road. "Never said you were."

Rita looked back at the boys. "So the house is purple? What else is wrong with it?"

Stu and Vic exchanged a look.

"The door's open," Stu said.

"And how's that wrong?"

"Well, he's not exactly the social sort."

"Yeah," Vic said. "He never leaves it hanging open like that. So we was worried something happened to him."

Rita glanced over her shoulder. Stu gave her a wobbly smile, and Victor dabbed some sweat from his forehead. She figured they knew more than they were letting on.

She faced forward again as Jason pulled into the driveway. Gray paint with black trim gave the decades-old bungalow a contemporary look.

"Definitely not blurple," Rita said.

A cleanly swept walkway and neatly pruned shrubs gave the home an overall appearance of tidiness.

"Nice flower beds," Jason said. He pointed to a hydrogen with blooms as big as dinner plates. "Those are blurple."

"Someone's taking care of those." She glanced at the boys in the back again. "Wait in the car, okay?"

Stu and Vic nodded. Then she and Jason got out.

As they walked together to the front door, she leaned into his shoulder. "Those two are spooked about something."

Jason nodded. "Uh-huh."

Rita arrived at the steps to the front door. It stood wide open.

"You think Stu and Vic saw their chance to loot the place?" She pulled her weapon. "Or were they truly concerned citizens?"

Jason pulled his weapon, too, and they mounted the steps to the door.

"Name's Clark, is it?" Rita asked Jason.

"Not sure," Jason said, as they crossed the stoop to the front door. It didn't appear to be kicked in, the lock intact and the wood panels undamaged. "I've never met the owners of this house. But that's what the boys said."

Rita knocked on the open door and called out. "Hello, Mr. Clark?"

No answer.

Seeing no signs of forced entry, she stepped into the foyer. The polished floor and windows gleamed, and the shoes by the door were arranged with precision, indicating an orderly lifestyle.

Jason followed. "Mr. Clark?"

Still no response.

They moved through the one-level house, clearing the spaces, clearing the house room by room: the living room, the kitchen, the bedroom.

In the bathroom, a strong pong of bleach clung to the air. Rita coughed, then moved on to the last rooms. They cleared a guest bedroom, a linen closet, then entered the office.

A man lay on the floor wearing a cotton shirt and khakis. And yet something didn't quite look right. For a moment, Rita didn't understand what she was looking at. And then something in her brain shifted and she saw: the man's head had been removed, and it now sat upon the desk.

Jason darted out of the room and crashed into the bathroom, where she heard him vomit.

Rita withdrew from the room, walking backwards as though she expected the cadaver to move.

In the hallway, she paused to lean against the wall, still gripping her gun. It was possible the killer was still in the house. But all she could think about was breathing.

Inhale.

Exhale.

She heard Jason clear his throat, then turn on the faucet and gargle water. She made her way to bathroom and collected him.

Outside, she deposited him on the lawn.

She rubbed his back. "I don't have any water for you," she said, her own mouth feeling dry.

"It's okay," Jason said. "I had some."

Rita patted his shoulder, then pulled out her phone and called Casper Forensics. She was aware that Stu and Vic were watching from the back of the cruiser.

"I got a body," she said. "Beheaded. Gonna need Dylan Bruce."

The message was swiftly received, and Rita was informed the medical examiner and Tilda's team would be underway momentarily.

Rita disconnected and looked at Jason. "I gotta go back inside. Clear the property."

Jason nodded. "I know. I'll come."

Rita shook her head. "I got it, Jason, you catch your breath here. We cleared most of the rooms, but still, I gotta make sure there's no one inside who needs help."

Heart pounding, Rita walked back inside the house. She stared down the hallway that led to the office. A shudder ran up her spine.

She pushed down the fear and told herself she was back in New York, clearing the floor of an apartment block, suite by suite. And this was only a rancher. Easy peasy, right?

She cleared a laundry room and the garage, then checked each of the rooms they'd cleared earlier. Although she let herself off the hook from returning to the office. After all, there'd been no closet or piece of furniture large enough in the room to obscure someone hiding.

She lowered her gun and walked out of the house.

Jason lay on the grass while Stu and Vic messed around in the back of the cruiser. Where was Walter when you needed him? Rita didn't often have thoughts like that. But she could really use him right now. Instead, she was stuck with Apex.

Sighing, Rita pulled out her phone and swiped for Ken Saunders' number.

Chapter Twenty-One

NEXT, Rita rang Mary Lou.

"I'm bringing in Stu and Vic in," she said. "Please arrange to have a parent for each of them at the station."

Mary Lou sighed. "What in the blazes have them two done now?"

"Nothing, I suspect," Rita said. "Or at least I hope so. They're witnesses."

"Roger," Mary Lou said, then disconnected.

Rita put away her phone as an Apex-branded pickup truck pulled up to the property.

The driver got out and walked up to Rita. "Sheriff."

"Thanks for coming, Ken," Rita said. "Please give my deputy a hand maintaining the scene of the crime here."

Ken stayed where he was, looking up at the gray and black house through his reflective sunglasses. Then he glanced over his shoulder down the street. Lastly, his mirrored gaze turned to Rita.

"Does this have anything to do with the stolen Apex vehicles?" he asked.

Rita blinked at him. "I don't know that yet."

Ken flattened his mouth. "Hmm."

Rita narrowed her eyes at him. "Is that a condition of this agreement?"

Ken rolled his shoulders, looking uncomfortable in a suit jacket. "I can offer my assistance with that, and only that."

"Well, you didn't tell me that before, when you were telling me about your cooperative spirit." Rita folded her arms. "So can you do us a favor this time instead?"

Ken hesitated, shifting on his feet. "Sure, Sheriff. Suppose that means I might call in a favor from you sometime, too."

It was Rita's turn to flatten her mouth. "Sure, Ken." Then she wagged a finger toward the cruiser. "I've got two witnesses I need to take into the station."

Ken lifted his sunglasses to peer closer. "They look unruly."

"You have no idea."

She turned and walked over to Jason, who'd managed to elevate himself into a forty-five-degree angle, propped against the Cottonwood tree in the front yard.

"You're looking better," she said.

He grimaced. "Not sure I'm feeling all that much better."

Rita slapped his shoulder. "You're upright. Sort of. And that's a good sign."

Jason gave her a wavering smile and nodded.

Rita called Ken over and told him to find some water for Jason. Then she headed back to the cruiser and took the driver's seat.

She twisted to talk to Stu and Vic in the back seat. "We'll get through this as swiftly as possible. Plus, there's coffee and cookies at the station."

Stu and Vic visibly brightened.

As they drove, Rita asked, "So, did you guys go into the house?"

In the rearview mirror she saw them shake their heads.

"Nope," Stu said. "We was just concerned because we saw the door open."

Rita fell quiet, confident Stu was lying.

They arrived at the station, where Rita directed Stu into her office and Vic into the bullpen.

"Their parents are on the way," Mary Lou said.

"Thanks, Mary Lou," Rita said. "Oh, and those two are gonna need cookies."

Mary Lou bobbed her silver head. "Ten-four."

Rita stepped into the narrow hallway leading to the back door. She pulled out her phone to call Hunter Green.

But the call rang through to his voicemail.

"Hunter, it's Rita. I've got a situation here and I need some full-time help. And Ken Saunders from Apex isn't it. So send me someone today, or I'm going to Casper myself to pick up a cop and I'll send the bill directly to you."

As Rita shoved away her phone, a short man with a shaved head walked through the front door.

"What the hell kind of shit has my son been up to this time, Sheriff?"

Rita crossed the room to him. "Mr. Gardner. Thanks for coming in."

Stu's father rolled his shoulders. "Call me Peter. And what's all this about?"

"Stu is a witness to a murder." Rita leaned in and lowered her voice. "And he can use all the support he can get right now."

Peter's shoulders slumped. "Jesus, murder." He paused. "Wasn't Vic, was it?"

Rita's eyebrows shot up. "Who, the victim? Hell, no." She nodded into the bullpen. "Vic's right there."

Peter gave him a look. "So where's Stu? You stick him in the cells?"

Rita lowered her brows. "Of course not. I told you, Stu's a witness. He's waiting in my office, probably eating cookies." Rita cocked her head toward the door. "Let's go."

Peter traipsed after her into the office. Rita closed the door behind them while Peter gave his son an awkward hug. Then Stu sat down again, and Peter sat in the chair with the broken leg beside him.

"Mind the chair," Rita said. "That one's broken."

"They're both broken," Stu said, gestured with his mug. A stream of coffee sloshed out. "But that's one broke worse. So I sat in this one."

"Gee, thanks," Peter said, adjusting his posture.

Rita sat at her desk and opened the top drawer. She took out a voice recorder, plus a pad of paper and a pen.

"I'll be recording your statement," she said. "Please tell me what happened."

Stu selected an Oreo from the package. "We was just messin' around, looking for somethin' to do."

Peter cleared his throat. "Instead of messin' around, Stuart, you shoulda been workin'. Or the Gas N Go's gonna fire ya."

"I don't work at the Gas N Go."

"What?"

"I don't work at the Gas N Go."

"Since when?"

"Since Chester fired me."

"When he'd do that?"

"Two weeks ago."

Peter leaned back in his chair, folding his arms. "So you ain't workin'?"

"Yeah, I'm workin'. I'm just on days off."

"Where ya' workin?'"

"At Thrift-O Gas."

"At the other end of town?'"

"Yeah."

"Didja know Chester's wife's cousin's husband owns that place?"

"Yeah."

"And you're workin' there anyway?"

Stu nodded.

"As interesting as this is," Rita said, "I'm the one conducting the interview. If we could get on with things, I'd appreciate it."

Peter sucked his tongue for a second. "The thing I don't understand, Stuart, is the Thrift-O Gas is practically in Beaumont. How the hell you get there? Ride your bike?"

Stu shook his head. "Skateboard."

Peter screwed up his nose. "Skateboard?"

"You'd better be wearing a helmet," Rita said.

"Sold my bike," Stu said.

Peter's eyebrows arched. "When you'd do that?"

Stu shrugged. "Couple months ago."

"Why?"

"Needed some cash."

"Didja think of gettin' a job?"

"I did. At the Gas N Go."

Peter frowned. "Till two weeks ago."

"That's why I got a job at the Thrift-O Gas."

Peter scratched this jaw. "I heard it's closing shop."

It was Stu's turn to look surprised. "Oh, yeah?"

"Yeah," Rita said, "is that right? Because I use that station all the time."

"Not often enough, I guess," Peter said.

"Guess not," Rita said. "Even though I hate guessing."

"So why were *you* down at the Gas N Go when it was my shift?" Stu asked, looking at his father.

"To talk to ya," Peter said.

"About what?"

"Doesn't matter."

"Why not?"

"'Cause you weren't there, were ya?"

Stu folded his arms. "But I was supposed to be."

"That's right. So it's a goddamned May Day parade that you got yourself another job."

"So what'd you want to see me about?"

Peter sighed. "About maybe quittin' the Gas N Go."

"Why would I want to quit the Gas N Go?"

Peter stared at him for a moment. Then he said, "'Cause I met this guy who sells lawnmowers."

"What kind of lawnmowers?"

"What does that matter?" Peter said, gripping that armrests of his chair. "The kind you ride."

"I don't wanna push 'em."

Peter sighed. "He wants sales reps."

Stu looked offended. "I don't do reps, Dad. That's your jam."

"I'm not talkin' about bicep curls, Stuart." Peter curled back his lips as he enunciated his words. "I'm talking' about bein' a sales *representative*."

"How can I be a sales *representative* if no grass grows around here?" Stu took another Oreo. "We only got Christmas trees in Still. Pinecones and needles and shit on the ground."

"Do you want to work at the Gas N Go or do you want to sell lawnmowers?"

"I don't work at the Gas N Go," Stu said, spraying chocolatey crumbs, "I work at Thrift-O Gas."

Peter ground his teeth for a moment. "Forget pumping

gas, Stuart. Lawnmowers. Riding ones. Easy peasy. You're always runnin' 'round town as it is. May as well sell some shit to the neighbors while you're at it."

Rita cleared her throat. "Speaking of calling on neighbors—"

"No thanks, Dad," Stu said, waving a hand. "When I said I don't wanna push lawnmowers, I mean I don't wanna sell 'em. And I don't know shit about pushing one around neither."

"Well, that's obvious since you never mow the back yard," Peter said.

"We don't have a back yard," Stu said. "That's why I run around town."

"Well, what do you call the area out behind our house, if it ain't the back yard?"

"The driveway."

Peter's face turned red. "Just because no grass grows out there don't mean it's a driveway. Do you see me parking my truck out there?"

"No." Then he shrugged again. "But if no grass grows out there, why do you care if I don't mow it?"

Peter ran his hands over his hairless head and looked at Rita. "Sheriff, you got some questions?"

"I do indeed," she said, shaking out her foot which had fallen asleep. "Otherwise we'll all be here till midnight."

"Midnight?" Stu said. "That ain't gonna work. I got a night shift at the Thrift-O Gas. I was plannin' to sleep this afternoon, but then…" The color drained from his face, and he took another cookie.

Peter blinked at his son. "You're workin' tonight? Well, you ain't gonna make that. Police business gotta come first."

Stu pulled the two halves of the cookie apart. "Shit, Chester's wife's cousin's husband is gonna fire me."

Peter took a cookie, too. "Well, then you can sell lawn—"

"You're not gonna get fired 'cause we're not gonna be here till midnight," Rita said. She fixed her eye on Peter. "*If* we get on with things." She pulled up her voice app, set it to record, and placed the phone it on the desk. "Please speak clearly."

Peter grumbled his agreement and Stu nodded, silent.

"So we've established you weren't working this morning," Rita said, addressing Stu. "Why were you messing around on Lodgepole Street?"

Stu shrugged and a stream of cookie crumbs cascaded down the front of his T-shirt. "Like I said, Sheriff, we was just messin' around. And we ended up in that part of town. Noticed Mr. Clark's door was standing wide open, which was weird."

"What was weird about it?" Rita asked.

Stu swallowed some coffee. "It's never open. That guy never goes anywhere."

"You don't live on Lodgepole Street," Rita said, "and you know this?"

He sipped again. "Walk over there often."

"Any particular reason?" Rita asked.

Stu shrugged. "We go all over town often."

Peter smirked. "Ain't that the truth?"

Rita sat forward, folding her hands on the desk. "Look, Stu, I know you went inside the house. I know you saw the body. And it's fine that you did. Anyone might. You were curious."

Stu shook his head. "Didn't."

Rita sighed. "Casper Forensics are on their way. If they find any of your fingerprints or DNA inside, you move from being a witness to a suspect."

For a moment, Stu was quiet. Then he said, "Yeah, I

went inside. But it wasn't only my idea," Stu said. "Vic thought we should check, too. We was just being neighborly, worried that maybe somethin' happened to the guy, like a heart attack or somethin'."

Peter's forehead buckled. "You two weren't lookin' to loot the place?"

Stu cut him a look. "Jesus, Pete, you my dad or a cop?" Then he glanced at Rita. "No offense, Sheriff."

"None taken," she said. "So what happened next?"

"We knocked. Truly, Sheriff, we wasn't tryin' to loot him. We knocked and tried to raise him. When no one came to the door, I went in."

"And Vic?"

"He waited for me outside."

Peter made a sound in his throat, folding his arms again. "What the fuck, Stu?"

Stu looked at his dad. "What?"

Peter lowered his brow. "You're always hangin' yourself out for that guy."

"I ain't hanging myself out," Stu said. He looked at Rita. "It's true. He waited outside."

"Scared, that's what," Peter said.

"No, he weren't," Stu said. "He was lookin' out for me."

"Sounds like a good friend," Rita said.

"The best," Stu said.

Peter grunted again.

"So you went in," Rita said, flashing an encouraging smile. "Then what?"

"I called around the house for him. But I didn't hear nothin'."

"So you checked the rooms."

Stu gave a nod.

"And—?"

Stu swallowed. "I saw…"

Rita nodded. "I understand. Did you notice anything odd about the house? I mean, aside from…"

Stu shook his head. "Nope. Just the open door."

"Did anyone pass by on the street?"

Stu thought for a moment. "Guess we'd have to ask Vic." He took another Oreo. "Since he was outside."

"Good point," Peter said.

"When you left, did you notice any neighbors around?" Rita asked. "Or service people?"

"Um, didn't notice much after I left," Stu said. "Guess 'cause I was runnin' hard."

"You were in shock," Rita said. "Is there anything else you can remember?"

Stu thought for a moment. Then he shook his head.

Rita shut off the voice recorder. "Thanks, Stu." She opened her drawer and took out a card. She passed it to him. "Sometimes, when we're in shock, we forget things. Details that might come back to us later. If you remember anything else, please call."

"Sure will, Sheriff," Stu said. "Though I think I'd rather forget about all of this."

Rita gave him a sympathetic smile and got up from her desk. "Eat all the cookies you want, Stu. I'm going to step out with your dad for a moment."

Rita met Peter Gardner's eye and gestured toward the door. He gave a nod and rose from his chair, exiting the office with Rita.

Rita closed the door behind them. "Thanks for coming in," she said.

"Sure thing, Sheriff."

"We're going to need a set of exclusion prints from Stu. Then you can take him home."

Peter nodded. "Sure thing."

"Stuart's seen something horrific," she said. "Give him some extra TLC today, huh?"

Peter pulled on his chin. "He likes the Runnin' Nuggets from Chicken Bun on the Run."

"Sounds great," Rita said through her teeth. "And call Chester's wife's cousin's husband at the Thrift-O Gas. Let him know Stu can't make his shifts for a couple days, but then he'll be back. By the end of the week, the distraction will do him good. But he's gonna need a couple days to recalibrate."

Peter nodded again. "Sure, Sheriff."

"Great." Rita opened her office door and poked in her head. Stu was removing the last Oreo from the package. "Thanks for waiting, Stu. Mary Lou's ready to take your exclusion prints. Then your dad'll get you out of here."

Stu came into the bullpen, licking his fingers clean. He looked across at Mary Lou's desk, then back at Rita. His teeth were stained dark brown. "Um, should I wash my hands first?"

Rita nodded. "Good idea."

Chapter Twenty-Two

"HUNTER GREEN'S on the line, Sheriff," Mary Lou said, holding out the receiver.

"I'll take it in my office," Rita said, giving Stu a final pat on the shoulder as his dad led him over to Mary Lou's desk.

Rita walked into her office and closed the door behind her. Then she sat at her desk and picked up the receiver. "Hello, Hunter."

"Rita," he said, with a note of impatience. "Sounds like it's taking some time for you to get used to small-town policing."

"Yes, Hunter," Rita said, dryly, "it does take some time to get used to doing nearly everything yourself."

Hunter grumbled something under his breath, then sighed. "I get it. These circumstances are somewhat exceptional. I'll send you an officer for seven days, and then I'll review the investigation."

"Thanks," Rita said.

"You're welcome. And you'll get used to it."

"Used to what?"

"Doing nearly everything yourself."

"I ain't in New York anymore, that's for damn sure," she said, matching this sigh. "Jason's a gem, but I still miss my partners."

"How's Dale these days?"

Rita smirked. "You should know. You probably see him more than I do."

"You know what I mean."

"Yeah, well, those weren't the kind of partners I was referring to."

"Cheer up, Sheriff," Hunter said. "You've got Apex to help you."

"Right. 'Cause they're real helpful. I'll carry on dealing with this beheaded guy, while Ken helps me help him find his own damned company's missing vehicles."

"Play nice."

"Hey, that usually my line," she said. "You forget I'm not the only one around here lacking enthusiasm about Apex."

"Goodbye, Rita."

"Thanks, Hunter," Rita said, squeezing in her words. "Have a good weekend."

Hunter hung up and Rita returned the receiver to its cradle. Then she went out to the bullpen. A dark-haired woman was gesticulating at Mary Lou while she closed the front door behind Stu and his father.

"I been called away from work, and it's been a hell of long day, let me tell you!" the woman said to Mary Lou. "And I got a husband at home with kidney failure who needs me there, taking care of him after shift. Instead, I'm here 'cause my goddamn kid got into some goddamned trouble again."

Rita approached, smiling. "Hello, I'm Sheriff Jonas."

The woman scowled at Rita, deepening the lines that radiated from her lips, from a lifetime of smoking or perhaps frowning. "I know who you are."

"And you must be Vic's mom," Rita said, continuing to smile.

The woman's nostrils flared. "Francine Nelson."

"Thanks for coming in, Francine. Like I said, there's no trouble. Please come into my office so we can have a brief chat, then you can be on your way to your husband." Rita gestured for Francine to proceed, then turned to Mary Lou. "Bring in Vic, please? And we're gonna need some more cookies."

The woman gave Rita a pert nod, then Vic the hairy eyeball. The kid sprang to his feet, following his mother and Rita into the office. Rita closed the door behind them.

"Vic, why don't you take this chair," Rita said, pointing to the chair with the wobbly seat back.

Francine was working out a way to sit in the chair with the broken leg when Mary Lou popped in.

She deposited a pack of Fig Newtons on the desk. "Sorry, no more Oreos." Then she slipped out.

Rita sat down at her desk and smiled at Stu. "Help yourself." She motioned to the cookies, then she looked at Francine. "Your son is a witness in a homicide investigation. I need to ask him a number of questions and I'll be recording his answers." She turned on her voice recorder. "Vic, please tell me what happened."

Victor hesitated.

"On Lodgepole street," Rita prompted.

Francine slapped him across the head. "You answer her at once."

"Do that again," Rita said to her, "and I'll arrest you for assault."

Francine folded her hands in her lap and puckered her mouth.

"Please, Victor," Rita said, "go ahead."

"It's like Stu told you," Victor said. "We was walkin' down Lodgepole Street and we saw the door wide open. Which was weird."

"And what was your reason for messin' around on Lodgepole?" Rita asked.

Vic glanced at his mother before answering. "Um, sometimes he leaves empties at the end of his driveway."

Francine narrowed her eyes at him. "You was collectin' empties like that bum Arbuckle?"

"Well I don't have a job like Stu does," Vic said, frowning back at her. "And Arbuckle's not a bum."

"And did you collect empties today?" Rita asked.

Vic paused. "Um, nope. Which makes sense, right? 'Cause he couldn't have 'cause … well, you know…"

"So you saw the door standing open," Rita said, "and you thought it was unusual?"

Vic nodded, taking a Fig Newton. "Like, maybe it was a home invasion."

"Were you frightened?"

"Of a home invasion? Hell, yeah. I wasn't goin' in there."

"But Stu did," Rita said.

Victor nodded. "He thought maybe the guy was sick or somethin'. Like a heart attack. He wasn't real old, but he wasn't real young, neither."

"So Stu went inside and what did you do?"

"I stood at the bottom of the steps, in case anybody came by."

"Were you expecting anyone to come by?" Rita asked.

Vic glanced at his mother. "No, Sheriff."

"These questions sound leading," Francine said. "Didn't you say my boy's just a witness?"

Rita gave her a tight smile. "I'm need to make sure I get all the information." She looked at Vic. "Did you go inside the house, Vic?"

Victor shook his head. "Nope. Already told you that, Sheriff."

Rita nodded and gestured to the voice recorder. "You did. But just for the record. And what happened when Stu came out of the house?"

Again, Vic hesitated, glancing sidelong at his mother. "Um…"

"It's okay," Rita said. "No one's in trouble here. We just need the information so we can put together the crime scene."

Victor cleared his throat. "Stu barfed in a planter."

Rita nodded, taking notes. "At the house?"

Vic shook his head. "No, about three or four houses down. Maybe more. We were runnin' and I didn't count."

"Okay," Rita said. "That sounds like a normal response."

"Yeah, I coulda run for hours," Vic said.

"I meant, it's a normal response to vomit," Rita said. "And then phone for help."

Vic's cheeks flushed. "Well, it ain't normal to puke in a mailbox."

Rita's eyebrows arched. "Did Stu also vomit in a mailbox?"

"Yep," said Vic, selecting another Fig Newton. "The one on the corner of Lodgepole and Ponderosa."

"Busy intersection," Rita said. "That mailbox must get quite a bit of use."

"Sure as hell does," Francine said. "That's why Victor put dog poo inside it."

Rita's eyebrows couldn't go any higher. "You put dog poo in there, too?"

"Not today," Vic said. "When I was eleven."

Rita laughed. "Well, that must have caused an upset."

"Sure as hell did," Francine said. "And none of my checks that week got to where they were going. Power and cable were shut off three weeks later."

"Thank goodness bygones can be bygones," Rita said, shutting off the recorder. She took out another of her cards and gave it to him. "If you remember anything else, Vic, please give me a call."

Nodding, Victor pocketed her card. Then he followed her to the door.

"Please head over to Mary Lou," Rita said. "She'll take your prints."

Vic nodded and headed across the bullpen. Francine stayed put for a moment, glaring at Rita.

"You're printin' a witness?" she asked.

"Exclusion prints," Rita said. "He was at the scene of the crime. A matter of formality."

"What for?"

"To find out whether he's telling the truth about not going inside."

Francine stiffened. "My boy may not always be obedient, but he always tells the truth."

Rita smiled wider. "And I'm sure you'd beat it out of him if you had to."

Francine bared her teeth, then loped after her son.

Rita gave Mary Lou a wave, then headed out the back door to the parking lot. She slid into the driver's seat of her Honda and texted Jason, telling him she was on her way back to the crime scene. He sent her a thumbs up.

Rita started the ignition and pulled out into traffic. As

she drove, she called Casper Hospital and navigated the menu to the nurses' station.

"I'm calling about Otto Jonas," she said. "How's he doing?"

"No change since yesterday," the nurse said. Rita didn't recognize her voice.

"Thank you," Rita said. "I'll get in to see him as soon as I can."

"Your father's doctors are hoping to speak with you," the nurse said. "They're wondering if you've made a decision."

"Not yet," Rita said.

"I'll let them know," the nurse said.

Rita thanked her and repeated that she'd be in soon to visit. A minute later, she was pulling up to the address on Lodgepole Street. Casper Forensics had already arrived and were packing their gear up the steps.

Dressed in white Tyvek, Tilda raised a hand and waved to Rita.

"We're goin' in," she said.

"Good luck with this crime scene," Rita said. "It's been a busy one."

Tilda glanced raised an eyebrow. "Oh, yeah?"

"Jason and I were both in the house," Rita said. "Jason vomited in the bathroom."

Tilda gave a nod. "Thanks for the heads up."

"And a teenage witness was inside. Maybe two, if the other one wasn't telling the truth about waiting outside. We'll send through their prints ASAP."

"Sounds like a party," Tilda said.

"Well, you can be thankful the teenager didn't empty his guts inside and instead decided to wait till the corner of Lodgepole and Ponderosa."

"That's good news I'll take," Tilda said.

Rita grimaced. "Not such good news for the Postal Service." Her gaze caught on a young cop in a Casper uniform. She hovered near the property fence line, repeatedly tucking her short hair behind her ear.

"One of yours?" Rita asked.

Tilda shook her head. "Nope."

Rita walked over to the cop. Her nametag read *V. Logan*.

"Morning, Officer Logan," Rita said.

"Sheriff Jonas," the cop said. "Casper PD sent me to assist with the investigation."

Rita gave her a wooden smile. "Welcome to Still. And to one hell of a grisly crime scene."

Swallowing, Officer Logan glanced at the house.

"How long have you been a cop?" Rita asked.

Logan squared her shoulders. "A week."

"Jesus," Rita said, making a mental note to thank Hunter for sending his best. "You worked a murder investigation before?"

She swallowed again. "Sure."

Rita smiled. "Well, we won't get your hands too dirty today. Come on."

Leading the young cop around the front of the cruiser, Rita crossed the yard to Jason.

"Jason," Rita said, "this is Officer Logan. Hunter sent her to help us."

Jason smiled. "Hi. I'm Jason."

Logan read his nametag. "Please to meet you, Deputy Perry."

"You can call me Jason," Jason said.

"Yeah," Rita said. "We don't really do the title thing around here."

Jason cocked his head. "Although I do call you Sheriff sometimes."

"True," Rita said. "But I think you're usually sarcastic."

Jason crinkled his nose. "I'm not sure I'd say I'm sarcastic. It's more like … not serious."

"Okay," Rita said, rolling her shoulders, "he doesn't take me seriously. But that doesn't mean we don't take him seriously just because we call him Jason. And we call Mary Lou Mary Lou, and we take her very seriously."

Logan blinked at Rita. "You can call me Vee."

"Vee," Rita repeated. "Great. Call me Rita, okay?" She turned and pointed up the street. "You and Jason talk to the neighbors, please. Find out what they know about Clark, and if they witnessed anything odd in the past few days."

Jason and Vee headed down Lodgepole, each taking a side of the street.

As they walked away, Tilda and Bruce emerged from the house. Bruce looked refreshed enough to head out on the golf green, while Tilda's complexion was the color of one.

Rita walked over to them. "How's it going?"

"Not sure I can slice the ham come Easter," Tilda said. She paused to think for a moment, her eyes cast up and her lips pressed flat. "Yep, I think I might be done with ham. Used to eat lasagna, you know. Loved it, in fact. But can't eat it anymore. Nope, not after that Ferris wheel incident."

"I hope Jason's vomit doesn't turn you off shepherd's pie," Rita said.

"I'm having shepherd's pie for dinner, actually," Bruce said.

Rita pulled a face. "I can't take any more talk of food. Got any info for me?"

"The dismembered head belongs to the body in the

room," Bruce said. "Or should I say, the body belongs to the head."

"Either way, I'll take it," Tilda said. "Otherwise, imagine the paperwork."

"Got a name that belongs to the head?" Rita asked. "And body?"

"Sure do," Tilda said, handing Rita a driver's license. "His name's David Clark."

Chapter Twenty-Three

RITA SHUT down the mobile data terminal when Jason and Vee approached the cruiser.

"What you'd find out about David Clark?" she asked getting out of the car.

Jason pulled out his notebook and flipped through the pages.

Rita eyed his notebook. "You're rather old-fashioned, aren't you, Jason?"

He blinked at her. "I am? I thought I was quite progressive."

Rita shrugged. "What do I know? Maybe handwriting is coming back in style."

Jason read from his notebook. "He was a bachelor who kept to himself."

"A divorcee," Vee said, consulting the notes on her phone. "Although he didn't go out much."

"Meaning he didn't date, or he worked from home?"

Vee nodded. "Both."

"Any recent sightings by neighbors?" Rita asked.

"Not really," Jason said. "Shopped at the Pantry every week but rarely spoke to anyone."

"Folks say they'd see him in the yard from time to time," Vee said. "He mowed regularly. Like clockwork, neighbors said."

Jason flipped back through a few pages, rereading his notes. "Every two weeks, a blue Toyota shows up, stays overnight, and leaves by the morning."

Vee nodded. "Or could be a Hyundai or Honda. Neighbors have differing opinions."

"So we've got a blue car," Rita said. "Any other distinguishing features?"

Vee shook her head, and Jason flipped through his notes again.

"Nope."

"Well, you got more than I did," Rita said. "I ran his ID. No criminal record or any other information. Of course, Google offered up a million David Clarks. But none in Wyoming." Then she gestured over Jason's shoulder. "Body's coming out now."

The medical examiner's department carried out the bagged body on a gurney.

In white Tyvek and rimmed glasses, Dylan Bruce looked like the Invisible Man. He said, "I'll make a date with Mary Lou to go over everything with you, Rita."

"Works for me," Rita said.

Then she glanced at Jason and Vee. "Let's go in and see what Tilda has for us."

They waited till Bruce and the others had loaded David Clark's body in the van, then they walked into the house.

Tilda met them at the door, holding two boxes. One contained nitrile gloves, and the other, facemasks. "Come on, I'll take you for a walkthrough."

After they'd donned masks and gloves, Tilda started in the foyer. "No forced entry." She gestured to the door, security plate and door latch intact. "Clark let his killer in."

Then she turned and headed down the hallway toward the office. "It seems they walked together to the office." She paused, waving the box of nitrile gloves to indicate a mark on the wall. "This could indicate a struggle. But the majority of the violence occurred in the office."

"Do you think the killer intended to take something that was in the office?"

Tilda shook her head. "If they did, they would have known where to find it. Nothing much is disturbed. Not even a throw pillow. It's like a goddamned Sears catalog in here. Only thing out of place is David Clark's head. And a large quantity of his blood." She waved them onwards. "Come see for yourselves."

Rita followed Tilda into the office, thankful to be wearing a mask as the pungent odor of blood soaked the air, as it did the short-pile beige carpet.

"The attack started here," Tilda said, pointing to blood spatter, radiating like tree branches.

Rita swallowed back the acid in her throat. "Did Clark fight back?"

Tilda's hooded head nodded. "Bruce noted some defensive wounds. But the attack was short and brutal."

Jason turned green again, while Vee's face held a stony expression.

"Thanks, Tilda," Rita said. She turned to Jason and Vee. "Please search the living room and kitchen, looking for anything that might explain why someone wanted to kill David Clark. I'll search the office."

Jason and Vee left the room, and Rita walked behind David's desk, where a filing cabinet stood next to the window. It was locked, but she found the key in the top desk drawer.

In the cabinet, the foremost folder contained invoices for accounting services made out to Angel Holdings Ltd. It appeared David was an accountant. And Angel Holdings Ltd. looked to be his only client. She flipped through folders of ledgers, but she didn't understand what she was looking at. She had a hard enough time keeping track of her own bills. She photographed the letterhead.

The next folder contained old pay stubs from Meadowlark Investment Firm. It also contained a letter thanking David for twenty years of service and outlining the terms for leaving the agency.

Rita closed the drawer and opened the next one, labeled household expenses. It contained a series of manila file folders filled with bank statements and bills. She didn't think anyone kept paper like that anymore.

She photographed each of the utilities: electric, telephone, and internet. No cable. She paused. And no cell phone. Odd.

Rita closed and locked the filing cabinet. Above it, a framed certificate hung on the wall. It declared David Clark a CPA who had graduated from Cornell University. She'd noticed a mousepad with the same crest on his desk.

Stepping around Tilda still photographing blood spatter, Rita returned to the desk. The crest on the mousepad was indeed Cornell. But there was no mouse on the pad, least of all a laptop.

She replaced the filing cabinet's key to the top drawer, then opened the second drawer. It contained extra stationery (neatly categorized) and a backscratcher. The bottom drawer held more Cornell-branded paraphernalia: pens, an ancient-looking binder, and a pair of fuzzy dice that would have more use hanging off a rearview mirror, if that were even a use.

Clearly, David Clark still felt some connection with his alum. But what of the other connections in his life? Scanning the office, Rita saw no obvious indications of family or friends.

She moved to a bookshelf, running her fingers over the titles. Most were accounting books. There were also a handful of best-selling novels, a field guide for Wyoming birdlife, and a half-dozen new crossword puzzle books, their spines not yet cracked.

On the top shelf, Rita found a couple of greeting cards, both addressed to "Dad, with love from Karen." One was for Father's Day. The other for his birthday.

Rita asked Tilda for one of her Zip-loc bags. "For evidence, please."

Tilda passed her a bag and Rita dropped in the cards. Then she left the office and found Jason and Vee in the kitchen, sifting through papers on the kitchen table.

"How's it going?" she asked.

"Nothing suspicious yet," Jason said. "The living room is a study in beige, with nothing to do in there aside from look out the window or choose one of the many crossword puzzle books on the coffee table."

"I'm noticing a theme," Rita said.

"The kitchen hasn't offered up anything suspicious, either. Healthy food in the fridge. Only liquor we found is an ancient bottle of Canadian rye, probably a past Christmas gift."

"Or long-time service gift for an employee," Rita said. "How about pharmaceuticals?"

Jason shook his head. "Nothing here stronger than antacids."

"Found this," Vee said, gesturing the stack of envelopes on the table. "Some unopened mail."

"Any bills from a mobile telecommunications company?" Rita asked.

Vee shook her head. "Mostly flyers. A subscription crossword magazine. But the top one is personal."

Rita picked up a pale blue envelope. The back bore a Hallmark logo and a return address for K. Clark in Carlsbad, California.

"It's another card from Karen," Rita said. "I wonder what's the occasion."

"Karen?" Jason asked.

"His kid," Rita said. She showed them the Zip-loc. "Got a couple cards here signed 'Karen.'" She passed the card back to Vee. "Please enter this into evidence, then call Mary Lou at the station. Ask her to request Carlsbad PD to search for Karen *née* Clark, for a next of kin notification."

"Yes, Sheriff," Vee said, stepping aside to call Mary Lou.

"Any chance either of you found a laptop or computer in the house?" Rita asked Jason.

He shook his head.

"And what about a cell phone?"

"Nope. Stolen?"

"The laptop, maybe," Rita said, "because surely a CPA would have one. But I'm not sure he even had a cell phone. Landline, yes. But I didn't see any bills for a mobile carrier, and David's finances were highly organized. I took photos of his records. On Monday you can have the pleasure of looking into his accounts."

"Looking forward to it already," Jason said.

Rita motioned for him to join her in the hallway. "Let's

keep going. I'll take the master suite. You take the guest room."

Jason nodded and entered the room opposite the David's bedroom. Rita entered the master suite.

A queen-sized bed was neatly made in denim-blue bedclothes. She opened the drawer of a bedside table. It contained a box of tissues, a coaster, some sharpened pencils and a rubber eraser, and a stack of crossword books. She flipped through the stack. Only the first one had been used, half the puzzles completed in consecutive order. She returned the book and closed the drawer.

She walked around the bed to check the other side-table. Also sparsely filled, the items inside rattled as the drawer opened. No lube, sex toys, porn, or handguns. She let out a sigh. Only an almost-empty tube of moisturizer, an unopened box of tissue, a dull pencil, and a half-filled crossword book.

Rita thumbed through the pages. The puzzles (all incomplete) were attempted out of order, and the penciled block letters didn't appear to be made by the same hand as those in the other book. Rita made a mental note and moved onto David's dresser drawers.

Again, no firearms. She found only his neatly folded clothes, mostly blue and khaki.

In the closet, the garments were organized not only by color, but season as well. She closed the closet door and took a final look around the room. On the wall hung a nondescript mountain landscape. Blue curtains flanked a small window, through which Rita was able to see into the back yard. Here, more tidy shrubs grew, and potted plants lined a terraced brick patio.

She stepped away from the window and crouched to check under the bed. Nothing. Not a single sock or even a dust bunny. Rita exited the bedroom and met Jason in the hallway.

"Find anything in the guest room?" she asked.

"A comfy looking queen-sized bed. A bedside table with nothing in it but a box of tissues, a brand-new crossword puzzle book, and a pencil. Winter coats hanging in the closet. Nice view onto the backyard. And enough room to swing a cat. I reckon Otto's entire camper could fit inside the room."

"What does that mean, to swing a cat?" Rita asked.

"I dunno," Jason said. He raised his lean arms above his head. "But sure is nice to be able to put my hands above my head and not bang my knuckles on the roof."

"Speaking of wheels," Rita said, "let's go search the garage."

Vee joined them, and they went through the adjoining laundry room into the garage. There, they found a ten-year-old charcoal Chrysler with very low mileage. They also found a shiny riding mower, called the LAWN-EX 300.

Rita patted the red machine. "This is a big beast for such a small patch of lawn."

"Maybe he was a gardening enthusiast," Jason said.

"The yard's tidy," Vee agreed.

"It might be tidy," Rita said, looking through the cabinetry, "but there aren't any gardening tools in here. And I didn't see a shed out back."

"Maybe he hires a landscaping company," Jason said.

"When he mows his own lawn?" Rita tapped her lip. "Maybe. Although I didn't see any invoices, and David seems to have kept every piece of financial paperwork."

The sparsely packed cabinets didn't reveal any other household tools, either. They found a few strands of

Christmas lights, an emergency kit, and some four-gallon jugs of distilled water. On a shelving unit where someone else might keep off-season camping equipment, they found several cardboard boxes labeled by year.

"More accounting ledgers?" Rita asked.

Vee flipped open the lid of the most recently labeled box. "Nope" she said, setting the box on the floor.

Rita squatted beside it. Crossword puzzle books, completed and dated, filled the box to the top.

"There must be eighty in here," she said, sifting through them. Yellow Post-Its stuck on random pages on about a third of the books. "Maybe a hundred."

"In this box, too," Jason said, opening another banker's box. "They all contain books."

"He completed a book every two weeks," Rita said, reading the dates marked with Sharpie marker on the covers.

Vee's eyes bugged. "Every two weeks? That's like…"

"Seven puzzles a day," Rita said, holding up a book with a splashy cover. "If there's ninety-nine in a book for $5.99."

Vee let out a low whistle. "I hear crosswords are good for the brain." She tapped her forehead. "Thinking exercises."

"My head's spinnin', just thinkin' 'bout what David Clark could do with his," Jason said. Then he flushed. "It's a shame about, you know — what happened to his head."

Vee cleared her throat.

Rita rubbed hers. "Mine's spinning, too, Jason. Maybe I can get rid of this headache with a crossword puzzle. 'Cause nothing else seems to shake it."

"Head spins are just what happens in a murder investigation, Sheriff," Jason said. "It's happened to me before."

Rita sighed. "Shit. You're right."

They returned the box to the shelf and left the garage. Outside, it had grown dark. Rita dusted her hands as if she could brush away the murder scene.

"That was a big day, team." She glanced at Vee. "You at Still Haven tonight?"

For a moment, Vee looked startled. Then her forehead puckered. "I beg your pardon?"

"Are you booked at the Still Haven Inn?"

Vee gave a nervous laugh. "I thought you were talking about a moonshine distillery." She cleared her throat. "I'm not staying overnight."

Rita raised her eyebrow. "You're driving back to Casper tonight? That's not gonna work."

Vee swallowed. "The department won't pay for my accommodations. And I don't have the money to get a room here."

"We'll figure out something," Rita said. "And don't worry, it doesn't have to be the Still Haven Inn."

"I've honestly never heard of it," Vee said.

"I'm not surprised," Rita said.

"Depends who you talk to," Jason said. "According to some folks, there's a lot goin' on there."

Rita looked at Jason. "You don't say?"

Jason blushed. "Sometimes there're stories about it in the paper."

"I see," Vee said. "Prostitutes?"

Jason shook his head. "No. You gotta go to the laundromat for that."

"Let's just say you couldn't pay me to stay there," Rita said. "Bring an overnight bag when you come on Monday, and I'll sort you out a place."

Vee nodded. "Thanks, Sheriff."

Rita smiled, but when Vee turned to go Rita let out a sigh.

Exhale.

God, she was beginning to feel like she was collecting lost souls.

Chapter Twenty-Four

WHEN RITA GOT BACK to the SCSO, Walter sat stationed at his desk, scrolling through his email. He looked up when they entered.

Jason sat at his own desk and Rita approached Walter's.

"Walter," she said, "what's up? It's late."

"I've been waitin' all day."

Mary Lou rolled her eyes. "It's true."

"You're in uniform?"

"Heard you replaced me with another cop."

"Of course you're not replaced," Rita said. "But you're still on leave."

Walter swiveled in Otto's chair, turning his back to his monitor. He looked Rita in the eye. "I want to help."

Rita nodded. "I know, but where you're really needed, Walter, is back in Beaumont with your family."

Walter lowered his brows. "Winnie's not my family."

Rita cocked her head. "True. You're not much of a bliss bunny, are you? More like a bison." She slapped him on the back. "But your kid needs you."

Reluctant, Walter nodded. "I know."

Rita patted his shoulder again, this time more gently. "Your job will be here for you when you return. But take all the time you need to take care of Adrian. And take all the time you need to take care of yourself."

Walter pushed up from his chair. "All right, Jonas. But the minute you need me, you call me, y'hear?"

Rita gave him a smile. "You bet."

As Walter made his way out, Rita grabbed a bottle of water from the staff room, then headed into her office.

Seated at her desk, she googled Angel Holdings Limited. But she found nothing relevant. She called Mary Lou's extension.

"Sheriff," Mary Lou said. "I was happy to hear Hunter sent someone in from Casper."

"She's as green as they come, but I'll take her," Rita said.

"First homicide?"

"Dunno," Rita said. "But I'd place bets it's her first beheading." She swallowed some bite in the back of her throat. "I know it's mine. And there was some rotten shit that went down in the Big Apple."

"Officer Logan needs somewhere to stay. Would you be able to put her up at your place for the week, starting Monday?"

"Well, only fools rush in where wise men fear to tread," Mary Lou said. "But anything to help the case."

"Thanks, Mary Lou."

"As Elvis said, 'My future starts when I wake up every morning.' And I happen to agree. Everyone deserves to start their day well rested."

"If she can *get* any sleep. I didn't pause to consider the copious posters in your apartment of shirtless men. When I stop by, I can barely focus on the conversation topic."

"I think Ted has the same problem. When I'm trying to feed him dinner and instead he's staring at Ryan Gosling."

"I don't like Ryan Gosling," Rita said.

"Maybe that's Ted's problem, too," Mary Lou said. "Sometimes I catch him hissing at that poor man."

"Sounds like Ted might appreciate having a visitor around the place," Rita said. She rubbed her face with her palms. "Especially with all these long hours we've been pulling. He must miss you."

Mary Lou blew out a breath. "He just don't purr as much when he ain't comin' into the station day to day."

Rita laughed. "Then it's a win-win for everyone. So you got any updates? I don't want you to have to stay here any later than you already have. Jason's probably falling asleep on his keyboard, so I'd better get him home."

"Only news you need to hear tonight is I followed up about Helen. Lydia, she says she ain't been back to her old residence since it sold. None of her friends heard from her, neither. I called George's parents, as well, but no word from Helen."

"Thanks for trying. I haven't got any leads on David Clark's killer, either," Rita said.

"Have you got a cell phone number for me to bring up the records?"

"Nope. Couldn't find one, and couldn't find any documentation to suggest he even had one."

"Well," Mary Lou said, "at least you can enjoy the weekend without having to think on the results of that."

"You're right," Rita said. "You always see the silver lining, Mary Lou."

"Silver's my *thing*," Mary Lou said. "I like silver earrings, silver bullets, and silver foxes. Not to mention my own beehive. Now get on outta here to the bullpen instead o' makin' me talk on this infernal phone, as if I don't do it enough all the day long. I mean, Jesus! Why the hell you just don't walk out here on your legs to talk to me is beyond me. If you don't walk around in life, you ain't gonna find nothing. How do you think I got to Graceland? If I didn't do that, I never would have met Elvis."

"Ten-four," Rita said. She gathered her laptop and water bottle and headed out to the bullpen.

Jason pulled up in his swivel chair.

"Good work, everyone," Rita said. "And thanks for staying late. Next week we'll have Vee around for more hours."

"You're welcome, Sheriff," Mary Lou said, smacking her lips still as glossy and pink as the morning.

"I'm coming in tomorrow," Rita said. "But neither of you need to feel obligated to do the same."

Mary Lou met Rita's eye. "I was thinking I'd go see Otto."

Rita's mouth went dry. "That's a good idea, Mary Lou."

"I'll be here with you, Sheriff," Jason said.

Rita swallowed her emotions. "Thanks. Let's head home now, everyone. I want to call the hospital."

As Jason drove them back to Otto's place, a text came in on Rita's phone. It was Cash.

There's a strange woman living in your apartment

A friend, Rita texted.

Didn't know you had any of those

Ha ha.

She put her phone on silent and stared out of the passenger window. But all she could see was a pale reflection of her own face, as ghostlike as Otto. Then a dark shape moved in the corner of her eye.

Her gaze shifted to the side-view mirror. A black minivan appeared to be following them. Was it the same as she'd seen the other night? Or was her imagination running wild?

"Can you bring down our speed for a moment, Jason?" Rita said.

Easing off on the gas, he glanced at her, then in the rearview mirror.

The minivan pulled out and passed, then signaled and took the exit ramp, breaking away from the artery of traffic.

"Never mind," she said. "I thought I recognized that vehicle. But I was mistaken."

They pulled into Otto's driveway. As Jason turned off the ignition, Rita's phone pinged. She swiped open her texts.

"It's Walter," she said. "They're going to Winona's mother's in Cheyenne."

Then she moved her thumbs across the screen, returning a text to Walter.

Please text when you arrive

Walter gave it a thumbs up.

Rita put away her phone, and they popped the door to get out.

"G'night, Sheriff," Jason said.

"Aye, aye, Deputy," Rita said. Then she stumbled up the steps to Otto's house and went inside.

She locked the door behind her and kicked off her shoes in the foyer. Then she trudged upstairs, stripping off her uniform as she went.

She ran the shower to a scalding heat before stepping beneath it. And the pounding drops on her skull drummed away her headache at last.

With her head feeling clear, she stepped out of the shower, toweled off, and pulled on her bathrobe. She was using her palm to clear the condensation on the mirror when the doorbell rang. She froze. What would she say to one of Otto's friends, if they asked after his condition?

"It's probably Jason," her reflection said. "Bringing by dinner."

Rita wrapped a towel around her damp hair and shuffled downstairs. She should probably tell him he needn't bother feeding her, because she'd a strange turn of appetite. Maybe it was the autopsies. Or discovering a decapitated body for the first time. Whatever the reason, she wasn't sure when she'd feel enthused about food again.

She padded through the foyer and answered the door.

But it wasn't Jason.

It was Cash.

Chapter Twenty-Five

CASH STOOD ON THE STOOP, his eyes soft with concern.

"Are you gonna let me in?"

Rita hesitated, then pulled the door wider. "I'm tired. Been a long day."

He cracked a smile. "More trouble with Stu and Vic?"

Rita gave a half-shrug and pulled the towel from her head. "Not quite." She shook out her damp hair. "But it's true they were a big part of my day."

Cash closed the front door, then kicked off his shoes. "We need to talk, Rita."

She sighed. "We do?" She hung the towel over the stair banister and headed to the kitchen. "About what?"

Cash followed her. "I'm having flashbacks."

Rita glanced over his shoulder at him. "What, acid?"

Cash laughed. "Jesus, no. I'm talking about you."

"Me?"

"Yeah. You're all prickly and withdrawn. What am I doing that's grindin' your gears?"

"Grinding my *gears*? Are we talking about us? Or your business?"

His jaw tensed. "I'm talking about the fact that everything that's going on reminds me of our wedding."

"You mean the wedding we never had?" Rita opened the door of Otto's fridge and stared at the shelves. But nothing appealed to her.

"Exactly," Cash said. "I'm feeling like you're going to take a runner on me again."

Rita gave a bitter laugh. "Where the hell would I run to now?" She took two cans of beer from the fridge door. "Although New York City doesn't seem so unappealing at the moment. But that has nothing to do with you and everything to do with this homicide investigation. Do you know I once investigated stolen hotdogs at the corner of West 49th and 5th Ave? Street vendor couldn't figure out who the hell was stealing them."

Cash gawked at her. "What the hell are you talking about?"

"A seagull. Can you believe it? A goddamned stealthy seagull was snatching them right out from under his nose, whenever he was counting out change."

Cash scratched at his stubble. "And your point?"

"My point is, I could be tracking down stolen hotdogs at the Rockefeller Centre right now, instead of dealing with headless cadavers in Still."

Cash's eyes widened. "Headless?"

Rita smacked her palm against her forehead. "Shit. I'm not supposed to tell you things like that."

"I'm not gonna say anything. You know that."

She sighed. "I know."

"So can we talk now?" Cash sounded both sincere and scared.

"Okay, we'll talk." Rita passed him a beer. "But not without a drink."

They sat at the table and cracked their cans.

"Let me start by apologizing for the other night," Cash said. "For my temper, on the phone. But I'm telling you, my dad has nothing to do with this."

Rita took a sip of her beer. It tasted tinny and thin. "How can you be sure? Considering he's…"

"An inmate?" Cash's voice had an edge.

Rita avoided his eyes. "I had to check it out. You know I have to follow every lead. And he's the only one I know in town who's involved in drugs." Her gaze flickered over Cash. "Besides you."

"Hey, that's not fair. I did him only one favor."

Rita frowned at him. "So you admit you took the drugs out to Apex for your dad. Why'd you do it?"

For a moment, Cash didn't answer. "I needed the money."

Rita laughed in spite of herself. "Cash needed cash."

He glared at her. "Heather needed the money."

Rita's eyebrows arched. "Heather Bannister?"

Cash frowned. "She's the only ex-wife I got."

"So Tom anted the money for Heather?"

"I asked his lawyer, Crawford, for the loan."

"Did it come with a red bow?"

"Rita…"

"You gonna tell me why she needed it?"

Folding his arms, Cash leaned back in his chair. "At this moment, I can't really figure out why the hell I *should* tell you. But since you're the goddamned Sheriff in town, I will. Not that you'd think I need to. I think it's pretty damn obvious. She wanted to leave Max, the city-slickin' fancy-pants councilor. But with the kids, where was she gonna go? I knew the Myers place was available and she and the kids could move in right away, fully furnished. So I helped her put together a down payment."

"I see," Rita said, nodding. She took a sip of beer, but

it didn't taste any better than the last mouthful. "Did you help her get her the job at Chattum Realty, too?"

"It's only part-time," he said, "when the kids are in school. But at least it's something."

For a moment Rita was silent. "You're a good friend to her, Cash."

Cash looked down at his hands, studying his beer can. "I didn't come here to talk about that. You gotta respect Heather wanting her privacy right now."

"Here's something you can tell me," Rita said. "How'd you find out so fast I'd been to see Tom in the first place? He said you haven't even talked to him in years."

Cash narrowed his eyes. "There's some truth to that. His lawyer called me — Crawford — and told me you'd been by."

"So then how do you know your dad has nothing to do with Arnold's death?"

Cash's gaze hardened. "Because he's never dealt meth. Tom doesn't touch that shit. And you know that. Jesus, Rita, why won't you drop it? And why are you so damn mad at *me* about it?"

Rita's gut knotted up. She was being way too hard on Cash. "I know I'm not being logical. But when my mind chews over this matter, it keeps coming back to Tom."

"Sounds like goddamned speculation to me."

Rita let out a breath.

Exhale.

"I know," she said. "I'm sorry. I feel all shaken up about Otto. I barely know which way is up or down." She shivered. Her hair and bathrobe were damp, and the cold beer didn't help. "I'm tired. I'd like to go to bed."

Cash exhaled, too. "I'd like to think that was a direct invitation for me to join you. But I suspect not."

Rita couldn't help but laugh.

Cash drained the last of his beer. "Max Bannister's a piece of shit. He treats Heather like a piece of shit. And those kids shouldn't be around all that." He met her gaze, his blue eyes burning. "I'd beat the shit out of that shithead, too, if I thought it would help. But unfortunately, I'd only get tarred with the same brush as Thomas Gabriel." He set his jaw. "I already live my life under that man's shadow."

Rita's chest tightened. She touched his hand. "Tell me."

"Jesus Christ, I can't take one goddamned misstep, can I? Every decision in my business, every exchange with the neighbors, every interaction with you — well, I gotta look clean and smell clean and be fucking clean all the time, don't I?"

Rita closed her fingers around his. "I'm sorry. I'll go easier on you."

He laughed. "Well, that's a fucking relief."

She blushed. "I'm sorry. I'm trying to do my job while also figuring out—" She waved her hand in the air between them. "All this."

He ran his hands through his hair, but he was smiling. "It's not easy being in love with the town — well, shit, you know how it is. Folks around here watch and talk a whole lot."

Rita nodded. "I noticed."

She also noticed Cash had used the L-word.

"But look at us." He grinned. "You left my life years ago, and yet here you are again, back in Still."

Rita forced a smiled. "Here I am. Still in Still."

And so was Heather Bannister.

Inhale.

"Everyone deserves a second chance," Cash said.

Rita nodded. "Yes. Heather's lucky to have you. And so are those kids."

Still holding hands, Cash squeezed hers. "I was talking about us."

Rita swallowed. "Some things change. And some things don't. It feels strange." Avoiding his gaze, she glanced around the kitchen. "Like sitting here. Together. In Otto's kitchen that looks the same as twenty years ago."

"I saw him today," Cash said.

She met his eye. "And?"

"No change. But I'm sure you already know that."

Nodding, Rita licked her lips. "Dr. Albright told me there isn't likely to be any improvement."

Cash put her hands to his mouth and kissed her fingers. "I'm sorry, Rita."

She opened her mouth to thank him. But instead a sob escaped, taking her by surprise.

Cash got up from his chair and came around to her side. He crouched to put his arm around her shoulders.

Another sob tore free of her throat. "It's my fault."

Cash's arm stiffened around her, pulling her close. "Definitely not, Rita. A lifetime of smoking was Otto's choice."

"I don't mean the cancer." Rita swiped at her tears. "I mean the stroke. He was … I was … upset. I made him upset. And then he had a fight with Helen. He kicked her out. And that night—"

"You can't think like this, Rita."

"That's what Helen thinks."

Cash made consoling sounds as he stood and pulled her out of the chair.

"Come on, I'll take you upstairs. You'll feel better with some sleep."

She cried as they trudged up the treads, his strong arms supporting her.

In the guest bedroom, he turned down the sheets while she slipped off her robe. He took it from her and hung it on the back of the door while she crawled under the covers. Her head settled into the pillow, and a wave of exhaustion rolled over her.

Cash returned to the bed and lay next to her, holding her tight though the sheets. She gripped his forearm. His shirt smelled like motor oil, and his skin like sunshine and sweat, a fragrance both familiar and comforting.

And before long, she was asleep.

Chapter Twenty-Six

WHEN RITA AWOKE in the morning, Cash was gone.

But he'd propped on her bedside table, a note written in blue ballpoint ink: *I'll check in later.* A lopsided blue heart encircled the words.

Rita got up and stumbled into the main bath. She washed her face and brushed her teeth, then returned to the guest room to dress in jeans and a t-shirt. Then she went downstairs to make breakfast.

As eggs sizzled in the pan, she leaned against the counter and picked up Otto's cell phone. He had a heap of unread text messages.

She swiped open the phone, but it was password-protected. She tapped her lip, thinking. He can't possibly still have the same password as before.

One, two, three, four, five, six.

Yep. Rita scrolled through the messages, all of them from Helen.

I am so sorry Otto
Please get back to me
Why won't you return my calls?

Rita tried calling Helen from his phone.

No answer.

She sent a text telling Helen that Otto was still in the hospital. Then she sent another one.

I'd like to talk with you Helen

Please get in touch

It's important

And urgent

She set down the phone, realizing she was sending nearly as many texts to Helen as Helen had sent to Otto.

Rita ate her eggs out of the frying pan, standing in front of the stove. They landed heavy in her stomach.

She spilled some water around her mouth and popped in some chewing gum. Then headed out to the driveway, locking the house behind her.

A silver Nissan she didn't recognize sat parked in front of the camper. The door popped open, and Blaze Wright emerged.

When he saw Rita, he froze. His curly hair looked particularly mussed.

She gave him a wave. "Good morning."

Blaze nodded, then scurried to the driver's side of his Maxima. Spitting up gravel, he drove away.

Rita walked across the driveway and knocked on the door of the camper. Half a second later, Jason's head popped out.

"Hi, Rita."

"Good morning. Ready to go?"

Jason stepped out of the camper, closing the door behind him. He was dressed in a T-shirt and pair of athletic shorts. "Sure," he said, headed for his Kia. "I'll drive."

"Thanks, Jason," Rita said, "but I'm bearing up okay

today. A good night's sleep seems to have cured my headache."

"That's good," Jason said, following Rita to her Honda. "I had a good sleep, too. But I thought you might have had a rough night."

Rita glanced at him. "Why's that?"

"When I took out the trash, I saw Cash's truck here. And heard raised voices. Then in the middle of the night, I heard Cash drive away."

Rita gave a half-shrug. "We're fine. Just old shit." She unlocked the Honda. "Did Blaze stay over last night?"

Jason flushed, nodded, and ducked into the passenger seat.

Rita slid behind the wheel and buckled her belt. "Did he ask about the murder?"

Jason nodded. "Of course. But I didn't tell him nothing."

Rita studied him for a moment. "Good." Then, trying for levity, he asked, "Did you feed him oyster mushrooms, too?"

Jason flushed even deeper. "Blaze eats a lot of Chicken Bun on the Run, so I gave him an elevated experience — Portobello mushroom burgers."

Rita's eyebrows shot up. "Damn, where the hell did you get those?"

"The Gourmand's Garden in Beaumont," Jason said. "Simmer the caps in wine for an hour, and they'll make anyone weak in the knees."

Smiling, Rita turned the ignition. "I got to take more dating tips from you, Jason."

"Sure," he said. "I know some guys you should meet."

Rita pulled out of the driveway. "I already met your cousin Rod. Twice. It's not going to work, Jason. I like teeth. And conversing with words."

Jason cocked his head. "He does grunt a lot."

"A lot? He should be put in the pig pen."

"To be fair," Jason said, "he was Edith May's pick."

"Hang on a minute," Rita said. "My deputy's little sister is matchmaking me? No wonder this endeavor is doomed."

"*'This endeavor is doomed?'*" Jason laughed. "Don't you think you're being dramatic? You sound like Trixie Belden."

Rita grinned. "You read her, too?"

"Of course," Jason said, "but The Hardy Boys were where it was at."

Rita grinned wider. "Me, too. I had such a soft spot for those brothers."

Jason looked thoughtful. "I wouldn't call what I felt for them was in any way soft."

When they arrived at the SCSO, they unlocked the building and turned on the lights. Their footsteps echoed across the linoleum.

"Though I'm happy she's with Otto today," Rita said, "it's not the same in here without Mary Lou."

"Nor without Ted," Jason said. "I think I miss him more than Walter."

Rita laughed and took a seat at Walter's desk. Pulling out a pad of paper and pen, she jotted a list of things for Jason to do on Monday morning, which included checking David's telephone and banking records, as well as finding out if Cornell alumni had any up-to-date information about him.

While Jason logged into his email, Rita checked David Clark's vehicle registration. He'd had the same Chrysler for the past ten years, with no insurance claims or traffic fines.

"He certainly lived his life in the slow lane," Rita said to herself.

Then she checked social media for chatter about David Clark's death. Nothing.

"There's an email here from David Clark's insurance provider," Jason said. "Jeff's party van for the Rawhide Revue was never registered after it was sold."

Rita tapped her lip. "So there's a good possibility it became the phony Apex van, huh?"

The telephone rang at Mary Lou's desk. Jason answered it.

"Still County Sheriff's Office," he said. After a moment he asked, "Can you hold, please?" He flicked the switch, then replaced the receiver to the cradle. "It's Karen Clark."

"I'll take it my office," Rita said, getting up. She walked across the bullpen into her office, closing the door behind her.

She sat at her desk and picked up the landline. "Hello, Sheriff Jonas speaking."

"Hello, Sheriff Jonas. I'm Karen Clark, David Clark's daughter."

"Thanks for returning my call," Rita said. "I am so sorry for your loss."

"Thank you." Karen's voice trembled. "I just have no idea who would want to kill my father. He was an accountant," she said, as if the occupation exonerated him from potential enemies.

"Were you informed how he died?" Rita asked.

"No," Karen said.

Rita let a moment of silence pass, then asked, "Do you care to know?"

A moment of silence passed as if Karen was nodding. Then she said, "Yes."

Rita took a breath. "I'm sorry to tell you, he was beheaded."

Karen gasped. Then sobbed. For a few minutes, she cried and Rita remained silent. Then Karen drew in a ragged breath. "Who could commit such violence? He was a very peaceful man, Sheriff."

"Please tell me about him," Rita said.

"He was an accountant in Casper for many years. Then he retired and moved out of town where it was quiet."

"When did he move to Still?"

Karen took moment before answering. "A few years ago. Four, I think. I'm sorry, I don't quite remember. I've only visited him once at his new home, and that was two years ago."

"Has he always lived on his own?" Rita asked.

"I think so," Karen said. "At least I don't think he has a girlfriend. He never talks about women. Never been the type to comment on their appearance or mannerisms. He's a gentleman that way. If he's dated since the divorce, I've never heard about it."

"When did he divorce?"

"Mom left him years ago, when I was only three."

"Why did your mother leave him?"

"Over the weather," Karen said with a laugh. "Can you believe it? But Mom hated the cold Wyoming winters and moved me out to California. The divorce didn't really have anything to do with Dad at all." She paused. "Unfortunately."

"And you've lived there ever since?"

She gave a little laugh. "Once you experience the sea breeze out here, Sheriff, it's hard to go back to freezing temperatures."

"Fair enough," Rita said. "Though nothing compares to mountain air."

Karen's laugh was a little bolder this time. "You're not

wrong about that. Sometimes I think Mom was just depressed being stuck at home with a little kid, and if she'd stuck it out a little longer, she wouldn't have had to run away to find her happiness again."

Karen fell silent, and Rita gave her a moment. Often, following an initial grieving period, a bereaved person will talk in detail about their deceased loved one's life. She imagined it was because they wanted to reaffirm every memory of that life, for now memory was all that remained of it.

Her thoughts turned to Otto and sudden, hot tears burned inside her nasal passage. Rita inhaled to hold them back.

"Did he visit you often?" she asked, steadying her own voice the way Karen was steadying hers.

"In Carlsbad?" Karen asked. "No, he hated to fly. Or sail. Or do any sort of travel, really. Only if he absolutely had to."

"So he didn't take a lot of tropical vacations?"

"Hardly left his house, far as I know," Karen said. "Not that he was phobic. He was just very frugal."

"Although he made a good salary as a CPA, did he not?"

"Yes, it's the reason he was able to retire early, after twenty years. He wasn't supporting any kids, and he had zero interest in travel. Wasn't interested in seasons tickets of any kind, or collecting or remodeling anything."

"So what did he spend his wages on, if not his passions?" Rita asked. "Did he gamble?"

Karen gave a sudden laugh. "Throw away money? Definitely not! I'm fairly certain he was saving it all, Sheriff."

"Who inherits his estate? Is that you?"

"Yes," Karen said.

"You knew the contents of his will?" Rita asked.

"Yes," Karen said again. "I have a copy of his will, actually. He was very organized."

"Do you have an idea of how much his estate is worth?"

"No. And I don't think I'd even accurately estimate. He hasn't worked for a few years, though he's also likely not spent much. And the numbers out here in Southern California real estate are so much bigger than Wyoming. He's got a modest little house compared to the two air-conditioned beasts that me, Murray, and Maverick occupy."

"Who are Murray and Maverick?" Rita asked.

"Maverick is a labradoodle," Karen said, "and Murray is my husband. Although usually I refer to him as my handyman."

"How long have you been married?"

"Two years, even though I'm still getting used to the idea. But I'd better — we're expecting a baby in four months."

"Congratulations," Rita said with genuine warmth.

"Thank you. Only—"

"Yes?"

A sob cracked Karen's voice. "Dad might not know. I sent him a card with the news. And there's a puzzle inside, and when he solves it, he'll know the due date. But if he hasn't received it by now, he'll ... he'll have never known he was going to be a granddad."

"I'm sorry," Rita said. "You will always think of him at the special moments in life. Did your father walk you down the aisle when you were married?"

Karen gave a light laugh, clearing her tears. "I'm too modern for that, Sheriff. Although there's a part of me, now, that wishes he had."

"Is that the same reason you haven't taken your husband's name?" Rita asked. "Your modernity?"

"Sure," Karen said, still sounding sad. "Mostly convenience, though. I'd established myself professionally before I met Murray. And it didn't make sense to change my name to his."

"So no particular allegiance to your father's family name?"

"Not really," Karen said. "In fact, when I was a teenager, I considered changing my surname to my mother's. Not because I'd had a falling out with Dad or anything. But with just me and Mom living together out west, I thought it would simplify things."

"But you didn't," Rita said. "Why not?"

"Mostly because I knew I'd never live down being called Karen McLaren."

Rita laughed. "So he didn't walk you down the aisle. Did he attend the wedding?"

"Sure did. We got married at City Hall, which was just his style and mine. A small crowd, and he could wear his chinos and denim shirt. Afterwards, he bought everyone Chinese food."

"That was kind of him," Rita said.

"Generous, too," Karen said. "With my stepdad and step-siblings' families, there were twelve of us altogether."

"Did he often do things like that?" Rita asked. "Treat others to dinner?"

"No," Karen said. "Though he used to like to eat out at this one diner in Casper. He said he used to tip them well, on account of their lasagna being the best outside of Italy. Not that he'd ever been to Italy or had any intention of crossing the Atlantic. I'd fly around for work and invite Dad all the time, but he always declined. Wouldn't even come to England, where they spoke the language of crossword puzzles."

Rita laughed. "What do you and Murray do for work?"

"Murray's in set dec."

"Which is?"

"Building and decorating film and TV sets. He mostly does the building part of that equation."

"And you?"

"Special effects."

"Like spaceships and explosions?"

"Not quite. More like the aliens on those spaceships, and what actors would look like after an explosion. I'm a makeup artist."

"So you can handle grisly sights?" Rita asked.

Karen's laugh tinkled again. "Not in real life. I can't even watch my own films. Once I've designed the makeup for a character, I never look at it again. As soon as an actor brings it to life, it's just too creepy for me. And Murray never pays close enough attention to the actors on screen to tell me if my work is any good, so I always rely on Dad's review."

"Your father viewed your work?"

"As much as he could."

"Although he didn't have a television set in his house."

"That's right," Karen said. "Television rotted your brains, whereas crossword puzzles strengthened them. He'd drive into Casper for the premiers at the Capitol Eight. After the show, he'd write me a letter, tell me his favorite parts. Sometimes he'd watch the movie twice, back-to-back." She laughed. "I always wondered if he paid for the second showing. But I never asked him. And now I can't." Karen fell silent. When she spoke again, her voice sounded brittle. "He's never going to write me a letter again." She sniffled. "I'm going to miss the way Dad did his best to provide critical feedback. Which was basically praise." She laughed but sounded sad. "It was his way of being involved in my life. And showing his pride."

Rita gave her a moment before asking her next question. "Did you ever talk on the phone about your movies?"

"No. He preferred writing letters to talking."

"I see. And do you know if he had a cell phone?"

"I'm sure that he didn't," Karen said. "At least, I've never had a number for one."

"Please tell me about his crossword puzzle books," Rita said. "We found bankers boxes full of crossword puzzle books in his garage."

"That doesn't surprise me," Karen said. "He dates a puzzle or a book when he completes it. And tabs any pages on which he's learned a new word. Not that I know if he goes back and rereads any of those books."

"Your father sounds very organized."

"He was that, all right," Karen said. "Organized. Simple. Tidy. Definitely not messy, like me at my job."

"Do you do crossword puzzles, Karen?" Rita asked.

Karen laughed again, then sighed. "No. But I probably should, given the number of times Dad left a post-script, giving me a hot tip to some obscure clue. I'd probably crush them."

"You have a healthy appreciation of your father's hobbies," Rita said, wondering if she understood Otto to the same extent Karen understood David.

"That's because all his puzzling over the years helped me realize that he didn't *not* love me as much as Mom, by not moving out west to be with us. Instead, I saw that he truly preferred keeping to himself. And I think Mom always sensed that he wanted to spend more time alone. To think. To do puzzles. Do math." She chuckled. "He sure loved bookkeeping."

"Can you tell me where he worked?" Rita asked. "You mentioned he's retired."

"Meadowlark something," Karen said. "Meadowlark Accounting? Something like that. Sorry I can't be more specific. They gave him a real nice watch, and he's never looked back."

"Did he moonlight or do pro bono work?"

"Not that I know of," Karen said. "But I suppose it's possible."

"Did he visit you in California?"

"He came out to LA for the wedding, like I said. But he hasn't visited us in Carlsbad yet. I mean — we only got our place here last year, when we started trying for a baby, and wanted a slower pace of life. When we're working, we stay in our apartment in LA."

"I see," Rita said. "Thank you for your time, Karen. I know this wasn't an easy conversation. Is there anything else about your father you can think of that would be helpful for our investigation?"

The telephone line went silent while Karen considered her answer. "No," she said at last.

"Have a good afternoon, then," Rita said. "If you think of anything, please be in touch. And when we find out more, we'll be in touch."

Karen said thank you, although the words were lost to her tears as Rita hung up the phone.

Chapter Twenty-Seven

ON THE DRIVE back to Otto's, Rita told Jason about her conversation with Karen Clark.

"Is she a suspect?" Jason asked.

"Hard to imagine," Rita said, tapping her fingers on the steering wheel. "Karen registered genuine shock when she heard about her father's beheading. And horror. I can't imagine her flying out to do the job, or making the arrangements in any way."

"She David's sole heir?" Jason asked.

"Yup." Rita sucked her lip. "And sounds like David has a lot of savings. But both she and her husband work in the film industry, and own places in Carlsbad and LA. Hard to imagine her killing him for his cash."

"Maybe her husband?"

"About as likely as Moses," Rita said.

Her gaze darted to the side-view mirror, checking for black minivans behind them. Thankfully, nothing appeared suspicious.

"The autopsy's on Monday morning," she said, "so I'm

heading into Casper tonight. I'll see my dad and stay for the night."

"Ten-four," Jason said.

Rita looked at him across the car. "You good to follow up on everything we got started today?"

"Yup." Jason took one hand off the wheel to count up his fingers. "Banking, utilities, and Cornell Alumni."

"Thanks," Rita said. "And when I'm in Casper, I'll call in at Meadowlark, where David used to work."

Rita rolled up the gravel drive at Otto's house and parked. Jason headed for the camper, while Rita went into Otto's to pick up her backpack. Before stepping out again, she scoured Otto's cabinets for some snacks. She settled on a jar of dry-roasted peanuts and headed back out to the Honda.

As Rita drove out of town, she made an impromptu detour to the Still Haven Cemetery. Fresh pink asters adorned Lisa's grave.

Helen, most likely.

Rita took out her phone and called her again. The call rang through to voicemail, and she left another message asking Helen to return the call.

Rita circled back to her car and headed for Casper. She drove straight to the hospital and parked in the visitor's lot.

Upstairs in the ICU, Rita passed several nurses and visitors on the way to Otto's room. But she made eye contact with no one. And she saw no sign of Mary Lou. She must have already been and gone. The day had gotten away from Rita.

Steeling herself, she walked up to her father's bedside. He looked the same as yesterday, only a little more fragile.

She sat in the chair beside the bed and took his hand. "I'm sorry, Otto." Then she added, "Dad."

She allowed her apology to sit in the space of silence

between them before speaking again. "I've been a shit daughter. I'm sorry for making things difficult between us. Your relationship with Helen ... well, maybe it's none of my business, but I care."

Her phone rang, but she silenced it. It was Cash. She rejected it, then sent him a text.

I'm with Otto

Cash texted back a heart emoji.

She silenced and put away her phone, then took Otto's hand.

"That's all, Dad."

Silence returned, crawling up her back.

Machines beeped.

She untied her shoes and slipped them off her feet. She pulled them up into the chair, settling in for the visiting hours.

But she didn't know what to say.

Inhale.

Exhale.

A faint knock sounded on the door.

Rita turned to look over her shoulder as a nurse stepped into the room. "Hi there."

"Hello," Rita said.

The nurse approached the bed to check the tubes entering and exiting Otto. Her nametag read *Josie*.

"You're Rita, I presume?"

Rita nodded. "Yes."

"I'm Josie. I understand you spoke with Dr. Albright the other day."

Rita nodded, still gripping Otto's left hand. "But I haven't made a decision." She inclined her head toward the ventilator. "I don't feel ready to take him off life support."

Josie straightened Otto's blanket. Not that it was in any

way disturbed as Otto had not in any way moved. "You got time, child, you got time."

Rita nodded again but said nothing.

Josie patted Otto's arm, then stepped back from the bed to check his machines. "You mustn't feel pressured into making a decision."

Rita's mouth felt dry. "I don't want him to suffer."

Josie gave Rita a warm smile. "Your father isn't suffering. He's comfortable." She patted the machine. "He's got some real nice assistance right here."

"It's not only the stroke," Rita said. She stroked Otto's hand. "Cancer's ravaging him while he lies here."

This time, Josie's smile was sad. "It does make things worse, honey."

"Honeybee," Rita said, the word bursting out before she knew she'd said it aloud. She blushed. "He calls me Honeybee."

Josie's smile brightened. "That's sweet."

Rita gave a bitter laugh. "I wasn't a very sweet child, though."

Josie's eye twinkled. "Oh, no?"

Rita sighed and stretched in the chair. "I was kinda dogmatic about the rules of the road. I used to ticket the kids that rode their bikes on the sidewalk."

Josie laughed. "Any of them pay their fines?"

Rita laughed. "Only one of them. This kid called Cash. And the fines were paid in candy, so since Sour Soothers were his favorite, I had a lot of canker sores that summer."

"Apple doesn't fall from the tree, does it, Sheriff?"

"Once, this kid Billy Miller rode his bike right into Edna Jones, knocking her down, library books and all. And what did I do?"

"You helped Edna Jones?"

Rita laughed. "Nope. I know that's what you would do, Josie. And I wish I could say that's what I did." She laughed again, still holding Otto's hand. "But, nope. I chased down Billy Miller and tied his hands behind his back with my knee sock. And left him on the front lawn at the post office. Then I dragged his bike to the SCSO and locked it up in the compound. I told my dad that my friend had gone on vacation and needed a safe place to store her bike because it kept getting stolen at the mobile home park."

Josie barked out a laugh. "When did poor Billy Miller get his bike back?"

Rita grimaced. "I left it there for two weeks. I have to admit I behaved more like a criminal than a cop." She wiped a tear born of laughter from her eye. "But Billy never rode on the sidewalk again."

Josie gave Rita a warm smile. "We all have a legacy to leave." She patted Otto's shoulder, then crossed to the door. "I'll let you two be now."

"Thank you," Rita said.

She stayed until visiting hours ended at eight. Outside, a bright full moon lit her way to the parking lot. She drove to the Best Western. Once inside her room, she looked up the accounting company David used to work for: Meadowlark Investment Firm.

She dialed the number, not expecting anyone to answer. And yet someone did.

"Hello?"

Caught off guard, Rita coughed. She cleared her throat. "Is this Meadowlark Investment Firm?"

"It is," a male voice confirmed. "But reception's closed."

"Understandable," Rita said. "I was calling to listen to the menu options, to find out who's who. But since we're talking, would you be able to answer some questions about your former employee, David Clark? I'm Sheriff Jonas from Still County Sheriff's Office."

"I'd be happy to, Sheriff Jonas," the cheery voice said. "Feel free to come by for a chat. I'll pull David's file."

"Now?" Rita asked.

"The front doors are locked, but I'll come down and let you in. My name's Randall Stockton." Then he gave her his number to text when she arrived, and the address of the firm.

Rita hung up and returned to the Honda. She punched the firm's address into the GPS. Meadowlark was a ten-minute drive to an unfamiliar part of town.

She texted Jason.

I'm meeting Randall Stockton at Meadowlark Investment Firm tonight. I'll let you know when I'm back at the hotel.

Jason gave the message a thumbs up. Rita wondered if he was with Blaze Wright again, making Mushrooms Neptune and avoiding questions about murder.

Ten minutes later, Rita arrived at a high-rise building. The sidewalks were empty, as were the parking spaces in front of the building. She parallel parked, then texted Randall that she'd arrived. Then she walked to the glass doors and waited.

A few minutes later, a tall man walked through the lobby. White hair neatly combed back from a high, tanned forehead, Randall Stockton appeared to be in his mid-fifties. But he walked with the energy of a thirty-year-old. He swiped a card across a panel and pulled open the glass doors.

Rita entered the high-rise and glanced around the lobby. Fancy vases of flowers and fussy tropical plants decorated the space.

Randall held out his hand for a shake. In white

Bermuda shorts and a pastel-striped golf shirt, he looked more like a tennis player than an accountant. "Pleased to meet you, Sheriff Jonas. Call me Randy."

Rita gave him a tight smile and ignored his hand. "Hello, Randy. You can call me Sheriff Jonas."

"Why don't we chat over a drink at the bar?" Randall said, gesturing toward a bustling taphouse branching off the left side of the lobby.

Rita gave him a polite smile. "No, thank you. We wouldn't want to be overheard."

Randall's lip twitched. "Suit yourself." He nodded toward the elevators. "My office is on the tenth floor."

Rita gestured for Randall to lead, circumventing any possibility of him suggesting that ladies go first.

He walked to the elevators, and she followed.

Chapter Twenty-Eight

RANDALL LED Rita into a large office comprising the entire tenth floor of the high-rise.

She scanned the open-plan layout, the desks arranged to allow each one a view through the floor-to-ceiling windows. The lights of downtown Casper twinkled beyond.

"Working alone?" she asked.

Randall laughed. "Sure am. It's Saturday night."

Rita raised an eyebrow. "And yet you're here."

Randall laughed again. "And to think, we could be having a drink downstairs." He motioned for Rita to follow him through the arrangement of desks. "My office is this way."

Two sandblasted glass walls cordoned off a corner office. Randall opened the door and ushered Rita inside.

Her seating options included either one of two red armchairs facing a cherrywood desk, or a sleek black leather sofa flanking one of the walls.

Not trusting the cleanliness of the leather sofa which may have functioned for more than mere reclining, Rita took a seat in one of the red leather armchairs opposite the desk.

Randall settled into a leather chair behind his desk. In his summer leisure outfit, he looked starkly out of place among the dark leather. He swiveled to face the windows.

"It's a beautiful night," he said. "Look at that moon."

"And yet somehow I don't think you came here to watch the moon rise." Rita shifted into the armchair, savoring its cushiness after the chair in the hospital. "You a workaholic, Randall?"

Spinning around to face her, Randall gave a boisterous laugh. "Takes one to know one, Sheriff."

He opened a desk drawer and pulled out a bottle of whiskey and two glasses.

Rita eyed the bottle. "No thanks."

Randall poured himself a draft. "Suit yourself. I don't mind drinking alone." Then he laughed again, this time self-conscious. "Must be why I'm divorced."

Rita smiled. "Must be."

"You too, Sheriff?" Randall asked.

"Me too, what?"

Randall shrugged. "Divorced. Here you are with me, working on a Saturday night. I can't imagine too many husbands who'd be happy about that arrangement."

"I aim to solve a murder, Randy."

Randall studied her for a moment, then threw back his whiskey. "What can I tell you about David Clark, Sheriff?"

Rita set her phone to record. "Please tell me about his tenure here."

"I pulled David's HR records," Randall said, tapping on a manila folder with a manicured fingernail. "He worked for Meadowlark twenty years." Then he slid it across the desktop toward Rita. "It's all here."

"Thanks," Rita said, picking up the folder and flipping it open. "What kind of clients did he have?"

"The regular," Randall said, sipping whiskey. "Lots of retail accounts, a gym franchise, a couple of dental practices."

Rita thumbed through the pages. "And did he get along with his clients?"

"Sure," Randall said. "Everyone seemed to like him, year in and year out."

"How about co-workers? Did he get along with the staff here at Meadowlark?"

"Sure," Randall said again. "He was one of our top employees. Naturally, we were surprised when he quit."

"Why's that?"

"'Cause David didn't seem like the kind of guy who enjoyed drumming up clients and keeping them happy." He winked at Rita. "Never enjoyed wining and dining the clients, like some of us do."

"He didn't retire?"

Randall laughed. "Retire? Hell, no. He left for his new clients. That's why his departure was so abrupt."

"Did he give notice?"

Thinking, Randall swirled his whiskey. "A couple days, I think. He didn't even take a severance package."

"But the firm gave him a gold watch?"

"Hell, yeah. We'd be dicks if we didn't."

"So his parting was amicable?"

"Very."

"What did you make of it?" Rita asked.

"What? David being a dedicated employee for twenty years, then suddenly taking off for some new gig, not even interested in leaving with benefits?" Randall grinned. "We should all be so fortunate."

"Did David tell you who his new clients were?"

Randall shook his head. "Nope. Never talked to the guy again after he left. But before he quit, I'd noticed a ledger on his desk with letterhead I didn't recognize."

"And that was suspicious?" Rita asked.

"I know all the clients at the firm," Randall said. "I'm friendly like that. So when I didn't recognize this one, I knew David was keeping an account for someone who wasn't with the company. Nothin' wrong with moonlighting. But it's not cool on the company clock."

"Do you happen to remember the account's name?"

"Absolutely," Randall said. "Because it gave me the creeps. Sounded like a funeral home. It was called Still Heaven."

Rita's ears perked up. To cover her interest, she said, "Or maybe it's a moonshiner distillery."

Randall laughed again and poured himself more whiskey. "David got pissed when he saw me looking at it. Snatched the ledger right out of my hand. I never figured out what Still Heaven was, but I figured it was illegal." Randall shrugged. "Why else react like that?"

"And he didn't tell you anything more at that time?" Rita asked.

Randall shook his head again. "David pretty much kept to himself. Never came to the company parties. Didn't join us for drinks on Friday night. He was divorced like most of us here, but he never seemed interested in playing the field."

"Do you know of any acquaintances he had here in town?" Rita asked.

Randall thought for a moment. "There's a diner David frequented. Ate there every day for lunch."

"Do you recall the name of it?"

"Sure," he said, pulling on his chin, "it wasn't half bad.

The Olive and something. It was Italian. Sort of. Lots of painted urns and fake plants."

"Did you go often with David?"

"Only a handful of times. He mostly ate alone."

"It sounds like he preferred his own company?"

Randall shrugged. "I just thought he liked to go solo because he was sweet on one of the waitresses." He scratched his jaw. "Can't remember her name though."

"Can you describe her?" Rita asked.

"Sure, she had these pert little titties that looked real good in her uniform." He cleared his throat. "If you don't mind me saying, Sheriff."

Rita stood. "That's all, Mr. Stockton, thank you for your time." She smiled with her teeth. "I'll see myself out."

Randall waved his hand in the air, a wedding band flashing. "No, no, I'll need to swipe my keycard to let you out of the lobby."

Rita pointed to his hand. "You said you were divorced."

A look of irritation crossed Randall's face. "I said I was divorc*ing*, Sheriff. I'm in *process*. But the damn paperwork has taken a year and a day. Not to mention an absorbent amount of my money."

"Then why do you wear it?"

Randall put his hands in his pockets as they walked. "If you really must know, Sheriff, it's because women are more apt to chat to me."

"As in, the bar downstairs?"

"Sure," Randall said, his jaw tense.

"I see," Rita said. The elevator doors opened and they entered. "And then you give them the same line you gave me, about being in the *process* of divorc*ing*?"

The doors closed and Randall hit the button for the

lobby. "Believe it or not, Sheriff Jonas, my intentions are purely professional."

"I couldn't imagine otherwise," Rita said, suppressing a shudder.

The elevator stopped and the doors opened with a ring. As they crossed the lobby, Randall stole a peek through the doors to the bar off the lobby, eyeing up the crowd.

"Night's still young," Rita said, wishing she'd gone to bed an hour ago. "I'm sure you can still make the most of it."

Randall grunted. Then he said, "Grape."

Rita paused. "I beg your pardon?"

"The Olive and Grape," he said. "The name of the diner. It's over on Whittaker Street. On the corner of Templeton."

"Thank you for your help," Rita said.

Randall swiped a card across the keypad and opened the glass doors for Rita. He wished her a good night, but she'd already walked away, enjoying the walk through the cooling evening air.

When she arrived at her Honda, for a moment she sat in the driver's seat, thinking. Still Heaven had to mean Still Haven Inn. She scrolled through her phone and called Milly.

"Evenin', Sheriff Jonas," Milly said when she answered.

"Hi, Milly," Rita said. "I'm calling to ask who your accountant is."

Milly hesitated before speaking. "I don't know."

"But you're the owner," Rita said.

"I'm sorry, Sheriff Jonas, really I don't know."

Rita rubbed her forehead. "How's that possible?"

"There's a silent partner who holds the majority

interest at the inn," she said. "He arranges for the books to be done."

"Who's the silent partner?"

"I don't know," Milly said again. "And I really can't talk right now. I've got a business meeting in Beaumont to get to."

"At this hour?" Rita asked.

But Milly had already hung up.

Rita called Jason.

This time he answered. "Sheriff."

"Everything go okay with Meadowlark Investment Firm?"

"The guy's a creep, but everything's fine, thanks. It's possible that David Clark may have kept the accounts for Still Haven Inn. Could you please head over there and ask Milly about it? She sounded evasive on the phone."

"Sure thing, Sheriff," Jason said. "I'll take care of it right away."

Rita could hear another voice in the background, deep and male. Blaze Wright.

"You know what, Jason?" Rita said. "Don't worry about it. It can wait until Monday."

Jason hesitated. "Are you sure?"

Rita sighed. "Yeah, I'm sure. We've all been working too steady. Enjoy your night off."

She hung up, reminding herself that simply because she used work to distract herself from other matters at hand, it was unrealistic to expect Jason to do the same. Besides, she didn't want him to burn out. She'd already lost Walter. And she couldn't be sure Hunter would be willing to send her a second replacement.

She swiped open Google Maps and charted her course. Then she turned the key in the ignition and headed for The Olive and Grape.

Chapter Twenty-Nine

It was a busy Saturday night at The Olive and Grape.

Since she wasn't in uniform, Rita pulled her badge as she walked up to the host, whose blue hair matched her blue-rimmed glasses.

"I'm looking for someone who might know a regular customer named David Clark," Rita said. "He was a regular here a few years ago."

"I'll get Brooklyn," the host said, "she'll know. She's been here longer than any of us."

A few minutes later, the host returned with a woman in her fifties, who had bottled blonde hair and cherry-red lips.

The host nodded her head toward Rita. "She has some questions."

Brooklyn blinked at her. She touched her hand to her chest, her fingers slightly trembling. "Questions *for me?*"

"I'll go clear your tables, Brooklyn," said the host, ducking away.

"Thanks, Piper."

"I'm Sheriff Jonas from the Still County Sheriff's

Office," Rita said. "I'm here to ask some questions about David Clark. Do you know him?"

Brooklyn hesitated. "Is he okay?"

"Can we talk somewhere private?" Rita asked.

Brooklyn nodded. "It's time for my break anyway. One moment."

Brooklyn flagged down one of the other servers, asking her to watch her table. Then she grabbed her coat from behind the host's counter and led Rita outside.

They found a quiet spot in the alley and Brooklyn took a pack of smokes from her coat pocket. Her hand trembled as she lit the cigarette and took a drag.

"Thanks for stepping away with me," Rita said. "I'm sorry to tell you that David Clark is dead."

Brooklyn suddenly coughed, dousing Rita in smoke. The aroma was both alluring and off-putting in one breath, reminding Rita of her own weakness. And the cause of Otto's death.

Doubled over, Brooklyn caught her breath. Then she straightened, her face red and wet with tears. "Jesus Christ." She swiped at her tears. "I beg your pardon, Sheriff, it's a bit of a shock." She wagged her hand, indicating the cigarette. "Combined with a bad habit."

Rita nodded. "I understand. I would also like to inform you that his death was a homicide."

Brooklyn's eyes widened. "Murder?"

Rita opened her phone to her voice-recorder app. "I'd like to ask you some questions about David, if that's all right?"

Raising the cigarette to her mouth, Brooklyn nodded. But said nothing.

"How well did you know David?" Rita asked.

Brooklyn took another drag before answering. "He was

one of the regulars." Her lips trembled. "One of the good ones."

"What do you mean by that?"

Brooklyn let out a shuddering sigh, blowing smoke. "Always tipped the bill. Gave me a little extra on holidays. Never pinched my ass." She gave a weak smile. "He was a real nice guy."

"I heard he was sweet on you," Rita said. "Did you date?"

Brooklyn avoided Rita's eye. "No."

"Did he ever proposition you in any way?"

Brooklyn shook her head again. "He was real shy, Sheriff. And not much of a looker. But I wouldn't have said no if he'd asked. Like I said, he was real nice."

"When did you last see David?"

Brooklyn tapped her cigarette while she thought. "Must have been a few years ago now." She coughed again. "He just stopped coming one day. Figured he moved out of town."

"He moved to Still," Rita said.

"How about that?" Brooklyn said. She tapped the ash from her cigarette. "Must be nice to retire. Makes me realize how long I've been here servin' spaghetti."

"Did David tell you he was planning to retire?" Rita asked.

Brooklyn gave a sad laugh. "He talked about retirement all the time, Sheriff. He tipped me real good, but every now and then he'd ask me if I was saving my tips. He was always telling me I could change my future just by saving my change."

"But you weren't a client of David's?"

Brooklyn laughed and shook her head.

"Did David ever mention his clients?"

Brooklyn squared her shoulders. "Not on your life. He

was real proud of his professional conduct. He was tight-lipped about all of his clients, even when his workmates would come in, wagging their jaws about this, that, and the other thing."

"Which work-mates were these?"

"Accountants. Bookkeepers. That set. They all worked at a place called Meadowlark. Sometimes we'd cater retirement luncheons and such for them."

"Was there a luncheon in honor of David when he left Meadowlark?"

Brooklyn crinkled her nose, thinking back. "No. At least I don't think so. It was a while ago now." She looked sad again. As if she hoped life had taken a different turn. "Even if he had a party, I'm sure he wouldn't have enjoyed it." She glanced at Rita. "He was a quiet type."

"Did you see David again after he moved away from town?" Rita asked.

A shadow fell over Brooklyn's eyes. "No."

"Did you know he sometimes came into town to go to the Capitol Eight Cineplex?" Rita asked.

"No, I never knew," Brooklyn said, sounding even sadder. She nodded toward the far end of the alley. "That theatre's just up the way. But no, he never stopped in."

"He came for Friday night premieres," Rita said. "A few times a year."

Tears shone in Brooklyn's eyes. "Guess I would have missed him anyway. I work breakfast and lunch, Monday through Saturday." She studied the burning end of her cigarette. "It takes a while to get used to a regular not being regular no more." She took a long pull on her smoke and exhaled. "Can't help missing him, you know?"

"Is there anything else you can tell me about David?" Rita asked. "That might help the investigation?"

Taking a moment to think, Brooklyn fished an Altoids

tin from her coat pocket, popped the lid, and ground out the stub of her cigarette. Then she closed the lid and returned the tin to her pocket.

She met Rita's eye. "Curtis Farstad."

"Farstad?" Rita confirmed for the recording.

"Yes," Brooklyn said. "He's David's financial planner."

Rita's interest piqued. "How do you know the name of his financial planner, considering David was so tight-lipped about his affairs?"

Brooklyn laughed, though she still sounded sad. "Because he gave me the card of this guy, Curtis Farstad, and told me to tell him David had sent me."

"And did you?" Rita asked.

Brooklyn nodded. "Sure did. Save up all my tips one year, just like David said to, and went and met this Farstad fellow. He usually only deals with the folks with the big bucks. But he took me on, as a favor for David."

"Thank you for the contact," Rita said.

"Anything to help David. That is, to find out who did this."

Rita turned off the recording app. "We're giving this investigation all we've got." She pulled out a business card and passed it to Brooklyn. "Please be in touch if anything comes to mind."

Brooklyn nodded and together, they walked back to the front door of the diner.

As they stepped inside the vestibule, Rita asked, "What's good to order?"

Brooklyn didn't hesitate. "Anything pasta. Avoid the risotto."

"All right," Rita said, "I'll take a lasagna to go."

"I'll put in your order as soon as I wash up," Brooklyn said. "See you in a minute."

She headed into the restaurant and Rita sat on a bench by the window to wait.

She pulled out her phone and texted Ken Saunders.

Does Apex have a financial stake in Still Haven Inn?

A minute later, Ken responded. *How should I know?*

Rita rolled her eyes and typed a response. *Please find out.*

Two minutes later, Ken texted back. *I'll get to it Monday.*

Rita tapped her nails on her phone case, thinking about the silent partner Milly had mentioned at Still Haven Inn. It was hard to imagine anyone being silent about anything in Still. Which meant it had to be Apex.

Brooklyn arrived with Rita's lasagna in to-go container. It smelled delicious. She paid and tipped the blue-haired host called Piper, who told her to "have a chill one." Then she drove back to the hotel, the aroma of lasagna permeating the Honda.

That's when she noticed a black minivan behind her. Was it the same one that she'd noticed in Casper a few days ago?

She changed lanes and then made a quick turn right. The van followed. She turned again, taking random lefts and rights. Each time the van did the same.

She bit down on her lip. "Shit."

She returned to one of the main arteries through town and pulled onto the double-lane road. She slowed to forty, then twenty miles per hour, waiting for them to pass.

But the van kept its distance, too far to read its license plate. Honking, other Casper drivers passed her, while the van continually changed lanes, disguising itself amongst the traffic. Was it going to hang back there forever?

A moment later, the minivan revved its engine and gunned past her in a cloud of blue exhaust. She didn't catch the license plate, but she had confirmation. Someone had been following her.

Inhale.

At least she knew she wasn't imagining things. She drove back to the hotel. Before getting out of the car she called Walter. But there was no answer. She left a voicemail message, hoping they'd settled into Cheyenne okay.

Then she climbed out of her Honda, taking the food to her room. She sat down to eat on the foot of the bed. The lasagna was actually pretty tasty.

Chapter Thirty

SUNDAY MORNING, Rita ate cold leftover lasagna. Then she brushed her teeth and pulled her hair into a ponytail. After dressing in a hoodie and leggings, she called Curtis Farstad on the off chance the financial planner was another workaholic.

The call rang through to his voicemail. Rita left her name and a message introducing herself, and that she'd like to meet with him on Monday afternoon to talk about David Clark.

She popped on a ballcap and headed outside. The day was warm, but not the sweltering variety they'd recently endured. As Rita drove to the hospital, she frequently glanced in the rearview mirror, scanning the road for black minivans. When she arrived at the hospital having seen none, she let out a breath.

Exhale.

As she rode the elevator to the ICU, she studied the toes of her sneakers, then briskly walked the hallways, hoping not to bump into Dr. Albright or any familiar nurses.

In Otto's room, she pulled up the chair and sat in it, legs crossed beneath her.

"Hi, Dad … Otto … it's Honeybee."

The ticking and whizzing and beeping ventilator answered back, and for a while, Rita listened.

Then her listening shifted to her own breath. She hadn't realized she was quietly sobbing.

"Sorry for the tears, Dad. I'm dealing with a tough case."

Inviting her to share, Otto stayed silent.

"Local teenagers got shot. It's Arnold Myers, dad. He's dead. And Adrian, Walter's kid. He's caught up in it too. In fact, a few days ago he was here in the hospital, just like you are. But he's gone home now." Rita paused, swallowing back a sob. "I'm … I'm not sure you're gonna go home, Dad. I'm not sure if you're going to be leaving here."

After a while, a nurse stopped by and offered Rita some food. It wasn't much, but Rita happily accepted the tray of applesauce, cookies, crackers, and cheese, instead of breaking vigil at Otto's side.

After she had lunched, she told Otto about staying in his house. And how she liked the slipcovers Helen had made. And how she appreciated him leaving her childhood bedroom as it was. She told him Jason was grateful to stay in the trailer, too.

Rita laughed. "You're still takin' care of everyone at the SCSO, Dad."

Rita stepped outside and turned off her phone's airplane mode. A message from Jason asked Rita to call him at her earliest convenience.

Rita called, and he answered right away.

"Hey, Rita," he said. "Called to tell you I stopped by Still Haven Inn."

"What'd you find out?"

"Not much. Milly had gone to Cheyenne, and the housekeeper didn't know when she would return."

"Cheyenne?" Rita asked. "Not Beaumont?"

"That's right," Jason said. "So I left her a message, trying to arrange a meeting for Monday morning."

"Thanks, Jason."

"I also touched base with Ken Saunders."

"And?"

"No luck on finding the Apex decoy truck yet."

"Thanks for the update," Rita said.

"How are you doing in Casper?" he asked. "How's Otto?"

"About the same. And so am I — damn tired. Enjoy the rest of your day off, Jason. You've definitely earned it."

Rita rang off, then called Milly.

No answer.

She disconnected without leaving a message since Jason had already done so. Rita tucked her phone into the pocket of her hoodie and headed back inside the hospital. Without saying a word, she returned to Otto's bedside and tucked up her legs in the chair.

Around six, Rita left the hospital. She used the McDonald's drive-thru and took her order back to the Best Western. She ate in the room while watching TV, but no shows held her attention. Instead, she went for a walk, thinking about Otto's condition.

And the decision in her hands.

When she got back to her room, she showered, washing away her tears, and conflicted feelings. She thought about texting Cash, but she fell asleep before making up her mind.

The next morning, she woke early. She ate a power bar

for breakfast, then dressed in khakis and a cotton shirt. She grabbed her backpack and headed downstairs.

"I'm checking out," Rita said, handing her keycard to the hotel desk clerk.

He chuckled. "Are you sure, Sheriff?"

Rita returned the laugh, but it felt hollow. "You never know when I'll be back." She rolled her shoulders, thinking about Otto. Every time she thought about heading back to Still, a leaden feeling overcame her. She forced a smile. "But I don't mind. I've slept better here than at home."

The desk clerk thanked her and offered her coffee from an urn on the sideboard. Rita declined and headed out of the Best Western. She put her backpack in the trunk of the Honda and drove out of the lot.

On the way to the hospital, she stopped at The Moon-Bean, a twenty-four-hour coffee shop that the Casper cops frequented. Its roast wasn't as good as Skyler's but came in a close second.

At the hospital, Rita parked in the visitor's lot. But this time she chose a spot on the opposite side to where she'd parked yesterday, when she'd spent the day with Otto.

Rita walked toward the morgue and gave a wave to Dylan Bruce, who'd come out to the parking lot to meet her. As she approached, her cell phone rang. She paused to check it.

But it wasn't the ICU. Or Cash. It was Jason. She rejected the call and continued on her way.

Jason called again. She gave Bruce a signal that she needed to take the call.

"Hi, Jason."

"Rita," Jason said. "Still Haven Inn burned down last night."

Rita's tongue took a moment to work. "What?"

"New fire chief suspects it's arson."

Rita blew out a breath. "Is anyone hurt?"

"Not sure yet," Jason said. "The housekeeper says there are no guests at the moment."

"That's encouraging," Rita said. "Hopefully our arsonist has a heart and chose a night with wide-open vacancy."

"I think it's vacant most nights," Jason said. "Rooms are mostly rented during business hours."

"Is that a fact?"

Jason grunted. "That's what Blaze says, at any rate."

"Blaze is an expert on this subject, is he?"

"He's lived in town a long time."

"So have you," Rita said. "You were born here."

A voice mumbled in the background.

"Blaze says the rooms are all right, so long as you get one with a view."

"What view?" Rita asked.

"The mountains, I suppose," Jason said.

"But that's the view everywhere around here," Rita said. "You can't stop looking at mountains if you wanted to."

Jason laughed. "Missing the skyscrapers, Sheriff?"

Rita shrugged, even though he couldn't see her. "Not really." She looked around at the hospital buildings. "Just feeling cagey, is all. Make sure it's Blaze who's feeding information to *you* Jason, and not the other way around, okay? Only feed him mushrooms and other edible things."

"I know," Jason said.

"I don't suppose any ledgers survived the fire?" Rita asked.

"Accounting ledgers?" Jason asked. "Do you think the arson has anything to do with David Clark's murder?"

"I'd hate to guess," Rita said, "but seems like an awful

big coincidence that first David is murdered, and then his client's business — if that's the case — is incinerated."

"And now Milly is missing," Jason said.

"Milly is missing?"

"Whether she's in Cheyenne or Beaumont, no one can get a hold of her."

"Perhaps to meet the silent partner," Rita said, thoughtful.

"Still Haven Inn has a silent partner?" Jason asked.

"Milly mentioned it yesterday," Rita said. "And we're gonna find out who it is."

Chapter Thirty-One

AFTER SPEAKING WITH JASON, Rita called Milly. But as expected, there was no answer.

Rita left a voice message:

"Hi Milly, it's Sheriff Jonas. I'm calling because the Still Haven Inn has burned down. And as no one has been in touch with you, I'm concerned. Please call as soon as you can."

Then she hung up and met Bruce's eye. "We got an arson."

The medical examiner gave her an empathetic smile. "You got some bodies to go with that?"

Rita sighed. "Hopefully not."

Rita and Bruce walked into the morgue where they donned PPE. Then Bruce set to work.

For three hours, Rita watched him work on David's headless cadaver. The head, thankfully, Bruce had already processed and stored out of sight.

When he was finished, Bruce washed up and invited Rita to join him in his office to go over the results.

"Coffee or tea?" Bruce asked, pointing to a Keurig machine and electric kettle.

Rita raised her disposable coffee cup. "Picked one up on the way over, thanks."

"Well, if you were planning to stop at The Moon-Bean, why didn't you say?" Bruce said, choosing a bottle of water. "They have fantastic crullers." Sitting at his desk, he cracked the lid and took a sip. "Shall we get down to it?"

"Please do," Rita said.

"Looks like David Clark was beheaded while he was alive," Bruce said.

Rita couldn't help but cringe.

"The job was done in two blows, either side of the neck, obliterating C3 and C4. Probably done with a machete."

"Shit," Rita said. "Sounds like that would require some strength."

Bruce nodded. "Strength *and* determination. Administering two clean blows like that requires a level of … detachment. Pardon the pun."

Rita felt her heart constrict. "Clark didn't have a chance."

This time Bruce shook his head. "Nope. Though he had defensive wounds on his hands and forearms."

"Time of death?" Rita asked. It was strange to imagine she had the chance to schedule's Otto's death. And how clean it would be, compared to David's.

Pushing his glasses up the bridge of his nose, Bruce consulted his papers. "Clark was deceased approximately sixteen hours when found. Reports will be in the system by the end of the day."

"Thanks," Rita said. "And how about Adrian?"

Bruce sifted through the paperwork on his desk. "I have the tox results right here."

He handed her the report.

Rita scanned the findings. No sign of drugs in Adrian's system. George would be happy to know. And Helen, if Rita ever talked to her again.

She got up and thanked Bruce again. Then Rita showed herself out of the morgue and returned to her Honda. She considered calling Tilda, then decided an air-conditioned drive to her office was a hell of a lot more appealing than baking like a lasagna in her car.

Tilda welcomed Rita into her office with a smile. "Boy, am I glad to see a head attached to a body." She bugged her eyes. "I definitely need a break from staring at a screen. Quite the case, huh?"

"It's got my attention, that's for sure," Rita said, rubbing her temples. "And now I've got an arson to go with it."

"Good times," Tilda said, leaning back in her chair. "How was the autopsy?"

"I missed the head, but caught the body," Rita said. "Bruce says the weapon was most likely a machete."

"Didn't find a machete or blade of any kind," Tilda said. "Kitchen knives were all in their block, with traces of kitchen grit all over them. The killer must have taken the weapon with him."

"And since he was beheaded while alive," Rita asked, "it would have been a bloodbath, yeah?"

Tilda nodded. "Blood spatter confirms that most of Clark's blood probably drenched the killer." She sat forward, resting her elbows on her desk. "And I believe the killer came prepared for the mess, because blood wasn't tracked throughout the house. We found a shred of Tyvek in the bathroom. Presumably the murderer wore the suit to do the deed."

Rita frowned. "Sounds professional. Was it one of the city's suits?"

Tilda shook her head. "Nope. We checked it against all of our gear and it's not ours. But it's easy enough to buy a Tyvek suit online."

"No doubt," Rita said.

"The bathroom also gave us a couple of other things," Tilda said. "We found some bloody water in the shower. Bleach was through everything."

"I remember smelling it," Rita said.

"We also found a single hair on the back of the shower curtain, with the root intact, so we should be able to get some DNA."

"There's some good news," Rita said. "Thanks for the update."

"You heading out of town now?" Tilda asked.

"No," Rita said. "I've got a few more folks to talk to in town. Including my dad."

Tilda walked around her desk, arms outstretched. "Of course. Hug?"

Rita leaned in and took the hug. "Thanks."

Tilda patted her on the back. "Take it easy, Rita."

Rita smiled. "You too, Tilda."

Before leaving the station, Rita went to the cafeteria and ordered a sandwich to go. Not in the mood to answer questions about Otto, she slipped out to the parking lot to eat in her car.

While she ate, she listened to a voicemail that had come in while she'd been talking with Tilda. It was from Curtis Farstad, inviting Rita to come find him by the Casper Golf Course between two and four that afternoon.

Rita started the Honda and headed to the golf course, traveling the broad avenues under a vast, uninterrupted sky. For several minutes she drove past columns of cottonwoods, their summer-green leaves shimmering in the breeze like coins in a wishing pond. Then the trees gave way to a cleared expanse of jewel-green grass.

She turned onto a black asphalt drive and traveled another quarter mile before arriving at the clubhouse. She parked and got out her phone to call David's financial planner, Curtis Farstad.

"Afternoon. Curt speaking."

"Hello, Mr. Farstad," Rita said. "It's Sheriff Jonas. I'm at the course now."

"And I'm on the third hole," he said. "See you soon."

Rita showed her badge at the front desk of the club and walked out onto the course. It was a nice day for a walk, and despite having little experience with the game, she appreciated the neatly trimmed hills and pruned evergreens.

She spotted two men, both wearing cotton pants and polos. One them appeared to trek the course more often than his portly companion. The tall slender one sunk his ball in the hole, and the heavy-set man congratulated him.

Rita called out, "Mr. Farstad."

Both men turned, but the tall one with blond hair turning gray at the temples stepped forward.

"That's me." He gave her a polite nod. "Pleased to meet you, Sheriff. Call me Curt."

"I'd like to speak with you privately, Curt," Rita said, taking out her phone to record his answers.

"Excuse us for a minute, Barry," Curt said, stepping to the side while the other man aimed his ball toward the hole. It rolled past by a foot.

"Barry could use the practice," Curt said, good-naturedly. "He doesn't get out here too often. Too much time at the desk."

Rita arched an eyebrow. "Workaholic? I heard it takes one to know one."

Curt chuckled as they stepped out of earshot. "How can I help you, Sheriff?"

"You're David Clark's financial planner, yes?"

"That's me."

"We looked through David's financial paperwork, but we didn't see anything with your name."

"I don't send my clients a lot of paper reports," he said. "David could track all of his accounts online. What would you like to know about David?"

"What services did you provide him?"

"Estate planning."

"Meaning investments?"

"Yes."

"What kind of investments?"

"Nothing risky, that's for sure," Curt said. "A very conservative portfolio. But I can't tell you anything else, due to client confidentiality."

"David Clark is dead," Rita said.

Curt turned pale and pushed a hand through his hair. "Oh, shit."

Rita watched him for a moment. A sheen of sweat had broken out on his forehead.

"Did you know David well?" she asked.

Curt tapped his club against the grass. "Not really. Congenial small talk, mostly. He liked to talk about crosswords puzzles he'd cracked. Like, if he figured out a commonly used word."

Rita peaked an eyebrow. "Like what?"

Curt's brow wrinkled. "I don't remember. I don't do crossword puzzles. I like to exercise my brain with numbers. And in my leisure time, I exercise my body. Even if Barry refuses to admit golf is a form of exercise."

Rita gave him an obliging laugh. "Did David ever tell you about his private clients?"

Curt shook his head. "Definitely not."

"Did you ask?"

"Definitely not," Curt said again. "You're suggesting a breach of client confidentiality. We shared a cash account, and I purchased commodities on his behalf. That's it."

"I need to notify David's lawyer," Rita said. "Do you know who that is? We didn't find any legal documents on the premises either."

Curt pointed to Barry, now teeing off at the fourth hole. "Barry."

Rita pointed. "Barry's his lawyer?"

Curt put his fingers in his mouth and whistled. Barry looked and Curt waved his arm, ushering him over.

Barry walked over and joined them.

"Hi, Barry," Rita said. "I'm Sheriff Jonas from the SCSO. I'd like to chat with you about David Clark." She indicated her voice recording app. "You were his lawyer?"

Barry nodded. "Barry Arnott," he said. "And what do you mean by 'were'? David's been my client since his divorce." Then he cracked a smile and laughed. "Are you telling me I'm fired?"

"David Clark is dead."

"Oh, shit," Barry said. "What happened?"

"Murdered," Rita said.

Barry and Curt looked at one another but said nothing. Their reaction, Rita thought, was unusual.

"What types of services did you provide him, Barry?" Rita asked.

"Estate planning."

"Those close to David say he was a planner," she said. "Organized."

Barry chewed on his lip. "Very. He had a plan, in fact.

A happy plan, he called it. It involved moving out west. I think he said Southern California. And that takes a chunk of change."

"Carlsbad?"

"Might have been."

"Did he plan to move after he retired?"

"It's hard to imagine he'd ever retire," Curt said.

Rita glanced at him. "Why's that?"

Curt hesitated. "He worked a lot."

"Perhaps all the more reason to retire," Rita said.

Curt rolled his shoulders. "I suppose some of us like to slog 'til we're pushing up daisies."

Rita narrowed her eyes. "Do you work a lot of over-time, Curt?"

Curt barked out a laugh. "Not me, Sheriff." Grinning, he tapped his golf club against the lawn. "I happen to think we're meant to spend our days on this good green earth doing as we please."

"Not everyone has the luxury of leisure time," Rita said. "And some choose to spend their leisure time working toward an honorable outcome." She smiled. "Like solving crime."

Curt and Barry shifted in their golf togs.

"It was his line of work," Curt said.

Rita met his eye. "What do you mean by that?"

Curt cleared his throat. "His client was generous." He swapped another look with Barry. "Would be hard to give that up."

"You knew this client was generous, even though you knew nothing else about them?"

Curt nodded. "I saw David's cash deposits."

"Did David have lot of savings?" Rita asked.

Curt and Barry swapped a look.

"Close to five million dollars," Curt said.

Rita tried not to show her shock. "Five mil?"

Curt nodded. "Like I said, he was paid well by his client."

Rita looked between them. "And neither of you has an inkling who it was?"

"I sometimes thought David worked for the mob," Curt said. "It was odd that he only had one client and made a shit ton of money. But I never caught wind of him doing anything illegal."

"Me neither," Barry said.

"Though he was private as hell," Curt said. "Not one word about clients or cars or vacations or women."

"Did he ever talk about family?"

"Said he hoped to have grandkids one day," Barry said.

Curt looked at him. "Oh, yeah? He never told me that."

"Probably because you don't have kids," Barry said.

"What about his will?" Rita asked. "Who inherits?"

Barry shrugged. "Probably the kids. That's usually how it goes. But I don't remember. It's been a while since we drafted it."

"I'd appreciate you checking and letting me know," Rita said. Barry nodded and she gave them each a card. "And please call me if you think of anything else."

"I thought of one," Curt said.

Rita blinked at him. "I beg your pardon?"

"*Iota*. That was one of the words David told me to remember. Because I could easily think a four-letter word for '*a little bit*,' could be *atom* or *mite*. But it'll probably be, '*iota*'."

Rita smiled. "Thank you for your time, Curt, Barry. Enjoy your game."

Then she turned and walked back to the clubhouse, wishing she had an iota of an idea as to who'd killed David Clark.

Chapter Thirty-Two

RITA LEFT the Casper golf course and took the connector to the freeway, heading straight for the Still Haven Inn.

She rolled up in her Honda to a smoking ruin, where a crew of firefighters worked to contain the damage. All that remained standing was the inn's sign, spray-painted with Arnold's neon legacy: "Fuck the rich."

Rita walked over to Jason, who was reading on his phone. As she approached, he looked up.

"Still Haven Inn's silent partner is Angel Holdings Ltd.," he said.

"So there we have it," Rita said, spreading her hands. "Our confirmation that David Clark worked for Milly, and whoever her silent partner is."

"Though I'm still waiting on the Secretary of State for more information," Jason said.

"Escalate the request," Rita said.

Jason nodded. "You bet, Sheriff."

Then Rita asked after Vee.

"She's back at the SCSO trying to track down Milly," Jason said. "She put out a BOLO for her vehicle."

"Good work," Rita said. Then she pumped her thumb toward the crew of firefighters. "I'm going to go see what the new fire chief has to say."

As Rita picked her way toward the smoking pile of debris, one of the figures broke away from the group and walked toward her. He wore a helmet marked with the chief's insignia.

The man removed his goggles and mask. "Hi there, Sheriff Jonas. I'm Paul Bastian."

"Pleased to meet you, Chief," Rita said. "I'm Rita. Take me through the scene?"

"Definitely arson," Paul said. "A liberal amount of an accelerant was used."

Rita surveyed the smoldering debris. "My deputy says no sign of any bodies."

"Thank God," Paul said, releasing a sigh. "We'll be wrapping up here within the hour. I'll let you know if we find anything unusual."

"Thanks, Chief," Rita said, turning to walk away.

"Oh, and Sheriff?" Paul said. "Do you know how George is doing?"

"Sure," Rita said. "I saw him recently. He's grieving his son, of course. You should go visit."

Paul looked taken aback. "At the prison?"

Rita nodded. "He would appreciate seeing a friend." Then she thanked him and wished him luck with the site before heading back to her Honda.

Rita drove to Sarah Thorpe's rental on Windset Lane. She parked on the shoulder of the road and walked onto the property, retracing the steps the supposed surveyors had taken. Maybe they'd been out here trying to find another access to the property in order to torch the inn. It wasn't like they could walk up to the inn's front door; Milly had increased security after the vandalism, and now cameras overlooked the parking lot, facade of the building, and the spray-painted sign.

She followed a narrow, trampled path through the brush which led all the way to the back of the inn. There stood a series of charred metal boxes which had recently housed functioning pumps and filters. Two more firefighters were working in the area as well.

Rita walked along the edge of the bushes, scanning them for anything that may have been thrown out of sight.

Something reflective caught her eye.

She pulled aside a branch and found an empty gas can. Using a sturdy stick, she hooked it through the handle and lifted it, hopefully preserving a set of fingerprints.

She returned to her Honda and stored the gas can in the trunk. Then she walked back to the property and knocked on Sarah Thorpe's door.

The door creaked open and Sarah's head poked out, her hair in a hundred directions. The baby gurgled, redfaced, on her hip.

"Sorry to disturb you, Miss Thorpe," Rita said. "But I have a couple questions. It shouldn't take much of your time."

Sarah nodded, though she remained wedged in the doorway without inviting Rita in. "Okay."

"Did you see or hear anything unusual last night?" Rita asked.

"Nothing until the sirens started," Sarah said. "Then neither me or Finn could sleep."

"Not surprising," Rita said. "Could you see the blaze from the house?"

"We could see the sky lit up real bright and saw some of the flashing red lights through the trees. The sirens kept coming and the light in the sky just kept getting brighter. So since Finn wasn't sleeping anyways, I strapped him in the carrier, and we walked over to have a look."

"Did you walk through the bush?" Rita asked.

Sarah gave a nervous laugh. "I might be a mushroom picker, Sheriff, but I ain't bold enough to walk through the woods in the dark with my baby. There are wolves in these parts, you know."

"So you went around, by the road?"

Sarah nodded. "I do it all the time, to get him to settle. Takes me about twenty-five minutes to get to the inn."

"So you witnessed the fire?" Rita confirmed.

"Yeah. I asked the firefighters if I should evacuate. But they said things were under control."

"In the past, did you ever hear much from the inn?"

"I don't hear much of anything, over Finn's crying," Sarah said. She gave a half-desperate laugh. "He's cutting a tooth, you know."

"You mentioned," Rita said.

Sarah grimaced. "It's probably a new one. I wear earplugs at night, so my eardrums can bear sleeping with him."

Rita smiled. "I hope you can get a nap today. Thanks for your help, Miss Thorpe."

Then Rita drove back to the SCSO, passing the Bighorn Mining building. The renovation was coming along. She spotted Stu talking to the red-headed construction worker. Maybe Stu was applying for a job there, since things at the gas stations didn't seem to be working out so well.

Her phone rang and she pulled over to take the call.

"Hello, Sheriff Jonas. This is Officer Duclos with the Casper PD. I'm following up on a burglary."

Rita turned off the ignition. "Yes?"

"Do you know Arlene and George Myers?"

"Yes," Rita said. "Those are the grandparents of Arnold Myers, our shooting victim here in Still."

"Apparently their daughter-in-law, Helen Myers — who lives in Still — broke into their house here in Casper and stole one of George's handguns."

Rita bit back a curse word. "Thanks for the info, Officer."

Then she called Helen. Again, the call rang through to voicemail.

"Helen, it's Rita. Whatever you're planning, you need to stop. Leave it to the police. Everyone's working to find Arnold's killer — the SCSO, Casper PD, Beaumont, Apex."

Rita wasn't so sure about Apex, but she wanted Helen to feel supported on all sides. "And no one wants you to get yourself killed, Helen."

Rita disconnected and put away her phone. Then she twisted in the seat, looking back at the Bighorn Mining construction site. Stu and the red-headed guy were now gone.

She started the ignition and drove to the office.

"Mary Lou," Rita said, coming into the bullpen, "need you to do something."

Mary turned away from her monitor, fingers still on the keyboard. "What can I do for you, Sheriff?"

Rita dropped her voice. "Helen is armed."

"Shit," Mary Lou said. "Helen plus a gun ain't a good equation."

Rita bit her lip. "Agreed. It's a priority that we pick her up and bring her in. But she won't talk to me. I think you might be the only one who can bring her in."

"Ten-four, Sheriff."

"Thanks," Rita said. "And Mary Lou?"

"Yeah?"

"Be careful."

Mary Lou smiled. "Of course. When things go sideways, I don't go with 'em." She winked. "The King taught me well."

Rita turned to face Vee, who was sitting at Walter's desk. "How's it going, Vee?"

"Good," Vee said. "Milly's vehicle was clocked a day ago near Great Falls. Officer issued her a speeding ticket."

"In Montana?" Rita said.

Vee nodded.

"Well, that's definitely not Beaumont or Cheyenne," Rita said. "I wonder where she's going? Please follow up with the officer who pulled her over."

"Will do," Vee said.

The phone rang and Mary Lou answered. After a brief call, she hung up and swiveled to face Rita.

"Beaumont found the fake Apex vehicle. The one used in the shooting of Arnold and Adrian. They've just towed it to their impound yard."

"This will hopefully answer some questions," she said. "And hopefully not create any new ones. I'll head over now."

But Rita paused. "Mary Lou," she said, "another favor?"

"What's up, Sheriff?"

"I've got a gas can in the trunk of my Honda that needs to be printed," Rita said.

"Gimme your keys," Mary Lou said, getting up from her desk. "I'll do the paperwork and get it on over to Tilda."

"Thanks, Mary Lou, you're a godsend."

Mary Lou straightened her shoulders. "That's what most of 'em say. Especially the electrician. I lit that man up like a Christmas tree."

Rita smiled through her teeth. "How charming." She nodded to Vee. "I'll take the truck into Beaumont. See you both later."

Vee and Mary Lou waved her off, and Rita returned to the parking lot. She took a moment to air out the truck before getting in and driving to Beaumont.

As Rita walked into the PD, she noticed a missing person's poster for Carly. She tore it down, then introduced herself at reception. The dispatcher asked Rita to wait while she called.

A minute later, an officer came to meet her.

"Hi, Sheriff Jonas, I'm Tal Jackson. I'll show you the vehicle."

Rita shook his hand. "Thanks." Then she showed him the poster of Carly. "Also, this individual on the poster isn't missing. She's a victim of domestic assault and doesn't want to be found at this time."

"Thanks for the tip, Sheriff," Officer Jackson said. "I'll close the missing person file after we meet. Let's head out to the impound."

Tal led her to the fenced yard with three impounded vehicles. They walked past two sedans to the phony Apex truck.

"Here it is," Officer Jackson said. "Emptied and incinerated."

"No plates, I assume, since it wasn't registered?" Rita said.

"Right," Jackson said. "And once again, the VIN was removed."

"Of course it was," Rita said, blowing out a breath. "DNA?"

"We're checking it over. But it's not very promising, burned out as it is."

Rita scanned the blackened hull. "No doubt."

"But one can always hope," Jackson said. "We'll let you know what we find."

"Thanks," Rita said. "How's the meth situation here in Beaumont?"

Jackson gave a slight shrug. "Same as everywhere else: bad."

"Do you know who's running it?"

Jackson rolled his shoulders. "I figure it's coming out of Casper. Small players around here dried up years ago."

"But someone would have picked up the slack," Rita said, thinking out loud. "What about Thomas Gabriel?"

"That guy's got a lock on everything," Jackson agreed. "But not meth. He's never liked the synthetics."

Rita nodded. "Right," she said, biting her lip. "I heard that too."

Chapter Thirty-Three

As Rita drove out of Beaumont, she received a phone call from David's lawyer, Barry Arnott. She pulled over on the shoulder to take the call.

"I have the information about David's will," he said.

"Thanks, Barry, go ahead," Rita said.

"One benefactor is his daughter, Karen Clark. She inherits the bulk of the estate. The other benefactor is a woman named Brooklyn Graff."

Rita hadn't expected to hear Brooklyn's name. "What did he leave her?"

Barry whistled. "A cool million."

"Thanks, Barry," Rita said. "You've been a great help."

Rita rang off and tapped her fingernails on the steering wheel. Could Brooklyn have killed David in order to inherit? But why wait all these years?

Rita swiped open her phone and made another call.

Mary Lou picked up. "What can I do for you, Sheriff?"

"Nothing, Mary Lou. I called to let you know I'm headed back to Casper."

"Shit, Sheriff," Mary Lou said, "you need another room at the Best Western?"

"I don't think so," Rita said. "Or at least I hope not. I plan to be back in Still tonight."

Rita drove a little farther down the highway until she arrived at a rest stop. She swung in and turned around the Honda, heading back the other way. God, she was getting sick of this drive — even if beyond the verdant, velvet hills, the clouds rose like snowy mountains in the bluest sky she'd ever seen.

She turned off the AC and opened the car window, swallowing the sweet pine-fresh air.

Inhale.

Dropping her shoulders, she loosened her grip on the steering wheel.

Exhale.

She needed a holiday, one that didn't involve getting into a vehicle for at least a week.

When Rita arrived back in Casper, she drove directly to The Olive and Grape. The lunch rush had ended, leaving the parking lot relatively vacant. She chose a spot by the door and headed inside.

Piper, the blue-haired host, stood at the front desk, spritzing laminated menus, then wiping them clean. Rita scanned the restaurant, looking for Brooklyn Graff. She spotted her near the back, washing a table.

Brooklyn felt Rita's gaze and looked up. An expression flickered over her face. Then she dried her hands on her apron and approached.

"Good afternoon, Sheriff."

"Hi again, Brooklyn," Rita said. "I need to ask you a few more questions. Can we step outside for a minute?"

Brooklyn hesitated. "I already had my break this shift. But I've only got another hour till I'm off. I can talk then."

"Then we'll chat here," Rita said.

Brooklyn glanced over her shoulder. "The manager—"

"This is important," Rita said, giving Brooklyn a knowing look.

Brooklyn bit her lip and nodded. "Okay, Sheriff, we can talk here."

"Can you tell me where you were last Thursday night?"

Brooklyn glanced over her shoulder at the host. "I was here, working."

"Even though you work the breakfast and lunch shifts?" Rita asked.

"I'd swapped shifts with Lonnie that night. She worked my morning shift."

"Why the swap?"

"We had a special event that night. The manager likes to have his experienced servers on the floor."

Piper set down her spray bottle. "It was a birthday party for an 80-year-old, Sheriff." Then she held up a small whiteboard. "Here's the shift schedule."

Rita crossed to the desk and looked at it. Thursday night's list of servers included Brooklyn's name. And similarly Lonnie's occupied the morning slot. But all the names were written in whiteboard marker.

"It's not a very permanent record," Rita said.

Piper pulled out her phone. "Brooklyn's in the birthday photos on the restaurant's Facebook page." She swiped through her phone, then handed it to Rita. "We all are."

Rita thumbed through a couple of pictures, spotting Brooklyn in several. Rita handed back Piper's phone. "Thanks."

"Why all these questions, Sheriff?" Brooklyn asked. Her fingers fiddled with her apron ties. "Do you think I had something to do with David's death?"

"David Clark included you in his will," Rita said.

Brooklyn's jaw trembled. "What? He did?" She dropped the ties she'd been worrying. "What ... what a sweetheart."

"You didn't know?" Rita asked.

Brooklyn blushed. "He used to ask me these 'would you rather' questions. Sort of a game we played. Like, would you rather visit Hawaii or Italy? Or would you rather ride a sailboat or an air balloon? But it wasn't creepy in any way. He never made me feel like he expected to be part of the fantasy. It was just daydreaming, you know? Which was nice. Because sometimes life can be real hard, you know? The day-to-day bits of it."

"David's ability to manage the day-to-day bits of life should make your life easier now. "

Brooklyn managed a wavering smile. "He managed things, all right. Always told me to save and have a plan. A happy plan, he called it."

"What's a happy plan?" Rita asked.

Brooklyn's smile became steady. "A plan for my happiness. And it didn't have to be a grand plan. He'd say, find something that makes me happy. The way crossword puzzles made him happy. He'd do 'em while waitin' on his order. And he told me more than once, he never minded waitin' 'cause he always had a book with him. And if he could die doing them puzzles, he'd die happy."

Then, realizing what she'd said, she clamped a hand over her mouth.

"What's your happiness plan, Brooklyn?" Rita asked, trying for levity.

Brooklyn gave a little laugh. "Probably sounds silly, Sheriff, but I'd like to build a greenhouse. And a real nice gazebo. Maybe a goldfish pond, too. Call it a bucket list. You got one of those, Sheriff? A bucket list?"

"Yup," Rita said. "It's got a vacation on it."

Brooklyn laughed. "Yeah, I'd like one of those too. I'd like to go to London. To the Kew Gardens."

"Good choice," Rita said. "Especially since David left you a million dollars."

Brooklyn choked on a cough. "He — what?"

"He left you one million dollars."

Brooklyn blinked and moved her lips, rather like a goldfish. But no sounds came out. Then she burst into tears. Piper came over and put her arms around her.

"A lawyer named Barry Arnott will be in touch with you to make the arrangements," Rita said.

Brooklyn blew her nose and nodded.

"Take care of yourself, Brooklyn," Rita said.

Brooklyn nodded again and Piper told Rita to have a chill one.

Rita returned to her Honda and headed to Casper to see Otto. Her feet carried her through the hospital as if on autopilot. Everything about the ward felt as familiar as the SCSO or the Bighorn Bean. And it had only been a few days since Otto had been here.

She pulled up the chair beside his bed and settled in.

"Hi, Dad. It's me."

Only the beeps and whirs of the ventilator responded to her words.

While Rita sat vigil, Mary Lou texted: *Don't matter what you say I've booked you a room at the BW*

Rita shot back a text. *Thx. Still got my bag with me*

Mary Lou sent a thumbs up.

Rita put away her phone and returned to sitting in silence, listening to the ventilator.

"What do you want, Dad?" she asked in a whisper.

Otto didn't respond.

Although she sat as still as a snow peak, Rita soon felt

her exhaustion. And hunger. But she knew nothing in the hospital cafeteria would appeal to her. She wished she'd brought a lasagna from The Olive and Grape.

She pried herself out of the chair, kissed Otto's forehead, and said goodbye. Then she left the hospital to check in at the Best Western.

A shower reinvigorated Rita. She put on a fresh t-shirt, sweater, and jeans. Then she headed down to the reception desk to get a lead on supper.

"O'Malley's Irish Pub is a good choice," the desk clerk said. She wore a pair of large-framed eyeglasses in leopard print.

"Is it close?" Rita asked.

"It's only four blocks, if you'd like to walk."

"Work for me," Rita said. "Thanks."

The desk clerk winked. "Even a sheriff needs to tie one on sometimes."

Rita gave her a weak smile. Tying one on sounded like a terrible idea. If anything appealed at the moment, it was warm milk.

But Rita knew some exercise would fire up an appetite. She thanked the receptionist for the recommendation and headed out into the warm evening.

The moon she'd viewed from Randall's corner office shone down on her. She walked the four blocks to the pub, identifying it by a green neon sign in the shape of a shamrock.

Inside O'Malley's, a rowdy crowd drowned out a riff of pre-recorded fiddle music. Rita chose a booth in the corner and read the specials written on a blackboard above the bar. When a server came by her table, she ordered fish and chips and a draft beer.

Scrolling through her phone as she waited, she felt someone's gaze. It wasn't an uncommon feeling for a law enforcement officer in a drinking establishment — except tonight she wasn't wearing her uniform.

She looked across at the bar, where a man in a baseball cap sat on a stool, staring at her. She didn't remember him being there when she'd walked in. He must have arrived after her. Still watching her, he raised a bottle of beer to his lips and drank. Then he slid off his stool and threaded his way through the tables, approaching her booth. He looked to be in his midthirties.

"Oh, hell," she said under her breath.

The man arrived at her table. He smiled down at her. "I know you."

"No, you don't," Rita said. "I don't live in town."

He smiled down at her. "Maybe not, but I know you're from around these here parts."

"And I know that I was having a better time before you showed up." Rita craned her neck, looking for the server with her beer. She tapped her nails on the table with impatience.

But the man didn't go away. Instead, he slid onto the opposite bench in the booth. "Rita Jones."

Rita narrowed her eyes at him. "So if I'm Rita Jones, who the hell are you?"

The guy looked taken aback. "It's me, Marcus." He adjusted the bill of his cap. "Don't you remember me, Rita?"

"No, I don't remember you."

"Marcus Dwyer." He straightened his shoulders. "We took algebra together."

Rita blinked at him. "You took algebra?"

"I remember you got the top grade. You were the smart kid in class. And a good girl, too. Cop's kid, right? Kind of untouchable, if you know what I mean." He raised his beer bottle to her, then frowned. "You ain't drinkin' nothin'?"

"Am now," Rita said, as the server delivered a steaming basket of fish and chips and a sleeve of beer.

"I'll have another," Marcus said to the server, indicating his bottle. "I got a tab at the bar going."

The server gave him a nod and said she'd be back in a minute. When she'd walked away, Rita looked at Marcus.

"I'd like to eat alone, please."

"Hey, now, Rita, I ain't tryna come on strong." Marcus leaned back in the booth, as if settling in for winter. "You goin' through a tough divorce or somethin'?"

Rita gave him an annoyed look. "Why does anyone think I'm getting a divorce? I've never even gotten fucking married."

"Jesus, you sound sore about that," Marcus said, rolling his shoulders. "I've been married twice. Divorced both times." He sounded proud.

Rita dug her fork into the crust of her fish, releasing the steam. "Somehow I'm not surprised."

"So you living in Casper now?" Marcus asked.

Rita bowled at him. "I'm here because a family member's unwell. So I'm not exactly in the mood for taking a stroll down Nostalgia Lane."

Marcus nodded. "Got it, Rita Jones." He shimmied out of the booth and picked up his beer bottle. "Well, have a nice life. Maybe I'll see you around Wyoming sometime."

Rita bit into her fish, spraying bits of crispy batter. "See you around."

Chewing on her fish, she watched Marcus weave through the tables and back to his bar stool. She kept her eyes on him the entire time she ate. But he never looked back at her, instead chatting to the bartender.

Rita used the last of her french fries to wipe up the

ketchup on her plate, then she licked her fingers. It was quite possible she'd eaten more ketchup than french fries, but something about the sweet sticky sauce seemed irresistible tonight. And she'd barely even touched her beer.

She slid out of her booth, settled the bill, and slipped out the door before Marcus could notice. Then she headed back to the Best Western four blocks away.

While she walked, she called Walter.

"You get to Cheyenne okay?" she asked.

"Yep," Walter said. "We're comfortable enough here."

"How's Adrian doing?"

"A lot better, physically. Physiotherapist says he's turned a corner. But now it's really hit him that his best friend is dead."

"I can imagine," Rita said. "You're a good dad to be there for him, Walter."

"Winnie and me are doin' the best that we can," Walter said. "And Adrian's grandparents too, pitching in making meals and shoring up his spirits."

"That's good to hear, Walter," Rita said. "Take all the time you need. Vee's finding her way around the ropes well enough."

"Thanks, Sheriff." Then Walter gave her his new address in Cheyenne.

Rita hung up as a black minivan pulled up in front of her, the side door already open.

She took a step backward and bumped into a figure. She flinched, unaware that she'd been followed.

Spinning around, she reached for her cross body. "Stop where you are, I'm a cop."

"Take it easy, Rita Jones," said the man, stepping back. He raised his hands. "It's me, Marcus Dwyer."

Rita's hand stilled on her weapon. "It's not Rita Jones,"

she said, though gritted teeth. "It's Sheriff Jonas of the SCSO."

"I know," Marcus said. "And no one's planning to hurt you. Thomas Gabriel just wants to have a conversation."

Rita stared at Marcus. "This is all about having a conversation with Tom Gabriel?"

Marcus spread his hands as he smiled. "That's it. Just talking."

Rita crinkled her nose. "I just talked to Tom last week."

Marcus cocked his head, gesturing to the open minivan idling at the curb. "If you don't mind—?"

Rita pointed at the vehicle. "This is your minivan?"

Marcus frowned. "Nothing wrong with a minivan. They handle real well and are easy to park while still accommodating several passengers plus cargo."

She peered inside the van. A man wearing a denim jacket sat in the driver's seat.

"I was remarking less on the fact that it's a minivan," she said, "and more on the fact that you and your friend here are the ones that've been tailing me."

Again, Marcus gestured toward the van.

Rita hesitated.

Then she sighed — *exhale* — and got in the van.

Chapter Thirty-Four

RITA STEPPED up into the van and took a seat. Marcus Dwyer followed, buckling in next to her.

"Nice upholstery," Rita said.

"Only forty thousand miles and no stains when I bought 'er," Marcus said, patting the door of the minivan.

"I imagine you got it for a steal," Rita said wryly. She glanced at the man in the driver's seat, but he didn't turn around.

Marcus dug in the pocket of his jacket and passed Rita a blindfold. "Here, put this on."

Rita ignored him.

"Please."

Rita gave him a look.

"Look, I already said I ain't gonna hurt you. But if you don't put it on, we ain't goin' anywhere."

Rita bit back a comment and tied on the blindfold. Then she put her hands on her crossbody, in case Marcus or his co-conspirator tried to remove it.

The van lurched into motion, and Rita was slammed back against the headrest. She tried to follow the route, but given the number of sharp turns, the driver clearly intended to throw her off the trail.

Eventually, the van rolled to a stop. Marcus pulled open the sliding side door, and Rita yanked off her blindfold.

The van had parked inside a warehouse. Between the towers of crates were two plastic patio chairs. A man in a silver suit occupied one, reading on his phone. He looked up as Marcus slammed the van door shut behind Rita.

The man in the silver suit put away his phone. "I apologize for this less than comfortable location, Sheriff Jonas." He stood and put his hands in his pockets. "But I dislike meeting in public."

Rita recognized his voice. "I'll take the apology, Alan," she said, striding over to the plastic chairs. She dropped into one of them. "I see I'm not actually having a conversation with Tom tonight, since he's in lockup."

"No false pretenses, Sheriff Jonas," Alan said. "Talking with me is as good as talking with Tom. I'm here to answer your questions about Angel Holdings Limited, then you can be on your way."

"Why do you think I care about Angel Holdings?"

Alan straightened his tie. "I know you put in a request for business details with the Secretary of State."

Rita narrowed her eyes at him. "Go on."

"I'd prefer you chat with the source."

"By the source, you mean Tom."

Alan inclined his head.

"Which means talking to you."

He nodded again.

"Okay," Rita said, "I'd like to hear about Still Haven Inn."

"Thomas Gabriel is a silent party."

"Know that already," Rita said. "Can you confirm that David Clark was the inn's accountant?"

Alan nodded. "Yes."

"And Tom's personal accountant?"

Alan cleared his throat. "David Clark is the accountant for Angel Holdings Ltd."

"*Was,*" Rita corrected.

Alan lowered his brows. "*Was.*"

"How unfortunate for David," Rita said, "that he's Tom's employee."

Alan furrowed his brow. "What do you mean by that?"

"It's risky going into business with Tom. Look how it turned out for David."

"If you're inferring I'm in danger, Sheriff, I can take care of myself."

"That's good," Rita said, "because I'm not inferring anything. The harm that came to David was most certainly indisputable."

Alan tapped his fingers on the plastic armrest. "I think you fail to understand that Angel Holdings Ltd. is a completely legitimate business."

Rita tapped her lip. "And yet for some reason I doubt that. Maybe it has to do with the fact David's head is no longer attached to the rest of him." She stood up, scraping the plastic chair across the concrete. "Thanks for the information, Alan."

"Please don't leave yet, Sheriff," Alan said. "A conversation is a two-way street."

"You're the one that wanted to have a conversation," Rita said.

"Correct. Which is why I'd like you to share some information with me."

Rita crossed her arms. "Is that right?"

Alan's face remained impassive. "Do you any leads on David's laptop?"

Rita shook her head. "Nope."

Alan's forehead creased. "We'd like to retrieve our account files."

"I would imagine so," Rita said.

Alan studied her for a moment. Then he said, "Thanks for your efforts, Sheriff Jonas." He stood and buttoned his suit jacket. "And now that you know who owns Angel Holdings Limited, you can stop asking so many questions."

"Why would I do that?" Rita asked. "I've got a murder to solve."

"And you think it's connected to my client?"

"I need to check out all angles. And I suspect someone's targeting Tom."

A muscle tightened in Alan's jaw. "Targeting Tom?"

"It's no coincidence that both Tom's investment property and employee were hit. Tom's the real target. But he's unreachable in prison." Rita shrugged. "So someone's sending a message another way. Inflicting maximum pain."

A shadow flickered in Alan's eyes. "Do you have any leads?"

Rita rolled her shoulders. "If I did, I wouldn't be sharing the results of an active murder investigation with you, Alan." Then she paused, studying him. "But I was going to ask you the same question. Has Tom pissed off anyone lately?"

The lawyer scoffed. "Presumably plenty, on the inside. But outside the pen? How much pull do you think he has?"

Rita shrugged. "Well, I'm sitting here, in a not-so-abandoned warehouse in God-knows-where, Wyoming."

Alan waved his hand. "We're done. Feel free to go. Enjoy your night in Casper."

Rita gave him the stink eye. "Yeah, I'll do that." Then she turned on her heel and marched toward the minivan. "Good night, Alan."

"Oh, and Sheriff?"

Rita paused, rolling her eyes. Then she turned. "Yes?"

"If you get any leads…"

"Yes?"

The lawyer shrugged. "Well, feel free to give me a call."

"You're expecting me to disclose the identity of my prime suspect, so that Marcus and his silent partner can go pick them up?" She laughed and shook her head.

Alan approached her. "Mr. Gabriel has instructed me to assist you in any way you require." He spread his hands in a generous gesture. "You need only ask."

"Fine. If I have a question, I'll pick you up for a blindfolded, nausea-inducing drive to a warehouse in Still, where we'll talk."

Then she stalked back toward the van and pulled open the side door. Marcus flinched at the sudden noise, dropping his phone.

Rita climbed into the bench seat. "We're done here. Take me back to the bar."

Marcus handed Rita the blindfold.

"Seriously?" she said.

Marcus gave her a sheepish look. "Can't have you knowing the location of the warehouse."

Sighing, Rita snatched the blindfold and tied it on.

Marcus rapped on the roof on the van and the driver turned the ignition. "Take her back to the hotel."

Rita yanked off the blindfold, meeting Marcus's eye. "You know where I'm staying?"

"Of course," Marcus said, sounding equally frustrated. "The Best Western at the west end of town."

"East end," the driver said, speaking for the first time.

Marcus grunted. "East, west, whatever. I'm not a goddamned sailor."

Rita replaced the blindfold. "You can drop me at O'Malley's, thank you very much."

Marcus rapped on the roof of the van again. "Take her to the pub."

Ten minutes later, the van drew to a stop. Rita took off her blindfold and tossed it at Marcus.

He caught it and stuffed it back in his pocket. "Too bad we never had that drink together first." He pulled open the sliding door. "Might have made the whole night a little funner."

Rita stepped down from the van. "Fuck off."

Then she walked into the pub, shaking. She headed for the bar and sat on the stool Marcus had occupied earlier.

The bartender took notice of her right away. "Hey, you okay? You look a little shaken up."

Rita folded her trembling hands on the bar top and took a deep breath. "Had a bad date."

The bartender gave her a tender smile. "I gotcha. Whatever you want, it's on the house."

"Thanks. I'll take a whiskey."

The bartender poured generously. As he slid the glass toward her, he leaned over the bar to speak close to her ear. "If you need a way out of this place, you can leave through the kitchen."

"Thanks," Rita said.

The bartender straightened up and winked. "I'll leave you to it, then."

As he left to serve another customer, Rita took a sip of her drink. The whiskey was warm and smooth and as good as a hot bath and a back rub.

She pulled out her phone and texted Cash: *Why the hell didn't you tell me you knew David Clark?*

Cash texted back right away. *Can we talk?*

But Rita wasn't in the mood for another conversation.

She just wanted answers. She ignored his message and threw back the rest of her whiskey. Then she dropped a tip on the bartop, slipped off the stool, and pretended to head to the bathrooms. At the last moment, she veered to the right and into the kitchens.

A couple of cooks glanced at her but said nothing as she walked directly to the back door, keeping an eye over her shoulder. When she stepped outside, unfollowed by Marcus or any other of Tom's buddies, she let out a pent-up breath.

The moon was now high in the sky, casting bright light on the sidewalk. Walking briskly, she headed back to the Best Western.

Inside her room, she locked the door and placed a chair beneath the handle. She checked the window casings too, ensuring that none could be opened. Through the window, she glimpsed the black minivan in the parking lot. She sighed and pulled the blinds.

Kicking off her shoes, she sat on the bed and took out her phone.

"Evening, Sheriff," Jason answered. "Everything okay?"

"Yep," Rita said, not ready to talk about what had happened. "I'm back at the hotel now, and I need you to do something for me, please. Could you go back to David Clark's house and get all the files for Angel Holdings Ltd. into evidence? I'll explain in the morning."

"Right away, Sheriff," Jason said. "Sleep well."

Rita put her phone on the nightstand, close at hand. Then she put her service weapon under the pillow. Too on edge to shower or undress, she laid on the bed and turned out the light.

Sleep didn't come easily.

Chapter Thirty-Five

ON HER WAY to the SCSO, Rita stopped in at the Bighorn Bean for a coffee and a muffin. When she walked in, Skyler gave her a wave.

"Good to see you back in town, Sheriff. The usual?"

"Yes, please."

As Rita approached the counter, she noticed Carly sitting at the back of the cafe sipping a coffee. Her bruises had darkened to greenish-black, but the swelling had gone down.

Rita walked over. "Carly. How are you doing?"

Carly flinched at Rita's voice, then looked up and smiled. "Hey, Rita. I'm okay." She shrugged and glanced around. "Feeling better, I guess. Feeling like I want to get out."

"That's good," Rita said. "Do you feel ready to talk about what happened?"

Carly shook her head. "No thanks. I value my beating heart."

Rita offered a smile. "I know Jeff has a long reach, but I'd make sure that nothing happens."

Carly mirrored her smile, though it was weak. "I appreciate that. But ... I don't want to overstay my welcome."

"Do you have family who can shelter you?" Rita asked.

Carly hesitated, then shook her head. "Got kicked out when I got pregnant." She gave a half shrug. "Lost the baby anyway."

"I'm sorry," Rita said.

"It was probably for the best, in the end." Carly snorted, then winced, fingering her cheekbone. "I mean, look at me."

"Looks like you've made some smart choices to me," Rita said. "Getting out of an unsafe situation. Building a career when you didn't have many options. Your mom should be proud of you, and you'd be a great mom, too."

Carly stared at Rita, unblinking. "Th-thanks."

"I know the courage it takes to shake off someone like Jeff Jeffries," Rita said. "Mary Lou's always quoting Elvis: 'When things go wrong, don't go with them.' It strikes me that you're like that, Carly — that you know when to stay true to your path, even when things go sideways."

Carly blinked, breaking her stare. "That's really wise."

Skyler whistled and gestured that Rita's order was up.

"I should go," Rita said. "If there's anything you need, reach out, okay?"

Carly smiled. "I'm fine, thanks. But I sure do appreciate you checking in."

"Of course," Rita said. "And I'll continue to do so."

She squeezed Carly's shoulder, then crossed to the counter to claim her coffee. As she lifted the cup from the counter, Jason called.

Juggling her coffee and phone, Rita answered.

"I got news about Angel Holdings Ltd.," Jason said. "Email came in from the Secretary of State." Over the line, she could hear his mouse click. "Says here that Angel Holdings Limited owns seven businesses in total. Still Haven Inn is one of the names."

"Confirming the connection we suspected between the arson and David Clark's murder," Rita said. "What are the other six businesses?"

"ARCH Junk Removal, Cherub Bros. Auto Body, Heaven Sent Delivery Services, The Lawn Ranger, Lawless and Sons Lease Management, and The Rancher's Pantry."

"Only one I recognize is the grocery store," Rita said.

"Dunno none of them other ones neither."

"Do you type your reports like that, too?"

"Like what?"

"Never mind," Rita said, taking a sip of her coffee. "Please find out what you can about the other five businesses. I'll head over to The Rancher's Pantry after we kiki at the office. See you at HQ in five — I'm just fueling up on caffeine."

"What's kiki?" Jason asked.

"It's a New York thing," Rita said. "You know I don't like sounding like a local."

Coffee in hand, Rita got into her Honda. She settled the cup in the beverage holder and rolled out of the lot.

At the SCSO, Vee sat at Walter's desk. Jason sat at his, almost invisible behind a stack of cardboard file boxes. Mary Lou hung up the phone and spun in her swivel chair.

"Morning," Rita said, raising her coffee in a salute. "Let's have a meeting, everyone."

She pulled up a spare chair and arranged it between Jason and Vee. Mary Lou poured and passed out glasses of lemonade, then sat back down at her own desk.

Rita gestured to the towers of boxes on Jason's desk. "Looks like you got the ledgers from the inn."

Jason patted the closest box. "Seven years of accounting." He removed its cardboard lid and handed Rita some papers.

Rita scanned the documents, then passed them back to Jason. "I have no idea what I'm looking at." She looked at Mary Lou. "Please package these up and send them to Casper for the Financial Crimes Unit to review."

Mary Lou scribbled a reminder on a hot pink Post-It, then slapped it on one of the ledger boxes. "Ten-four."

"So we've got confirmation that David Clark was the accountant for Angel Holdings Ltd.," Rita said, nodding toward the cardboard boxes. "And we know that the silent partner in the inn is Thomas Gabriel."

Mary Lou made a sound like a horse. "I didn't expect that."

Rita took a sip of lemonade, its tartness inducing tears. "One of Still's better-kept secrets."

"So this Tom Gabriel is head of Angel Holdings Ltd?" Vee asked.

"Looks like," Mary Lou said.

"And what we need to figure out now," Rita said, "is who knew David Clark was working for Tom."

"That will help narrow the suspects, since no one seems know much about David," Jason said.

"Who's this Tom Gabriel?" Vee asked. "Aside from the head of Angels Holdings?"

"He used to run the drug trade here in Still, back in Otto's day," Rita said, surprised Vee hadn't heard the gossip. "Although according to his lawyer, Alan Crawford, Tom's a legitimate businessman now."

Mary Lou let out a laugh. "Ha! Legitimate, my ass."

"I'm inclined to agree with Mary Lou," Rita said. "I think there's more to these businesses of Tom's than meets the Secretary of State's eye," Rita said.

"Maybe someone is trying to move in on Gabriel's turf," Vee said.

"That makes sense if Gabriel's still running drugs," Rita said.

"Maybe Gabriel's using the inn to launder money," Jason said. "That would explain the low vacancy rate and the lights still being on."

"Plausible," Rita said. She swallowed some more lemonade, her tastebuds becoming accustomed to its acidity. "What'd you find in David's phone and banking records?"

Jason clicked through some tabs on his computer, bringing up the records in question.

"He paid his bills on time, most of them automated payments. Nothing abnormal in his deposits or withdrawals."

"That adds up," Rita said. "When I was in Casper, I met with his financial planner, Curtis Farstad. He never detected any illegal activities. Neither did his lawyer. What about his phone records?"

Jason clicked to another tab. "He never owned a cell phone. Landline doesn't show any calls."

"Not even a call to Karen in Carlsbad?"

"No, which means he either used a burner or email."

"Or snail mail," Vee said.

"Right," Rita said. "And are we still missing his laptop?"

Vee nodded. "Yep."

"Alan Crawford confirmed its existence," Rita said, grimacing. "And made it clear Angel Holdings wants it."

Mary Lou folded her arms. "For all those legitimate business records, I reckon."

"Do you think David was killed for it?" Jason asked.

Rita gave a half-shrug. "I don't think so. While Crawford expressed his eagerness to have it returned, he didn't seem urgent. He seemed irritated, not frantic."

"Did he have any idea who might have taken it?"

Rita shook her head. "He dragged me to a warehouse because he thought *I* could give him that information."

"Warehouse?" Mary Lou asked, mascaraed eyes blinking.

"A creepy one," Rita said. "Except for the plastic patio furniture."

"Yikes, Sheriff," Jason said, "are you okay?"

Rita rubbed her temples. "Let's just say, I'm glad to be back in Still. Vee, please head on over to David Clark's and take another search for a laptop. And also look for a receipt or a serial number or anything else that might give us a lead."

"On it," Vee said.

"Thanks for hitting the ground running," Rita said. "I've sent you all over town and you've barely just got here."

Vee grinned. "You're welcome."

"Are you staying at Mary Lou's now?"

Vee nodded and threw Mary Lou a smile. "She's been feeding me, too."

"Did she make you stuffed capsicum?" Jason asked.

Vee shook her head. "Eggplant Parmesan."

"Oh, no." Jason dropped his head into his hands. "I'm getting food FOMO."

"I could bring you some leftovers," Vee said.

Mary Lou's hair silver beehive wobbled. "*I* decide about the leftovers."

Vee glanced at her. "Um, okay…"

Mary Lou fixed a stern eye on Jason. "Are you getting fed properly these days, Jason?"

He shrugged. "Doing my best. Although the portobello

mushroom burgers were disappointingly dry. I'm cooking on a hot plate in a camper van."

"The hot plate don't have nothin' to do with that," Mary Lou said. "It's the marinade. Did you use Pinot Noir?"

"Cabernet."

"Cabernet?" Mary Lou threw up her arms. "For the love of Elvis, you gotta use a Pinot Noir." She fixed an eye on him. "Jason, would you like some leftovers?"

Jason's face lit up. "I'd love some, Mary Lou."

"How many times do I have to tell you, just say so? I hear your tummy growlin'. But you gotta speak up." She refilled his lemonade. "Ain't right for me to meddle."

Rita laughed. "Meddling is half the reason you're paid, Mary Lou."

Mary Lou denied Rita's comment the dignity of an acknowledgment and instead fluttered her eyelids at Jason. "I'll have Vee bring you some leftovers tomorrow."

Jason smiled. "Thanks, Mary Lou, I appreciate that."

Mary Lou patted his shoulder as she passed him on her way to the kitchen with the empty lemonade pitcher.

When she was gone, Vee turned to Rita. Her nose crinkled with confusion. "Isn't that what I offered to do in the first place?"

Rita winked. "I wouldn't worry about it," she said. "I'm still getting used to things around here."

Chapter Thirty-Six

RITA WALKED into The Rancher's Pantry. She scanned the checkout counters for Helen.

But seeing no sign of her, she continued to the back of the store and took a narrow corridor to the staircase that led to the manager's office.

Halfway up the narrow stairwell, she knocked on the wall. "Hi Peter, it's Sheriff Jonas."

A chair scraped against the floor above and she continued up the treads. A moment later, a door opened and Peter appeared on the landing.

His face wore a look of irritation. "This ain't the best time for me, Sheriff."

"We can go down to the SCSO if that works better for you?"

Peter mumbled something under his breath. "Come on up."

Without waiting for Rita, he turned and retreated back into his office. Rita followed.

Stu sat in his dad's office, in a chair that was sturdier

than either one in Rita's office. A large window looked out over the grocery store floor, but it looked like the blind had never been lifted, its metal slats coated with sticky brown dust. Beside Peter's desk, a recycling box overflowed with empty boxes of various granola bar brands. Hanging above an empty water jug (growing white fuzz inside), a calendar from last year showed a rugby player getting a face full of turf while a floating caption read: *Failure is Not Fatal.*

Rita pointed at the image. "I'm not sure about that." She shuddered, thinking back to the things Dylan Bruce had told her during David Clark's autopsy. She cleared her throat. "Not if he destroys his cervicals."

Peter blinked at her. "Huh?"

Rita turned to Peter's son. "Hi, Stu. Good to see you."

Peter flicked a hand toward Stu. "Go on, Stuart, get out of here."

"Please stay," Rita said. "I actually want to talk to both of you."

A muscle in Peter's jaw tensed. Then he pulled out a rolling office chair and dropped into it. Rita took the chair beside Stu. It was definitely cushier than anything back at the SCSO.

"What do you want to ask me?" Peter said.

"Why didn't you mention that you knew the identity of the homicide victim your son discovered?" Rita said.

Stu stiffened beside her.

"Because you didn't ask," Peter said.

Rita puckered her brows. "Well, I'm asking now."

Peter gave a noncommittal shrug. "David's our accountant."

"*Your* accountant?" Rita said. "Or Thomas Gabriel's?"

Peter didn't respond.

"Tom Gabriel," Rita repeated. "The person who actually owns The Rancher's Pantry?"

The color drained from Peter's face.

"Do you launder funds for Angel Holdings Limited?" Rita asked.

White-knuckled, Peter gripped his armrests. "Angel Holdings Ltd. is a legitimate silent partner." He moistened his lips. "Everything's on the up and up."

"I find that hard to believe," Rita said, "when the primary investor's in prison for illegal trafficking."

"Tom Gabriel's a changed man."

"Funny, I heard that recently," Rita said. "But I'm still not convinced." She paused and made a point of looking around the office. "So how's business?"

Peter swallowed. "Up and down."

"Helen Myers works here," Rita said. "She's mentioned the downs."

"Yeah, well, she don't work here no more, so her opinion don't count."

"So you're saying the store isn't barely staying afloat? Contrary to rumor?"

Peter scowled. "Times are hard." Then he cleared his throat. "No good help to hire around these parts."

Rita pointed at Stu. "What about your son?"

Peter screwed up his face. "He's already got a job."

"Are you sure about that?" Rita asked.

"And are you sure about him workin' here?" Peter said. "Got to have a head on your shoulders."

Rita felt her face flinch the thought of heads not being on shoulders. "I bet if he can pump gas," she said, recovering, "he can tong croissants."

"We already tried him in the bakery," Peter said. "But Stuart won't wear a hairnet."

Rita glanced at Stu and looked him over. "That would be a problem."

"Fuckin' right," Peter said.

"How about a haircut?" Rita asked.

Stu glowered at her. "No."

"See?" Peter said.

Rita shrugged. "Yeah, I don't know what you do about that. Guess there's a reason I don't have kids." She looked back at Stu. "What were you doing with the red-haired man at the Bighorn building?"

Peter sat forward, interested in Stu's answer to the question.

Like his dad, Stu turned pallid. "I was doing a favor for a friend."

Peter folded his arms. "You bailin' out Vic again?"

Stu shook his head. "Not this time."

"What kind of favor?" Rita asked.

"You buying drugs?" Peter said, turning red. "Or selling them?"

Stu pressed his lips together, looking like he wanted to crawl into a hole.

"What'd Tom ask you to do?" Rita asked.

Peter thumped the desk. Rita gave him a look. "Jesus Christ. Tom Gabriel?"

Stu straightened his shoulders. "It weren't no big deal. He just wanted me to find out if Brent's dealing drugs."

Peter popped out of his chair, rolling it back against the wall. The calendar shifted.

"How dare Tom get you involved in this shit?" He ran his hands over his shaved head. "Goddammit, Stuart, you're just a kid."

"I didn't actually buy any drugs," Stu said. "I *could* have. I probably *should* have. But I chickened out when I saw Sheriff Jonas roll past."

"What other favors have you done for Tom?" Rita asked.

Stu was quiet again.

"So help me God," Peter said, fisting his hands, "I'm gonna—"

"Take it easy, Peter," Rita said. "We already got one kid in town dead, and another one injured." She snapped her attention back at Stu. "What other favors?"

Stu groaned and dropped his head in his hands. For a moment, he rocked to and fro. Then his head popped up again. "I got a call to check on David Clark because he hadn't made his monthly meeting."

"What does that mean?" Rita asked. "What monthly meeting?

"Dunno," Stu said.

"Who does David meet?"

"Dunno. All I was to do was go to this address and check on him. That was it."

"Who called you asking for this favor?" Rita asked. "I doubt it was Tom Gabriel himself."

Stu shook his head. "Can't say."

For a moment, Rita studied him. It was clear he was frightened of retaliation. "Did Tom ask you for any other favors?" She paused for a beat, reminding herself to soften her voice. "This is your opportunity to tell me."

Stu shook his head again. "Nope. But I know Vic did some work for him."

"Jesus Murphy," Peter said, dropping into his chair and rolling back up to the desk.

"Such as?" Rita asked.

Stu shrugged. "Deliveries and shit."

"And shit?" Rita pressed.

Stu shrugged again.

Rita blew out a breath. "Thanks, guys." She met Peter's eyes. "Keep an eye on Stuart."

Peter nodded. "I'll keep him in line."

"That's not what I mean," Rita said. "I mean keep him safe. Someone's targeting Thomas Gabriel. The Rancher's Pantry could be next. There's a shooter out there who ain't afraid to pull a trigger on a kid."

Chapter Thirty-Seven

Rita left The Rancher's Pantry and walked out to the parking lot. A black minivan pulled into the space beside her. She stiffened.

Marcus Dwyer sat in the driver's seat. He hopped out while the man in the denim jacket who'd been driving the other night got out of the passenger seat. He walked away, lighting a cigarette while Marcus stayed where he was, grinning at Rita.

She narrowed her eyes at him. "Are you following me?"

Marcus laughed. "Of course not. I'm only out for a drive."

"All the way out here? You're not in Casper anymore, you know."

Marcus cocked his head at his companion, who continued smoking in a strip of shade along the side of the building. "We got business."

"Got anything to do with protecting Thomas Gabriel's assets?" Rita asked.

Marcus laughed again. "Only asset I see at the moment is you, Sheriff Jonas."

Rita snorted. "If I catch wind of anything illegal in Tom's business operation, I'm going after him."

Marcus's grin widened. "You ain't gonna find nothin'."

Another vehicle pulled into the lot and a woman got out. She glanced at them as she rummaged in her trunk for reusable shopping bags.

"Your uniform's makin' people gawk," Marcus said. "Let's talk in the van."

It was Rita's turn to laugh. "No thanks, Marcus. You have a habit of taking me to unknown locations."

Marcus frowned. "It ain't a habit if it only happens once."

"Well, I'm not about to give you a second chance," Rita said. "We can talk in my wheels."

Marcus bugged his eyes at the SCSO-issued vehicle. "I ain't gettin' in that carousel ride. My minivan or nowhere." He dug in the pocket of his jeans, then tossed his keys to Rita "You can hold on to those."

She caught the keys and glanced across the lot at Marcus's partner, still smoking in the shade. Then she sighed and pocketed the keys. "Fine."

She walked around the back of the minivan to the passenger seat, pausing to photograph the license plate.

"Here we are again," Marcus said, sliding behind the wheel.

Rita sighed. "At least I get a front-seat view this time. Or rather, a view at all."

"So what d'you want to talk about, Sheriff?"

"I want Tom Gabriel to stop bothering Stu," Rita said. "It's obvious someone's targeting Tom and those associated with him, and I'm worried about Stu. I've already got one dead kid and another one seriously wounded."

Marcus nodded. "I'll put in a word."

"Thanks," Rita said. "I also want to know who Tom Gabriel's enemies are."

Marcus's face grew impassive. "Gabriel doesn't have any enemies."

Rita laughed. "You and I both know that's bullshit. Whoever's going after him knows his business. Did he have a falling out with anyone recently?"

Marcus screwed up his face, thinking. "I dunno."

"You don't know?" Rita asked, studying him. "Or you're not going to tell me?"

Marcus grinned. "What do you think, Sheriff?"

Rita rolled her eyes and popped the door.

"Wait."

Rita paused, holding open the door.

"I'm staying in town for a while," Marcus said. "If you got any more questions, you can call me."

"And are you going to answer them?" Rita asked.

Marcus shrugged. "Dunno if I'll know if I'll answer your questions, but I'll answer your call." He ran the tip of his tongue over his teeth. "Wanna show me where to get some good grub around here?"

Rita got out of the minivan. "Depends which end of town you're at," she said. "Where you staying?"

Marcus set his jaw. "None of your business, Sheriff. Unless you're changin' your mind about that dinner invitation?"

"Just checking, is all," Rita said, "because the inn burned down." She smiled with her teeth. "Call it small-town hospitality."

Marcus growled and spoke in clipped words. "I am aware. That the inn. Burned down."

"Oh, of course you are," Rita said, smiling wider. "It's one of Tom's enterprises, isn't it?"

"Don't play coy with me, Sheriff, 'cause I'll be coy with you."

"You're very coy about where you're staying," Rita said.

"Well, where do you think I'm layin' my head?" Marcus asked.

Rita sighed. "I dunno. A bedroll in the back of the minivan, parked overnight in a rest stop?"

Marcus sat back and smiled at her. "At Cash's, of course."

Rita tossed back his keys, slammed out of her vehicle, and slammed into hers.

As she buckled, she watched Marcus's companion stub out his cigarette and return across the lot. Marcus emerged from the minivan and the two men entered the grocery store.

Rita blew out a breath. God, she'd love to be a fly on the wall during that conversation.

She pulled out her phone and called Thomas Gabriel's lawyer.

"I want to speak with your client again," Rita said.

"Good day to you too, Sheriff," Alan said. "And by my client, I assume you mean Thomas Gabriel?"

"It's my understanding you don't have any other clients," Rita said.

For a moment, Alan was silent. "It's not going to happen, Sheriff. Talk to me."

"I already did that," Rita said. "I want to talk to Tom this time."

"Sorry, Sheriff." Then Alan hung up.

"Fuck," Rita said, putting away her phone. Then she turned the key in the ignition and headed back to the SCSO.

As she drove, she debated calling Cash. But she

couldn't trust herself to keep apart professional and personal affairs. She decided to wait for him to break the news about his houseguest.

She pulled into the lot outside the SCSO and went inside.

"Howdy, Sheriff," Mary Lou said.

"Hi, Mary Lou," Rita said. "Could you please make an appointment for me to chat with Vic Nelson again?"

"Ten-four," Mary Lou said.

"Thanks." She turned to Jason. "I'm headed to the Bighorn Mining Building to talk to the red-headed man. Can you join me?"

Jason nodded and pushed away from his desk. "Yup."

"And Vee, could you please run Marcus Dwyer?" Rita passed Vee her phone, open to her photo gallery. "Here's the plate number for his black Chrysler minivan."

Vee took the number from Rita's phone, tapping on her keyboard. "On it."

"Thanks," Rita said. "I want to know what he's been up to since algebra class."

Chapter Thirty-Eight

RITA PARKED the SCSO truck beneath the graffitied sign still standing out front the Bighorn Mining Building. As she unbuckled, a call came in from Vee.

"I got an update on Milly," she said. "Her passport was used thirteen hours ago at the Canadian border. Then she took a flight from Calgary to Mexico City."

"Please follow up with Mexican authorities," Rita said.

"On it," Vee said, hanging up.

Rita shared the news with Jason.

"You think Milly killed David and fled?" he asked.

"Maybe," Rita said. "Or was she spooked by the arson and ran off?"

They popped the doors and stepped out into the heat of the day. Walking quickly, they crossed the sandy lot and stepped inside the building's shady interior. Sawdust and drywall dust clung in her throat. Somewhere, a drill echoed.

Rita called out. "Hello?"

No one answered.

"Come on," she said, motioning to Jason as she followed the sound of the drill.

"Know where we can get hardhats?" Jason asked.

Rita glanced at him. "Huh?"

He pointed to a sign on the wall stating hardhats were mandatory on site.

Rita fiddled with her bun. "Shit, I don't know."

Jason frowned. "I feel like I'm cruising down the highway on a motorbike without a helmet."

"Well, thankfully we're not cruising very fast," Rita said, picking her way through the construction materials. "Keep a look out and you'll be all right."

Jason's frown deepened. "It's hard to look out when I have to make sure I don't trip on all these cords." His toe kicked something metal, which rang out as it pinged off the wall. "Or puncture my shoe on a giant nail."

"You're not wrong that this place could use a visit from an Occupational Health and Safety officer."

Jason grunted. "That's what my sister does."

Rita paused to look at him. "What?"

"Occupational Health and Safety," he said. "She's an officer."

Rita knit her brow. "Which sister?"

"Loraleigh."

"She's eleven."

Jason clucked his tongue. "Girl Scouts is riskier than you'd think. When they were earning their seamstress badges, she organized thimbles for the entire troop."

Rita blinked at him. "And that's an eleven-year-old's responsibility?"

"Not entirely. She had Edith Mae's help, of course." He shrugged one shoulder. "Loraleigh had to get the thimbles from somewhere."

Rita shook her head. "Naturally."

They rounded a framed-in wall and came upon a man working the drill. He wore a white Apex branded hard hat, safety glasses, and yellow ear-protectors. When he saw her, he lowered the drill and removed his earmuffs, letting them drop around his neck.

Rita recognized the man's stooped posture, identifying him as someone she'd previously seen on the site. A few yards past him, a similarly dressed man she'd not seen before was measuring some lumber.

"Can I help you, officers?" the man with slumped shoulders asked.

"I'm Sheriff Jonas," Rita said. "This is Deputy Perry. We'd like to ask you a few questions."

He pushed up his hard hat, wiping sweat from his brow. "Okay."

"Your name?" Jason asked, recording the conversation.

"Dwight Wilson."

"We're looking for a red-headed man, Dwight," Rita said. "I saw him here working with you last week."

"That's Brent Hollander," Dwight said. "But he didn't show up for work today, so Moe took the shift."

"I'm Moe," the man measuring lumber said.

"Was it unexpected for Mr. Hollander not to turn up?" Rita asked.

Dwight shrugged his slumped shoulders. "Not really. He'd injured himself the other day and he's been gripin' ever since."

"How did he injure himself?" Jason asked.

"Dunno." Dwight glanced at Moe. "You know, Moe?"

Moe shook his head. "Nope."

"Was his injury severe enough to seek medical attention?"

Dwight shrugged again. "Dunno. Boss didn't think he needed time off."

"Does Brent live in town?" Rita asked.

"Somewhere in Beaumont, I think," Dwight said. "But I don't really know."

"So Brent Hollander is from around these parts?" Jason asked.

Dwight shook his head. "I don't really know."

"Do you know if he has family?" Jason asked. "A partner of any kind?"

"We're just co-workers," Dwight said, "not friends."

Rita tapped her chin. "What *do* you know about Brent Hollander?"

Dwight thought for a moment. "He worked for Apex."

"You mean on the payroll?" Rita asked. "Not a contractor?"

Dwight nodded. "Yeah."

"And the same for you two?" Rita asked, wagging a finger between Dwight and Moe. "You both work for Apex?"

The men nodded.

"On payroll?"

They nodded again.

"Did you always work with Mr. Hollander?" she asked Dwight.

"Met him on this site," he said. "We was assigned this gig together."

"And you didn't find out much about him during your shifts?" Rita asked.

Dwight tapped the ear protection hanging around his neck. "Wear these most of the day."

"Is Mr. Hollander a good employee?" Rita asked.

Dwight gave a half-hearted shrug. "Got his work done. Never gave me no trouble. Not that I'm his foreman or nothin'."

"What do you know about Mr. Hollander dealing drugs?" Rita asked.

The men exchanged a glance.

"Haven't heard nothin' 'bout that," Dwight said.

Moe shook his head. "Me neither." He scratched his jaw. "I don't even know who Brent Hollander is."

"Thank you for your time," Rita said, handing them each one of her cards. "If you hear from Brent, please let me know."

The men took the cards, but Rita suspected they'd be lost to the drifts of debris on the floor before the end of their shift.

Rita and Jason returned to the police truck, where Jason ran Brent Hollander's name through the portable data terminal.

"He's got some minor misdemeanors," Jason said, reading the screen. "Couple DUIs. But nothing related to drugs."

Rita called Ken.

"Hello, Sheriff Jonas."

"Ken," Rita said. "I need to talk to you about one of your employees possibly being related to our case."

"Come on over, I can see you now," Ken said.

"Already on our way," Rita said, hanging up. She glanced at Jason. "He sounds especially cooperative today."

Jason drove them to Apex HQ. They checked in at reception and were directed upstairs to Ken's office.

Rita nudged Jason on the glass staircase. "I know why he was so quick to invite us on over."

Jason leaned in so she could lower her voice.

"He wants to show off how important he is, occupying Boyd's old corner office with a view."

Jason grinned.

They walked to Boyd's old office in question. Rita rapped her knuckles on the door.

Ken cleared his throat and called them in. "Come on in, Sheriff. Deputy."

Rita strolled in and glanced around Boyd's old office. "Nice digs."

"Have a seat," Ken said, settling himself behind his desk.

Rita lowered herself into a chair, scanning the framed posters of Michael Jordan and Shaquille O'Neal that had now replaced the watercolor paintings that had hung during the previous occupant's tenure. "You've put your touch on the place, Ken."

Ken shifted, then folded his large hands on the desktop. "How can I help you, Sheriff Jonas?"

"We're here to ask about your employee, Brent Hollander."

"How's he involved in your case?" Ken asked.

"I'm hoping you can help with that," Rita said. "What do you know about Brent?"

"Let me look at his HR records." Ken tapped on his keyboard. "Looks like he didn't show up for a shift this morning."

"Is that odd?" Rita asked.

Ken shook his head, reading further. "No. There's a note here saying he'd been injured in the workplace. Looks like we're dealing with a shit-ton of paperwork regarding compensation."

"Does it say how he injured himself?"

Ken nodded. "Burned his hand. Blowtorch."

"Is Brent a welder?" Jason asked.

Ken read more of Brent's record. "A carpenter."

"But he was using a blowtorch on-site?" Rita asked.

Ken shrugged. "It's what the report says." He looked

away from the screen to meet Rita's eye. "You thinking he might be involved in the arson?"

"I'm thinking a lot of things these days," Rita said. "Can you tell me anything else about him? Vital statistics? Place of residence?"

"Thirty-two years old," Ken said. "Local hire. Lives in Beaumont. Nothing more here about him."

"Thanks," Rita said. "Can we have his address please?"

Ken jotted it down, then stood and pocketed the slip of paper. "I'm coming, too."

Rita swapped a look with Jason and together, they headed downstairs. Ken followed at their heels, which is when the gunshots rang out.

Chapter Thirty-Nine

RITA PULLED her service weapon and followed the curving wall of the staircase. Jason followed one step behind her, Ken keeping as close as his shadow.

Before they reached the final tread, the glass front doors shattered. The gunfire ceased, and a woman screamed. They crossed the empty lobby and headed outside, crunching over the shards of glass like diamond gravel.

Loud voices shouted. Two security guards near the gate to the parking lot aimed their firearms at someone lying on the ground. Rita broke into a run.

Helen lay spread eagle, her cheek pressed to the pavement and her blonde hair splayed. One of the guards used his boot to pin her hands behind her back. A handgun lay on the ground.

"Back off," Rita said, closing gate distance.

The guards hesitated.

"Now."

The guards swapped a look, then lowered their weapons and stepped back.

Rita pushed past them and crouched next to Helen. "Hang on, Helen, I got this handled."

Helen let out a shuddering sob, while Jason collected the handgun without a word.

Ken stepped up. "Helen Myers, I'm arresting you for—"

"What?" Rita sprang to her feet. "You're doing nothing of the sort."

Ken's eyebrows lowered. "We're on Apex property."

"Back the fuck off, Ken," Rita said. Then she bent over and helped Helen to sit. "I'm gonna get you outta here, Helen. Do you think you can stand?"

Helen took a ragged breath, then nodded. Rita helped her up, then walked her to the truck where Jason had placed the firearm. When he saw them, he opened the rear door and helped Helen inside. Then he offered her water and tissues.

Footsteps approached. Rita turned to see Ken.

He glared at her. "Helen Myers is Apex's prisoner."

"On what grounds?"

His face turned purple. "On the grounds that *this* is Apex grounds." He used a thick digit to point down at the pavement. "Whatever goes on here is Apex's business to conduct."

Rita flared. "Then Apex should conduct its goddamned business on Apex grounds, instead of spreading its shit all over Still." She turned and handed Jason the truck keys. "Take Helen to the SCSO, please, and get her processed into the cells."

Jason nodded and climbed into the driver's seat.

Ken stepped behind the vehicle, blocking Jason from backing up. He crossed his arms. "You're not taking her anywhere."

Rita rolled her eyes. "I'm not interested in your turf war."

He gave her a steely look. "Get her out of the fucking truck."

Rita sensed the guards watching on. She sighed and motioned for Jason to wait. Then she cut her eyes back to Ken. "Let's discuss this somewhere private."

Ken stayed where he was, looking confused.

"Out of respect for Helen," Rita said.

Ken grunted, then loped over to her. "We can go behind the guards' hut." Then he stalked off.

Rita caught up to him. "What the hell's wrong with you, Ken?"

"Wrong with me?" Ken said. "I'm doing my job. What the hell's wrong with her, shooting the shit out of the place?"

"There's nothing wrong with her. She's bereaved."

Ken grumbled. "And that's a license to go bat-shit crazy?"

"She has two dead kids, and as far as she's concerned, Apex killed her daughter. And given the rumors around town, Apex killed her son, too."

"So you think it's okay she goes on a shooting rampage?"

Rita laughed. "Don't tell me you're gonna charge Helen over some shot-up glass doors?"

Ken squared his boxy shoulders. "She could have killed someone."

"Jesus, Ken, she took a .38-caliber Special to the giant Apex logo. She wasn't trying to kill anyone. She was trying to mess up some shit. Fuck you around a bit. Like mother, like child, right? Think about what Arnold was up to in his last living days."

Ken blinked back at her.

Rita let out a sigh. "Look, Helen needs help, and I'm gonna make sure she gets it. If you agree not to press charges against her, I'll drop the charges I have against you … for that *rendezvous* out at the reservoir."

Ken's eyes stopped blinking and stared at her. "You'll do that?"

Rita took out her phone and called Hunter Green.

Hunter sounded mid-sigh as he answered. "What is it now, Sheriff Jonas?"

Rita put the phone on speaker. "Ken Saunders is here with me." She met Ken's eye. "In the spirit of cooperation, what would it take for me to drop the charges against him?"

For a moment, Hunter was quiet. Then he said, "Say the word, Rita."

She glanced at Ken. He gave her a slight smile and a nod.

"Do it," she said to Hunter. Then she disconnected the call and put away her phone, looking Ken in the eye. "If you fuck me over and go after Helen, I'm reinstating these charges. And then I'll be a rabid dog, and I don't let go until there's no meat on the bone. Got it?"

Ken nodded.

"Good," Rita said. "Now go tell your guys that it's your idea Helen gets some professional help. And after we get Helen sorted out, we'll go pay a visit to Brent Holland."

"Deal," Ken said, shoving past her. He stalked past the guards' hut and strode out to the parking lot. He waved at Jason and a minute later, the police truck pulled out.

Then he punched a fob, and a vehicle beeped in the parking lot. "Let's go," he said. "We'll take the Audi."

Rita followed him across the lot. "Thanks."

Ken grunted as he opened the driver's side door. "I suppose I should be thanking you."

Rita's eyebrows arched. "Wow, that *is* cooperative."

Chapter Forty

As KEN DROVE AWAY from Apex, Rita texted Jason: *How is Helen?*

Jason texted back. *Calmer. ML made her lemonade with chamomile and ginger.*

Rita's shoulders relaxed. *Where is she?*

ML is taking her for psych eval.

Good to hear, Rita texted. *Anything else to report?*

Courier just left with David Clark's ledgers. I told Casper PD ETA this afternoon

Thx, Rita texted. Then another: *Vic?*

Coming in this afternoon

Please take the meeting if I'm not back, Rita typed.

Jason gave her message a thumbs up, and Rita put away her phone.

Ken glanced at her. "How's Helen Myers doing?"

Rita smiled. "Getting the care she needs, thanks. We can head to Beaumont now."

Ken dutifully drove the freeway speed limit, then took the off-ramp by a lone aspen among the cottonwoods, cutting through Beaumont's grid of streets. He flicked the turn signal and rounded a corner.

"This is it: Churchill Street." He cocked his head to peer through the side window of the Audi. "We're looking for 1363."

"I know this street," Rita said. "The owners of the Rawhide Revue live here."

The two-story brick houses running down the north side of the street were nearly identical to the ones on the south, as if they were reflections of one another.

As they rolled past Carly and Jeff's place, Rita took a look at the property. Jeff's Jeep wasn't in the driveway. He must no longer be on sick leave.

Ken pulled up to the curb in front of Brent Hollander's address. Parked in the driveway was a black pickup, and behind it an old white van sat on blocks.

Rita got out of Ken's Audi and walked to the back of the carport. She studied the van. "Give it a lick of fresh paint and a decal, and it could pass for an Apex-issued vehicle."

Ken grunted.

Rita took photos of the plate and VIN number, as well as other views of the truck. Then she texted Vee and asked her to run the vehicle.

Ken led the way to the front door and knocked. When no one answered, he knocked a second time.

Next door, a screen door banged open and a woman's voice said, "It's about time you lot showed up."

Rita looked over her shoulder. "Hello. Can we help you?"

The woman put her hands on her hips. "Could have used your help last night — when my fucking peace was disturbed."

"What happened?" Rita asked.

The woman threw up her hands. "Jesus Christ, I told y'all on the phone already."

"Please tell us again," Rita said.

"Bunch of screaming and yelling and hollering."

"Is Mr. Hollander a noisy neighbor?" Rita asked.

The woman shrugged. "Sure, when he's drinking with his friends. But I didn't see no friends last night. Lights weren't even on."

Ken looked at Rita. "Could have been game night. Or MMA."

The neighbor scrunched up her face. "What's that?"

Ken craned his muscled neck and raised his voice. "I said, it sounds like you might have overheard mixed martial arts."

"It sounded like someone was getting fucking murdered, that's what."

"Maybe someone sustained an injury," Ken offered.

The woman scowled. "It went on for at least fifteen minutes. I couldn't fucking sleep."

"What time did you call?"

The woman folded her arms across her chest. "Around midnight."

Rita looked back at the house. "Shit."

"You think we're dealing with another crime scene?" Ken asked.

She pointed to a brownish smear on the door. Ken's eyes widened and he leaned in to look closer, while Rita pulled out her phone and called Beaumont PD.

The dispatcher patched her through to an officer. "Yeah, we got a call and went out last night. But it was just some guy with his TV on too loud. Officers told him to keep it down."

Rita continued to stare at the door. "Well, I'm looking at a blood smear right now."

"Forensics will determine that — *if* we're actually dealing with a crime scene," the officer said.

"Call me suspicious," Rita said, "but I've got a headless corpse back at Still. Are you sure you don't want to send someone back out here to double check?"

A moment of silence ensued. "We're sending a car," the officer said. "Thanks."

Rita put away her phone and looked at Ken. "They're sending someone." Then she turned and waved at the neighbor, who was still glowering at them from her front stoop. "Hey! Beaumont PD is sending someone."

The woman mumbled something unintelligible, then retreated inside, the screen door banging behind her.

"You really think there's a headless body in there?" Ken asked, his voice lowered even though the neighbor had left. His face was as white as a snowcap.

Rita leaned against the low stone wall running along the side of the driveway. "Dunno, but there was one at the last place. And you should thank your lucky stars you didn't have to see it." Rita's phone rang and she answered it. "Hi, Vee."

"Hi, Sheriff. I'm calling to confirm that the white van is registered to Brent Hollander. He has a pickup truck registered as well and no other current vehicles. However, there was one other white van formerly registered to him."

"And now?" Rita asked.

"Insurance lapsed four months ago," Vee said. "No indication if it simply expired, or there was a vehicle transfer."

"Thanks," Rita said. "Good work."

As Rita pocketed her phone, a Beaumont patrol car pulled into the driveway. Two officers got out, one male and one female, both young.

"Hi," Rita said, "I'm Sheriff Jonas. This is Ken Saunders from Apex. Were you the officers that came out last night?"

The officers shook their heads.

"That was Night Watch," Officer Bergstrom said.

The pair walked to the door and knocked. When there was no answer, they called out their names and declared they were going to enter.

"Would you like me to assist?" Rita asked.

"It's all right," Officer Cortez said. "We've got it."

They pulled their weapons and tested the doorknob. It was unlocked. Bergstrom and Cortez prepared themselves, then entered the house.

Outside, Rita paced while Ken stood like a statue, hands folded, his facial expression hidden behind his mirrored sunglasses.

A few seconds later, the Beaumont officers barreled out of the house. Cortez hit the ground vomiting, while Bergstrom pulled her radio. But all she could say before retching was, "We got a body."

Chapter Forty-One

RITA ZIPPED up her Tyvek suit and entered the house.

She followed the lights down the hall to the master bedroom. A headless corpse sat tied to a kitchen chair. Judging by the red-haired head on the pillow, the body belonged to Brent Hollander. His right wrist was secured with an athletic sock (likely one of his own) to the chair's armrest. All four fingers lay on the carpet.

Rita withdrew, walking backwards out of the room, then retraced her steps down the hallway. Outside, she stripped off her suit and put it in the designated bin.

Also in Tyvek, Tilda approached. "What did we do to deserve the honor of you pitching in around here?"

Rita blew out a breath. "I called in the crime scene."

Tilda gave her a consoling smile. "Lucky you."

Rita sighed again. "And I only wanted to talk to him."

"This seems a little different than the last one, huh?" Tilda said.

"Is it?" Rita asked. "I mostly noticed the common thread of decapitation."

"Well, this guy was tortured," Tilda said. "Lost one finger at a time."

Rita rubbed her hands on her face. "Machete?"

Tilda gave a grim shake of her head. "We found a bloody hatchet under the bed. Though it's not the best tool for removing a finger at a time."

Rita grimaced. "Sounds like a lot of blood again."

"Not really," Tilda said, shrugging. "Not nearly as much blood spatter at this scene. It'll take further investigation to determine if the victim was dead before beheading, but I have my suspicions."

"Well, whichever way it plays out, please send me a copy of all the results."

"Of course," Tilda said. "Wouldn't do it any other way."

Rita bade Tilda goodbye, then pulled out her phone and called Jason.

"We found Brent Hollander," she said. "Deceased. And —" She broke off as bile rose in the back of her throat.

"Beheaded?" Jason asked, sounding as sick as Rita felt.

"Uh-huh," Rita said. "I want you to warn Peter and Stu and Vic when he comes in. Call Walter as well. He's in Cheyenne with Adrian."

"Right away," Jason said, then hung up.

As Rita put away her phone, Officer Bergstrom approached, looking less green than before.

"Officer Dawson, who was on shift last night, is at the station now if you'd like to talk to him, Sheriff Jonas."

Rita thanked her and walked over to Ken, who was sitting on the stone wall beside the driveway.

"Can you drop me off at Beaumont PD?"

"I'm not sure I can do that," Ken said.

Rita threw up her hands with impatience. "Goddammit Ken, these Apex policies—"

"That's not what I mean," Ken said. "I mean, I'm not sure I can drive." He handed her his fob.

"Okay," she said. "But … you didn't actually go in the house, did you?"

Ken wiped a hand across his forehead. "Hell, no. Cortex told me everything I need to know."

"Okay," Rita said again, "let's get out of here."

She got in the Audi and started the engine. Ken slid into the passenger seat and rolled down the window. As she drove to the station, Ken hung his head outside, then said he'd wait for her outside.

Rita left Ken in the shade of a juniper and went inside the station, where she was escorted to a conference room, where she met Officer Dawson and his sergeant. The sergeant looked like he'd taken a stripe off Dawson.

Rita extended her hand to both men. "Sheriff Jonas, SCSO," she said. "I appreciate you taking the time to tell me about last night's call out to Churchill Street."

Officer Dawson nodded. "You're welcome, Sheriff Jonas." He consulted his notes. "We got off the call just after midnight. Noise complaint from the neighbor, so we checked out the address. Rolled past about twelve-thirty."

"Yourself and—?" Rita asked.

"Officer Knoll, who's on leave today," the sergeant said.

"When we arrived at the house, it was dark. But as soon as we approached the door, we could hear the noise the neighbor complained about. The TV was blaring. Knoll recognized the movie. It was a horror flick."

"Which one?" Rita asked.

"The one with the tools," Dawson said.

"What tools?" the sergeant asked, furrowing his brow.

"You know," Dawson said, "construction tools."

"Is it the one with the drill?" Rita asked. "Or the saw?"

"The one with the drain snake," Dawson said. "Anyway, Knoll knocked, and the homeowner answered."

"He gave you his name?" Rita asked.

Officer Dawson consulted his notes. "Identified himself as Brent Hollander."

"Did he show you his ID?"

A micro-expression flickered across the sergeant's face.

Dawson folded his arms. "We never asked him for it. Figured we were dealing with a noise complaint."

"Fair enough," Rita said. "Can you describe the man who answered the door?"

"White, about five ten, average build."

"What color was his hair?"

"Couldn't tell you. He was wearing a baseball cap."

"A ballcap?" Rita said. "Did he have stubble?"

"Dunno." Dawson shifted. "It was dark."

"How dark?" Rita asked. "There are streetlights on that road."

"Porch light was burnt out, and the guy was backlit by the TV."

"It's a big TV," Rita agreed, recalling the contents of Brent's living room, which amounted to a threadbare futon and a giant flat-screen TV. "So then what?"

Officer Dawson consulted his notes, then closed the folder. "He apologized and went and turned down the volume."

"And nothing else seemed amiss?"

Dawson shook his head.

"And you didn't go in?" Rita asked.

Another micro-expression flickered across the sergeant's face.

Dawson set his jaw. "We didn't have a reason to."

"Thank you," Rita said. "I don't have any other questions."

She excused herself from the interview room and paused in the hallway to text Tilda.

Could you please confirm porch light at the crime scene isn't working?

Then she put her phone away and headed outside. Ken waited in the grass beneath the juniper, his forehead resting on his drawn-up knees.

"Thanks for waiting, Ken," Rita said, approaching.

"No problem," Ken said, pushing up from the ground. "Fresh air did me good."

"Can I ask another favor?" Rita asked. "Can you stop by the Rawhide Revue on our way back to Still?"

"Sure thing," Ken said. "Except…"

"You need me to drive?"

Chapter Forty-Two

RITA PARKED Ken's Audi outside the Rawhide Review and glanced around the lot.

"Don't see Jeff's Jeep here," Rita said. "But it wasn't at his house on Churchill Street either."

Rita unbuckled and got out of the Audi. She walked up to the front door of the strip club, where Ollie stood post.

"Hi Ollie," Rita said. "I'm looking for Jeff."

"He ain't here."

"I figured," she said. "Do you know where he is?"

Ollie curled his lip. "His bitch took off, and he's trying to track her down."

"So not recovering from a black eye anymore," Rita said.

Ollie blinked at her. "Huh?"

"Never mind," Rita handed Ollie a card. "Please have Jeff give me a call when he's back."

Ollie grunted and dropped Rita's card, allowing it to flutter to the ground.

Rita gave him a tight smile. "I'll take that as a yes."

She walked back to the Audi and pulled out of the

parking lot, Ken still slightly green and resting his head out the open window.

As they neared Still, they came upon a collision on the freeway. A courier van lay on its side, the driver's side smashed in. Vee directed traffic, rerouting it into the other lanes. Rita pulled over and parked Ken's Audi.

"I'm getting out here, Ken," she said. "I can get a lift back with my people. Are you okay to drive?"

Ken gave her a feeble nod and got out of the passenger seat. As he walked around to the driver's side, Rita handed him the fob.

"Thanks, Ken." Then she made her way over to Jason, who stooped over the courier driver, who sat shaking on the ground.

Jason noticed Rita approaching and said something to the courier driver. Then he patted his shoulder and stepped away to meet Rita.

"What happened here?" she asked.

"Driver of the courier truck got forced into median," Jason said. "Van flipped and rolled."

"Shit," Rita said. "He the only passenger?"

Jason confirmed with a nod and motioned her to follow him to the van. The back doors of the vehicle stood open. Inside, packages and parcels lay everywhere.

"Perpetrators made the driver open the back at gunpoint." Jason's voice held an edge. "And guess what was taken?"

Rita set her jaw. "I hate guessing. But I have a feeling this was the courier transporting David Clark's files to Casper."

Jason gave a grim nod. "Yep. And now they're all gone."

Rita kicked the van's tire. "Fuck." Then she blew out a breath, steadying her nerves. "I'll talk to the driver now."

They walked back to the shoulder where he sat, huddled in a blanket even though the day was warm.

Rita dropped to her haunches beside him. "Hi, I'm Sheriff Jonas. I'd like to ask you about what happened."

Nodding, the driver swallowed back tears. Some blood rimmed one of his nostrils, as well as matted the hair above his left temple.

"You were injured in the crash," Rita said, more of a statement than a question.

The driver nodded. "Hit my head."

"EMTs are on their way," Jason said.

"What do you remember?" Rita asked, touching his shoulder. "Take your time."

The courier took a shuddering breath. "I was forced off the road by another vehicle. I already told Officer Perry I didn't catch the license plate. All I remember is it was black. A van or a truck."

"Did you see the driver?"

"Only that there were two of them. They both wore masks."

"Men?"

"Yes."

"Armed?"

The courier let out a sob. He buried his hands in his face and nodded.

"What did they do?" Rita asked. She touched the man's arm. "I know it's hard to go over this."

The driver let out a shuddering breath. "They dragged me out at gunpoint. Held the gun to my head and made me unlock the back."

"And then what?" Rita asked.

The driver started to tremble. "They made me lay in the dirt, made me put my face in it. I heard them rummaging around in the back. They took some packages and left." The blanket slipped from the driver's shoulders as he trembled more vigorously; Jason pulled the blanket back onto his shoulders and rubbed his back.

"I thought I was going to die," he said.

"I know," Rita said, meeting his eyes and giving him a smile. "And now you are safe." A siren drew near. "Ambulance will be here any minute." Then she slipped her card into the breast pocket of his uniform. "Please call if you remember anything else."

The driver nodded. "I need to call my boss," he said. "Need to tell him what happened."

"Leave that to us," Rita said, pushing back up to standing. "We'll take care of it while you go with the EMTs, okay?"

The courier nodded and Rita stepped away. Jason joined her.

"You'd make a good mom, Sheriff."

"Be professional, Jason," Rita said. "I make a good sheriff, okay? I'm sheriffing."

Jason cleared his throat. "I'm good at spotting good moms because I don't have a particularly good one. I just think you should know my opinion is not unfounded." Then he pulled out his phone and searched for a number. "Hello, Ace Delivery?"

While Jason spoke to the courier company, Rita called Randy at Bighorn. "I've got a courier van that needs to be towed to Casper PD." She gave Randy the location and a thank you, then hung up.

Then she called Thomas Gabriel's lawyer, Alan Crawford.

"Good day, Sheriff Jonas."

"How did you find out we were moving the files?" Rita asked, skipping the salutations. "Is Marcus Dwyer following me?"

Alan laughed. "I think you're jumping to conclusions about why Marcus is in town, Sheriff."

"So you *do* know Marcus is in my neighborhood," Rita said. "In that case, why don't you tell me why he's really here? It's not to have a meeting at The Rancher's Pantry, but to keep tabs on what I'm up to, isn't it? Well, fuck you. I'm going to rip the cover off Angel Holdings and nail Thomas Gabriel to the cross."

"Don't flatter yourself, Sheriff. Marcus isn't in Still to watch over you. He couldn't care less what you're up to. He's simply catching up with an old friend."

Rita scoffed. "By old friend, you mean Cash."

"Obviously."

"Somehow, I doubt any friend of Tom's is a friend of Cash's by default. Tom told me that Cash doesn't even visit him anymore."

"Tom tends to exaggerate," Alan said.

"Exaggeration or not, tell him it's a two-way street," Rita said. "Why doesn't he send Cash a letter?"

"Don't hold your breath waiting for that to happen," Alan said. "Besides, you give me too much credit. I can't change Tom's mind."

"You have some very persuasive tactics," Rita said. "Maybe you should try them on your client."

Chapter Forty-Three

RITA DROPPED into the passenger seat of the cruiser, while Vee took a seat in the back. As Jason headed for the office, Rita pulled out her phone and dialed Casper Forensics.

"Rita," Tilda answered. "I've got some news for you."

"Me too," Rita said. "I'll go first. Randy's picked up a courier van and is delivering it to Casper PD. Should be there within the hour. Any DNA from the van would be helpful."

"Sounds good," Tilda said.

"What have you got for me?"

"Brent Hollander killed himself," Tilda said.

"What?" Rita said. "But he was decapitated."

Jason glanced at her.

"Posthumously like I thought," Tilda said. "Which is why there wasn't a crap-ton of blood everywhere."

"So how'd Brent do it?" Rita asked.

"We found a pocketknife embedded in his heart. It's possible that when the killer was interrupted, Hollander grabbed the knife and killed himself."

"Shit," Rita said, her stomach turning. "Was it the same knife used to remove his fingers?"

"When the killer went to the door, Hollander must have got a hold of it."

"And self-inflicted the wound?"

"With his left hand," Tilda confirmed. "The entry point came from below. If whoever took his head off had done it, he would have had to have been kneeling. And all other injuries to the deceased came from an overhead angle. But Bruce is gonna be the one who will pin down those details."

"Right," Rita said. "It's a busy week at the morgue."

"I'll let you know as soon as we find more," Tilda said.

Rita disconnected and put away her phone.

Jason glanced at her again. "What'd Tilda have to say?"

"That Brent Hollander killed himself," Rita said. "Knife wound to the heart."

"Jesus," Vee said from the backseat.

Jason frowned, pulling into the lot behind the SCSO. "So why behead the body?"

"I have the same question," Rita said, getting out of the cruiser. "Maybe to give the impression it was the same killer?"

"A copycat?" Jason said. He pulled open the back door, and they filed inside. "If that's the case, the killer must have had some inside knowledge about David's death."

"A fact which would definitely connect the two murders," Rita said, walking into the bullpen.

Mary Lou paused typing as they entered.

"But are the murders connected?" Vee asked, taking a seat at her desk. "Brent Hollander was a blue-collar worker twenty years younger than David Clark, a white-collar professional who never left his house. What did they have in common?"

"Thomas Gabriel," Rita said.

"And the lack of a head," Jason said, sitting at his desk.

"Brent Hollander also lost some fingers along the way," Rita said.

Mary Lou winced.

"Damn," Jason said. "And the poor guy's hand was already burned."

"Victim had a burned hand?" Vee asked. "Why's that matter?"

"Documented as a workplace injury," Rita said. "But it could have happened setting fire to the van. It's also possible that Hollander was one of the shooters in the Apex van. We found a similar vehicle at his property. I've tried to get a hold of Jeff Jeffries at the Rawhide Revue. Carly confirmed that Jeff sold the van to Hollander. So why'd he lie about selling it to John Doe?"

"'Cause Jeff Jeffries ain't straight up about nothin'," Mary Lou said.

"What've you two got for me?" Rita asked, glancing between Jason and Vee. "Deputy?"

"I spoke to Vic and his mother, Francine," Jason said. "Vic was hired to pick up the financial records for The Rancher's Pantry and the Still Haven Inn, then deliver them to David Clark's address. He did that once a week on Saturday mornings."

"Every Saturday?" Rita said. "So much for those two saying they didn't know David Clark."

"Apparently David never talked to Vic. Or left out empties. Vic says David Clark just answered the door, collected the records, and closed it again."

"Once again proving the rule that David Clark kept to himself," Rita said.

"I talked to Mexico City police," Vee said. "Nothing yet on Milly's whereabouts. I also talked to Moses Grant about Angel Holdings Ltd. But he didn't have anything to offer, aside from saying Angel Holdings was interested in buying into the project, but at the moment the project's on hold."

"Good work, Vee," Rita said.

"I also have some information on Marcus Dwyer," Vee said. "He lives in Casper and hangs out his shingle as a private security professional. But he mostly works for Gabriel's lawyer, Alan Crawford."

"Thanks. Marcus Dwyer is hanging around town," Rita said, "and he doesn't play nice. So keep an eye out." Then she looked at Mary Lou. "Any news on Helen?"

"Doctors have moved her to Casper. They put her under a mental health watch."

Rita nodded with understanding. "She's committed."

"For the time being."

"Thanks, everyone. See you back here tomorrow."

Rita swiped open her phone and texted Carly: *How are you doing?*

Carly replied immediately: *A little stir crazy. Could use a change of scenery*

Rita smiled to herself. *That's an encouraging sign. Want to go out for food?*

Carly sent a thumbs up.

I'll pick you up in an hour, Rita texted. Then she headed to Otto's, where she showered and changed into jeans and a black t-shirt. Then she drove back into town, to the Bighorn Bean parking lot. She texted Carly when she arrived.

Carly came downstairs, her bruises more or less obscured by a thick layer of make-up.

Rita smiled. "You look great."

Carly scoffed. "You don't need to say that. I know what I look like."

"Then you know it's a big improvement," Rita said.

As she drove them across town to The Shaft, they chatted about Rita's apartment (the dryer had indeed burned the bedsheets; most of the plants had moved to sunnier perches, if that was all right with Rita; and the water pressure was surprisingly good for a building its age).

Pulling open the door to the restaurant, the rich aroma of roast beef made Rita salivate. They entered and scanned the room for a vacant table.

Above the din of banter and laughter, one voice called out above the others: "Hey, Dallas!"

A barrel-chested man in checked shirt approached. "Ain't seen your tits out at the Revue lately."

Carly ignored him while Rita cut him a look.

Chester laughed. "What, you friends with the sheriff now, Dallas? You got a new line o' work?"

"Buzz off," Carly said, ducking into a booth. "That's not my name."

"Sure it is, hot stuff, I'd know you anywhere." He let out a bark of laughter. "Even with your clothes on!"

Rita slid into the booth next to Carly. She glared at Chester. "Shove off, Chester."

"Now I get it, Sheriff." Chester leaned over the table. "You're the one in the new line of work, ain't ya, not Dallas." He hooked his fingers through his belt loops and rocked back on his heels. "Your uniform got them tear-away seams?"

Rita rolled her eyes and looked at Carly. "You wanna get out of here?"

Carly nodded.

"Okay, you can wait in the car while I order the food." Rita have her the keys. "I'll get you a burger."

"You can't leave yet," Chester said. He raised his arms and clapped his hands twice. The restaurant fell silent. "Dallas is gonna give us a little show, ain't she?"

A scattering of patrons hollered, and Chester winked at Carly. "It's about time Dallas traded that puny little pole up in Beaumont for Still's famous *shaft*."

Rita slammed her fist on the tabletop. "She said that's not her name."

Chester frowned at Rita. "Well, she's got it tattooed on her ass!"

"Hey!" Ruby Joe shouted from the back of the restaurant. "Knock it off over there."

Carly slid out of the booth and squeezed past them, ducking out of the restaurant.

Rita wagged a finger in front of Chester's nose. "Stop talking about your shaft, Chester, or I'll write you a ticket for public indecency faster than Destiny can swing around a pole."

Chester blinked at her. "Destiny? Who the fuck is Destiny?"

"A future date," Rita said.

Chester blinked again. "I'm married, Sheriff."

"You don't say," Rita said, turning on her heel. "As such, you should make better choices." She crossed to the bar and ordered two burgers from Ruby Joe.

"You're supposed to eat less o' these things, Sheriff," Ruby Joe said. "Not double down on 'em."

"You'll be glad to know the beef one's not for me," Rita said.

Ruby Joe's eye sparkled. "Cash?"

"Sure," Rita said, digging in her pocket. She fished out a twenty and some loose ones and paid for the burgers.

"I meant Cash Gabriel," Ruby Joe said, depositing Rita's money in the cash register. "You got a date?"

"Already had one of those in Casper the other night," Rita said. "And that was enough for the month. Maybe the whole year. Tonight I'm staying in with a friend."

"Well, enjoy," Ruby Joe said with a smile. "Order'll be up in ten minutes."

"Thanks. And sorry about the noise a few minutes ago. I was putting Chester in his place."

Ruby Joe laughed. "Sounds about right. That guy needs to be put in his place. I'm glad it was you raising a ruckus, Sheriff."

Rita walked back to the vestibule and scrolled through her phone. She had two unread texts from Cash.

"Speak of the devil," she said to herself. She swiped open the messages: *Saw Otto today.*

The second one had come in ten minutes after the first, likely prompted by her lack of response: *Chat to you later.*

She sent back a thumbs up, then surfed the internet while she waited for their food. Her surfing led her to websites for local funeral parlors.

She was reading an information package about cremation when she was delivered a warm paper bag. She thanked the server and headed out to the parking lot.

"Smells great," Carly said, taking the bag to place on her lap.

"I've lived off those burgers for entire weeks," Rita said, driving them back to her apartment.

They walked up the back steps, Carly carrying the bag. At first, she headed straight to the door, familiar with the place. Then she paused and stepped back, giving Rita a half-smile.

"After you," she said.

Rita winked, unlocking and opening the door of the apartment. She entered, noting a slight change in the apartment's aroma. It still smelled familiar, like home — only lighter and fresher.

Carly followed her inside as Rita pried off her shoes and tucked them against the wall. The usual drifts of dust have been swept up along with all the other dirt that usually tracked in after a long shift.

"I'll get us some drinks if you set the table," Carly said. "Skyler dropped off some bottled sodas earlier."

"Skyler's the best," Rita said, padding into the kitchen. "But let's eat in the living room. I miss it more than my dining room table."

"It's a nice table," Carly said, referring to a white desk painted with a giant sunflower.

"It came with the place," Rita said.

She opened a cupboard to get plates. Carly had stacked them in tidy pillars and aligned the mug handles in one direction. Rita smiled to herself and closed the cabinet door, then grabbed the ketchup from the fridge and the paper towels from the counter.

In the living room as well, Carly had applied her organizational magic. The drapes were tied back, framed photographs arranged for better viewing, and the book spines aligned according to color and size. The room seemed brighter too, thanks to a repositioned mirror that caught the window's light.

Rita sat on the couch as Carly tore open the paper bag and removed two paper cartons, both marked with Sharpie ink.

"This one's mine," she said, holding up the one marked 'HB.' She handed the box marked 'PB' to Rita. "What'd you get? Peanut butter chicken?"

"The Portobello mushroom burger," Rita said. "I haven't tried it before, but my deputy inspired me. Plus, I didn't want to deal with any more comments from Ruby Joe about my cholesterol."

Carly looked perplexed. "I wouldn't think you have a problem with cholesterol."

"Me neither," Rita said. "But I figure I must since she's informed me more than once that I eat a concerning amount of burgers." She took a bite.

Carly swallowed a bite of her own hamburger. "How is it?"

"Delicious," Rita said through her mouthful. She cleared her mouth with a swallow of soda. "Do you know there are people who make a good living picking mushrooms?"

"What do you mean?" Carly asked. "Picking them out in the woods?"

Rita nodded, taking another bite. "Yup."

Carly puckered her brow. "Like a pig, snuffing out truffles?"

"I think they use different methods of deduction," Rita said. "But yeah, that kind of thing. Anyway, you can make a decent living."

Carly raised an eyebrow. "Oh, yeah?"

Rita swallowed another bite. "Pickers around here sell to gourmet restaurants."

Carly nodded slowly. "That makes sense."

Rita swallowed another bite. "Have you ever thought of another line of work?"

Carly picked at her food for a moment. "It's true I've been thinking about kicking off the stilettos. Marriage aside, I've had it with bosses like Jeff." She snorted. "And patrons like Chester. I was thinking I might go to California. I've always wanted to go there."

"I hear Carlsbad is nice," Rita said. "What are you going to do in California?"

Carly shrugged. "Something in the tourist industry, I guess. Maybe serving. Or hosting."

"Have you heard of set dec?"

Carly shook her head. "I haven't been around boats."

"It means set decoration. There are these people who stage the sets for movie productions and TV shows."

Carly's eyes sparkled. "I never thought of doin' nothing like that."

"Never say never," Rita said. "I like what you did around here."

Carly blushed. "I was hoping you would."

"Of course," Rita said. "Last time we talked, I remember saying you should call me" — she waggled her finger around the room — "to do something about this situation."

Carly laughed.

Rita pointed to a framed photo of herself that used to sit on the bookshelf, now displayed on the wall. "Why'd you hang that there?"

Carly turned to look. "Oh, the photo of the woman?" She shrugged. "I liked the way she was smiling, with her eyes squeezed shut like that — I'm sure she's laughing." Carly turned back to Rita, wearing a sad smile of her own. "I'd like to feel that happy one day."

Rita smiled. "It'll happen. I know that doesn't mean much coming from a stranger, but I believe in you."

Saying nothing, Carly nodded and took another bite.

"That's me," Rita said. "The woman in the photo."

Carly's brow puckered. "Really? I'm sorry, I didn't recognize you."

"It's okay," Rita said, taking another bite of burger. "I used to wear my hair a lot longer." She swallowed. "And not talk while I was eating. But New York changed everything."

Carly laughed again, and Rita's heart warmed. She was glad to take Carly's mind off of her worries. At least for a little while.

"What made you so happy?" Carly asked. "When that photo was taken?"

"My friend had put an ice cube down my back. I'm not sure I *was* laughing. I was probably fucking mad. But my friends thought it was so funny, so they decided to further embarrass me by memorializing the moment with a framed five by seven." She smiled. "Cops are like that. I imagine we bond different than dancers do."

Carly nodded and Rita could tell there were dancers' stories to be told. Or not be told, as the case may be.

"Thanks for hanging it up," Rita said. "I'd forgotten about that photo, and it's nice to remember those times. That friend who put the ice cube down my back. She was a good pal."

Carly looked sad again. "You're not pals anymore?"

Rita shrugged. "It's not so much that. We were together at the Academy. But then she ended up going down to Florida, and we lost touch after that. You meet a lot of people in my business."

"Mine too."

"Which is kind of wild," Rita said, "because sometimes you gotta rely on these folks to save your life. And yet you might never see them again after your next shift."

Carly nodded. "I know."

"It's odd to think our salvation can be in the hands of strangers. And yet our loved ones can hurt us the most."

"True," Carly said, picking some lettuce from between her teeth.

"What's happened between you and Jeff?"

"He's always stressed about the business. Fewer and fewer customers, money gettin' tighter all the time. He relies on the dancers' tips to keep the lights on. And naturally those are gettin' fewer all the time."

Rita took another sip of soda. "So he made you his punching bag."

Carly's eyes shifted.

"Not much of a problem-solving tactic," Rita said.

Carly gave a bitter laugh. "Lotsa guys do worse."

Rita pulled a face. "Do you know someone named Brent Hollander?"

"Asshole lived down the street from me and Jeff."

"He was a bad neighbor?"

"More like he was a bad customer. He came into the Revue a few times. Every time, he harassed the girls real awful."

"Every time? Didn't Ollie throw him out?"

"Nope."

"Why not?"

"Because Jeff seemed to like him."

"Why do you think that was?"

"Dunno."

"Did Jeff ever sell him a vehicle?"

Carly laughed. "Yeah. That dumb eyesore of a party van that Jeff parked out back of the Revue."

Rita took a bite. "The umber one?"

"Umber?"

"Brown."

Carly nodded toward one of Rita's throw cushions. "It was kinda that color."

"Do you remember when that was?"

Carly thought for a moment. "Sorry, I don't. It was a few months ago."

"Ever notice anything unusual taking place at Brent's house?"

Again, Carly thought for a moment. Then she shook

her head. "He had a few parties there." She shrugged. "But I never went."

"His neighbor mentioned his place could be noisy when his friends were around."

"Sure," Carly said. "But he never had much of a turnout. The scene at his place never compared to Jeff's."

"How so?"

"Brent's one of those fly-by-night types. He's only in town until he shits the bed, and then he'll be gone for good. But Jeff's a fixture, you know? A pillar in the industry."

"I suppose so," Rita said, compelled to agree that Jeff was rigid and had rocks in his head, if that's what Carly meant by being a pillar. Instead, she thanked Carly for telling her about Brent.

"Thanks for telling me about Brent. If you remember anything else about him, please let me know."

Carly nodded. "Okay."

Rita wiped her hands dry on a sheet of paper towel, then crumpled it and dropped it on the plate. "That was delicious. Do you think I ruined my mushroom burger with ketchup?"

"If you ruined your burger with ketchup," Carly said, "I obliterated mine with aioli. You're like this guy I sat next to in seventh grade. Tim Grimsby ate ketchup on everything."

Thoughtful, Rita crinkled her nose. "I don't actually like ketchup that much. I've just had an odd craving for it lately. How was yours?"

Carly blotted her mouth. "A hell of a lot better than Chicken Bun on the Run. I've eaten an awful lot of that lately."

"No doubt," Rita said. "I hope you ate up the salad in the fridge?"

"I did," Carly said. "And appreciated it."

"I have a friend who leaves a lot of salad in the fridge."

"That's nice."

Rita shrugged. "Yeah, well, it keeps him in good shape. I can't help it if I'm addicted to muffins."

Carly laughed. "I think I am too, now. I dream about muffins."

"Me too," Rita said. "Every morning at four a.m. when the ovens fire up."

Carly laughed again. "Thanks for supper. You helped me forget my troubles for a while."

"You're welcome," Rita said. "And you helped me forget mine for a while. I don't often have dinner guests in my place, so I really enjoyed it." Then she laughed. "Even if *I* was the guest."

Carly got up, wiping her hands on a paper towel. "Then I'll walk you to your own front door."

Rita unfolded herself from the couch and they took their dishes and trash to the kitchen.

"I'll wash up," Carly said.

"Thanks," Rita said, returning to the foyer. She pulled on her shoes. "Whatever you get up to, Carly — muffin baker, mushroom picker, interior decorator — you'll do great."

"Thanks, Rita."

Then Rita let herself out the door, closing it behind her.

She drove toward Otto's, taking a detour past Cash's place. Marcus's black minivan parked in the driveway. She didn't see Cash's pickup.

She circled around his block, scanning for his vehicle. When she didn't see it, she pulled into his driveway and parked next to Marcus's black minivan. She got out and went and knocked on the front door.

It opened. The man who'd ridden shotgun to The Rancher's Pantry and who'd driven to the warehouse stood facing her.

"Your sidekick here?" Rita asked.

He rolled his shoulders in his denim jacket. "I don't got to tell you nothing, copper."

"So he's not here," Rita said. "Where is he?"

The man crossed his arms. "Wouldn't tell you if I knew."

"Well, do you know when he'll be back?"

He glowered at her. "I ain't his babysitter."

"But you're his partner, yeah?"

The man grunted.

"Can you take a message?"

He growled and slammed the door.

"Well, it was worth a try." She turned on her heel and headed back down the stoop. She got back behind the wheel and drove to Otto's house.

And let out a sigh when she saw Cash's truck in the driveway. She got out and walked up to him, sitting on the front porch.

"What are you doing?" she asked.

"Looking at the stars."

Rita sat down on the step next to him. "Except the stars aren't out yet."

"They will be soon," Cash said.

Rita leaned back and looked up. "It's a beautiful sky."

"Well worth the wait tonight."

"Stars are always worth waiting for," Rita said.

"I meant it's worth waiting for you."

Rita fell silent, enjoying the scent of him.

After a moment she said, "You saw Otto today."

Cash nodded. "He ain't lookin' good."

"No."

He touched her hand. "No."

Rita watched the sky, searching for stars.

"It's getting dark," she said at last.

Cash nudged her ribcage. "Told you we'd see the stars."

"You planning on spending the night?" she asked.

Cash sighed. "If you'll have me. Gabriel's crew showed up and want to use the house. Not that I have a say in the matter."

"Marcus Dwyer, for one?" Rita said.

Cash looked at her, surprised. "How the hell did you know?"

She gave him a look. "I'm in the biz."

"I didn't mean it like that," Cash said. "But that guy's bad news."

"I know," Rita said. "I've had a few run-ins with him. Possibly back in high school as well, but thanks to my better judgment, I may have erased algebra class from my memory."

Cash laughed, and Rita's heart felt lighter. She put her head on his shoulder. "I appreciate you visiting Otto."

Cash was quiet for a moment. Then he wrapped his arm around her. "Your old man deserves it."

Hot tears welled in Rita's eyes. "You're a good man, Cash Gabriel."

He rolled his shoulders, jostling her cheek. "You might even call me angelic."

She laughed. "Devilish comes to mind more easily." She admired the stars for a heartbeat, then dropped her head back on his shoulder. "I'm glad you can stay — whether Marcus had anything to do with that or not."

Cash kissed the top of her head. "Me too."

Chapter Forty-Four

Rita awoke to a bearded jaw nuzzling her.

She grinned. "You're fuzzy."

"I haven't shaved in a few days." Cash plumped the pillow beneath their heads. "Long hours at the hospital, combined with everything else going on around here."

"Well, I like it," Rita said. "You couldn't do that back in high school."

"There were a lot of things I couldn't do back in high school," he said, a mischievous twinkle in his eye. His hand moved over her hip beneath the covers.

"You had a lot of stamina in high school," Rita said. "Both on the track and off."

Cash returned his beard to her neck and nuzzled some more. "Maybe I had stamina, but I didn't have style. I got style now." He moved his hand in a way that made Rita gasp.

"That is stylish," Rita said.

"When do you need to get into the office?"

"Half an hour ago."

"But it's six-thirty in the morning," Cash said.

Rita laughed. "It's a murder investigation, Cash. I'm always running behind."

"What, can you spare twenty minutes?"

"For you, sir, I can spare thirty."

A half hour later, they were both in the shower, then toweling off one another's backs. They ate another breakfast of eggs and toast in Otto's kitchen, then kissed at the door before parting ways.

"We're like an old married couple," Cash said.

Rita crinkled her nose at him. "Speak for yourself."

He frowned at her. "What do you mean?"

"Call yourself old all you want," Rita said, "but I ain't havin' it."

"That's a relief," Cash said. "I thought you were talking about the married part." Then he gave her another quick kiss and headed out.

Rita locked up the house and got into her own car. Before going into the office, she stopped at the Bighorn Bean and picked up her regular, plus three more coffees.

At the SCSO, she passed them out to Mary Lou, Vee, and Jason. Jason popped off the plastic lid and blew on the steaming liquid.

"Thanks, Rita," he said. "Skyler always does it just right."

Mary Lou stiffened. "Are you saying I don't?"

Jason shook his head vigorously. "Not at all, Mary Lou. Your coffee's second to none, just like your eggplant parmesan and chicken cordon bleu. It's just that I could use a little extra today."

"You look exhausted," Rita said, pulling up a chair.

"Been here all night looking at vehicles," he said. "Tryna track down white vans. I cross-referenced all our witnesses with vehicles. And guess what?"

Rita took a sip. "Hate guessing."

"I ran Brooklyn Graff," he said. "She's got a blue Hyundai."

"Though none of the neighbors were actually sure about the make," Rita said.

"True," Jason said, "but she ran a stop sign at Lodgepole and Spruce, which is four blocks away from David's house."

Rita arched an eyebrow. "So much for saying she's never been to Still."

She picked up the receiver of Jason's landline and called Casper PD. "Please bring in Brooklyn Graff for questioning. I'll be there in a little over an hour to interview her." After she'd hung up, she asked, "What else is there to talk about before I head to Casper?"

"I have an appointment to talk with Mexico City police in about an hour," Vee said.

"Great," Rita said.

"And I'll be meeting with the fire chief to get his final arson report," Jason said, rubbing his face.

Rita patted his shoulder. "Get some shut eye too," she said. "You've already called in a solid day's work, Deputy."

He yawned. "Thanks, Sheriff."

Rita headed back outside with her coffee cup and settled into the cruiser. It was a beautiful morning for a drive, making for a swift trip.

At the Casper PD, Officer Dawson escorted Rita to the interview room. The officer who'd been waiting with Brooklyn took his leave, and Rita entered the room. Brooklyn sat pale and shaking while Dawson gave Rita a rundown of the recording equipment. Then he left, closing the door behind him.

Rita gave Brooklyn an encouraging smile and took a seat.

Brooklyn burst into tears. "I didn't mean to lie, Sheriff

Jonas. I was just so shocked that David was dead. I didn't understand why. And what it would mean for me."

"Please explain everything," Rita said, "starting with why you held back the truth that you'd visited his home."

Choking back a sob, Brooklyn nodded. "David and I were having an affair." She cleared her throat. "I'm married, y'see."

"You don't wear a wedding band," Rita said.

"My husband thought the same thing when I stopped wearing it. That maybe I was tryna hide the fact I was hitched. So I told him when I didn't wear it, I earned more tips."

"And was this the reason you didn't wear it?" Rita asked. "Or because you wanted David to think you weren't married?"

"No," Rita said, "I wasn't fishin' for men, Sheriff. I couldn't wear my ring. I washed my hands so much at the job, I got a real fierce rash under the band. Doc said skin couldn't dry out. Some kind of fungus got up in there."

"I see," Rita said. "You mentioned David was generous with tips — both cash and investing tips. Did David give you any other money?"

Brooklyn shook her head. "No."

"Gifts?"

Brooklyn shifted. "Shit, Sheriff, I'm sorry, I lied about that, too." She chewed on her lower lip for a moment. "Didn't want to tell you in case you guessed about our relationship."

"What kind of gifts?"

"Little things that Mike — that's my husband — things he wouldn't notice. Gardening tools, some nice hand soap, chocolate treats I could eat on my break, things for my car, like a bamboo backrest and some fancy sunglasses I keep in the console. A few gift certificates, too, for the spa."

"How long had you been seeing each other romantically?"

"It didn't actually happen until he moved to Still." Brooklyn scoffed. "Isn't that ironic? But the last time he came in for lunch, he said he'd miss me. And I said I would, too." Tears welled in her eyes. She swiped at them with a trembling hand. "So he suggested we have dinner after my shift … and things went from there."

"And your husband Mike doesn't know?" Rita asked.

Brooklyn flushed. "We're separated now. Have been for more'n eighteen months."

"Because of the affair?" Rita asked.

Brooklyn's gaze skated away. "Because of his gambling. He never knew about David and don't imagine he ever will, 'cause he never gave two shits what I was up to. He was in his own damn betting world. And we don't talk no more."

"So if you'd separated from Mike, why did David continue the affair in secret?" Rita asked, even though she knew the answer.

"He was very private," Brooklyn said.

"Was he married?" Rita asked.

"Hell, no!" Brooklyn said, looking horrified. "Er, not that I'm anyone to judge him. But no, infidelity wasn't the reason. He had a high-profile client that expected him to live a shuttered life. And he liked it that way, anyway, so what was the harm? After years of Mike making public disturbances, I was happy to hide away at David's bungalow."

"Neighbors report seeing you visit on regular intervals. Every weekend, is it?"

"I visited every second weekend," Brooklyn said.

"Two weekends a month?" Rita clarified.

Brooklyn nodded. "I didn't mind seeing him part-time."

"Why is that?" Rita asked.

Brooklyn took a sip of water. "My mom's starting to ail. I spend every other weekend with her in Douglas, cleaning the house and doing her shopping. The alternate weekends, I spent with David."

"And always in his home?" Rita asked.

Brooklyn nodded. "He didn't like to go to hotels or nothin'."

"So no dinners out?"

"We stayed home, Sheriff." Tears welled up again. "Chili and cornbread for dinner. Breakfast in bed." She gave a little laugh. "Probably sound like an old married couple. He used to do crossword puzzles Sunday morning while I worked in his garden."

"I noticed how tidy it was kept," Rita said.

Brooklyn managed to smile. "Thank you. It was a real pleasure puttering out there. Mike never appreciated my efforts, but David liked things tidy and praised my green thumb."

"A talent of yours," Rita said.

Brooklyn blinked. "What's that?"

"Horticulture," Rita said. "You're good at growing plants."

Brooklyn shifted and looked away. "Oh, I don't know about that, I just like doing it. And David's place is real easy to take care of 'cause he had a southwestern aspect. Shrubs really love it." Then her gaze dropped. "I'm gonna miss his garden, Sheriff. Nothing quite so divine as the perfume of a Japanese honeysuckle."

"And you never knew anything about David's work?" Rita asked. "Please consider your answer. Some people's lives are in danger because of their connection with David's employer."

Brooklyn's eyes grew wide. "All he ever said was that he worked for important people and was very well paid."

"Do you know what he spent his money on?"

"Like I already told you, Sheriff, David was an investor —" Brooklyn's voice broke off, and she dropped her head.

"What is it?" Rita asked.

Brooklyn swallowed her tears. "We're supposed to be in London right now. It's the first trip he'd booked for us." Her voice trembling. "He'd always wanted to go, but said he'd never do it on his own."

"What was there for him in London?" Rita asked.

Brooklyn shrugged. "He liked Sherlock Holmes a bit, and them Charles Dickens books, too. But mostly he wanted to sit in Trafalgar Square and do his crossword while the world bustled by." Brooklyn laughed again. "He liked to feel like an island in the busy river of life. He was that way in the diner, focused on his puzzle during the lunch rush, and it was easy to imagine him that way in a pub or on the tube."

"Not much of a people watcher, huh?" Rita asked. "His nose being buried in a puzzle book."

"Suppose not," Brooklyn said. "I ain't no looker, Sheriff, and I sure ain't rich. That's how I know David liked me for me." Her voice shook. "He loved me just the way I was."

Rita smiled. "Were you running away together?"

Brooklyn's eyebrows arched. "Of course not."

"So you and he intended to return?"

Brooklyn nodded. "He knew I'd never leave Mom. And he'd never leave Karen."

"You knew Karen?"

Brooklyn shook her head. "No, I never met her. He only told me about her."

"And did he tell her about you?"

Brooklyn shook her head. "No. He was very—"

"Private," Rita finished. "I understand. And he never visited you in Casper?"

"Nope," Brooklyn said. "Not even after me and Mike split, and I'd come down with a cold. Then he'd send me some DoorDash, and we'd talk over Zoom."

"Is that how you communicated with David?" Rita asked. "You Zoomed?"

"Uh-huh," Brooklyn said. "He hated tech, but COVID had forced him to get online. He always said it was 'cause he wanted to look at me. But I know it's 'cause he was familiar with how to do it, and didn't want to give in to gettin' a smartphone."

"When you Zoomed," Rita asked, "where was David?"

"Just in his house," Brooklyn said. "You know, in a private space."

"So he had a computer?"

"Sure. A laptop."

"We didn't find a laptop in the house," Rita said. "Can you describe what it looked like?"

"Not really. He kept it in his office, and his office door was usually locked. I never spent any time in there."

"And no smartphone?"

"Nope. He was a bit of a dinosaur that way. Preferred snail mail. Pen and paper."

"He wrote letters to Karen," Rita said.

"Yes. Karen sent cards and postcards and occasional notes. She wasn't a letter writer the way he was. She has a busy life, out in California."

"You said you never met Karen. Did you ever meet any of David's other family or friends?"

"No."

"Did you ever see anyone else at all at David's house?"

"Only once."

"What happened?"

"A man stopped by and they had a brief conversation."

"Can you describe him?"

Brooklyn shook her head. "I never saw him. David asked me to wait in the bathroom with the fan on. So I never saw or heard him neither."

"What did you make of that?" Rita asked.

Brooklyn shrugged. "That's when I figured out the very important people who paid a lot of money were unsavory sorts."

"Did you ask David about it?"

"No. Though I probably should have — you know, given what's happened."

"You can't think that," Rita said. "Especially since it's a really good thing you don't know anything about these unsavory sorts. All the same, you might consider spending a bit of time up at your mom's these days. Or any other address you don't normally frequent."

"Are you saying I'm free to go?" Brooklyn asked.

Rita nodded. "Yes, but let's stay in touch by phone."

"All right," Brooklyn said. "Mom's been asking to see her cousin up in Buffalo. She ain't gonna make that trip much longer. We can head up there this weekend."

"Good idea," Rita said. "For both of you."

Chapter Forty-Five

RITA WALKED out of the Casper PD parking lot and drove across town to the hospital. As before, she beelined through the corridors to her father's room without stopping by the nurses' station.

Otto looked like little more than a skeleton.

"Dad," she said. But only a sob escaped. His hand in hers felt half its former size.

"Miss Jonas?"

Rita turned.

A nurse approached on soft footsteps. Another face Rita didn't recognize. Her nametag read "Lynda."

"Hello, Lynda," Rita said.

Lynda smiled. "Evening." She proceeded to check Otto's tubes, making a couple of minor adjustments.

"How does it work?" Rita asked. "I mean, when we take him off the ventilator — how do we do that?"

Lynda paused to look at her. She smiled. "When you're ready, we'll remove his lines to the ventilator. But we'll keep him on an oxygen respirator so he's comfortable."

Rita nodded. "I see. You need to — I need to — we need to wait. Until some others can get here."

Lynda gave Rita a nod. "That's a good plan, Miss Jonas. I'll leave you to make some arrangements for family to arrive." Then she departed, leaving Rita with Otto.

For a few minutes, Rita stroked his hand.

"It won't be long now, Dad. I'll make sure Helen is here, too."

Then Rita cleared her tears and left Otto's room, headed to the psychiatric ward. At the nurse's station, she asked to see Helen Myers.

The admitting nurse showed Rita into a small, quiet room containing two armchairs flanking a small table. Potted bamboo, pale blue walls, and a small trickling water-feature added a tranquil tone.

"We'll bring Helen out to visit with you here," the nurse said. "We prefer not to have uniforms on the floor. It can be upsetting for some of the patients."

"I understand," Rita said, taking a seat in one of the gray armchairs.

The nurse departed and returned a few moments later with Helen. Helen's hair hung limp, and her eyes appeared vacant. The nurse helped her into the other armchair.

"I'll leave you two for a nice chat," she said with a smile.

When the door of the quiet room had closed, Rita reached out and took Helen's hand.

"Helen—"

Helen began to cry. Rita came out of her chair and moved to Helen's side, encircling her shoulder with her arm. "It's been a difficult time," Rita said. "You've lost so much."

Helen gulped back her sobs. "What's going to happen to me?"

For a moment, Rita said nothing. "You're going to get some help. That's all that matters now. That you feel supported."

"But what about charges?" Helen began to cry again. "Apex is pressing charges."

Rita shook her head. "They won't press charges. Take my word for it." She flicked the crest on her sleeve. "I don't wear this ugly-ass uniform for nothin'."

Helen cracked a smile, and Rita passed her the tissue box on the table.

"Thank you, Rita," she said, taking a tissue. And Rita knew she meant it in every sense of the word. Helen blew her nose. "How's Otto?"

"Not well," Rita said. "Dr. Albright thinks there's nothing more we can do for him. He isn't likely to come out of the coma."

Helen began to cry again. Rita gripped her shoulders harder. "I won't do anything while you're here. I know you'll want to see him ... to say goodbye."

Helen stiffened. "But…"

"What is it?"

"Otto ... may not want me here."

Rita let out a bitter laugh. "Well, he might not want me there either. He was pretty pissed off at both of us."

Helen gave a tentative nod.

"So maybe we're the perfect sendoff," Rita said. "Just what Otto needs. His two favorite nags."

At that, Helen laughed a little.

"You've still got forty-eight hours here on your seventy-two-hour hold," Rita said. "After that, we need a plan. Where will you go?"

"I've got a sister in Arizona."

"Good."

Helen picked at a seam. "But I haven't spoken to her in years."

"I'll call her for you."

Helen's fingers picked harder. "I don't know her number. I never memorized it. It's in my phone. But they took that away from me."

"I'll get your phone," Rita said. "What's its passcode?"

"Lisa's birthday," Helen said.

For a moment, Rita was startled. Then she understood. She swallowed her emotions before speaking. "I don't know the date of her birthday."

Helen's eyes seemed to clear for a moment. "Of course you don't," she said. "It's 1-8-0-9."

"Thanks," Rita said. "What's your sister's name?"

"Susan McPherson."

Rita thanked her and kissed her and promised to return as soon as possible. Then she left Helen in the quiet room and returned to the nurses' station, where she asked for access to Helen's phone.

"I don't need to take it with me," she said. "I only need to get a number."

The nurse nodded and went to fetch it from Helen's locker. A moment later, she returned and handed it to Rita.

The phone's wallpaper featured a photo of Lisa and Arnold laughing by a river on a sunny day. Helen wouldn't want to see that when she opened her phone. Rita swapped it for a generic sunset, then unlocked the phone and swiped through the contacts to find Susan McPherson.

When she had the number, she passed the phone back to the nurse and headed downstairs. Inside her vehicle, she dialed the number.

"Hello?"

"Hello, Susan McPherson? This is Sheriff Jonas with the SCSO in Wyoming."

"Yes, this is Susan," the woman said, her voice quivering. "How can I help you, Sheriff?"

"I'm calling in regard to your sister, Helen Myers."

Susan inhaled a breath. "Yes?"

"Helen is recently bereaved," Rita explained. "Are you aware?"

"Bereaved?" Susan said. "Oh, I'm sorry to hear of George's passing. I haven't talked to Helen in years, but I can only imagine what she put up with."

Rita cleared her throat. "George Myers in very much alive. And compliantly serving his sentence. But both their children are deceased. Murdered. And Helen's romantic partner is preparing to pass. At this time, she needs a great deal of support."

"Oh my God," Susan said, stammering. "I had no idea. I'll come straight away."

"Thank you," Rita said. "Helen is currently in a psychiatric ward at Casper Hospital. She's being held there for another day or so."

"Thank you," Susan said.

Rita shared some more details of Helen's care, then rang off and called back upstairs to the psych ward. "Helen's sister, Susan McPherson, is on her way," she told the nurse. Then she recited Susan's phone number for the nurses' station's records.

"Thank you, Sheriff," the nurse said.

"Oh, and Helen could probably use the good news about her sister coming to visit."

"Of course," the nurse said. "I'll tell her right away."

Rita put her phone away and drove back to Still.

Chapter Forty-Six

ON THE DRIVE back to Still, Rita's phone rang. She took the call, hands-free.

"Deputy."

"The Shaft was broken into last night," Jason said.

"Shit," Rita said, boosting her speed. "I didn't expect that, given it's not on the roster for Angel Holdings Ltd."

Rita arrived at The Shaft, a one-level building set back behind a large parking lot. A shingled roof and decorative window shutters gave it an antiquated aura. She got out of the cruiser and walked up to the entrance. Someone had kicked in the front door.

Inside, Jason took photos amidst a jumble of overturned tables and chairs. Rita crossed to him, picking her way through the silver maze of flatware.

"Someone sure made a mess," she said. "Anything stolen?"

Jason scratched his ear. "Only damage. Ruby Joe doesn't leave any cash on the premises, and we didn't account for any other missing valuables."

"What about the security cameras?" Rita asked,

pointing to a large unit hanging from the ceiling. "Were those damaged?"

Jason looked up. "Vee's looking at the tapes now with Ruby Joe in her office. Instead of contracting it out, Ruby Joe's got an ancient analog system. They're watching the footage on her desktop computer."

"Was the office door kicked in, too?"

Jason shook his head, motioning for Rita to follow. "Looks like someone tried, then decided it wasn't worth the effort." He led her to the rear of the building. "This is Ruby Joe's office."

Rita entered. Ruby Joe sat at her desk, drinking a mug of steaming tea. Vee stood behind Ruby Joe's shoulder, reviewing the tapes with her. Vee looked up and nodded at Rita.

"How are you doing, Ruby Joe?" Rita asked.

Ruby Joe sighed. "Well enough, Sheriff. Can't own a pub and never expect it to get busted into it."

"We've got footage of the burglar," Vee said. "Come have a look."

Rita and Jason came around to the other side of the desk. A paused security footage frame showed a masked man inside the building.

"Ruby Joe was just bringing up the footage from the exterior cameras," Vee said.

Ruby Joe clicked the computer mouse. "This here's the footage for the parking lot."

The video played, showing a jeep pull into the lot and park in the shadows. Rita didn't need to be able to read the pair of stickers on the rear bumper to know the curly script said "Charity" and "Destiny."

"That's Jeff Jeffries in the driver's seat," Rita said.

Ruby Joe peered closer at the screen. "Why the hell is that dimwit breaking into my pub?"

"He's trying to find Carly," Rita said. "Chester recognized her at the Shaft the other night."

Ruby Joe looked up at her. "Chester?"

Rita nodded. "He obviously told Jeff where he saw her."

Ruby Joe folded her arms. "So he came here to confront me about it?"

"Or he thought she was bunking here," Jason said.

Ruby Joe scowled. "Well, Chester can consider himself cut off."

"I need to go let Carly know Jeff's in town looking for her," Rita said. "I'll pick her up and bring her to the SCSO. Then I need you to take her to the women's shelter in Cheyenne, Vee."

Vee nodded.

"Thanks," Rita said. She looked at Jason. "Jason, please seize all the security footage. You printed the place already?"

"Yeah, though I'm not hopeful we got anything clean off the doors." He rubbed his neck. "But I'll be thorough, Sheriff."

"Thanks," Rita said. "See you soon."

She drove to her apartment and parked behind the Bighorn Bean. Rita ran up the stairs and knocked.

For several minutes, no one came.

"Shit," Rita said under her breath. She pounded again. Relief flooded her when she heard the security chain on the door slide.

The door opened a crack, and Carly's wide eyes looked through. When she saw it was Rita, she removed the chain and pulled the door wide. She wore one of Rita's spare bathrobes. She'd cut her hair short and bleached it blonde.

"Thanks for waitin'," she said, running her hands

through her damp yellow locks. "I was just doin' my hair. You know, 'cause Chester made a scene?"

"Smart thinking." Rita stepped into the apartment, closing the door behind her. "Especially since Jeff's in town looking for you."

Carly gave a small cry and covered her mouth with her hand. "What should I do?"

"We've got a place for you to stay in Cheyenne. You can come with me now."

Carly spun and ran to the bedroom. The bureau doors slid open and slammed closed as she packed her belongings.

As she waited, Rita looked around the apartment. Carly had made more adjustments. The throw rug in the hallway now lay in the living room. A houseplant Rita had sometimes wondered was artificial appeared to have grown twice in size. And the remotes on the coffee table were arranged in descending length next to a laptop with a Cornell sticker.

A chill ran down Rita's spine.

This wasn't Carly's laptop.

Carly came out of the bedroom, now dressed in jeans and a black hoodie and carrying her bag.

Rita turned. "Carly Jeffries, I'm arresting you on suspicion of murder."

Chapter Forty-Seven

RITA CLOSED David Clark's laptop with a *click* and stepped back from Mary Lou's desk.

"I can't get into it either," she said. "Passcode protected. Please put this into evidence."

"Ten-four," Mary Lou said.

"Thanks," Rita said. "I'll talk to Carly now."

While Mary Lou called down to the cells, Rita returned to her office. She closed the door behind her and leaned against it to breathe.

Inhale.

Exhale.

Someone rapped on the door.

She pushed off from it and retreated to her desk. "Come in."

The door opened and Vee's head poked inside. "I've brought Carly for her interview."

"Thanks." Rita pulled open the top drawer to get out her voice recorder. "Bring her in."

Vee entered the office, escorting Carly, who gripped a bottle of water. Her face was swollen with tears.

Rita invited her to take a seat and passed her a box of tissues. Carly took one and blew her nose. Once Vee had closed the door behind her, Carly crumpled the tissue and looked at Rita in earnest.

"I didn't kill no one."

"Let's talk about it." Rita turned on the recorder. "Tell me about the laptop in your possession."

Carly swallowed her tears and nodded. "I took it from Jeff."

"What was he doing with the computer?"

"I dunno. But I knew it was important to him. He never took his eyes off it. So the one time he wasn't watching it like a hawk, I took it."

"Why?"

Carly frowned. "For ransom."

"You took the laptop to negotiate money from him?" Rita clarified.

"In a manner of speaking." Carly curled her lip. "Jeff said if I walked away from him, I was walking away from the business, too. And that's bullshit. I own half the Rawhide Revue, and nothin' can change that. I don't got to stay sleepin' under his roof to be his business partner. So I took the laptop to negotiate with him. I'd give him it back if he let me go, once and for all."

"And I take it he said no?" Rita asked.

Carly gave a bitter laugh. "Wouldn't you know it, he agreed? Over text." She held up her phone. "I got it in writing. But then, the more I thought about it, passing the hours in your sunny little apartment, I realized, I don't want to be in business with him neither. Especially not since I know he'd keep goin' after all these dirty little side businesses. With guys like Brent Hollander. Maybe even more hustles, 'cause I wouldn't be there talking' him out of it." She shook her head, her short locks flying. "So I asked him for money instead. To buy me out. And I'd never trouble him again. But he hasn't replied since."

"Tell me about these dirty little side businesses of Jeff's."

Carly gave a little shrug, as if choosing a flavor of ice cream. "Well, he started dealing drugs about six months ago."

"You weren't involved in the scheme?"

She scowled again. "I was against the idea from the get-go. Dancers got enough to deal with, without those types comin' around the club."

"Why did Jeff get into trafficking?"

"Because the Revue was going bankrupt. I wanted to introduce escort services to make ends meet. Sometimes those Apex bigwigs are in the area and like to step out, all fancy-like. They know all the right small talk and tables manners and shit. I know some girls who'd do that kind of work."

"But Jeff didn't agree?"

"He never even listened to my ideas. He was all starry-eyed 'bout whatever Brent had to say."

"So the drug truck was Brent Hollander's idea?"

Carly nodded. "Yup. Brent converted the van. One of Jeff's bank friends bankrolled the product. And the business took off."

"This friend that bankrolled the plan," Rita asked, "is it Thomas Gabriel?"

"Nope." Carly grimaced. "Max Bannister."

"Can you confirm that?" Rita asked. "Did you see him at the Revue anytime?"

Carly let out a bitter laugh. "That fucking asshole beat me up."

Rita's jaw dropped. "It wasn't Jeff?"

Carly shook her head.

"Why?" Rita asked.

"Because I sold Heather my old car. Max was angry *at me* because that's how she packed up the kids and left him without anyone noticing. He tracked me down to teach me a lesson." She pointed at her eye socket, still faintly green. "This was the lesson."

"Did he harm you in any other way?" Rita asked, her jaw tense.

Carly shook her head, a genuine look of relief on her face.

"Could you please answer for the recorder?"

"No, he didn't harm me in any other way."

"And did he threaten to harm you in the future?"

"He said if I ever helped Heather again, he wouldn't be so easy on me."

Rita bit back several colorful comments.

"So Max financed Jeff's venture," Rita said. "Please tell me about the other players involved."

Carly drank some water, then licked her lips. "Brent Hollander and that goon Ollie drove the vans."

"All the business was operated out of the vans?" Rita asked.

Carly nodded. "Thank God. Jeff wouldn't allow any sales on the property, which was his only smart idea about the whole thing."

"So Ollie and Brent drove around conducting sales, and the profits were funneled back into the Revue?" Rita asked.

Again, Carly nodded. "That's right. But then about a week ago, Jeff got real scared."

"Why?"

"He lost one of the vans."

"By lost, he meant stolen and destroyed?"

"Right," Carly said. "He lost all the product, which he

meant wasn't going to be able to make his payment to Max."

For a moment, Rita tapped her lip, thinking. Then she picked up her landline and dialed Mary Lou's extension.

"What can I do for you, Sheriff?"

"Could you please run the telephone number for Max's lawyer?" she asked. "The one he called the night we brought him in for battery?"

Silent, Mary Lou tapped her keyboard. Then she said, "The number belongs to the Rawhide Revue."

Rita thanked her and hung up.

"Do you remember Jeff receiving a call from Max Bannister last week?" Rita asked.

Carly nodded. "Sure do. Max called Jeff, and for the first time since the van was gone, Jeff seemed to chill out. He called Ollie and Brent over to our place and told them Max would cancel the drug debt — if they did a favor for him."

"Do you know what the favor for Max was?" Rita asked.

Carly scoffed. "Nope. But let's just say I was plenty scared when I saw Jeff give Ollie a machete."

"And Ollie left your house with it?"

"Yep," Carly said. "Though I pretended I didn't see nothin'. I stayed awake that night, half-dressed beneath the covers in case I needed to leave in a hurry. I always keep a small bag packed with some essentials, ready to go."

"What happened next?" Rita asked.

Carly fiddled with her newly shortened locks. "Just before dawn, Ollie and Brent came back. They talked with Jeff out in the driveway. I couldn't make out what they were saying. But I could see the machete was bloody, and figured something really bad had happened."

"You figured right," Rita said. "Did you witness anything else?"

"Ollie and Brent gave the laptop to Jeff as proof the job was done," Carly said. "Then they both took long showers."

"Was the laptop for Jeff?" Rita asked. "Or Max?"

"Not sure," Carly said. Then a smile twisted her lips. "But Jeff tried all day to get into it."

"And failed?" Rita asked.

Carly laughed. "He was so pissed. At one point, he went out to the garage to blow off steam. So I grabbed the laptop and ran."

"And ran where?" Rita asked, for the sake of the recorder.

Carly met her eye. "Still. I ran here."

"To the SCSO," Rita said.

Carly kept her gaze on her. "Here," she said. "For help."

Chapter Forty-Eight

"IT'S NOT THE BEST WESTERN." Rita gestured to the cell. "And it most certainly ain't the Still Haven Inn. But this is the safest place I can think of for you for the night."

Carly put her backpack on the cot and sat down. "I understand," she said. "I'll be fine."

Rita wished her a good night, then headed upstairs to the bullpen.

"I've got the Mexican police on the line," Vee said. "They have Milly at their headquarters. They can put her in a Zoom room, if you'd like to talk to her."

"Yes, please," Rita said, heading for her office.

"I'll email you the link."

Rita went into her office and closed the door behind her. She sat at her desk and entered the Zoom room, the meeting already being recorded. Milly looked out through the screen, her eyes wide and dark.

"Hi, Milly," Rita said.

Milly blinked a couple of times. "Is it true the inn's gone?"

"Yes," Rita said. "Please tell me what's going on."

Milly exhaled. "Shit."

"Why did you flee?" Rita asked. "Because of the arson?"

Milly nodded.

"Why?" Rita asked.

Milly dropped her gaze. "Because I found David."

Rita stilled. "You saw the body?"

Milly took a deep breath. "Tom Gabriel asked me to go check on him."

"At his house?" Rita asked.

Milly nodded again.

"When was this?"

"On Thursday," Milly said. "In the morning."

"What time?"

Milly avoided Rita's eye. "Early."

"How early?"

Milly flushed. "Before dawn."

"That's an unusual time to check in on someone," Rita said.

Milly bit her lip. "I don't make a habit of saying no to Tom."

"Did you talk to Tom personally?"

Milly shifted. "Talked to his lawyer."

"Alan Crawford?"

"Yes."

"Why did Alan Crawford ask you to check in on David Clark?"

"Because David hadn't responded to an email Alan had sent David the night before. And when Angel Holdings wants an answer — well, they expect you to answer. So when David didn't, Alan called me to go have a look."

"Was that an unusual request from Alan?" Rita asked. "Checking up on David like that?"

Milly gave a little shrug. "A little, because it wasn't like

David to not respond. But it wasn't unusual for Alan to ask us to keep an eye on each another."

"And by 'each other,' do you mean everyone involved with Angel Holdings Ltd.?" Rita asked.

Milly nodded again. "Yes."

"Please tell me what happened when you arrived at David's house."

Milly moistened her lips. "I knocked, but he didn't answer. So I tried the door." Her gaze flicked away. "I know I probably shouldn't have, but I did. Tom — Alan — would've expected me to."

"Go on," Rita said.

"I called out to David first." Milly paused to steady her voice. "Then I went to his office. And ... that's where I found his body." Milly paused to take a sip of water. "Then I ran out of the house. I don't even think I closed the door behind me."

"Did you see anyone?" Rita asked.

Milly blinked at her. "At the house? No."

"Did you notice any neighbors?"

"No neighbors," Milly said, "because it was early. Didn't see no one when I was running back to my car."

"Did you park in David's driveway?"

Milly shook her head. "I parked a block away."

"Why?"

"Because David liked things private," Milly said. "Because Tom wants things private. I didn't want anyone to recognize my car in his driveway."

"So you don't recall passing anyone as you ran back to your car?" Rita confirmed.

"No," Milly said. "But I sure remember that goddamn Apex van."

Rita stilled. "Where was the Apex van?"

Milly thought for a moment. "Maybe at Lodgepole

and Spruce. I don't really remember the roads I took. I was scared shitless."

"What happened with the Apex van?" Rita asked.

Molly folded her arms. "They almost ran me off the road."

"Were they following you?"

Milly shook her head again. "No, they was just driving like a couple a hellions. I don't think they noticed me at all, until I yelled at them."

Rita raised an eyebrow. "You yelled at them?"

Milly squared her shoulders. "I told 'em I'd report 'em to Apex."

"And did you?" Rita asked.

"No."

"Because you discovered David?"

Milly hugged her own arms. "I was spooked."

"I can imagine," Rita said, "seeing your colleague like that. Did you see the driver of the Apex van?"

"Yes. It was a construction worker I'd recognized around town."

"A construction worker where?" Rita asked.

"At the Bighorn Mining Building," Milly said.

"Can you describe him?"

"Tall, thin. He's got red hair. Although he was wearing a skullcap when I saw him driving."

"Was there anyone else in the vehicle?" Rita asked.

"Yeah," Milly said, "in the passenger seat. A big, ugly guy made of muscles."

"Did they stop when you yelled at them?"

Milly looked annoyed. "No. They drove outta there faster than me."

"And what did you make of David's murder?" Rita asked.

Milly took a moment before answering. "I figured Tom killed him."

Rita tapped her lip. "In which case, Tom wasn't really asking you to check on David."

Milly shook her head.

"So why would Tom want you to see David's body?"

Milly chewed on her lip. "To send me a message."

Rita's eyes widened. "That's quite the message. Seems more like a threat. Is there a reason Tom Gabriel would threaten you?"

Milly drew herself up. "He's a shrewd businessman, Sheriff Jonas."

"You didn't quite answer the question, Milly. Is there a reason Tom Gabriel would threaten you?"

"A couple years ago, he loaned me the funds to keep the damn doors open."

Rita nodded. "I see. And you couldn't make the payments?"

"Last year I missed a few. That's when I signed over the property to Angel Holdings Ltd."

"So if Tom owned the inn," Rita asked, "why would he need to send you a message?"

Instead of answering, Milly dropped her head.

"Were you skimming profits?"

Milly's head snapped up, her eyes burning. "Skimming? It was *my* business. *My* property."

"No," Rita said, "it wasn't your property. Not if Tom Gabriel owned it."

"Well, it should have been," Milly flared. "I worked hard to keep that place running."

"Do you have thoughts on who may have set fire to the inn?"

For a moment, Milly was silent, avoiding Rita's eye. "No."

"Do you think Tom is responsible?"

She snorted. "No. Tom's gonna be mad as hell it burnt down." Heat flashed in her eyes. "Why the hell d'you think I'm here?"

"Can you please tell me where you're staying?" Rita asked.

Milly gave her the address of a small beachside resort.

"Thanks," Rita said. "If you relocate, please let me know."

"Okay," Milly said, although Rita doubted her compliance.

"Thank you for all the information, Milly," Rita said. "Now can I please speak to the officer with you?"

Milly looked over her shoulder, and a uniformed man approached the camera.

"I'd like to email you a lineup to see if Milly can identify a suspect," Rita said to him.

The officer agreed. Rita punched Mary Lou's extension into the phone on her desk. "Mary Lou, please email a lineup with Ollie Anderson to Mexico City police."

Mary Lou's fingernails were already tapping on her keyboard. "Ten-four."

"Thanks," Rita said, hanging up and returning her attention to the Zoom room. She watched as the officer returned to the desk to present a printout of the lineup to Milly.

Milly studied the page, then identified number five: Ollie. Milly signed the document, and the officer told Rita he would scan and email it back at once.

"Thanks," Rita said to both Milly and the officer before leaving the meeting. Then to herself she said, "We got them."

Chapter Forty-Nine

Rita walked back into the bullpen and took a deep breath. Jason, Vee and Mary Lou looked up from their desks.

"We got them," she said. "Milly positively ID'ed Brent Hollander and Ollie Anderson from the Rawhide Revue at the scene of David's death. Plus we've got Carly's statement."

"So Jeff is targeting Tom Gabriel?" Jason asked.

"Not quite," Rita said. "I believe Jeff's been running the drug trade here in Still, not Tom Gabriel."

"But Jeff's not trying to take out the competition?" Vee asked.

"Right. This wasn't about competition, but revenge," Rita said. "When one of Jeff's drug trucks got destroyed, he sent Ollie and Brent to get even. Except he probably didn't know they were going after kids." She paused, swallowing her emotion. "But whatever Jeff said, Ollie and Brent did as instructed."

"So then Jeff was in a bind for the death of Arnold Myers and the attempted murder of Adrian Hutch," Jason said. "And he still owed Max Bannister because the van was out of commission."

"Exactly," Rita said. "Which is why the night we arrested Max Bannister, he called in a favor from Jeff, offering to pardon the payment."

"And this favor was to kill David Clark?" Vee asked. "As a strike against Angel Holdings Ltd?"

Rita nodded. "It all points back to Max Bannister. Carly's statement, too."

Mary Lou shuddered. "That's quite the way to do business."

"This isn't business," Rita said, "it's personal. Otherwise, why not just shoot David?"

"So what's the personal connection?" Vee asked.

Rita pulled on her chin. "Let's think through all the personal connections in this case. What about Sarah Thorpe's sister? She mentioned a sister in Casper who worked for the city. Maybe she knows Max Bannister."

"I can follow up on that," Jason said, pulling out his phone. "The phony surveyors who showed up at Sarah Thorpe's place on Windset Lane were probably Brent and Ollie, too."

"Right," Rita said. "Sarah Thorpe couldn't identify Brent's red hair because it was hidden beneath his skullcap."

"What about Brent Hollander's death?" Vee asked. "Ollie again?"

"Hollander was a casualty of Tom Gabriel leveling the playing field," Rita said. "When Tom found out Hollander was trafficking drugs on his patch, he sent someone to deliver a message. It was probably Marcus Dwyer who told Tom, and Marcus who showed up at Brent's place with a penknife and a hatchet. He tortured Brent to find out the name of his boss. Maybe Brent held out. Maybe he didn't.

But when the cops showed up and Marcus went to answer the door, Brent grabbed the penknife and killed himself."

"Yikes," Mary Lou said.

Jason ended his call. "Get this: Sarah's sister, Nadine Thorpe is Max Bannister's executive assistant."

Rita raised an eyebrow. "That's interesting."

"But she's off work at the moment."

"Also interesting," Rita said. "What's the reason?"

"HR manager said she's taken family-related leave — to take care of her sister, who's unwell."

"Sarah's only unwell because Finn won't let her get any sleep," Rita said. "Vee, you and I will head to Windset Lane to talk to Nadine." She looked at Jason. "Jason, I'm gonna need you to handle things in Beaumont."

Then she scooped up the receiver on Mary Lou's desk and punched in the number for Beaumont PD.

"Please pick up Ollie Anderson and Jeff Jeffries," she said, "for the murders of David Clark and Arnold Myers, and the attempted murder of Adrian Hutch."

Chapter Fifty

RITA PULLED up to the driveway on Windset Lane and idled the cruiser. Sarah Thorpe's Westfalia remained parked exactly as it had last time, collecting more dry summer leaves.

"Looks vacant," Vee said.

"It's definitely remote out here," Rita said. "If Nadine is here, she's not making her presence known." She pointed to a thick laurel hedgerow growing along the road. "I'm gonna park the cruiser behind the bushes. Let's peek around the side of the house before announcing our presence."

Rita and Vee followed the fence line onto the property. Blinds were drawn in most of the windows.

"There," Rita said, pointing. Between the house and the fence, a burgundy Toyota RAV sat parked on the scrubby grass.

"I'll go run the plate," Vee said.

"Thanks," Rita said. "I'll meet you on the veranda in five."

While Vee returned to the cruiser, Rita glanced around

for signs of anything unusual. But nothing appeared out of place. No fresh footprints led to the track through the bush, either.

She made her way toward the front of the house and met Vee as she came around the laurel hedge.

"Vehicle is registered to Nadine Thorpe," Vee said.

"Perfect," Rita said as they approached the front door. Inside the house, Finn hollered for relief. Rita rapped loudly enough to be heard.

The door cracked open and Sarah looked out, Finn planted on her hip. The infant fell silent when he looked at Rita and Vee, both in uniform.

"Hello, Sheriff Jonas."

Rita smiled. "How's the tooth?"

Sarah let out a nervous laugh. "Don't ask."

"This is Officer Logan," Rita said. "We're here to talk to your sister, Nadine."

For a moment Sarah said nothing, her gaze flipping between Rita and Vee. "My sister lives in Casper."

"Her car is parked out back," Rita said.

Sarah flushed.

"I don't want to arrest you for interfering with an investigation," Rita said.

Sarah pulled the door open. "Come in, Sheriff, Officer."

Rita and Vee stepped into the house, and Sarah closed the door behind them. Finn teethed on his knuckle, watching with wide eyes.

"Nadine's upstairs." Sarah shifted Finn to her other hip. "I'll go get her."

"It's all right, you two stay," Rita said. "I'll go up."

Sarah nodded and put Finn on the floor with his toys. "She's in the first bedroom."

"Thanks." Rita glanced at Vee. "Please wait with Sarah. I'll got chat to Nadine."

Rita went upstairs and rapped on the first door off the landing.

"Hello, Nadine, my name is Sheriff Jonas with the SCSO. I'd like to ask you some questions, please."

For a moment, it was silent. Then the door opened and a young woman who looked as sleep deprived as Sarah looked out with worried eyes.

"How can I help, Sheriff?"

Rita stepped through the doorway and scanned the room. A double bed and nightstand faced a small window that looked over the back of the property, affording a view of the inn's blackened roof.

"I'm here to talk about Max Bannister," Rita said.

Nadine stiffened. "Okay."

"You're his executive assistant?"

She nodded. "Yes. But … well, I'm on leave at the moment."

"Family-related leave, yes?"

She nodded again. "Sure. I'm helping out Sarah and Finn."

"I know Sarah really appreciates it," Rita said. "How long have you worked as Max Bannister's assistant?"

"Eighteen months."

"I know that Max Bannister is running drugs," Rita said.

The color drained from Nadine's cheeks as she sunk onto the edge of the bed.

"Were you aware?" Rita asked.

Nadine shook her head. "No."

"Did Max ever ask you to do anything that wasn't part of your job duties?"

For a moment Nadine picked at the coverlet. Then her

gaze met Rita's. "He made me to do his dirty work on the clock."

"What kind of dirty work?" Rita asked.

Nadine shrugged. "Looking up records about some guy so he could get revenge."

"Revenge?" Rita asked. "Which guy?"

"This guy who helped Heather."

"Heather Bannister?" Rita clarified.

Nadine nodded.

"Do you know the name of this guy?" Rita asked.

Nadine nodded again. "Thomas Gabriel."

"And do you know how he helped Heather?"

"Sure. He gave her the cash to buy a house in Still. He used to be her father-in-law or something like that. So she up and left with the kids without telling anyone." Her gaze flickered away. "Well, she told me."

"Are you friends with Heather Bannister?" Rita asked.

"Friends? Not really. We don't hang out or nothing. But it was hard not to be friendly when I knew what she dealt with, being married to that dick."

"Does Max know that Heather confided in you?"

"Hell, no," Nadine said, almost laughing. "He thought we were too scared of him to talk to each other." She flushed again and glanced at Rita. "But he's kind of stupid."

"Do you know how Max planned to enact revenge on Thomas Gabriel?"

She thought for a moment. "No. I only did the things he told me. Looking up records and stuff."

"What kind of information did he want you to look up?"

"He wanted to find out what businesses Thomas Gabriel owned. Names of his employees. Things like that."

"And do you recall the name of Thomas Gabriel's company?"

"For sure," she said. "I thought it was kind of sweet. Angel Holdings Limited."

"And what information about Thomas Gabriel's business dealings did you provide Max Bannister?"

"A list of the businesses he owned," Nadine said. "But then one of the businesses burned down." She pumped a thumb toward the window. "This inn here by Sarah's place. I thought Max might be responsible, so I called Sarah and told her. And she told me about the rumors here in Still, about an accountant who was killed. That's when I got scared."

"Why were you scared?" Rita asked. "You hadn't done anything wrong."

"I recognized the accountant's name, David Clark. I'd seen it on the paperwork for Angel Holdings. I was scared Max was gonna come for me next, because I'd been looking at those ledgers. Not that I even understood half of them."

"So you came here to get away from Max?"

Nadine let out a bitter laugh. "Hell, yeah. In case you don't know, Sheriff, he likes to hit Heather. That's why she left."

Rita took a breath. "I hate to tell you, you're not gonna be safe here either. You and your sister need to take Finn and leave now."

"Our mom lives in Montana," Nadine said.

Rita shook her head. "No, don't stay with family. Find a hotel you've never been to, in a town where no one knows you. Register under your mother's name."

Nadine nodded and opened her mouth to say something when Vee called out downstairs.

Rita stepped out onto the landing. "Yes?"

"Someone's arrived," Vee called up.

Rita walked across the landing to Sarah and Finn's room on the front of the house and looked through the window. Downstairs, a black BMW sat parked in the drive. A male figure popped open the driver's door and got out.

Rita ran back to the landing.

"It's Max Bannister," she called out. "Sarah, bring Finn upstairs."

What she didn't tell Sarah is that Max was holding a shotgun.

Chapter Fifty-One

RITA PULLED some tubes of gift wrap out of the closet and ushered in Nadine, Sarah, and Finn. He had started to bawl again — though this time Rita suspected it was from the darkness in the closet and not his tooth. Sarah whispered in his ear, cooing and kissing him into silence.

"We're going to pretend we're little mushrooms in here, Finn," she said. "Growing in the dark."

Rita gave the sisters her best reassuring smile. "Don't come out until I tell you." Then she closed the door on them and slid a bureau in front of it.

A shot rang out.

Rita headed for the stairs, pulling her gun.

Downstairs, Vee stood in the open doorway, service weapon in hand. "Stand down, Mr. Bannister."

Rita pounded down the final treads and joined her in the doorway. "Still County Sheriff's Office."

Max Bannister stood ten yards away, gripping a shotgun, sweat glistening on his face. His mouth twisted into a strange grimace that might have been a smile.

"Put down the weapon, Mr. Bannister," Rita said.

Instead, Max Bannister raised the scope to his eye and fired. Rita and Vee dove for cover as the shell exploded in the foyer ceiling.

This time Rita shouted. "Put down the goddamn gun, Max."

Another blast hit the ceiling, raining dust on them. Vee scooted on her belly and slammed the door shut. Then she jumped to her feet and bolted it while Rita radioed Beaumont PD for reinforcement.

Another blast from the shotgun shattered a living room window.

"Shit," Rita said. "Beaumont's on their way, but we can't wait out Councilor Bannister's trigger finger."

Another window shattered and Vee glanced over her shoulder. "He's circling the house."

"Probably looking for another entrance," Rita said. "We gotta secure the ground level."

Vee nodded, already headed for the kitchen. Rita followed. But there was no back door in the kitchen.

Vee spun around, her brow knit. "Maybe the house doesn't have a second entrance. Ground floor's not much bigger than a bungalow."

Rita walked out of the kitchen and into the hallway. "Seems unlikely. This place may not be up to code, but it's old, bound to have another door somewhere."

She opened the nearest door off the kitchen. It led to a small laundry room with an apartment-sized washer and dryer. A door on the far side of the room led outside.

"Here it is."

Before their eyes, the doorknob jiggled.

Rita spun, pushing Vee out of the laundry room. "Hurry. Door's locked now, but not for long." Vee exited, and Rita closed the laundry door behind them. "Let's barricade it."

They returned to the kitchen and dragged the heavy, wooden table into the hallway, shedding bits of dried Play-Doh as it bumped over the uneven floorboards. They shoved it against the laundry room door as the shotgun fired again, blasting a hole through the back door to the laundry room.

"This table ain't gonna stop him," Rita said. "But hopefully it'll slow him down."

"I'll sneak up behind him," Vee said. "He won't expect one of us outside."

Rita chewed on her lip. "Sounds risky. At close range, that shotgun's gonna do damage."

Vee tapped her lip. "Then we need an element of surprise. I'll go out an upstairs window."

"If you think you can do it." Rita rapped her knuckles on Vee's bulletproof vest. "Buckle up, Officer Logan."

Vee set her jaw and headed upstairs. Rita followed her into the bedroom where the Thorpe sisters hid with Finn. Stepping over the rolls of gift wrap, they crossed to the window.

"You sure?" Rita asked.

Downstairs, Max's footsteps echoed in the laundry room. Then he fired several rounds into the kitchen table.

Vee opened the sash. "I'll see you on the flip side, Sheriff."

She squeezed through the small opening and crept onto the roof. Staying low, she jumped to the lower roof of the veranda. With one more jump, she was on the grass. She rolled, somersaulted, and jumped to her feet.

"Jesus Murphy," Rita said, as though Otto were standing beside her, "she's a goddamned stuntwoman."

Vee gave Rita a quick wave, then disappeared around the corner of the house.

Finn let out a sudden cry. Below, the footsteps stopped. Then they moved again, this time on the staircase.

Rita opened the bedroom door to peer through the crack.

Max Bannister stood on the stairwell, paused halfway up. He bent over his shotgun, reloading it.

Rita swiped a roll of giftware, then slipped through the door and across the landing.

"Shouldn't have used so many shells on the kitchen table," she said to Max, tossing the roll of giftwrap down the stairwell. As it flew through the air, the paper unfurled, fluttering like a flag.

Startled, Max glanced up, fumbling the firearm. "What the—?"

"I'll take that," Rita said, darting forward to grab the weapon.

The giftwrap roll bounced down the treads as Max took a step back. His heel caught the tube, rolling his foot. Max teetered, then fell, bouncing his way to the bottom of the stairs.

Rita followed, and as Max hit the last tread, Vee flew through the front door, pouncing on top of his six-foot frame. Rita set aside the shotgun and piled on after her, wrestling Max Bannister's hands behind his back. Vee snapped on a pair of cuffs.

"Max Bannister, you are under arrest for the attempted murder of law enforcement officers, and under suspicion for collusion in the murder of David Clark."

Then they guided him out of the house and down the front steps of the verandah. As they walked him to the cruiser behind the laurel hedge, Rita read him his Miranda rights.

Max spat in Rita's face. "Fuck off."

Rita sighed and rolled her eyes at Vee. "Get the spit guard on him."

Vee popped the trunk of the cruiser to get the spit guard. Max pulled away, stretching his neck. They wriggled it onto his head, then lowered him into the back seat of the cruiser.

"Can't stop Heather from getting what she's owed," he said.

"Making threats isn't going to help your situation, Councilor," Rita said. She held out Max's shotgun to Vee. "Pack it up for the SCSO."

She took the weapon. "Sheriff."

Rita returned to the house, and went upstairs. She pushed aside the bureau and opened the bedroom closet. Warily, Nadine emerged. Sarah and Finn followed.

"It's all over," Rita said. "Max Bannister is arrested and about to be driven off these premises."

The sisters burst into tears and held onto one another, pressing Finn between them. Outside the window, gravel crunched.

Nadine stiffened. "Max is mixed up with a lot of bad guys. What if someone else comes?"

"A reasonable concern," Rita said, stepping up to look through the window. "But thankfully it's Beaumont PD."

The sisters visibly relaxed.

"Officer Logan will stay to take your statements," Rita said. "I'm gonna personally drive Councilor Bannister to the SCSO." Then she winked at Finn. "Good work on that tooth."

Then she headed downstairs and out onto the veranda. Two Beaumont patrol cars parked by the hedge, and four officers stood chatting with Vee. In the back seat of the SCSO cruiser, Max Bannister was thrashing against the seatbelt.

Rita walked up and thanked the Beaumont officers.

"Thank for showing up, guys," Rita said. "We've got gunfire and that BMW and some traumatized witnesses to process."

"Been a hell of a week for you and yours, Jonas," one of the officers said.

Rita sighed. "Tell me about it." She looked at Vee. "Please stay to take Sarah's and Nadine's statements? I'll take Mr. Bannister to the SCSCO."

Vee nodded. "You bet." Then she met Rita's eye. "Good luck with him, Sheriff."

Rita snorted. "Thanks. I'll take all I can get."

Vee and the Beaumont officers walked up to the house and Rita popped open the driver's door.

Max's shouts escaped the backseat.

"Would you knock it off?" Rita asked, her words drowned out by the ring of her cellphone. It was Mary Lou.

"We got another fire," Mary Lou said.

"Good grief," Rita said. "As if we don't have enough to do. Is this one arson, too?"

"Looks like."

"Let me guess," Rita said, "and I hate guessing. It's The Rancher's Pantry?"

"Nuh-uh."

"Are you okay, Mary Lou?" Rita asked. "You don't quite sound like yourself. Or the king."

"It's Cash's house, Rita," Mary Lou said.

"What?" Rita asked.

But she'd already disconnected and dropped her phone. She twisted in the driver's seat, straining against the seatbelt. Her eyes bored into Max.

"What the hell did you do?"

Max stopped struggling with his seatbelt and leaned back. "I dealt with Heather's ex, that's what."

Rita frowned. "Technically *you're* Heather's ex now."

Max growled. "Cash Gabriel paid for paying for that fucking house."

"*Tom* Gabriel footed the tab for her house," Rita said. "It wasn't Cash's money."

"Well, Cash did all the dirty work, running around and putting out everything else that she needs."

Rita felt the heat creep into her cheeks. "That's not true."

Then she flicked on her radio and called Vee. "Please tell Beaumont PD to take the Thorpe sisters' statements. I'm gonna need you to drive Max Bannister to the station instead."

"Ten-four," Vee said.

"Thanks," Rita said. "And send out whichever one of them's the best driver."

Chapter Fifty-Two

RITA CLIMBED out of the driver's seat and stepped aside for Vee.

"Take Mr. Bannister to the SCSO," she said. "But you're not to deal with him on your own, okay?"

"'Cause you won't be able to handle me," Max barked from the backseat.

Rita ignored him. "Get Ken to help you with processing him every step of the way."

Vee nodded. "Sure thing."

Rita gave her a slap on the back, then turned to the officer from Beaumont.

"I need a lift to another crime scene," she said. "Arson, not far from here. And we got to get there fast."

Officer Brentwood turned the ignition and hit the sirens and lights. As they pulled up to Cash's house, more strobing lights bathed the scene. The house Cash had lived in for twenty years was a smoking pile of rubble.

Without realizing it, Rita sobbed aloud.

Brentwood touched her arm. "You alright, Sheriff?"

"As good as I'm gonna be tonight," she said, hopping

out of the passenger seat. "I appreciate you all helping out at Windset Lane."

Brentwood gave her a salute, and Rita strode toward the blackened foundation. Cash's truck was parked in the driveway, but there was no sign of Marcus's minivan.

The fire chief crossed to her. "Stay back, Sheriff. It's not safe to approach yet."

She craned to see the damage. "Arson?"

Paul pulled a grim face. "Without a doubt. Pour patterns all around the exterior. Whoever did this didn't try to cover up their dirty work."

Rita ground her teeth. "Fuck. Where's the homeowner?"

"We found one body in the bedroom."

Rita's guts contracted. "Do you have a positive ID?"

The chief shook his head.

"I gotta make a call," she said, stepping out of earshot from Paul. She whipped out her phone and called Cash.

But there was no answer. Not even voicemail.

She tried again and again, feeling sicker each time she tried.

"He can't be dead," she said. "I'm already losing Otto."

Then Rita's phone displayed an incoming call.

"Jason."

"Rita." His voice sounded as hollow as hers. "In Beaumont ... when we went to arrest them ... there was a shootout."

Rita inhaled. "Jesus, Jason, are you injured?"

"No, but Reynolds is. Thankfully, he'll be okay. Other officers are okay, too." He paused. "But Jeff and Ollie didn't make it."

"Oh, hell," Rita said. "I'm sorry you've been through this, Jason."

"Definitely earned my paycheck today." His voice tight. "Oh, and guess what we found on the premises?"

"You know I hate guessing."

"A machete."

"Tilda will be glad to close the loop," Rita said.

"Forensics is already testing it against David's DNA."

"Thanks, Jason." She passed as her eye tracked an Audi pulling up to the curb. "Have you heard from Cash?"

"No," Jason said. "Why?"

"Arson. His house. One body found inside." Rita's voice felt weak. "I'm at the scene now. And I can't get a hold of him."

She heard Jason take in a breath. "You know Mary Lou'll be doing everything she can."

Rita nodded, even though Jason couldn't see her. "I know. Thanks. I gotta go now. Ken's arrived."

She hung up and waved for Ken's attention. He noticed her and approached.

"Heard about the fire," he said. "Came to see if it's connected to this drug business."

"You've already finished everything at the SCSO?" Rita asked.

Ken's forehead creased. "I don't understand."

"We arrested Max Bannister," Rita said. "He's a real live wire, so I told Officer Logan to call in your assistance."

Ken shook his head. "Never got that call."

"Shit," Rita said, already headed for the Audi. "I need a lift to the station, Ken."

"You got it, Sheriff," Ken said, jogging after her.

As he slid behind the wheel Rita pulled out her phone and dialed the station. Mary Lou answered.

"Where's Vee?" Rita asked.

"Taking Max Bannister to Natrona County," Mary Lou said. "Just like you ordered."

"I never authorized that," Rita said.

Rita rang off and called Vee, but there was no answer. Then she called Casper PD.

"Is Officer Logan there?"

But the answer was no. The same answer she received when she called Natrona County. No sign of Max Bannister either.

"Fuck," Rita said. "Fuck, fuck, fuck."

Ken glanced at her sidelong. "What's happened?"

Rita blew out a sigh. "All this time, I'd assumed Marcus Dwyer has been keeping tight watch over us, and that's how Thomas Gabriel knew about David's ledgers being taken by courier to Casper PD. But what if it wasn't Marcus? What if Officer Logan was the leak? And that's also how they knew we were looking into Angel Holdings in the first place?"

Ken blinked at her, then looked back at the road. "Fuck."

Rita dialed Casper PD again. "How did Officer Logan get seconded to us here in Still?" she asked.

"She volunteered," the officer said.

"I think Officer Vee Logan is working for Thomas Gabriel," Rita said. "And she's kidnapped our suspect, Max Bannister. I need you to put a BOLO on our cruiser."

"One moment, Sheriff Jonas," the officer on the line said. The receiver muffled, then the voice cleared on the line. "We just got a report on an abandoned SCSO patrol car on the highway."

Rita thanked him and hung up as Ken pulled into the lot behind the station and parked beside her Honda.

"Thanks for the cooperation, Ken," Rita said, popping the passenger door and hopping out of his Audi.

"Anything else I can do?" he asked.

"Appreciate you staying on standby," she said as she

crossed to her Honda. She unlocked the door and gave Ken a wave. "I'll be in touch."

He waved back and pulled out of the lot.

She got in her car and texted Jason.

You still in Beaumont?

He sent back a thumbs up.

Can you meet me at Casper PD?

He sent back another thumbs up.

Great. Find me that warehouse in Casper where I met with Tom's lawyer.

Then Rita started the ignition and drove up the freeway to the abandoned black and white cruiser. It sat on the shoulder of the road, with no visible signs of damage. At least, not at a distance.

She pulled over, parking her Honda on the shoulder in front of the patrol car. Inside, there was no sign of Max Bannister or Vee.

"Shit," she said, unable to hide her frustration. Then she popped the trunk. No one in there either. This time, she let out a sound of relief.

Chapter Fifty-Three

RITA GOT BACK in her Honda and drove to the Casper PD, where she found Jason and the Chief of Casper PD waiting for her.

"I checked out the cruiser," she said. "No sign of Vee or Max Bannister."

"Hell of a mix-up," the chief said. He spread his hands, giving her an encouraging smile. "We're out looking for them now."

"Thanks," she said, forcing a smile. She pulled on Jason's elbow, steering him toward the door. "Let's go, Deputy. I want to follow a lead." Over her shoulder, she said, "Thanks, Chief."

"Let us know if we can offer any other assistance," he said.

Rita gave him a nod as they pushed through the front-doors. Then she glanced at Jason. "It's not a mix-up," she said, under her breath. "It's a setup. And Vee's the plant."

"Jesus," Jason said, leading the way to the SCSO truck.

"What'd you find for Angel Holdings' warehouses?" Rita asked as she climbed into the passenger seat.

"Lawn Ranger's in the industrial district." He punched the address into the GPS.

When they arrived, the place looked vacant, with no vehicles parked nearby.

"I recognize that roll-up door," Rita said. "Crenshaw's probably parked inside, if he's here."

A rusted metal door swung inwards when Jason knocked. He and Rita exchanged a look. Then they identified themselves and stepped into the warehouse, clearing the foyer.

The foyer led to a cavernous building filled with cardboard towers and one olive-green Jaguar convertible.

"Nice ride for this part of the country," Rita said.

Jason grunted. "Nonsensical ride for this part of the country."

"Here's another fancy ride." Rita pointed to one of the cardboard pillars.

Jason read the label: "LAWN-EX 300 Riding Mower."

"Same model as in David's garage."

Behind them, footsteps echoed upon metal treads. Rita glanced behind her, where a narrow staircase led down from a small landing containing some offices.

"Hello, Sheriff Jonas," Alan Crenshaw said. Today, he wore a tan suit. "To what do I owe the pleasure of this visit?"

"Deputy Perry and I are here for Max Bannister."

Alan blinked at her. "Max Bannister?" He smoothed his silk tie with clean, tapered fingers. "I don't know who you're talking about."

"Don't play stupid," Rita said. "Max Bannister is a Casper City Councilor."

Alan gave a sly smile. "I confess I don't follow politics, Sheriff Jonas."

She smiled back with her teeth. "But I'm sure you've

seen his mug everywhere. Probably on a campaign mug. I'll get a warrant for the warehouse and find proof that you know everything about Max Bannister."

Alan's lip curled. "Go ahead and search it. You won't find what you want." He paused to fold his arms, studying her. "So why are we talking about Mr. Bannister?"

"Because he's the one targeting Thomas Gabriel," Rita said, reading his face for a reaction. "And you tasked Vee Logan to kidnap him, because Gabriel wants revenge for David Clark's death. Not to mention all the other headaches Mr. Bannister has caused."

Alan's face remained impassive. "It all sounds rather rash. Like child's play."

Rita arched her eyebrows. "Child's play? Have you told your client that Max Bannister killed his son?"

Alan froze. "What? When?"

"Earlier this evening," Rita said. "In a house fire."

Alan shook his head as if he could undo the fact. "I haven't heard about—"

But his words were cut off when Rita's phone rang. When she read the caller ID, she stepped back to answer it, almost too frightened to wish it were really him.

"Cash?"

"Rita."

At the sound of his voice, she stumbled and reached for the wall. She pressed her forehead against it. "I thought you were dead."

He laughed. "Dead?"

"Your house—"

"Fucking hell, tell me about it. Dad's crowd really is the worst."

"They found a body."

"Well, it's not mine," Cash said in rush. "Thank goodness."

"Yes," Rita breathed, "thank goodness. But your truck."

"Someone slashed my tires," Cash said. "So I borrowed Marcus's minivan. He'd been out all night and looked like he'd be sleeping all day."

She took another deep breath. "Where did you go?"

"To visit Otto," Cash said. "Damn minivan nearly didn't make it to Casper. Dunno why anyone buys those things. But I'm here now."

Rita pressed her head against the wall. "Thank God." She blinked, trying to clear her head. "You're there now? At the hospital?"

"Yeah, and you need to come, Rita. It's why I called."

"What's happened?"

"Otto woke up."

"I'm on my way," she said and hung up.

Rita put away her phone and looked at Alan Crenshaw. *Inhale.*

He lawyer put his hands in his pockets and grinned. "What are you gonna do, Sheriff Jonas?"

Rita bit down on her lip. She had zero evidence Alan had been involved in anteing the money for Heather Bannister's downpayment — let alone having ties to Vee Logan.

She blew out a breath — *exhale* — and shifted her gaze to her deputy.

"Jason," she said, "please take me to the hospital."

The End

About the Author

Lauren Street has always loved a mystery. As a kid growing up in bible belt country she devoured every whodunit book she could get her sticky little hands on and secretly investigated all of her (seemingly) normal boring neighbors. Sometimes their pets and farm animals too. All grown up now and living in the UK with her thoroughly unsuspicious (and often unsuspecting) husband, she writes domestic psychological thrillers about families torn apart by secrets and lies. And she sometimes still peers over garden walls to check up on the neighbors.

Also By Lauren Street

The Still County Thrillers

Still Here

Still Buried

Still Burning

The Bishop Smoky Mountain Thrillers

Hide Me Away

Fuel To The Flame

Closer By The Hour

A Gamble Either Way

Calling My Children Home

Too Far Gone

Here You Come Again

A Friend Like You

The Company You Keep

One By One

Come Back To Me

Replaced with Nolon King

Replaced

In Her Place

Irreplaceable

The Salazar Redwood Forest Thrillers

The Girl Who Couldn't Stop Dying

The Girl Who Couldn't Get Out

The Girl Who Couldn't Be Found

Standalone Novels

Postpartum